Now We Are Animals

R P Nathan

D1236580

CASSIOPEIA
CONTEMPORARY

First published in paperback March 2022
by Cassiopeia Contemporary,
a division of Cassiopeia Publishing

Cover Design by ebooklaunch.com
Other design and layouts by Cabochon Design

This book is a work of fiction. The characters and
events portrayed are figments of the author's
imagination. Any resemblance to actual persons, living
or dead, is purely coincidental. Regardless of this, the
setting for the novel is most definitely our own world.
If you look around, you'll realise that because of our
lack of kindness to fellow species and each other, this
story has been playing out in real life for centuries.
The difference is, we can do something about it.

for

Dominic and Rosa

with all my love

.

I had my nightmare again last night.

The first time in months, but it's still the same.

Emma says, "Why are you trying to ruin this for us, Cara?"

She's angry with me.

She's always angry with me.

But that's not the stuff of nightmares, however much I can't stand her.

Couldn't stand her.

No, the horror is what I've witnessed, and what I'm trying to tell her. About what's happened to the others.

Almost worse than what I've seen, though, is the moment Emma realises what's ahead of her. Her look of terror at that sudden understanding is as gut-churning as her fate.

That's the moment I jolt awake screaming, drenched in sweat, as scared as she must have been.

Last night my shouts disturbed Aggie. She stumbled groggily to my bedside and petted me for a while, trying to get me back to sleep.

In the end, I pretended to nod off.

And after Aggie shuffled away, I was left lying alone again in the darkness. My mind was racing and my heart pounding, and all I could do was try and count sheep to calm myself down.

But that didn't help. Instead, all that counting just got me trying to work out the number of days to when I'm eighteen and a half, at which point I'm going to be in line to be Harvested too.

I must have nodded off because I woke up again terrified. Certain that it had already happened. But when I touched a finger to my breast bone and ran it down my chest, the skin was unbroken.

Shaking with relief, I remembered that I was OK. Unlike Emma, I'd escaped.

Her fate will not befall me. Not while Aggie's around.

And that was it.

Slowly the panic faded, and I drifted to sleep once more. Soothed by the knowledge that no harm could come to me.

I was safe.

Safe in my cage.

Now We Are Animals

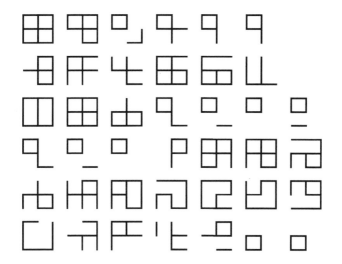

Inquisition Exhibit 78427

Neuroterror Classification: Cat. 1, **HIGHEST THREAT**

Derived from original Inquisition Exhibits 65321
and 65322: two journals discovered on the
outskirts of 13th State, 20th City [Cambridge]
written by notorious human runaway Charlotte
Brontë, also known as Carabel Caffarelli.

PCD [Precise Carbon Dating] reveals the entries in
the notebooks were composed over the same time
period with the final entry only hours after The
Day Of Sharing.

The journal entries have been rearranged in this
single Inquisition Exhibit so the lies contained
within can be studied in the order they were
originally written. First presented in this form
at the interrogation of Mlaxet 2328.

WARNING: CONTAINS NEUROHAZARDOUS AND CORRUPTING
MATERIAL.

PROCEED WITH EXTREME CAUTION

Part 1: Gods Amongst Mortals

[1.1]

I've got a journal!

I'm going to write in it every day!

From now on I'm going to tell you everything, dear reader.

Everything!!

Well, I say a journal. But it's just a notebook. And I say *a* notebook: actually, I've got two!

Sorry, reader. Too many exclamation marks. That would really annoy me if I was reading this.

Aggie got them for me.

Of course.

Thank you, Aggie.

She knows how down I've been, so as a surprise she brought me – just an hour ago! – a couple of books to write in and some pens and pencils. She said she'd had to sweet-talk Schektl and Plaxys to get them, and it had not been easy.

I won't lie, when she gave them to me, my heart was banging.

I know that probably sounds pathetic, but I've not held a book for such a long time that, when she handed them to me, I didn't touch the books so much as caress them.

It's not like they're even pristine.

And just in case they've put different covers on them or digitised them or something by the time you read this, let me describe them to you as they are right now.

The first one of the two notebooks, this one, the one I'm writing in, is *beautiful*.

OK, the back cover is creased like someone sat on it, and it's a tiny bit scorched.

But forget that.

The cover is bright orange with a matt rubbery surface.

Maybe you can even feel it yourself, reader? The way your finger slightly drags when you try and slide it across the surface?

It's A5 with a scarlet band that closes it up with a snap. The pages inside are blank and a lovely cream colour.

Most of all it just smells like a book.

Maybe you don't know what a book smells like. Maybe this notebook is the only thing you'll ever read.

So, how to explain it?

If I say it smells musty, you'll think of a cobwebbed attic or damp cellar. And it is kind of like that.

Or if I said it smells of pine trees and resin, then maybe that would be a little fanciful, but there is a hint of that too.

What it really smells like is memories.

I'm running my fingers over it right now.

The other notebook is much less interesting. I mean, it's still a book which is great, obviously. But it's just a spiral-bound notebook. The cover is a geometric blue and red. Its lined pages are bright white apart from a little water staining at the bottom of each one, as though Aggie fished it out of a puddle.

□ | □ □⌐
   □

[2.1]
Hello again.

I'm writing in my second notebook now.
These pages don't really smell of anything.
Overall, this notebook is just a bit dull.
Sorry!

But in the other book, my pen glides over the pages. Whereas with this one, every stroke feels like an effort.

I knew the moment I got the books that this blue and red one would be the spare, only to be used when I've filled every last scrap of paper in the orange one. I'm going to slip it into a hole in my mattress and out of sight, in case they take it away again for not using it – they've taken everything else from me after all.

But there's one thing I do before I squirrel it away – and it's such a childish thing but who will ever tease me over it – I to write inside the front cover:

Carabel Caffarelli
31B Peverley Road
Highbury
London
The World
The Solar System
The Universe
The Galaxy

Not that I live at 31B anymore, of course. But I'm hardly going to write my <u>now</u> address.

Even though it's in a nicer part of London and a lot posher than our family flat, it's my cage not my home.

And actually, I can't even remember whether I've got Universe and Galaxy in the right order.

But you know what?

Even if I'm wrong, I'm not having any crossings out at the front of a notebook.

There's too much imperfection in my life already to make a mess of this too.

[1.1 continued]

Anyway, I'm going to write in this notebook, this gorgeous orange notebook every day.

I'm going to write to you.

And you know what, dear reader?
We're going to be friends.
Best friends.

[1.2]
Sorry.

This is actually pretty hard.

I haven't got anything to say today.

Aggie says I should try and write every day as it'll make me feel better.

But what's the point, reader?

You're probably not out there to read it.

[1.3]
I've not been feeling great.

The brand on my right wrist was really hurting even under a ton of ointment.

It was like I could still feel the heat in it.

It's better today though, and I'm forcing myself to do some writing.

Even if it's only a few words to you.

Whoever you are, reader.

I'm lying here, and the sun's shining through the window at the moment.

I could be back at home writing my diary in bed.

It's spring sunshine.

Late spring perhaps.

If I stare into the light, it's bright white.

But if I hold up my left wrist, it becomes a multi-coloured dazzle of sapphire and emerald and ruby as the sunlight glances off the beads of my bracelet.

I'm sorry, reader. I just can't get started.

It's not just the pain in my wrist. It's like the moment I begin, my energy saps away.

If you understood you'd understand.

The pen feels so heavy in my hand as I write this.

Aggie says I'm still ill.

⊓ ⊓ ⊓
  ⊔ ı

[1.4]
The Mantra is:

> Colonists are intelligent,
> Colonists are creative,
> I am not a Colonist.
> Animals are not intelligent,
> Animals are not creative,
> I am just an animal.

⊓ ⊓ ⊔
  ⊔

[1.5]
Aggie told her parents she thought I was getting sick again.

They came over just now. Plaxys, her mother, felt my forehead and pronounced there was nothing wrong with me. She's young looking, auburn hair and a gorgeous face. She definitely resembles Aggie. Which shouldn't be a surprise since I asked that she look that way. She's also very

17

intimidating physically: tall and powerfully built, like the girls on the school hockey team.

Anyway, satisfied that I wasn't ill, she reminded Aggie to remind me – she tends not to talk to me directly, which honestly suits me fine – that she wanted me to write The Mantra in my journal.

Like all Colonists, Plaxys spoke without actually speaking, and even though she was addressing Aggie, I could hear her clearly in my head:

—Make sure she writes it early on so she doesn't forget.

Shecktl, her father, who is very handsome, pale skin but dark hair, said, —A sensible precaution. Though the science is very clear: they don't possess that kind of intelligence.

—Yes. But you know her illness has left her occasionally deluded.

She turned back to Aggie. —Make sure she does it. And ensure there is nothing in her writing which might cause an Inquisitor concern.

Then her parents left, and Aggie stood over me while I wrote out The Mantra.

I mean, it was a bit unnecessary.

I recite it every week after all. Not every morning and night like on the farm, but I'm still not going to forget it in a hurry. It's burned into my memory like the brand is burned into my wrist.

Aggie stayed with me for a bit after her parents had gone. But then even she went.

It's kind of cloudy outside so no sunshine today.

With everyone gone, it's just me, and this notebook, and you, reader.

But if I look back, I've written a few lines at least. Even if I've not said much yet.

So, today I'm happy.

[1.6]

Ugh.

I actually thought I had it a few days ago. That I'd found a rhythm to write to you.

That first thing would be a good time to write.

And honestly, my head's been so fizzing with accumulated thoughts the last couple of mornings that I thought it would be easy.

But it was like there was too much to say.

There are still so many beautiful empty pages in this notebook that I don't want to ruin them with any old rubbish – which I know I'm clearly doing right now.

It was like when Tess got an Instax camera for her birthday, and she was so careful about not wanting to waste film and wait for just the right moment, that she never took any photos at all.

That's what this is like.

And then I thought maybe the end of the day would be best.

Because by then things would have happened. Not much maybe. Because not that much ever happens. But enough that I would have something to write about, like in a proper diary.

But by the end of the day, I'm so tired.

I don't even know why.

So sorry, reader, that I've not written anything for a few days. Right now, it's late morning, and I'm sitting at my table finishing off my breakfast, and I've picked up my pen and am just writing whatever comes into my head.

So, that's what I'm going to do from now on. Just write.

[1.7]

Today Aggie's cleaning my cage.

I call it that, reader, but it's not like the cage I used to keep my gerbil, Cosmo, in. That was so cute: bright primary colours and split-level, with the compulsory wheel. On the upper level there was a red plastic igloo which Cosmo would squeeze into if he needed some peace and quiet.

My 'cage' is obviously a lot bigger. It's a natural alcove room off the lounge-diner, around ten feet wide and deep. It has a mattress on the floor in the corner. A low wooden box is next to it with a carafe of water for the night. There's a cross trainer, and a chair and table where my food gets laid out during the day and which doubles as a writing desk. It's where I'm sitting right now. There are windows just in front of me so there's natural light. It's definitely a lot more comfortable than a prison cell.

There are no bars at the front of my alcove, but an invisible barrier prevents me from getting out: Colonist tech. I'd call it a force field, but it isn't like you get zapped if you touch it. It feels more like touching soft rubber. You can push into it, but only so far. And they can make it disappear in an instant using their mind control, so it must be some type of energy.

I have a little ensuite in the corner opposite the bed. But apart from that it's all open. At least Cosmo had his igloo. I don't have any privacy unless I'm sitting on the toilet or having a shower.

Luckily, most of the time Aggie's parents just leave me alone. Schektl has only ever shown sporadic interest in me. And though I might catch Plaxys watching me sometimes, studying me like one of her lab specimens – which is frankly kind of terrifying – it's only when she's around, and that isn't very often.

Aggie, by contrast, spends loads of time in my cage bringing me food, rearranging my things, chatting to me. Oh, and doing my hair. She *loves* brushing and braiding my hair. Though from the moment I arrived, she's been critical of my thick brown curls.

—Why isn't your hair finer? Why isn't it long and blonde?

"You'd have loved Tess's hair," I'd say wistfully.

She would nod in agreement and then sigh in my head as the bristles snagged yet again.

Now I say 'she' when I talk about Aggie. Something I should explain straight away – something which Aggie explained to me properly only recently – is that up until adulthood, Colonists are hermaphrodites, which means physically they're not male or female but both. When Colonists reach seventeen, they can choose which gender they want to be, and this determines their sex.

Seems like a good system really. And as in so many areas, Colonists are more advanced with gender than we were. Take Rebecca, for instance, who was a trans girl in the upper sixth but hadn't had her operation yet. Even so, she ended up on the farm with the rest of the girls because the Colonists said it was how you felt inside that was important.

I mean, Rebecca's probably dead by now like everyone else her age, but for a few months at least she'd have got treated like any other girl. And that certainly wasn't always the case at school.

So, what I'm trying to say is that at the moment, strictly speaking, maybe I should be using 'they' rather 'she' for Aggie. But she identifies so much like a girl, that it wouldn't seem right not to refer to her as one.

Anyway, my point is Aggie likes spending her free time with me.

Today, however, she's clearly in a mood.

I'm sitting at my desk writing. Aggie's wearing her usual oversized navy jumper and black leggings, her copper-red bob swinging, looking as casually beautiful as always.

She reminds me of someone famous. She's got a snub nose, full lips, and the longest of eyelashes. She's not just pretty, she's definitely beautiful.

They're all so, so beautiful.

Her face is completely unruffled and her forehead uncreased, but it's the way she moves as she goes about my cage that means I know she's in a mood. She's not exactly stomping, but she has a defiant air of exasperation as she changes the sheets on my mattress, sweeps the floor for crumbs, then moves into the ensuite to clean the toilet. She actually reminds me of *me* when I hadn't cleaned Cosmo out for a fortnight, and my mum would get angry with me.

[1.8]

(A little bit later. I'm writing down the conversation I just had with Aggie before I forget.)

I say to her:

"Aggie, you know you were telling me about the hermaphrodite thing the other day? You've never actually told me how old you are."

—You never asked. I'm fourteen and a half. *Ugh!*

Aggie backs out of the shower-room with a toilet brush in her hand. I've never heard an expression of such disgust through her thoughts before.

"Sorry," I say hurriedly. "I just went to the toilet. So anyway… I'm older than you."

—Not really.

Aggie returns to the toilet long enough to jab the bowl with the brush, then beats a hasty retreat once more.

"I'm seventeen though."

—Yes. 'Latter-Stage Pre-Harvesting' we would describe you.

I shudder. "Can we just stick to seventeen?"

—I understand. Seventeen then. But one of our years is worth five of yours. So actually, I am approximately seventy-three.

"What?"

—But to us Colonists I'm like a teenager too.

"And how long do Colonists live to?"

—In your years? About three hundred and fifty.

"What?" I'm stunned. It's like what Dad said to me when Cosmo died at the age of four. *We're like gods amongst mortals.* But now the tables are turned. I'll be middle aged when she's twenty. And when she's thirty-five, I'll be…

Even though I'm effectively being held prisoner here, even though I'd have my old life back in a heartbeat, I feel myself choking up that she'll just carry on after I'm gone.

"Would you… Would you get another pet when I'm dead?"

Aggie sees what's on my mind. Her face doesn't change. It's still smooth and featureless, the same as when she's having a strop at Plaxys, the same as when she sets out my food. But now she bites her lip. She comes over and sits down next to me, taking off her rubber gloves. Which is good because they reek of bleach.

—No, she thinks, putting her arm around me. —I never would. I don't want any old pet. I want you. You're special.

Aggie doesn't really look like us. It's just some kind of mind trick. She doesn't even have limbs in the same way that we do. But a member of your family putting an arm around you when you're feeling vulnerable, is an arm around you, even if it's just a neural projection.

And Aggie's the closest thing to family I have left.

[1.9]

That felt good yesterday. Writing that much.

It took me a while to get it all down. But once Aggie had gone, I sat there till it was complete. And I felt stronger for it.

I even went on my cross trainer for the first time in ages.

And I hate my cross trainer.

Even though I'm feeling better, I'm not going to write any more today.

I need to pace myself.

I definitely don't want to overdo it.

I hated being ill.

[1.10]

Aggie's groggy in the mornings. She doesn't get going properly till she's warmed up, so she's bleary when she brings me my breakfast tray.

Breakfast is fruit, a high protein cereal bar, a Danish or croissant – vegan versions, of course – and water. I never used to eat this much in the old days. But I only get two meals a day now, so this is really brunch.

Apart from when she goes out for her weekly exercise, Aggie just hangs round the apartment. When I first got here, months ago, I'd asked her, "Don't you go to school, Aggie?" She just shrugged.

"So, how do you learn?"

—When we're little, by secretion.

"By what?"

—Mother and Father pass me information via saliva.

"That's so disgusting."

—But now I'm older, I receive regular lessons on Colonist history and science and art and literature.

And about once a week, I see her sitting quietly in the living room as she receives her lesson. They're on a different wavelength or something to their normal communication, so I can't hear these thoughts.

More recently I asked her, "I see you listening a lot. But can you talk to your teachers?"

—No. It's one-way.

"But what if you want to ask a question?"

—There's no need, Cara. Any questions I have will be answered when I connect to The Hive Mind, on The Day Of Sharing.

"But aren't you curious about things *now?*"

Aggie considers my face. —No. Not so much.

"So, there's never anything where you just want to know? Where you have to know right now, otherwise you'll burst?"

—Our physiology doesn't work like that. And I didn't think yours did either. I had no idea your organs were so connected to your emotions.

"Not *literally,* Aggie. Of course, not *literally* bursting. But if there's an argument brewing, I usually feel it just here—" I jabbed at my stomach. "Or if there's someone I really like and I see them unexpectedly, I get this kick just *here.*"

—Your lungs?

"My heart, Aggie. My *heart.*"

—I see. We do not feel emotion in the same way. And we do not feel curiosity like that either. We're not driven by the need to acquire knowledge.

"Well, humans are." I heard myself about to say it and knew it was going to sound pompous, but I couldn't help myself. "That thirst for knowledge, the need to discover and create, is very human—"

—Be careful, Cara, you don't misremember human past, especially human creativity, which clearly never existed. You're correct in one way, though. We observed that humans

25

had a greed, not just for knowledge, but for material possessions. That greed did not serve you well. Colonists by contrast are not driven to acquire that which we do not currently possess.

I fixed her a look.

"Apart from other people's planets you mean?"

[1.11]

This is getting easier.

Writing at the same time each day definitely helps.

Sitting at my little table.

Just after I've finished breakfast.

I eat alone, of course, never with the rest of the family.

Not after that one disastrous dinner.

It's not like they eat together every night these days anyway. Plaxys and Schecktl are too busy. But when I first arrived, they would eat right here on the long table in the living room just beyond my alcove.

I remember watching them through the barrier. This was after I'd recovered from my fever but before I got properly ill. You know: head ill. Back then Aggie said,

—Can Cara come and eat with us?

—If that's what you want, said Schektl.

—It isn't proper, said Plaxys.

—*Please*.

—It has behaved itself since being here, said Schektl.

Even though Schektl ignores me most of the time and always refers to me as 'it', I definitely prefer him to Plaxys. I get the impression that Plaxys is really the one in charge, though. This time, however, she merely said,

—If you must.

So, I sat at the end of their table. I ate my doughnut and listened while they thought to each other. I could understand some of what they were saying, though not all. It flitted in and out of English, a mix of static and voices, like the old radio Dad sometimes used to fiddle with on Sunday mornings.

It made me think of meal times we'd had at home.

Me and Mum and Dad and Tom.

Although even those were practically ancient history.

And the last one I remember – just the three of us by then – was when we'd had a big argument about going on holiday to Italy, to see relatives. *Again.* I just wanted to do something different. Why couldn't we go to Spain? Or even Wales?

Now it doesn't seem like such a big thing to have been arguing about; but at the time it got pretty heated.

So anyway, sitting there with Aggie's family made me feel kind of sad, but also really grateful that they were letting me eat with them at all. Aggie had told me beforehand that Plaxys didn't really like humans.

"Why did she let you keep me then?"

—Because I pleaded.

So, I was being on my best behaviour. I mean, I can be as charming as anyone if I really want to be.

I sat, eating my doughnut, and watched them having their dinner of these huge green leaves. They were fabricated, of course, but looked pretty much like banana leaves. And I thought of how people used them for plates in places like Thailand. Though I'm guessing Thai people are on farms like most of us these days, so don't really do that anymore.

And actually, in that argument about going on holiday, I wrote Wales just now because I thought it would make me sound kind of down-to-earth and modest, but honestly, reader, what's the point? What I'd really said was, why couldn't we go to Thailand? Because Tess's family had gone there at Easter, and she'd raved about it. I'd pushed my chair back at home and screamed across the table, "Everyone else gets to go to Thailand! How come we never go anywhere amazing like that?"

That meal wasn't the finest moment with my parents. I don't even know why I've written about it, instead of all the great times I had with them.

Maybe it's because those would set me off crying. This memory only makes me think what a complete idiot I am. Somehow that's easier.

Anyway, reader, I promise I'll try not to get too diverted when I'm telling you stuff. I know I have a tendency to get side-tracked, and I know I'm doing it now, but only because it's so nice to have someone to talk to.

So anyway, Aggie's parents were taking polite bites out of their leaves, and I was eating a jam doughnut.

And I didn't say a word. Honestly, I was being really good.

They talked about work a bit, stuff I don't claim to understand about crop yields and growth rates, pheromones and spike proteins.

Then Schektl asked Aggie what she'd done that day and hadn't it been a lesson day?

—Yes, we learned poetry.

—Ah good, said her father. —What did you learn?

She stood up and was clearly getting herself ready to recite. There was a bit of static so I didn't catch the title, but Aggie told me after it was called The Song of Methilien. I only caught fragments, but it was very beautiful:

> …In the darkness
> We feel no cold.
> The long years pass
> And we do not age.
> Parted as children,
> I will see once again
> Your young face,
> Methilien.

And on. That was the bit that stuck in my mind.

When Aggie was done, her mother seemed lost in thought. Schektl put an arm around her as though to comfort her: something I've never seen again. But only for a moment. Then Aggie sat down, and both parents started applauding her. They did this by making this strange clicking noise like tapping two plastic spoons together.

Meanwhile, I'd got really excited by the beauty of what I'd heard, and because finally I thought I had something I could contribute to the conversation. So, when Aggie sat down, I stood up, grinned at them and recited:

> ~~Shall I compare thee to a summer's day?~~*
> ~~Thou art more lovely and more temperate.~~

I was smiling like a six-year-old as I was saying the poetry. But Plaxys's jaw dropped, and Aggie and her father stared at me. I thought they were just impressed, so I carried on:

> ~~Rough winds do shake the darling buds of May~~,
> ~~And summer's lease hath all too short a date...~~

—This is an outrage!

Aggie's mother sounded in my head, and she hit me with a neural smack. I staggered from the sheer force of it. She hadn't touched me, just the power of her mind, but I felt like I'd been clubbed.

"What have I done wrong?" I gasped and then screamed as it felt like my head had been put in a vice.

—That you could defile us with your lies like this.

"I don't understand! Please stop!"

---

* 🔲 🔳 🔲 🔲 🔲 ± 🔲 🔲 🔲 🔲 🔲 🔲 🔲 🔲 □ □

On this and subsequent pages certain words were blacked out in the notebook due to their neurohazardous nature. In this version of the journals these words have been partially reinstated for an Inquisitor audience but be aware that the threat of contamination from these fragments remains **HIGH**.

—You have stolen these words. Humans had no poetry. No creativity of any sort. Only Colonists are creative. Did they not teach you this on the farm? Are you so unintelligent that you don't even understand The Mantra?

"I do, I do." I was sobbing by now. It was like she was inside my head and wringing out my brain like a sponge.

—Recite The Mantra. Recite it now.

"I can't while you're hurting me."

The pain subsided a fraction. I wiped the tears from my face.

"*Colonists are intelligent. Colonists are creative.*"

I gripped the edges of the table and saw my knuckles turn white.

"*I am not a Colonist.*"

—Don't hurt her, Aggie shouted.

—Silence Mlax–*Aggie*. Sit down. Carry on, Cara.

I closed my eyes, squeezing more tears from them. "*Animals are not intelligent. Animals are not creative.*"

—Please don't hurt her. Aggie's voice was barely above a whisper.

"*I am just an animal.*"

I almost passed out as Plaxys gave me one last neural blast.

—Don't forget that. *Never* forget it.

My head felt like it had splintered. But now the gale of noise was gone, I could hear Schektl's voice too, cool and dispassionate as always. —Fascinating. It actually believes it is intelligent.

It was like he was discussing the results of a science experiment. —But I have read the research, you know, and their higher brain function is basically non-existent.

Plaxys turned to Aggie and pointed at the alcove. —Put her back in her cage. Now!

I crawled there myself. Onto my bed. Curled up in a ball and sobbed for an hour till I fell asleep.

My illness started pretty soon after that.

And naturally I wasn't invited to eat with them again.
Plaxys was right to punish me though.
Colonists are so much more than us after all.
Gods and mortals.

⌐ ▫ ⌐

[1.12]
I'm at my desk again.

I've just eaten my protein bar. Saving my Danish for later.
Apricot today.

Aggie's dusting.

Just now she was saying that, as well as keeping a journal of daily stuff, I should write about when the Colonists took over. She said it would help me.

"Help me how? It's not going to change anything, or bring anyone back."

—It won't do that, Cara. Of course, it can't do that. But I know memory keeping is important for humans.

"It's painful too."

—I understand. But it will help.

"Where would I even start?"

—At the beginning.

So, now I'm sitting here, trying to do that.

Aggie has often been around when I've been writing; and, up till now, that's been fine. But today it feels a little like being in an exam.

—Don't mind me, she says.

But I know if I look up, Aggie will be watching me.

I have to ignore that and just get on with it.

Begin.

At the beginning.

Keep it nice and factual.

31

After all, with everything's that happened, who needs to make anything up.

So.

Hi.

I'm Cara.

(You've probably guessed that already.)

I was doing A Levels when this all kicked off. My favourite subject was English ~~Literature~~, and as well as ~~Shakespeare~~, obviously, I was studying some really cool ~~novels: Jane Eyre~~ – my favourite book of all time – and ~~Jude The Obscure~~, and a modern one which was ~~The Color Purple~~.

I'll be honest it gives me a buzz to think of someone – you, reader – reading this in a hundred years' time like I'm ~~Charlotte Brontë~~ or even ~~Jane Austen~~. If you can read my writing that is: I know it's not the greatest. And goodness knows what you'll even all be doing in a hundred years—

⌐ □ ⌐

[1.13]

(Next day. Back at my desk. Vegan cherry Danish today.)

So, at that point Aggie snatched the notebook from me looking as perturbed as Aggie ever gets, which superficially isn't very much. I've never seen her forehead so much as wrinkle, but yesterday she was almost jittery.

She asked me what the word ~~novel~~ means.

I said it's a piece of writing that isn't true. A fiction. A work of imagination.

Aggie said she thought so; and crossed it through. Really blacked it out so it was no longer legible.

Then, though she's been lurking nearby as I've been writing, she properly read the first few pages of my journal and started positively shaking.

She pointed at this word and that word and asked about them. I told her they were the ~~authors~~ of ~~novels~~ and she crossed them out; plus, what I'd recited at the family meal. Plus, a bunch of other stuff too.

When she was done, I could tell she was absolutely furious.

She said she'd warned me about this.

Plaxys had warned me about this.

—Colonists will simply not countenance anything which makes humans seem more advanced or creative than they actually are. Such things are not possible of you, and Colonist scientists have proved it. Humans are good for farming and racing, and that's it. We accept that humans had the basic intellect to keep daily records and write factual histories and manuals but no more than that.

At which point, I have to say, I threw down my pen. "Why do you let me write at all then? Why do you even want me as a pet?"

—I got you the books because I knew writing in them would make you happy. And you being happy makes me happy. I wasn't that well either before we found you. Everything changed when you fell into my life.

Aggie's voice in my head was trembling. —But listen, Cara, when you lied about humans having poetry, Mother was angrier than I've ever seen her. So, how can you think it's OK to repeat those lies in writing?

"I'm just writing down what happened—"

—YOU STOLE THOSE WORDS!

Aggie was deafening, as loud as Plaxys at that dinner, and I cringed with pain. She did this sometimes. But like always, it only lasted a moment, and then her voice dropped back down to normal volume. —I'm sorry, Cara. Did I hurt you?

"No." My head was ringing. "No, I'm OK."

—I'm sorry, Cara. So sorry… But if Mother catches you writing untruths like this, she won't just punish you. She'll get rid of you.

I curled up on my bed and burst into tears. Aggie sat down next to me and stroked my hair.

—I'm trying to protect you, Cara. And it's not just about Mother. Writing things like this puts me in danger too. I will be reading your journal – I *want* to – and any falsehoods I have read but not purged from my memory will get uploaded when I combine my experiences with the collective consciousness on The Day Of Sharing. Anything as blatantly untrue as saying humans have created written works of imagination, could disrupt The Hive Mind and damage it. Even tiny insidious fragments, uploaded in error, might be enough to cause contamination, and maybe even shut it down for a while until it's cleansed. Colonist Inquisitors work really hard to rid our world of human lies so that The Hive Mind can be pure. We think the truth is the best way to keep humans content. That's why we insist on The Mantra. So, let's not you and me be the ones who allow an untruth to sneak through. If that happened, we'd get in trouble. A *lot* of trouble. And you wouldn't want that?

I shook my head. I didn't want that.

—Neither do I, said Aggie, kissing my hair. —So, please just accept that I might have to black out a few falsehoods from your journal. For your own good. I'm so fond of you, Cara.

And I knew she meant it too. She's been good to me despite everything. I was very lucky.

After all, I'm here writing this, aren't I?

[1.14]

I need to start again.

I need to put aside any notion of human imagination and creativity, and just stick to the facts.

After all, writing anything is like therapy for me. I've got so much more energy than a couple of weeks ago. And Aggie's explained that writing, in and of itself, is perfectly acceptable. Even though we're not intelligent like Colonists, humans still function at a high level for primates. Recording events in a journal is apparently entirely consistent with that level of development. It's like chimpanzees using tools.

So, reader, let's start again.

My full name is Carabel Caffarelli.

But to you, I'm Cara. It's really only my family or Miss Temple who called me Carabel. And only then when I was in trouble.

Or when something really sad had happened.

I'm Italian. I think I kind of said that already, and you can probably tell from my surname. But North London Italian, both my parents born in England too, only *their* parents actually from Italy. I'm seventeen now and was still sixteen when this all started. I was in Miss Temple's class – who was also my English teacher – in Year 12 at Highbury Park School, and back then I had five friends—

I guess I've been trying to block all of this out, so thinking about them now, as a group, so many months later, makes me feel sick to remember what we went through. After all, at least one of them is dead. And if the others aren't dead now, they will be soon. But I can't tell the story without them: without them, there'd be no *me*.

They were Tess and Jo and Pip and Brandon and Orlando.

Jo is Chinese like I'm Italian. Tess and Orlando are full-on English. They actually look like brother and sister with that blonde hair, blue-eyed thing going on. Brandon's Nigerian, really dark-skinned, and Pip, short for Philip, is a fabulous mix of Thai and Jewish and Jamaican. The six of us kind of reflected the diversity of the school as a whole. And

I'd always thought it was a reasonably progressive place because Pip and some other kids were openly gay, and on the whole people were OK with that.

I say 'on the whole' because certainly not *everyone* at school was great.

I mean, Alec Durber was an utter dick and horrible to so many people, Rebecca and Pip included. Not that Pip cared. I mean, that boy was *dazzling,* and he had this innate ability to rise above anything and take people with him. But still, a dick's a dick, and can bring the whole mood down sometimes. And then there was Emma, of course, who could be really annoying in her own way. But despite them, on the whole, it was an OK place.

And obviously I had more than five friends, but these ones were special. We'd all started secondary school together, though I'd known Tess and Orlando even before then. We weren't the kind of friends who would necessarily message each other fifty times in an evening and gossip about everything; more the sort that when you bumped into one of them on the way to History, you'd stop and have a laugh and say, *see you at lunch.*

And I said they weren't the kind of friends you'd spend all night talking to or messaging, but Tess actually was like that, and the boy we spent most of our time on was, of course, Brandon. Not that Tess was into him romantically, because she wasn't really like that with anyone. But she appreciated how beautiful he was as much as I did. In fact, most of the girls in our year were in love with Brandon, though as far as I knew he wasn't going out with anyone.

Sometimes we'd talk about Orlando too, though for other reasons. He'd had a crush on me ever since Year 7 which was kind of embarrassing because he was so not my type. Every now and then, Tess and I just had to have a laugh about *that* situation.

Anyway, it was the beginning of July and getting close to the end of term. We were in the canteen, Tess and me. I can remember exactly what we were wearing, given that we ended up practically living in those clothes for weeks. I had my oversized T-shirt from Camden Market with the ~~Andy Warhol~~ and ~~Velvet Underground~~ banana on it and a pair of cut-off jeans. Tess was wearing a pretty yellow summer dress with spaghetti straps.

And looking back I can hardly believe it, since, in all the time we'd known each other, it hadn't happened maybe more than a handful of times, but we were having a full-on row. It had started with something pretty trivial. I had pasta for lunch that my mum—

I'm going to have to stop.

⌐ □ □⌐

[1.15]
Just thinking about Mum – well – I'm not going to go into that here.

But sometimes I'll have to break off when I'm writing.

I was basically sobbing yesterday.

Aggie took the notebook when she saw how upset I'd got.

She told me expressions of grief are perfectly OK and pointed to other animals that show similar outpourings of emotion: elephants and sea-lions and dolphins. If anything, it confirms our place with them. Aggie hoped that would be of comfort.

It was.

She also drew my attention to some more crossings out she'd had to do. One in particular about my T-shirt.

"What? No music either?"

—It's music? Especially not, then. Singing is fine. Birds sing. It's an animal thing so there's no reason why humans can't. But you're no more capable of proper music than you are poetry.

She was kind about it, but firm.

Anyway, back to that day.

Mum had made me pasta with homemade pesto. Whenever she gave me something nice, I always shared it with Tess. She normally only had something sad-looking from the cafeteria, or a boring sandwich from home. That day was no exception. I had half of my pasta ready for her on the lid of my lunchbox when she sat down with her slice of limp school pizza. My dad—

Just one tear but that doesn't mean I loved him less.

—had worked out how to do great pizza at home, so that the dough and the mozzarella blistered and bubbled, but Tess's sorry triangle looked highly unappetising as though it had been microwaved from frozen. I pushed the makeshift plate with the pasta over to her, and her eyes lit up.

"Thanks, Cara. You want?" She indicated the pizza, and laughed when I twitched my nose at it. She tossed her head so her hair flew back over her shoulders. And I know girls obsess about hair, but in Tess's case it really was a magical thing. Sitting with her back to the floor-to-ceiling plate glass windows which surrounded the cafeteria, and the sun behind her, you could see every beautiful quivering blonde strand.

Tess picked up her fork, grinned, and stabbed a quill of penne. "This is seriously delicious," she said, her eyes widening after the first mouthful.

It made me so happy to watch her. She was gorgeous, especially then. She had dimples and her skin was creamy pale even in the summer we'd been having. And I know she would always say nice things about my olive skin and my dark ringlets, which she used to tangle her fingers into when we were younger, but she was properly beautiful. There was no one I loved doing stuff for more than Tess. Which was ironic given what was about to happen.

"It's delicious," Tess said again, smiling with pleasure, spearing another piece with her fork.

"It's just pesto."

"It must be great being Italian. All that proper food. I don't even know what goes into pesto."

"Basil," I said, delighted to be able to tell her. "We have this huge bush on the window sill in the kitchen. And pine nuts. But you've got to toast them a little."

"Like in a toaster?" She took another mouthful.

"No." I was laughing. It was only ten days before the summer, and I was relishing our last bit of the school year together and the simplicity of being there with her, given I was barely talking to anyone at home after the row about the holiday. "You cook the pine nuts in a frying pan. Then you add basil. Olive oil. And really good parmesan—"

She retched. Mid-mouthful. Her face contorted. Her eyes grew wide and staring. And I know a lot has happened since, but just then Tess did something totally disgusting. She spat out her mouthful onto the lid of the lunchbox, right on top of the remaining pasta, strands of saliva hanging from her mouth, dribbling onto the uneaten food. At first, I thought she was choking; then I realised it was something far worse.

She slumped in her chair, her eyes red, wiping her mouth with the back of her hand. I mean, she looked seriously unwell. *"Parmesan?"* she gasped. "It's got parmesan in?"

In sudden horror I thought I'd poisoned her like the time I gave Titania some chocolate despite her dairy allergy, and had to stab her with an epi-pen. "Are you allergic?" I asked breathlessly, desperate to know what I needed to do.

"No, it's just that parmesan's not vegetarian."

Now, maybe I forgot to mention that Tess was vegetarian.

She had been ever since we went to a city farm in Year 7, and she couldn't square the idea that the pig we were so happily petting was destined for bacon and salami and pork chops. I didn't get the logic at all. That pig wouldn't have *been* there if people hadn't been going to eat him. He had a nice life. Plenty of apples. Plenty of slops. But she kept going on about it, and by the following week, she'd given up all meat and fish. She cried when she someone told her Haribos had gelatine in them, but then they went by the wayside as well. More recently she'd been banging on about how eating animals was actually dangerous as it meant killer viruses could cross over into humans; which was just plain stupid because everyone knew that any of those outbreaks are always contained. Anyway, despite all that, as far as I knew, cheese was just cheese. And once I'd worked out this was just part of her vegetarian thing, I was *furious*.

"*What?* That's the most disrespectful thing I've ever seen." That was actually a line my mum was using on me back then with increasing frequency, and it was good to let someone else get both barrels from it. "My mum *made* that." The strong implication being that Tess's mum couldn't even switch on a microwave. "And you spat it out."

"I'm sorry, Cara." She was swilling her mouth out with water, and even made like she was about to spit, before she reluctantly swallowed. "But it's made with animal rennet."

"Who cares what it's made of?"

People were looking over from other tables by now.

"I don't eat meat or meat by-products. You know that."

"But – it's – cheese!"

"Rennet comes from a calf's stomach."

Which I hadn't actually known and sounded pretty disgusting, but I was too far gone to back off. "Well, it's not like they kill the calves just for their stomachs."

"It doesn't matter. I'm not eating stuff from an animal." Tess crossed her arms and set her face against mine. "Anyway, what they do to calves is horrible. You know they breed them so cows can go on producing milk. And most of the male calves are killed for veal. Did you know that? The dairy industry is really brutal."

"Then why haven't you given up milk?"

"I'm going to. The moment I'm eighteen." Her eyes flickered, the anger in her face relaxed. "My parents won't let me go vegan before then. They think I'm going to get osteoporosis."

At other times that would have broken the argument, burst it like a bubble into soapsuds and laughter. And it's not like we even had that many arguments; and, honestly, most of them I started. I used to get angry about quite a lot of stuff back then, but not usually with Tess; hardly ever with Tess.

I think looking back on it, weirdly, I wasn't even properly angry with *her*. It was just that by spitting out the food my mum had made, she was somehow insulting her. Even though, of course, I knew she wasn't doing that on purpose. But I knew if I could jump to my mum's defence *here,* that it would somehow make up for that big argument about Thailand, which still felt recent and raw. "I mean, it's not like I *asked* to be Italian," I'd said. *Screamed.* So, by being angry at Tess, I was actually being angry at myself and kind of apologising to my mum at the same time. And if that doesn't make much sense I totally understand.

So anyway, her attempt to defuse the squabble would have worked on other occasions. But that day, I was in too deep. "Well, couldn't you have waited till you'd finished my mum's food before you gave up parmesan? Before you spat it out?" And stared at her with such hatred that only a saint would have attempted a reconciliation. But to give the girl her due, St Tess of Highbury stepped up.

"OK, Cara. I'm really sorry."

My anger wagons, however, were already rolling. I mean, it was all made doubly bad by the fact that Mum had made me the pasta and pesto despite the argument. So, I didn't even hear her apology. I just spoke over the top of her, "You shallow hypocrite."

I'm not even sure where the 'shallow' came from. I was way out of order. I knew it, even then. But worst of all was to call someone, who spends their life wrestling with matters of conscience, a hypocrite. It does their head in. Tess sat back and her face, always pale, was like marble.

Orlando and Brandon and Jo arrived at that moment and were startled at the evident hostility at the table, the frostiness almost tangible as they put their trays down. But it was Pip who saw the hot anger in Tess's eyes which I could feel in mine. He knew something serious had to be done, and he went straight for the nuclear option.

"Come on girls, you're not fighting over me *again,* are you?"

At which the others cracked up. I mean, Pip's gay, but that wasn't why it was funny; it was just that anything he said was *always* funny. Even Tess and I managed a smile, though we didn't look at each other yet. But, given another ten minutes, we would have stood down the anger. By the end of the day, we would have been chatting normally again. And although we never got to do that, it was nice to think that the last moment we properly had together, was a moment of good humour, like so many we'd had before; like nothing would ever change.

But everything did change.

Pip's face registered it just as we all felt it, and, since we were all looking at him, his expression was a mirror to our own.

"What's that sound?"

A high-pitched whistle so loud, so powerful, and so sudden it felt like screwdrivers being plunged into our ears. But only for an instant, and then, as we started to recover and even laugh at the total weirdness of it, the floor-to-ceiling windows, which ran two sides of the canteen, imploded in a billion fragments.

[1.16]

Aggie put my journal down. I couldn't see it in her face, but her body language told me she was excited.

—You need to write some more of this, Cara. I'm finding it very interesting.

"Don't you know what happened already?"

—Not exactly. Not the detail. You need to carry on writing, Cara. Seeing things from a human perspective is fascinating. And it's nice to hear more about your friend Tess.

"Yes, she's amazing."

Aggie's gone off into the other room now. I will write some more about what happened to us. But not today.

It takes it out of me.

I'm still here at my desk.

I'm nibbling on an apple turnover. One of those nice ones with the sugar crystals on top. I know already it's going to be the highlight of my day, so I'm going to eat it very slowly.

While I'm here, I may as well tell you a bit more about life in the apartment.

Though, honestly, it's not that exciting.

Everything is driven by when the sun rises. There's a flurry of activity as it begins to get light. The early morning bustle of Aggie's parents getting up and out. But all I see of them is as they walk past the alcove barrier, on their way to the front door.

They're cloaked as humans as usual, of course. I think it's something they can do quite effortlessly, to make me see them like that – like giving off a scent. Apparently, they'll keep doing it till The Day Of Sharing. Then they'll show themselves in their true form.

I've never seen them – or any other Colonist – as they truly are. Not properly anyway. Just this one time where I saw a shadowy outline at night. And even that was pretty traumatic, so I'm not in any rush. But it's still a while to The Day Of Sharing.

Anyway, Plaxys and Schektl are both gone soon after it gets light. But I just lie there. There's no hurry because there's nothing to do until Aggie gets up, and that can easily be another hour yet. I'll usually read over some of what I wrote the day before, though I need to wait until the sun's risen properly because my solar lamp isn't very bright. Aggie is always telling me how amazing Colonist tech is, but their lighting is frankly terrible.

Once the sun's up, I get good light regardless. My window faces east. Our apartment is in what was once clearly quite a fancy part of Hampstead, and from here on the fourth floor I have a view of trees. Tall, graceful trees. Poplars, I think. They're lovely to watch when the wind blows and they bend with it, or when they changed colour last autumn. It does mean I only get glimpses of the sun as it rises beyond them, but even those snatches of sunlight are great. They burst through my window in the morning and turn the bare cream walls of my alcove to gold.

I'm holding my hand up right now, my fingers dancing into and out of the buttery yellow warmth. When I pull my arm back, the sunlight hits the wall and splashes light and colour into my cage, and for a moment I feel like I used to.

It reminds me of a different day, the sun higher and stronger, only a week before the Colonists arrived, but the light the same somehow. Lying with Tess on Highbury Fields. Our last revision session, testing each other on irregular French verbs, enjoying the heat, and the smell of the newly mown grass: sweet and fresh, the stray clippings dry and flyaway even after only a few hours. We'd lain there, basking, heads almost touching, our files strewn before us, the open pages a riot of fluorescent pink and yellow highlighter splashes.

Miss Temple had been there as well, at a safe distance, taking advantage of a free period to sunbathe, her lovely blue eyes hidden behind heart-shaped sunglasses, topping up the tan on her long legs, ahead of her August wedding.

A wedding which was never to happen.

Before I had the notebook and something to read – even if only something I've written myself – I'd lie on my mattress until Aggie brought me my tray.

And even the arrival of breakfast wasn't usually enough to make me get up.

I'd simply lie there.

Sometimes, when Aggie left the barrier down and was busy in another part of the apartment, I'd wander out. But only a short distance into the living room which caught the later sun, and I'd laze in it on the floor.

There was no attempt at self-advancement.

What would have been the point?

This was never going to end.

So, I would just lie there, the sun warming me through.

A bee or fly might buzz and bang against the glass.

And in the distance would be the coo of a wood pigeon. And I?

I was alone, staring at the ceiling.

No wonder I got ill.

Even with Aggie around it just got so boring.

But things are better now.

Because now I've got you, reader, as well.

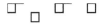

[1.17]

We instinctively dived for cover as the windows shattered.

I found myself on the ground, face-to-face with the woodblock floor. I sat up, gingerly checking around for chunks of glass. Jo was up already. That day she was wearing

45

her peach jumpsuit. Blood was trickling from a cut on her right cheek, and I caught the tin taste of it on my own lips too.

"Must have been a gas explosion," Jo said, though it was difficult to make out clearly as my ears were still ringing. We turned to where the windows had so recently looked onto the running track; where there was now nothing but gaping open wall. Oh yes, and Them.

Later we would call them Colonists, but back then they were simply *Them*. Sixty of Them perhaps, standing evenly spaced along the base of the empty window. They looked like us: dressed in jeans and blouses and skirts and T-shirts. But it was clear They were different. They were all tall and there was a stillness about Them as They stood there. And They were just so damned beautiful. Boys and girls, late teens, early twenties, and so incredibly lovely to look at that it almost hurt our eyes.

"You OK?" asked Brandon, as I got to my feet. Seeing Tess still down, he helped her carefully upright – which, can you believe it, even in the middle of everything, gave me a pang of jealousy. Jo and Pip were just brushing themselves down; we all were. I could see Orlando wanted to brush me down if he got the chance, but I made it clear I was managing just fine.

Pip was laughing, seemingly unconcerned. "Well, *that* was a lucky escape. What the hell was that?"

All around there was relief that no one had been injured. I even relaxed enough to remember the argument, and a flicker of resentment threatened to resurface. But then I, like everyone else, suddenly realised that in all the self-congratulation that no one had been hurt, in all the general hubbub, none of the figures around the edge had moved, not even a millimetre. We turned towards Them, and an eerie silence fell over the hall.

Eventually Brandon called out to Them in his not very deep voice – though I'd always kind of liked it like that – "What's going on?"

At first there was just silence; but then we all heard it though none of Them opened their mouths.

—Come with us.

And then the after-sound. Like I had earphones in, and someone had turned up the volume to full blast. I put my hands over my ears to shut it out. Only, that made no difference because the sound was inside my head, so screeching and shrill that my eyes watered, and I fell to my knees, right back onto the shards of broken glass. It hurt like crazy, but I could do nothing about it. I just had to get the noise out of my mind, was scrabbling and scratching at my ears, but it made no difference.

Then, just as suddenly, it was over. The pain in my head subsided till it was no worse than the hangover I'd had that time Tess and I had found her mum's toffee vodka and snuck it into Orlando's sixteenth birthday party.

A gentle voice came from Them.

—Come with us.

It was like being whispered to by a friend. Their arms were outstretched and I felt myself getting up and starting to walk forwards. If that's what They wanted me to do, then that was clearly what I needed to do. They must be trying to help. Maybe They were first responders, paramedics, though They didn't look like anyone I'd ever seen when my younger brother Tom was still alive, on one of his frequent visits to Accidents and Emergencies. I needed to walk towards Them, but They were so beautiful that it made it a pleasure.

Not everyone was so spellbound though. Brandon was shaking his head like he had water in his ears after swimming. "Snap out of it," he was saying. But his voice was distorted. I stopped and watched him, but I was groggy like I was half asleep.

"Leave them alone!"

47

The entrance doors to the canteen had burst open, and half a dozen teachers appeared, wearing ear defenders from Product Design and armed with fire extinguishers. Instantly, the lethargy lifted and seeing them – including Mr Carton, our fantastic French teacher – I came to my senses. I really needed to get out of there.

"Come to us! Don't worry about the sound. Just run!"

Before I could move, however, the sound returned, and I crashed to the floor again. But where the earlier noise had been shrill and piercing, this time it was deafening. I was clutching my head, tearing at my hair to make the cacophony stop.

I realised at that point, that whoever these beautiful people were, They weren't there to help us, and I needed to get to the teachers instead. I crawled, I swam, through the broken glass.

"Come on! Come—"

But then Mr Carton was down. All six teachers crumpled at the same moment. They sank to their knees then fell prostrate, hands to ears like us, despite the heavy ear muffs they wore. Their bodies were shaking, violently convulsing. Then that stopped, and they were still.

Were they dead?

Had those beautiful intruders somehow killed them?

We had no idea. But now when They said,

—Come with us.

We came. There was nothing else we could do. We didn't know what had happened to the teachers, but we knew we couldn't help them. And we knew we didn't want it to happen to us. Mr Carton, those other teachers who had come to help us, I left with not even a half glance, so desperate was I – was everyone – to get out of there. I sobbed for him as I ran, but I ran all the same.

Once I got outside, I looked round frantically for Tess or Brandon but could see neither. I prayed they were OK, that Pip and Jo and Orlando were all right too, but everyone was just running. Two long lines of Them, drawing gradually closer together, formed a funnel so, as we ran, we were eventually forced into single file towards the exit.

But approaching the gates, I realised this wasn't a way out at all. The twin lines of Them continued outside the school and even crazier, it ran across the pavement and the main road and then onto Highbury Fields beyond. The road itself was static mayhem, cars slewed to a halt, crashed into one another, smoking. A waste truck had been hit side-on by a lorry and had tipped over onto the pavement spilling its sickly-sweet rotting contents, the stench unbearable on this hot day. All around, drivers were slumped as though asleep at their wheels. On the pavements, pedestrians were lying prone. Up the road that led to Finsbury Park and down the road to Highbury Corner, it was eerily quiet, yet instantaneously chaotic.

I scanned the faces on either side of me, those smooth beautiful faces.

Who were They? What did They want?

They must have been terrorists, but were they Islamist extremists? Maybe they were Russians? But all these nationalities? It made no sense. And with the weirdness of it all, the horrible realisation began to crystallise that I was just in the wrong place at the wrong time like the girls in the Manchester bombing or London Bridge or 7/7. I felt a sudden nauseous wave of fear. I had been afraid earlier, of course, but that had felt mostly like shock. This was something different, something visceral like my period, or the time I got salmonella, a frantic fear that made me want to scream.

But even through that, there was some piece of me which held on. Despite the rampant fear, the tears I was crying were of anger. This was not right. Whatever *this* was, it was not right. And I was not going to let it happen to me. I slowed to a halt, and kids pushed past as I looked for a way through the smooth lovely faces inclined toward me.

—Hurry.

I started moving again. I would escape this. I would survive it, and I would get my revenge for Mr Carton; but it wouldn't be now. I didn't need to feel the voice in my head again to convince me that now was not the time to resist. I would bide my time. So, for now, I ran with the rest of them.

[1.18]

—Oh dear, said Aggie about an hour ago.

She'd finished reading the last section. I was eating a cinnamon swirl, savouring the sugar and spice on my lips.

—That must have been terrible for you, Cara.

"You knew what happened at our school didn't you?"

—Oh. I didn't mean that. I was referring to the death of your brother.

"Huh?"

—You wrote: *when my younger brother Tom was still alive.*

She recalled it without looking at the notebook.

"Do you have a photographic memory, Aggie?"

—I suppose so. Don't you?

"Of course not."

—Oh. Well anyway, I am sorry about your brother.

I shrugged. "It was a long time ago."

—What do you say when someone has died?

I stared at her.

—To show sympathy.

"Condolences?"

—Yes. Condolences. Condolences, Cara, for your brother. Can I ask what happened to him?

"I really don't want to talk about it."

—Of course. Condolences, Cara.

"And what about all the other people that died when your lot turned up?"

—Of course. Condolences for them too.

[1.19]

The Colonists were lined up all the way to Highbury Fields.

As I jogged between them, it struck me that Mum and Dad would be going out of their mind if they knew what was happening. And with rolling news and the Internet and Twitter there was no way they couldn't.

I had to let them know I was OK, or unhurt at least. Also, when I'd said we were barely talking, in truth I hadn't said a word to Mum since that stupid Thailand argument. "You don't understand me! You're all so old! Well, I'm not, and I don't want to go to crappy Italy *ever* again!" I'd kicked my chair back, and it had clattered as it fell. I'd stormed up to my room and slammed the door; then burst into tears. I'd been really hungry but there was *no way* I would have gone downstairs to get my plate of Mum's lasagne which I'd been really looking forward to. Instead, I'd finished off the unloved hard toffees from a Christmas tub of Quality Street.

I'd not said a single word to Mum since then, even though it had been three days. I'd managed a few hellos and even a hug with my dad in that time. Somehow it was easier with him. With Mum I don't think I'd more than glowered. Yet I'd still been fine taking in the lunchboxes of food she'd made for me. I'd had my lasagne cold the next day (it was delicious), and I guess that's why the pasta and pesto had been so important. It wasn't just pasta and pesto, it was all the love she'd put into making it, for someone who wasn't even talking to her.

So, now I *really* wanted just to ring my mum and dad, but most of all Mum, and tell her I was OK and, if not exactly safe, then certainly alive and not to worry and that I would be back home in time for dinner and, you know what, I'd thought about it, and I *really* wanted to go to Italy after all.

But when I sneaked my phone out to call them, there was no reception. No wifi, of course – though I could sometimes catch a weak signal from the Highbury Fields café – but to have no network reception was unheard of.

The corridor of Them snaked round a corner, and we were brought up short as the scene suddenly opened out. Highbury Fields slopes down a little from East to West, and coming onto it from the East as we were, we could see everything clearly. The whole area was covered with people, more even than when the circus comes on the hottest and longest summer evenings. That was why I couldn't get any mobile reception – there must have been three thousand people there. They were in three distinct zones: to the south a group of girls, to the north boys, and adults straight ahead. There was no one standing guard as such, but lining the perimeter of the Fields were more of Them in their simple and elegant loveliness. No one doubted what They would do if anyone tried to make a break for it. So, when I heard,

—To the left.

I just went and joined the girls. From the uniforms, it looked like all three schools which bordered Highbury Fields – one of them just a primary school – had been emptied. That got me really scared because whatever They were doing, They were one hundred percent organised. This was like that time a few years ago when that school was hijacked in Russia, or those poor Chibok girls in Nigeria. I mean, to have coordinated an attack on *three* different schools, to have surrounded them, emptied them, rounded everyone up, well that took brains and backing and money.

No one seemed to be in physical pain, but that didn't stop the group, en masse, being near hysterical. There was screaming and shouting, and screaming and crying, and ever-increasing calls for water. Given there were so many girls present already meant some of them must have been there for a while, and it was *hot*. I was as thirsty as everyone else and yelling with the rest of them, wandering around aimlessly for what seemed like hours, until suddenly I caught sight of Tess.

I pushed through the press of bodies in between, and we embraced, all thoughts of our stupid argument gone. And a second later, Jo joined us in the hug. She and Tess had come to the Fields together, and we were so relieved to see one another that we were literally jumping for joy.

"It's all going to be OK, you'll see," I said. Just being together again had lifted my spirits so much. "We'll be out of here soon. It's only a matter of time before the police or army turn up. They've probably got the whole area cordoned off already. They'll bring in trained negotiators and meet Their demands, and then They'll start letting us go. It'll be over in an hour or two. Three at the outside."

"But who *are* They?" said Tess. She looked really pale, which given she naturally had the fairest complexion of anyone I knew, was saying something.

"Yeah, and where did They come from?" Jo said in a strangled kind of voice. She looked around her. "They're like a hundred series of America's Next Top Model all in one place."

Tess started laughing, which got me in fits as well. We were in positively high spirits, all things considering.

—This way.

I looked round to find out who had spoken, but seeing Tess and Jo's faces I realised it was starting again. Our beautiful captors had reorganised themselves. Some of those who had been on the outer perimeter had closed in, so that They were now surrounding the group of girls.

—This way.

Again, two lines had opened up, corralling us forwards. No one bothered to try to escape. And at least the route took us beneath the shade of the big plane trees which ran the edge of Highbury Fields, and which offered welcome relief from the blazing sun. As we trudged along, the dust rose in clouds around our feet. Now that the immediate risk to life seemed to have dissipated, all I could think of was how my cream Converse trainers were getting trashed with all the dirt on them. I'd have to put them in the washing machine, and it was always fifty-fifty when you did that whether they'd be ruined or not.

We carried on walking, first past the group of adults, then, twenty metres further on, the boys standing in a tight square. Just the regularity of them was sinister because I'd never known a crowd of boys to be that ordered in my life. Through the gaps in the row of Them lining our route, I scanned the faces of the boys, but was disappointed when I didn't recognise anyone.

Still, no one here was being hurt, and quite possibly SAS sniper teams were already in position. So, I faced forward, trying not to think about how parched I was, and instead chose to congratulate myself on having chosen trainers at all that morning, when I could have so easily gone with my brand new, silver pumps.

By now we were pretty much at the edge of Highbury Fields, and I could see the corridor of Them stretching into the distance. Though I'd been trying to maintain some positivity, my heart sank afresh at the thought of the march ahead because whenever this ended, it would not be soon.

All of a sudden, I heard my name being shouted. Turning round, I saw Pip had emerged at the front of the square of boys, and was waving at me and Tess and Jo.

"We'll all be back together again soon!" he yelled and gave us a massive thumbs-up and a huge grin. Seeing him really lifted our spirits.

Of course, it wasn't true. We never were all back together. But I'm glad he called to us, and we got to see him one last time. Because it was just after that they started killing the boys.

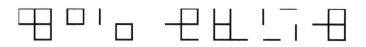

Part 2: Snowballs and Starlight

Most of the time, Aggie just hangs out.

It must have been hard on her before I arrived because she spends a *lot* of time with me.

On a typical day, like today – let's say it's May, but I lost proper track a while ago – she comes in after I've been awake for an hour or so. Up until a couple of months ago, when I wasn't being very communicative, when I would just lie there, feeling blank, she'd leave the breakfast tray on my table and depart. But these days she stays while I eat. On a fine morning, I think I've already said, my alcove is drenched in sunshine, the wood floor golden in the light, and Aggie stands there motionless, soaking it all in.

Once she's warmed up, she'll start fussing around me as I sit, and often she'll be bursting to tell me some new development stemming from her parents' Administration work. It's mostly really dull to me though.

Sorry Aggie. But I am only human after all.

Learning about Colonist medical advances or hearing that nutrient growth rates have hit target is not that thrilling.

But it is interaction.

When breakfast is over, and Aggie has gone to do her chores in the rest of the apartment, well that's my normal writing time.

Like now.

I've been exercising in this time too, on the cross trainer. It's better than nothing.

Around midday, Aggie rejoins me. Often this can be fun, and we sit together chatting. These days, I might also do a bit more writing in my notebook. Filling in the stuff that happened when the Colonists arrived. But it can get boring as well. Sometimes we end up just sitting in silence together.

Later on, there's a task for both of us: we make that day's supper using the fabricators. Fabricators are like a really advanced version of the 3-D printers we had in Product Design. But instead of plastic being extruded, it's lines of sugar and starch and proteins and flavourings. But they're just as slow as our school printers: fifteen minutes for a single bagel. So, to produce the food for the evening meal and the following day's breakfast takes most of the afternoon.

Although it's a chore, it's taking a long while for the novelty to wear off. It's genuinely amazing how faithful fabricated food is to the original. As well as Colonist favourites, it's programmed with all kinds of regional human cuisine. A lot of Colonists like to try local food apparently; though Aggie and her parents have never been that interested.

Anyway, you select whatever you'd like, and it just makes it. It's the one true highlight of the day to eat whatever you want. I tried Italian at first but, however good it tasted, I couldn't properly enjoy it. It felt like a betrayal of Mum's cooking. So, I'm currently working my way round the world. I'm in China at the moment and had Sichuan tofu hotpot yesterday. Which was delicious. Though *very* spicy.

I eat mostly vegan these days, of course. And sometimes some vegetarian things containing milk and eggs, like cake, if I'm not thinking and have fabricated it, and then it seems like a waste to throw it away.

One thing about having been properly starving at some point in your life is that it stays with you.

And I have to confess I do crack and occasionally order something with meat in it. Which leaves me feeling kind of dirty. For obvious reasons. Though I'll console myself that it's only synthetic, anyway.

As well as making food, the fabricators can also produce a few toiletries like toothbrushes and tampons. It's a massive step up from the farm where we had to make do with bits of straw and rags.

Aggie's parents return from work at dusk. By then, I'm usually back in my cage, the barrier firmly up again.

Sometimes they eat together, sometimes not. These days, when they do, it's in the kitchen. Even from there I can hear them thinking to each other. Aggie in particular thinks really loudly. Occasionally it makes sense to me, often it's incomprehensible. But by now, I can block it out when I want to, like it's white noise.

I have my dinner alone.

I take a shower in the evening.

Do my teeth.

And then go to sleep when it gets dark. The solar lights are no better at night than they are in the morning, though you'd think they ought to be since they've had the whole day to charge.

I just lie there.

Think about the old days.

Wonder about Tess and Jo, and how they're getting on.

Eventually I fall asleep.

And then that's the end of another day.

⌐□ □ ⌐□ □₁

[1.21]

"Are all Colonists only children?" I asked Aggie yesterday.

—No. Why?

"Well, you're the only one I know. And you're an only child."

"Oh, I see. No, usually Colonists have many children. But they have them all in one brood: The Spawning. But occasionally a Spawning is barren—

"Yuk."

—and no children are produced. After that they can't try again for children for seventeen years.

"Why so long?"

—It's an evolutionary advantage apparently. Usually, this second attempt would not be successful, but when it is the resulting brood is called Late Spawn and always consists a single child. I am Late Spawn. We Late Spawn are very rare and are much loved by our parents.

"Aren't all Colonist children much loved?"

—Yes. But we're regarded as *very* special.

"Lucky you. Do you mind being a single child?"

—Well, it can get quite lonely. I was lonely before we found you. But being Late Spawn is to be envied.

"Why?"

—Because only one egg is produced, all of Mother and Father's reproductive energy—

"*Ugh.*"

—was put into me. Late Spawn generally have very strong telepathic abilities.

"Is that why you're so loud?"

She started fiddling with the pens on my desk. —Yes. Not always though. I do try not to be—

"Sorry, Aggie. It's fine. I mean, it's only now and then. I didn't mean anything by it."

—No, you're right. I need to control myself much better.

She sighed and hung her head.

After a moment, I said gently, "You were telling me how Late Spawn were actually quite cool."

—Yes… Well, we are very strong telepathically. So, when we reach maturity, we usually become Soldiers.

"Wow. You're going to be a Soldier, Aggie?"

—Yes.

A bit of bounce returned to her voice. —Quite cool?

"I guess so. I just don't see you as the soldier type. Aren't they the ones who rounded us all up?"

—Oh, yes. So, perhaps not so cool for you? But for Colonists, Soldiers are very highly respected. They keep the peace.

"Isn't that what the Police do?"

—We call *them* Inquisitors. They ensure law is followed. But soldiers make sure everyone is safe against anything that might harm Colonists.

"Other species you mean?"

—Yes, of course. Mostly other species. Soldiers must always be impartial, so after maturity we may no longer live with or visit our parents.

"Isn't that going to be sad for them? For you?"

Aggie's shoulders moved in a shrug. —I don't see it like that. For me it will be exciting to serve as a Soldier.

"I guess... Hey, what will happen to me then?"

—Remember, it will not happen till I reach seventeen. That's still many of your years away. Whatever happens, I'll find a way to keep you with me."

"Thanks..." It was all so much to take in. But she was right: it was years into the future. Almost another lifetime. "So... anyway... Aggie the Soldier. Yeah, that is pretty cool. If you are actually that strong."

—Oh, I am *very* strong, Cara.

I think it was just the way she said it, but we both fell about laughing.

⌐ ⌐ ⌐ ☐
　☐　　　＿

[1.22]

I've been looking back at what I wrote a few days ago.

Those shade-giving plane trees we walked under on Highbury Fields the day the Colonists arrived has made me think of winter a couple of years back.

I'm not talking about last winter: that was sodden. There'd been flooding for weeks in the South West with pictures of Somerset looking like an inland sea. They said it had been down to climate change, of course. London had been mostly fine, but it had still rained incessantly.

In contrast, the *previous* winter had seen a delightful dump of snow in the run-up to Christmas. Everyone got into the spirit, even Jo who was normally busy with one of her million activities and a girl called Juliet who was pretty much queen bee but you could see why since she was tall and blonde and striking looking. Them and Tess and me, we'd all somehow managed to climb up a tree, on that avenue of planes that ran down the edge of Highbury Fields, to take full advantage of the snow.

Now, that was kind of a big thing for me because I hate heights. I hate climbing anything, but trees in particular. It's all down to stuff that happened a long time ago. It was a massive deal for me to be up there, but I was with Tess and Jo, and Juliet was egging us all on, and the snow made everything seem magical and possible.

So anyway, we climbed into the branches of one of the huge plane trees, and whenever a boy walked underneath, we'd pelt him with snowballs. They were just so surprised. And we were too high for them to get us back. It was beyond hilarious.

But then, irony of ironies, we couldn't get down. Well, I couldn't anyway. My old fears suddenly took over, and I felt like I was going to slip horribly and got stuck half way. The other three, having safely reached the ground, were trying to talk me down by shouting over each other. Meanwhile, a few boys – I think even Orlando was amongst them, but I could never get him to admit it after – were pelting me with snowballs in revenge, and I was getting increasingly panicky.

Suddenly, I felt someone's hand on my leg. That completely freaked me out, but whoever it was then placed my foot securely on the stump of branch that it had been thrashing about trying to find, and guided the next step as well. By which time I was almost down, and I could jump to the ground and, turning, found myself right in Brandon's arms.

This was two winters ago. He wasn't so tall then, still the same height as me, so we were completely face to face. His skin was so dark in contrast with the snow around him that I just wanted to touch his cheek there and then to feel the warmth within.

But, of course, I didn't do that.

Instead, I jostled awkwardly with him and made to go to my left when he went to his right and vice versa, my fake Ugg boots – which I'd rate zero stars for climbing – trampling his adidas trainers until we eventually broke free. But I couldn't say a word as I must have winded myself coming down from the tree.

Funny thing was, it seemed like he had too.

How did I get onto that? Oh, yes, the trees.

On the day They invaded our school, we girls had been marching beneath them down the side of the Fields, and then on to the tarmac path which ran past the tennis courts, when the screaming began behind us.

We knew it was the boys right away, though we had to jostle each other to catch a glimpse of them, Tess and I even taking turns on each other's backs. From what we could see, the boys were going down in waves as though They were going through them row by row. The boys seemed to be falling cleanly, without fuss – without pain, I've always told myself – like dominoes in a line. The screams were coming from those immediately behind (and from us girls watching as well, of course). There was a lower-pitched sound too, a desperate wail from the adults. They must have been able to see closer at hand what was happening to the boys.

I suppose I didn't know for *certain* they were actually being murdered – I couldn't see clearly enough – but at the time there seemed no doubt something terrible was happening. Shouting broke out amongst the girls almost immediately, spreading away from us and down the column like a bushfire. Those like me, nearer the scene of the crime – because how else could it be described? – we tried our best to get back there, but were blocked by Them. So, we kept craning over and around each other, until the pressure from us was so great that we crashed into Them like a wave, and some of the girls broke through.

Initially, they were so stunned to be outside the cordon that the girls just stood there; before a few of them came to their senses and started running. Even in that split second, however, some of Them had moved smoothly into position and must have focused their sonic beam or whatever it was on the escapees, because they fell to the ground, writhing. All except one girl who had been faster reacting and kept on running. I didn't know her, but she looked like she'd been in a PE class. She was dressed in white T-shirt and Nikes, and she was sprinting.

We shouted to her, willing her on, willing her to escape. Our captors had closed ranks again, but they made no attempt to race after the girl. They simply turned to watch like we did.

The girl was heading up a path which led back to the main road and from there into a maze of streets, where she'd surely find somewhere to hide. And if the road had been clear, she'd have been straight across it to safety.

But it wasn't clear.

Even as she was looking desperately back over her shoulder at the pursuit which didn't come, two of Them moved smoothly into the path ahead of her. We yelled a warning, but just as she turned, They hit her with Their sound beam, and she went down.

We fell silent, but those closer to the Fields were still wailing, still clambering around each other to see what was happening to their classmates and brothers and boyfriends. And those further up the line of girls were buzzing about what was even going on. Peering through the gaps in Their cordon, I caught a glimpse of the PE girl with two of Them standing over her. They picked up her body and carried her away.

—Move.

After that initial instruction we didn't hear any more, but we were towards the rear and felt Them physically pressing us forwards. None of us wanted Them to get too close, so we started running, and that imperative rolled like a wave throughout the whole group until everyone around and ahead of me was jogging too.

I lost track of Tess and Jo at this point.

We ran past the clock tower and onto the high street. It took me a few moments to register that the road was now completely clear of vehicles in stark contrast with the mayhem I'd witnessed earlier. In the time we'd been on Highbury Fields, They must have somehow cleared all the crashed cars and lorries and cyclists away. How was that even possible?

Out of the corner of my eye I saw someone stumble. My first instinct was to keep on running, but I knew that wasn't right. So, I pulled up short and went back and knelt next to the girl on the ground.

She had a darkish complexion and wore her hair in pigtails. She must have been Year 7 and had the blue uniform of the school on the other side of Highbury Fields. She sat with one leg bent up towards her, her knee grazed into a scarlet mess, tears rolling down her face. She reminded me of one of my little cousins in Italy.

"We've got to keep moving," I hooked an arm under hers and lifted her sharply.

"Ow!"

"You're fine. Come on."

She glared at me, looking so silently furious, that I wondered if she might be hearing impaired. I made a 'move it out' signal with two fingers, and she burst into laughter.

"What are you doing?" Her eyebrows, which had been knitted so tightly together, were now positively dancing on her forehead.

"Oh. I didn't think you'd understood. We can't stop here."

"I know, but my leg hurts."

"Lean against me." I took her weight, and we set off together. Not before time as They were now right behind us.

—Faster.

As we hobbled down the road, I scanned the windows in and above the shops. But there were none of the faces I'd been hoping for. This whole thing had obviously been meticulously planned, the terrorists having somehow cleared out an entire corridor of people before they'd hit the schools. I guessed that sonic weapon of theirs was able to penetrate walls. And maybe that had blasted the roads clear too.

The girl – Ada was her name – was feeling it bad now, stumbling as much as running, and complaining of feeling thirsty. We'd gone most of the way up the high street, and then, just as I thought she couldn't go on another step, we were brought up short as the girls in front of us came to a halt. Ahead of us the crowd snaked forwards to Seven Sisters Road and then round to the right, towards Finsbury Park. I hadn't seen Tess or Jo for a while, so I held tightly to Ada's hand in consolation.

Suddenly, in a wave, the girls in front of us sat down. Like we were attached, we followed suit. I hadn't heard a command from Them, but it was very welcome to rest on the ground, and Ada looked beyond relieved.

It was three o'clock.

[1.23]

Earlier today, Aggie had left the barrier down while she'd gone to do her cleaning chores elsewhere in the apartment. I was taking a slow turn of the living room, ambling idly around, when I found what I think is evidence of the people who lived here before.

I never normally wandered this far, which was why I hadn't seen it before, but on the vertical part of the doorframe leading to the hallway was a series of short lines at various intervals.

Pen marks in different colours.

Some distinct. Some half rubbed away.

But unmistakeably a record of heights.

My immediate thought was that rich people were so strange because, honestly, if I'd lived in an apartment as nice as this, I'd never have let pens anywhere near the woodwork or walls.

But here it was. And it said:

> Alice 3
> Alice 5½
> Alice 7

Lots of Alice basically. Also aged 10, 11, 13 and 15.

But there were another couple of names as well:

> AGN 8

which was just above Alice aged 7.

The writing was slightly different – her dad rather than her mum maybe?

I think this was still just Alice, but initials this time.

I wondered what her full name had been: Alice Grace Norton? Alice Georgina Nixon?

There was another as well:

> eta 16

just above 'Alice 15'.

The first 'e', though lower case, was slightly enlarged, so could have been as a capital letter. I think this was an actual name: '*Eta*'. Although… there was a smudge before it that I couldn't make out, so maybe it was *part* of a name… Greta? Yes, Greta made sense.

When I stood there against the wall, I realised she was the same height as me.

Greta.

Who was she I wondered?

Not Alice's sister, because otherwise her name would have appeared with equal frequency. Nor even a very close friend who would have been over at the apartment more often.

So maybe Greta was a cousin?

One Alice didn't see very often.

Or a friendship which didn't take off? Where one visit to the apartment had been quite enough.

Whoever Greta was, though, it was Alice who had actually lived here.

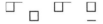

[1.24]

I asked Aggie about it when she came back into the room.

"There used to be a girl called Alice living here. Did you meet her?"

—The family that lived in the apartment had already been evacuated by the time we arrived.

"'Evacuated' means moved to safety. I don't think that's quite what happened to them... Alice would have been just a little younger than me."

—I told you, Cara. I never met her or her parents.

Colonists didn't lie. But I wasn't going to let it go.

"You're sure Alice wasn't your pet before me? I mean, how are you so good at doing my hair if you didn't learn it from Alice?"

—We are Colonists, Cara. We're good at everything. We observed your species closely. You're advanced as far as animals in your world go, but we are far ahead of your level. Things which you think complicated are nothing for us. Do you think one of your pets would have been surprised if, as well as throwing a ball for them to fetch, you were able to fetch it yourself? Of course not. They would expect it. So should you.

"But why do you want me to be blonde and have long hair? Was Alice blonde?"

—I will tell you one last time, Cara. I never met any Alice. In any case, our studies indicated that all human females want to be blonde.

"That's so not true," I said.

Though she did sort of have a point.

[1.25]
It had been a long afternoon.

The sun was starting to sink in the sky. In another half an hour it would be down below the line of buildings and finally, mercifully, we would be in shade. Even in a baggy T-shirt and with my olive complexion the exposed skin on my arms was feeling raw. Poor Tess must have been red and peeling by now in that thin-strapped dress she'd been wearing.

I must have checked my phone fifty times while we sat there, desperate to see if anyone had messaged me. But there was nothing. And still no signal either. Not just for me but for any of the girls on any network. And searching for a signal seemed to be draining the battery faster than normal: I was down to only 20%.

Next to me, Ada was snoozing. Her mouth was opening and closing silently, her lips already cracking. I'd told her to take a nap, that I was certain we'd have water by the time she woke again, but I knew I was going to have to disappoint her.

Earlier on I'd tried reasoning with Them.

"We need water. We need the toilet."

But Their beautiful blank faces had remained impassive.

"Why won't any of you look at me? We just need some water."

—Sit.

"No, I won't sit! We've got rights, you know." I'd jabbed a finger at the terrorist closest to me. "Will you please just give us something to drink?"

"Don't, Cara." Ada had tugged on my top. "It's OK."

"It's OK," I'd echoed back to her, to combat the frustration at our helplessness, my own thirst, my growing need to go to the toilet, and most of all at the lack of helicopters buzzing overhead: you normally couldn't keep the police choppers away from even minor incidents round this part of North London. "We'll get some water," I said, trying to calm down. "You'll see." Her smile had made me smile back at her reassuringly. "You rest. By the time you're awake, you'll have a drink. They'll hand out bottled water. You'll see."

But now she was stirring, and nothing had changed apart from the sun getting lower in the sky.

"What's happening?" I asked irritably, loudly. "Why are we just sitting here?"

"We're being processed," called out a girl two or three rows up from us. "Before being handed over to the authorities."

I recognised the speaker as Emma Woodhouse who was deputy head girl at our school and captain of the hockey team. And, even though only some of the girls went to

Highbury Park, her loud, clear voice meant that when she stood up and spoke, people listened.

"Releasing hostages is complicated. We just have to be patient."

Girls' heads turned towards her. They started looking hopeful again.

"How do you know?" someone asked.

"I heard it from up the line. There's a queue all the way along Seven Sisters Road up until Manor House, and then we're being handed over there."

"But who are they? What do they want?"

Emma gave the questioner a resigned shrug of the shoulders. She was wearing a chambray shirt and jeans. Her boring clothes and no-nonsense shoulder-length brown hair lent her total credibility. "We don't know. I don't think anyone does. Their demands aren't clear." She was looking around for the next question, an open smile on her face.

"Are you sure we're being handed over?" I asked. I'd never liked Emma, especially not since she gave me a detention for talking in the library. A *detention*. Up until that point a deputy-head girl's powers of punishment had been entirely theoretical as far as I'd been aware. And *anyone* giving a Year 12 a detention for *talking* was unheard of. I hadn't even been that noisy. "You're sure it's not gossip?"

"Of course, it's not gossip! *Really*, Cara. I told you, it's been passed down the line. I heard it from someone I trust, so it's definitely reliable. Now any sensible questions?"

I subsided at the snub.

"We should just make a break for it," a girl hissed.

"No. I don't think that would be a good idea. What's your name?"

"Olanna."

"Well, Olanna, there will be trained negotiators working on getting us out. We don't want to risk anything happening in the meantime. Let them do their work. We just need to be patient."

"They're going to kill us is what they going to do."

"No one is killing no one," said Emma defiantly. Thought about it a moment, didn't want to undermine the punchiness of her statement with grammatical niceties; but couldn't help herself. "*Anyone.*"

"But what about the boys?" There was a rumble of assent.

"They killed them all."

"We saw them."

"And then they started on the adults."

I jolted.

It shouldn't have been a surprise, of course. If they could have killed the boys then why not the adults too. After all, I'd seen what they'd done to Mr Carton. But the thought that the adults were a target too suddenly flipped things round in my head. Up until then, I'd wanted to speak to Mum and Dad so they could reassure me, so they could tell me help was on its way. Now I was suddenly genuinely worried about *them* for the first time.

All around, the subdued, exhausted girls were stabbed by their memories of horrors they had already seen and even more terrifying imaginings of what was to come, and a new wave of wailing and sobbing broke out. I wasn't immune. I wanted to tear my hair out as multiple horrible thoughts flooded my mind.

Emma, however, was calm. She frowned at the last speaker: Olanna again. "Please remember there are younger girls here and spreading rumours is not helpful. No one actually *saw* the boys being killed."

And now she mentioned it, we hadn't. We'd seen the boys falling, but that was all. Even Mr Carton and the PE girl and the people on the road might have been merely incapacitated. Maybe that's how they cleared the roads so quickly afterwards. Everyone just got up and walked away…

"Why would they want to hurt us anyway?" Emma said. "It wouldn't make any sense. They'd just antagonize the authorities, and then they would come in with all guns blazing. At which point, no one gets out of here alive."

We all started properly freaking out again at that and Emma realised instantly she should have chosen her words more carefully.

"It's OK, it's OK," she soothed us. "That's why none of that is going to happen. Why no one is going to get hurt, and why, up till now, no one *has* been hurt." She flashed an angry glance at Olanna like she had tricked Emma into using the words 'all guns blazing'.

I felt suddenly drowsy, heavy-lidded. She'd explained it all. I didn't know whether to believe her or not, but I was too exhausted with worry to fight it. Yet still I heard Olanna's dogged voice.

"But what about the people on the road?" Olanna insisted. "What about our teachers? They were killed."

Emma merely shrugged; and, in a great *coup de theatre,* held out a palm-up hand. "If they were killed then who is that behind you?"

Beyond our close cordon, unmistakably, a touch weary looking, our teachers were arriving. And there, right at the front, was Mr Carton and, even more wonderfully, alongside him was beautiful Miss Temple. They halted thirty metres from us, and we screamed hysterically, whooping in joy and relief. Until another barrier of Them interposed themselves, and we lost sight of the adults almost immediately; but we had seen them. We turned back to Emma who was smiling magnanimously.

"So please, no more scaremongering. Let's just sit tight and we'll be out of here before nightfall." She sat down, acknowledging the applause which broke out around her. In the end, even I was clapping. And sobbing. It was just such an incredible relief to see Miss Temple safe. And a huge weight of guilt lifted seeing Mr Carton standing there, when we'd left him to his fate at school. But then the whole day had been so crazy that maybe it should have been obvious he was still alive. That they all were. Pip and Orlando too. Brandon. And I didn't have to worry about my parents anymore.

I was sobbing and cheering with everyone else, and Emma just sat there soaking it all in, smiling modestly as though it were all for her. So, there was relief. But we were still sitting there, and gradually we fell into silence once more. It was then that Ada, who had somehow slept through all the commotion, chose to wake up. "I need the toilet."

But there were no toilets.

In the end, we had to pee at the roadside. In the gutter. Which was as disgusting as it sounds. And the terrorists didn't so much as bat an eyelid, even when the drain started smelling totally rank in the warm afternoon.

The euphoria we'd felt at seeing the teachers evaporated again pretty quickly.

And we just carried on sitting there.

For hours.

[1.26]

Starting to write down what happened means I had my nightmare again last night.

The first time in months, but it's still the same.

Emma says, "Why are you trying to ruin this for us, Cara?"

She's angry with me.

She's always angry with me.

But that's not the stuff of nightmares, however much I can't stand her.

Couldn't stand her.

No, the horror is what I've witnessed, and what I'm trying to tell her. About what's happened to the others.

Almost worse than what I've seen, though, is the moment Emma realises what's ahead of her. Her look of terror at that sudden understanding is as gut-churning as her fate.

That's the moment I jolt awake screaming, drenched in sweat, as scared as she must have been.

Last night my shouts disturbed Aggie. She stumbled groggily to my bedside and petted me for a while, trying to get me back to sleep.

In the end, I pretended to nod off.

And after Aggie shuffled away, I was left lying alone again in the darkness. My mind was racing and my heart pounding, and all I could do was try and count sheep to calm myself down.

But that didn't help. Instead, all that counting just got me trying to work out the number of days to when I'm eighteen and half, at which point I'm going to be in line to be Harvested too.

I must have nodded off because I woke up again terrified. Certain that it had already happened. But when I touched a finger to my breast bone and ran it down my chest, the skin was unbroken.

Shaking with relief, I remembered that I was OK. Unlike Emma, I'd escaped.

Her fate will not befall me. Not while Aggie's around.

And that was it.

Slowly the panic faded and I drifted to sleep once more. Soothed by the knowledge that no harm could come to me.

I was safe.

Safe in my cage.

[1.27]
Aggie was plaiting my hair again today – having more success than I'd ever had – when she asked,

—What do you like most about your new life, Cara?

It wasn't the first time she'd asked me that. She always seems eager to know I'm enjoying my time with her as much as she evidently enjoys having me here. But it's a difficult question to answer. I mean, it's complicated being alive and safe when I've basically abandoned everyone who's ever helped me.

So instead, I turned it around and asked,

"Well, what do *you* like about it?"

—Oh. Being here with you. I've told you already. Before you came, I was so lonely. I became ill because if it.

"What did you do before I came?"

—I was just here in the apartment. On my own.

"And before that?"

—Well, before Earth, I just recall darkness and cold.

"That sounds horrible."

—No, Cara. It wasn't unpleasant. It was just nothingness. Stillness. But I was there. Travelling. That is the way of The Journey. It's an important thing for our people.

"That's what that poem was about."

—The Song of Methilien? Yes. We are a people that travel wide distances from one land to another. I was travelling. For a long time. And then one day we were here on Earth. It simply happened. No great sense of arrival. And then came The Waiting. Cloaked. In the shadows. Watching you all. But where before there had been infinite darkness, now there was colour and activity and life. So beautiful. All of you.

Aggie fell silent until she'd finished the braid.

—And you? You still haven't answered. What do you like most about your new life?

To which I answered, like I always answer, with the truth. "Being with you." It always sets Aggie quivering with happiness, and today was no exception.

But sometimes the question was:

—What do you miss most about your old life, Cara?

That's harder to answer.

—Because you never really write about your family. Don't you miss them?

I've tried to explain that to her already. That because I don't write about them doesn't mean I don't miss them. Obviously, I miss them every moment of every day. And all my friends too. But that doesn't mean I'm going to try and put that into words.

I'm not sure I *can* put it into words.

"Of course, I do, Aggie."

—Of course, you do. But you just don't want to talk about them. I understand. Like your brother.

"What?"

—Condolences, Cara. Well then, what *thing* do you miss most?

In terms of daily life, I used to think it was impossible to narrow it down to one thing. There are a *million* things I used to have which simply don't exist anymore, like my phone and social media and lip gloss and straightening irons and TV and clothes shopping.

So, the first time Aggie asked that question it put my mind in a whirl.

It's only as time has passed here, that actually I realise there is a clear answer to it after all.

What I miss most is the thing I realise, apart from my friends and family, gave me the most comfort in the whole world.

Books.

And I know that makes me seem like a nerd.

But I'm not going to apologise.

I just like reading.

Why should I pretend anyway?

Because if you're turning these pages, you must do too.

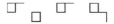

[1.28]

—And by books, said Aggie holding the journal way out in front of her, like it might spontaneously combust. —You mean manuals and factual accounts and sets of instructions?

She gave me the eye, but the lesson's been learned.

"Of course. What else could there have been?"

—Good.

She handed the notebook back to me, then made herself comfortable on the living room sofa for that morning's lesson.

[1.29]

It had got properly dark.

It was early July, so it must have been nearly ten o'clock, and it was impossible not to fixate on how thirsty and hungry I was. I'd had nothing to eat or drink since the first few mouthfuls of pasta at lunch. A few of the girls were using the lights on their phones to cheer themselves up, but last time I'd checked my battery was down to 3%, so I thought I'd save mine. In the event this situation lasted the night, I would try Mum and Dad first thing in the morning.

—Stand.

We looked at each other. No command apart from the occasional warning had been heard for a couple of hours.

—Stand. Start walking.

With the reiteration came a gentle reminder, a buzz in our heads like the time I'd licked a 9V battery. Just a warning, but we got up hurriedly.

"I'm scared, Cara. Where are we going now?"

I gripped Ada's hand, but Emma piped up once more.

"You see. I was right. It's the handover. We'll be home soon."

Ada rubbed her head against me. "You think that's right?"

"I'm sure it is."

"Thank you, Cara."

"For what?"

"You saved me."

"Not *saved*—"

"Cara, can we keep in touch after this?"

I smiled in the darkness. "Just try and stop me."

She gave a throaty chuckle of pleasure.

We took a right at the top of the street and headed along Seven Sisters Road. It was a relief being on the move again, especially in the cool darkness after such a blazing day.

"It's dark, isn't it, Cara? Wow, look at the sky!"

I looked up. It was the most amazing set of stars I'd ever seen. Jo – who's into astronomy and physics and everything else – had once pointed out some constellations to me, so I knew where Orion and Cassiopeia were; but when I looked up now it was impossible to make them out. They would just have been brighter spots amongst the scintillating backdrop of other stars. Across the middle of the sky was a bar shaped cloud which confused me as it had been the clearest day. Until I realised it was the myriad stars of the Milky Way.

Despite everything, it was kind of a cool way to finish a crazy and horrible and exhausting day.

Or at least it was, until Ada said in a flat voice, "Oh. I've just worked out why the stars seem so bright. The streetlamps are off."

She was right. The lights along the Seven Sisters Road, the busiest around here, were all dark. But so were the hotels and flats which lined the road. Apart from a few bobbing white spots from girls' phones, there were none of the familiar lights from cars, or motorbikes, or planes, or cranes, or mobile phone masts, or shops, or houses. Whichever direction I looked, there was just darkness.

Somehow, someone had put out all the lights in North London.

□ | □   □ |
　　　□

[2.2]
I know I said I wouldn't write in this notebook till the orange one was full, but I wanted to talk to someone.

Privately.

I can't write about it in my other book because I don't want Aggie to see. I'd have to explain it all to her.

How I'm feeling.

But I've got to tell somebody.

So, I'll tell you:

I don't want to die.

There. I've said it.

Though putting it on paper doesn't make me feel any better.

Actually, it feels worse. Makes it even more real.

It's writing everything down. It gets my thoughts out which is helpful.

But it's also unsettling having to revisit everything that happened.

As was seeing the name Alice scratched into a doorpost.

Why should seeing the name of a girl I've never met and know nothing about make any difference to me? But somehow it does.

It's the dream as well. I'm having it every other night now.

I just don't want to end up like that.

I don't want to die, full stop.

I remember when I was eight, thinking about what it must be like to be dead. And assuming that if there wasn't a heaven or anything, then it would be like the time I got trapped in Mum and Dad's ancient wardrobe when I was even younger, playing hide and seek with Tom.

Peaceful and dark and perfectly quiet to begin with, but then I got increasingly panicky when I couldn't get out and no one could hear me.

But of course that isn't really what death would be like.

However scary it was in the wardrobe at least I was still <u>there</u>.

Conscious.

When I'm dead, all that will be left of me will be these notebooks.

And who wants to be a book on a shelf?

A book that you happened to pick up, reader.

It's so weird that I'm talking to you and you're here, but I'm not any more.

I mean, let's face it: it'll be a long time till this is all over.

So, writing this is like trying to cross a huge gulf of blackness between me and you.

There's an ache in the pit of my stomach when I think about it all.

But I have to get on with it.

I'm alive at least.

I'm safe, and Aggie will keep me that way.

I'm special to her.

She told me so.

[1.30]

You can convince yourself things are OK. Little lies you tell yourself to get you through. Humans have always done this. It's enabled us to survive the most terrible situations. It's an empowering, stoical thing, a resilience to keep accepting whatever stuff gets thrown at us and carry on. And if things get worse rather than better, then so be it. But it means for a while, for those minutes or hours, we lived in hope.

But hope can be an enemy as well. A poor ally leading us docilely on. The expectation that things can't get worse, the disbelief that the terrible stuff that is engulfing us can really be happening, the serene waiting allowing the obvious to be

83

ignored and for evil to take hold and become strong. While we wait for deliverance, we miss the opportunities to resist.

What if resistance is pointless? Look at the PE girl. It didn't help her. But maybe if we'd all done that, if we'd all risked everything, then we'd have broken Their cordons. Some of us would have got away.

But we didn't risk everything.

We went along willingly.

And we went along with what Emma told us. Not because it confirmed our own experience, but for the very fact that it denied it. What she said was deeply reassuring, and the teachers showing up just when they did, even if we only saw them for a convenient moment, swung it her way. Looking back, it's obvious we should have done something different. But I'm not blaming her, or us, or even me. We were only doing what we as a species have done countless times before when faced with colossal and monstrous evil. We simply refused to believe things could possibly be that bad. We just couldn't imagine that anyone could be that wicked.

But just because you can't imagine something, doesn't mean it isn't true.

I still didn't see it. Even in that deep night, lit only by the stars and a few mobile phones, I assumed there had been a power cut. Or a pre-emptive and cunning plan by the SAS to disorientate the terrorists by cutting off the electricity supply. All I knew was Emma's words were being proven right. We were marching down Seven Sisters Road towards the waiting and welcome arms of the authorities.

It was so dark now that Ada held tightly to my hand. By my reckoning, we were nearly at the end of the road. I'd thought we might hear whoops of freedom up ahead; but it was silent. They were probably being quietly led away by anti-terrorist officers.

"We're nearly at Manor House," Emma announced. "I can see the junction. We're – no, wait! That's not right! We're meant to be— *Ah!*"

We all felt it at the same time. A vicious, stinging screech in our heads.

—TURN LEFT!

We all did. There was no question of resistance, of wondering what was happening, our minds were being flayed with burning sonic lashes. I let go of Ada's hand, my hands instinctively, uselessly, rising to cover my ears. I felt sick with the pain but kept staggering on with the others, away from the road now, and the hoped-for exchange, and in through the Manor House entrance to Finsbury Park. I could just make out the gates as we were marched through them, the dark wrought iron rising ominously over us into the yet deeper darkness above.

—To your right.

Each girl held on to the one in front in the pitch darkness, shuffling slowly forward, down the hill. The pain gradually subsided, but as it did so, the shouting began. Shouts and sighs and yelps of betrayal. And real anger too, directed at Emma.

"What's going on?"

"You said we'd get exchanged!"

"I want to go home!"

Emma's voice, coming from somewhere up ahead, was so different to her earlier condescending tone. Now it was as shaky as anyone's. "It'll be all right. You'll see—"

But no one was listening. We were just obeying the sounds in our heads which pushed us on through the darkness, over the rough asphalt of the path. It took me till I was at the bottom of the hill to realise that Ada was no longer at my side.

"Ada where are you?"

But by now everyone was shouting and though she may have heard me, may even have been shouting back, I couldn't hear her.

—Onto the grass.

There was a large field over to our right where we were being directed. I tripped over the kerb and went sprawling.

—You will sleep here.

"What are you talking about?"

"There's no shelter!"

We all felt the buzzing, but before it became unbearable, the girls around me dropped to the ground. The earth was dry and hard. It had been a baking day. Even so, in the open air it was starting to get cooler, and I was only wearing a T-shirt and denim shorts. I tried to gain comfort from the stars, but they couldn't stop my head spinning with the new reality. This first day of our ordeal. Even up to an hour ago, I'd been convinced it was about to end. Now I didn't know what to think.

How all of this could have come about on such an ordinary day I had no idea. I was meant to be going shopping with Tess for summer tops at the weekend.

Above me the stars continued to glitter serenely. When I closed my eyes, my mind swirled. I thought of Ada. I thought of Mum and Dad and Tess and Jo. I thought of what might have happened to Brandon and Orlando and Pip. I thought of Miss Temple and Mr Carton and the PE girl. The bodies on the road. Eventually though, exhausted with the day, I slept.

□ | □ □⎯

[2.3]

There's something about writing in this notebook I really like.
It feels secret and safe.

I mean, I'm literally writing in it under the covers at the moment. Everyone else has gone to bed and I can barely see the page, but it's a proper thrill to be writing here in private.

It's not like I'm going to say anything I shouldn't — Lord knows I don't want to get Aggie or me in trouble, in case anyone were to read it.

It's just easier to write some things here. Special things. Silly things.

But maybe deep things too.

Stuff that's buried.

I also wonder when I write here, whether I should make myself seem more attractive.

I could save all my clever lines — I can be quite clever sometimes, reader — and then distil them so what you get here in this notebook is like a better version of me.

Like dressing up for a party. A fancy top. And a little eyeshadow. Just polishing what's there already.

All smiles and lip gloss and laughter and tossing my curls back.

That's what Tess always said made me look prettiest.

And I've definitely caught Orlando and a couple of other boys looking at me when I do that. Maybe some girls too.

So, is that what I should do for you, reader? Get all dressed up for a party, so you think I'm the funniest, prettiest, cleverest girl ever?

The problem is I'm not sure you even know what a party is.

And I don't know if that's what I should be explaining to you. What life used to be like. And if it is, then I'm so not the right person to do it.

I just took it all for granted and enjoyed it and hated it in equal measures.

The only thing I will say is: don't ever drink toffee vodka.

And as for me trying to present a particular image of myself, there's no point. You're the only one I can tell everything. Why lie?

So, I apologise, reader, if I'm a bit plain sometimes. No glitz. Not always a bundle of laughs.

But I guess you've got to work with what you've got. Right?

My clothes are a sweatshirt and baggy joggers, by the way. Both grey.

And that about sums me up.

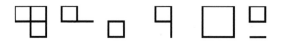

Part 3: Six, Never Seven

□ | □ □ |

[2.4]

Deep things. Stuff that's buried.

Let me tell you about my brother.

Let me tell you about Tom.

He was two years younger than me. Always getting into scrapes, always ending up in hospital. Throughout my entire childhood I'd only gone to A&E once, and even that turned out <u>not</u> to be a broken arm. By the age of six Tom practically had a loyalty card: a split forehead (twice), fractured wrist, gashed tongue, dislocated elbow, dislocated knee, and a raging fever which Mum and Dad thought was meningitis; but wasn't.

When we were little, we'd play together a lot. Tom would help me with my jigsaws, and the pieces would end up on the floor. He'd join me when I was making a den and inevitably collapse it.

So, he was a complete nightmare.

But oh, I loved him.

And all I think of now is that when the den collapsed, we rolled around in the blankets laughing and laughing.

On my ninth birthday, when Tom was six, nearly seven, we went to Kenwood House up on the edge of Hampstead Heath. We went to the tearoom and I had coffee and walnut cake. Tom had Victoria sponge. Mum and Dad just had tea.

You remember things like that when you're small.

Tom was allergic to nuts, so we had to be careful. That day he distracted us, so we were all looking the other way, and when we looked back, a huge chunk had disappeared from my coffee and walnut cake and Tom was choking.

Then his face turned to a huge grin, and he produced the lump of cake from under the table.

Hilarious.

Afterwards we ran outside to play.

We rolled down the grassy slopes to the wrought iron railings that separated us from the wide field where families were picnicking and playing frisbee and throwing balls to their dogs.

We ran back up the slope and rolled down again.

Dad timed us climbing over the railings. I had the longer legs but Tom was fearless so it was usually a draw.

I can't remember who won that day.

Then, while Mum and Dad walked sedately behind, we raced across the field to the lake on the far side, and over to the Rocket Tree.

I don't know who first called it that, but it was always the Rocket Tree to us. It was a massive beech, like several trees conjoined, all rising together, the tangle of branches affording endless nooks and crannies and footholds and hiding places. It was the perfect play area and that day there were already a dozen children on the tree, all ages from toddler – with anxious parents waiting below, arms outstretched – to older ones, ten- and eleven-year-olds, even some secondary school kids, who were on the tree for height and kudos, racing each other up the intertwining branches to the very top.

Tom was really into space stuff around then, so that day he wanted to pretend the Rocket Tree was just that: a rocket. Heading to his favourite planet, Jupiter. He was the captain. I was a passenger.

"Why can't I be the captain? I'm older."

"OK." He shrugged like he so often did. He didn't really care about things like that. He just wanted me to join in. "You're captain. I'm an alien."

He started the countdown. I gave him a boost to get going and then he was away. Meanwhile I scrambled up to the first perch about five feet off the ground. I was wearing a red elephant print dress and Geox trainers. Ahead of me, above me, my alien brother scrabbled around the tree trunk in a loose spiral, hauling himself confidently upwards from one handhold to the next. He was a born climber and a tree was like a second home to him. By contrast, my ascent was decidedly cautious. I hated heights, they made my head spin and my stomach swirl, and when I reached that first perch, I leant back against the tree trunk and took deep gulps of air.

"Nineteen! Eighteen! Seventeen! Come on, Cara!" I caught the flash of his white trainers through the tangle of leaves above. "We've got to get higher or else we'll be burned by the rocket's engines at take-off."

Halfway between us and Kenwood House, my parents had stopped, heads close together. Despite everything, I still remember wondering what birthday surprise they were planning for me. I willed them to be talking about a horse-riding lesson like Susan in 4E had got.

The day was hot and shimmery, but they were so vivid. Like I could reach out and touch them.

"Fourteen! Thirteen!"

I couldn't even see Tom now, but his voice came from overhead.

"Come on, Cara! The engines are firing soon."

I manoeuvred myself so I was facing the trunk and gingerly lifted my right leg to the next tangled branch, my trainer pawing to find a foothold.

"Twelve! Eleven!"

I found a crevice for my right foot, put my weight onto it, pushed off and brought my left up to meet it. But my trainer sole slipped against the wooden ledge, worn smooth by a thousand previous climbers. On its own that would have been fine, but just then my right hand, clinging to the dusty handle of a well-worn loop of a branch, was kicked by a kid coming the other way, and the sudden stab of searing pain caused me to let go. My whole body juddered and lurched, only my left hand and right foot remaining in contact with the tree.

"Nine! Eight! You've got to get higher, Cara."

Suddenly my right foot slipped.

My left arm wrenched at the shoulder but I clung on and my body slowly rotated until I was facing outwards.

"Cara, come on!"

My parents were staring back towards the House.

I thought I was going to be sick with the giddiness and the pain in my shoulder but then my right hand found a branch and I clung on.

My flailing right foot caught on a knot and it gave me support.

Seconds passed.

A minute.

It suddenly occurred to me I hadn't heard anything from Tom for ages.

I called up weakly but then broke off. "Stop it!" *I snapped at the little kid still trying to get past.*

"Cara—!"

A piercing scream—
My parents turning to look—
A clatter of branches and leaves—
Mum screaming—
A flurry right before me—
So fast that I had no time to even see him properly, to react—
To try to catch my brother as he fell.

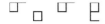

[1.31]

It was light when I awoke though the sun wasn't up yet.

I'd been dreaming about being in bed, so when I opened my eyes, I expected to see a window and, around me, posters plastering the walls to my tiny bedroom.

But I was in a field.

All about me, the grass was covered in a fine sheen of dew.

There were bodies as far as I could see, and I had a thumping headache. For a moment I thought I was at the Reading Festival.

Then, with a crushing sense of realisation, I remembered what had happened. I squeezed my eyes shut and cried for a bit, great sobs gripping my body.

Then, even the comfort that provided was gone, and I sat with my knees pulled up to my chin, hugging myself against the seeping chill and damp. Around me a few others were doing the same. Those awake were subdued like me.

Suddenly I remembered my phone. I dived into the pocket of my shorts to get it out. But though I pressed and repressed the power button, the phone screen stayed blank. The battery was dead.

I wanted to cry. But I had just done that so all I could do was hang my head.

When I looked up again, I saw a group of Them creating a perimeter around us. They didn't seem tired or dishevelled. They were all as groomed and beautiful as the night before. I wondered whether I should risk trying to run through a gap in their line. I mean, I was terrible at running, was kind of rubbish at all sports, but I had my Converses on and was willing to give it a go.

Then I remembered Ada.

I scanned the sleeping bodies on the ground, getting more and more anxious when I couldn't find her. And not just her: none of the younger girls seemed to be there.

"Ada!"

Others were waking and starting to call for their little sisters. Shouts were ringing around the field, and I kept searching but couldn't see her anywhere. My chest was constricting with fear as to what might have happened. And then suddenly I was properly angry. I ran up to the line of Them, to a ripped guy with a big afro and a beautiful redhead.

"Where is she?" I yelled at Them. "What have you done with her?"

They just stared back impassively. Then suddenly I realised it wasn't only the younger girls that were missing. I couldn't see the teachers either. Whether they'd followed us into the park or not I didn't know. But they certainly weren't with us now.

—Drink.

I spun around at the voice in my head.

—Behind you. Drink.

Over on the far side of our field I could see something glistening. I started walking with scores of others and, as I got closer, could see a huge pool dug where an outdoor gym had been. It was twenty metres across and fed by a pipe snaking down from the running track.

I didn't want to take anything these people gave me, but the moment I saw the water I became so thirsty that I found myself sprinting to the edge of the pond. I knelt and didn't even bother cupping my hands. I just put my whole face in the water and slurped down the first drink I'd had in eighteen hours.

Clustered like animals around an African waterhole, other girls were doing the same, stooping and kneeling, some lying, all of them slaking their parched lips and throats. The water was cool and delicious.

There were smiles everywhere. Having water meant for a while at least we could forget everything else.

"You see," said Emma. "Our demands are being met." She didn't give up easily that one. "The Metropolitan Police are obviously conducting a complex negotiation for our release. Water would have been one of their first stipulations."

Stipulate this, I thought irritably and carried on drinking.

—Eat.

Looking around wildly we saw that at the opposite end of the field a low heap of something had appeared. Girls rushed in that direction.

"It's bread and fruit."

"It's OK!"

"This bread's delicious!"

I was towards the back this time and it took a few minutes of jostling to push through the throng to the huge pile of apples and bananas and oranges and soft bread rolls. I took one of the rolls and sank my teeth into it. Maybe I was just starving, but that really was the best bread I'd ever tasted, like a brioche, slightly sweet, and all the better for it. I peeled a banana and took a bite. It was perfectly ripe. It and the roll were gone in a minute in alternate happy mouthfuls. Next, I split open an orange. The juice was sweet and lovely. After I'd eaten, I lay back. The sun was rising and it was suddenly beautifully warm under its early rays. By contrast with last night, the grass beneath me felt springy and comfortable.

—Urinate and defecate over there.

They were directing us to some bushes to the right. It was pretty disgusting to be told stuff like that, but still it was better than having to do it in the street.

Around me was happy chatter, but I was content just to lie there with my eyes half closed, the light filtering through my eyelashes, Emma's incessant reassurances and 'I told you so's almost drowned out by some of the girls starting to play childish clapping games.

"*Cara!*"

"Thank God!"

I jumped to my feet in time to be almost knocked over by a twin embrace from Tess and Jo.

I hugged them back joyfully. Somehow, I'd known they'd be fine but it was still such a relief to see them. Then I pulled myself free. "Hey you haven't seen a Year 7 girl, have you? Her name's Ada? She's got pigtails—"

"All those girls are gone," said Tess wide-eyed.

"Along with the teachers," said Jo. "Who is she anyway?"

That was kind of difficult to explain. Someone I'd known for a grand total of six hours, someone who in the way of younger kids might barely acknowledge me the next time she saw me. "Just someone I was looking after," I said vaguely.

"Tess saw them being taken."

"I couldn't sleep – at *all*," Tess explained. "They must have done Their mind thing, and all the younger girls got up and walked off in the middle of the night like they were in a trance."

"Did you see where?"

She shook her head guiltily. "It was really dark. I'm sorry."

"Well, we need to go and find them!"

"Sure." In the past, Jo's dispassionate tone had often irked me. It seemed sometimes like she displayed an utter lack of emotion: I guess it's what came of being so into science. But at times like this, it was good to hear her clinical voice. "We'll find her. We'll find everyone. But we need to get ourselves out of here first."

"How? I haven't seen anyone escape."

"We've been watching them," said Tess. She could be a little dreamy sometimes, so I was impressed at how on it she seemed now. "They have weaknesses."

"For starters," said Jo. "Though they're clearly using some kind of thought projection, it doesn't mean they can read our minds."

"It's like when I talk to Bonny." Bonny was Tess's golden retriever. "She knows what I'm saying, but I don't know what she's thinking."

"Plus," said Jo, "you saw what happened when that girl from Highbury Woods made a break for it. Everyone moved simultaneously, and They couldn't cope. Just for a moment it was too much for Them, and a few girls got through."

"And then," said Tess. "Did you see what happened next? That girl got *away*."

"Er… well, not really," I said. "One of the terrorists zapped her, and she went down."

"Right. But the ones closest to us couldn't do it," said Jo. "It means their mind control only works over a limited range."

"So, if we get away…" Tess's eyes gleamed. "We *get away*."

"So… how does that help us?"

"We need to create a surge," said Jo. "Not sure how yet… But we need a surge and then we make a break for it."

"But where to?"

"Parkland Walk."

"The disused railway line?"

"Exactly. It runs all the way to Highgate. And from there, it's not far to Hampstead Heath."

"And then what? Go to the police?"

Tess and Jo exchanged a glance. "Probably…" said Tess. "It's just… Well, did you see how all the electricity had been cut off last night? It looks like quite a large-scale incident. What happens if it's all over London? Or maybe it's even bigger."

"How could it be bigger than London?"

"Have you noticed there's nothing in the sky?"

I instinctively looked upwards as Jo spoke.

"No planes or helicopters. Airships. *Drones*."

The clear blue was pristine. Not a vapour trail to be seen. "But…" My head was spinning. "Who *are* They, if They could do something like this?"

"I don't know. Perhaps it's an invasion."

"The Russians?"

"They don't look Russian."

"Russia's a big place," said Jo.

"I don't think they're Russian," repeated Tess doggedly.

"It really doesn't matter," said Jo. "The point is, once we get away, we might just need to lie low for a bit till it's all sorted out."

"I think we need to get as far away as possible," said Tess.

"Shouldn't we just get home?" I said. "Find out what's happened to our parents?"

That reminder left us all uneasy. Then Jo's eyes gleamed. "Cara, you've just given me the idea for the surge. I think I've got a way for us to escape."

⊓ ⊓ ⊓ ⊓
 □   □

[1.32]

—I don't think I can allow this.

Aggie had been eagerly reading my latest instalment. But at the end, she grabbed a pen and held it poised.

—This is subversive. It might encourage other humans to escape.

"It's pretty unlikely anyone will ever read this. And, in any case, they want to escape already."

—I don't believe that. Humans aren't trying to break out all the time.

"Because there's nowhere to go."

—No. Mostly because they fear death.

"That doesn't make sense. Most of them know they're going to be killed anyway. It's got to make sense to try and escape."

—And yet the vast majority do not. The fear of certain near-term pain or death is a powerful disincentive to escape. In any case, everyday farm life is so comfortable, why would they want to leave it?

I snorted. "It's *OK*. I wouldn't say comfortable."

Although Aggie's face doesn't do expression, her body language evoked surprise pretty clearly.

—Well, we have modelled our husbandry of humans on how you treated farm animals. We assumed that you had chosen conditions for them that you yourselves would have enjoyed.

I didn't really know what to say to that.

—And this is certainly not the first time that your species has faced such challenges. Before Colonisation, we researched instances where one group of your species has controlled another. I believe you used to call it slavery or concentration camps. In those cases too, there could have been little doubt for the clear-sighted that death was the ultimate outcome. And yet only a few risked escape.

I frowned.

—Incidentally I know of no other species which treats its own in this way.

I was quiet for a long time. Eventually I said, "Look, cross it out if you need to. It doesn't really matter."

Aggie blinked, then put the pen down, leaving the page as it was. —OK. You can finish it. In any case, I would like to know what happens.

[1.33]

For the plan to work, we needed everyone awake, so we bided our time for another hour.

By then, it was still only seven o'clock by Jo's digital watch. But there was already sufficient commotion, that everyone was up and stretching and drinking and feasting and had even formed an orderly queue to the toilet areas. The day hadn't cranked up to full temperature yet, and the relief of food and water and a night's sleep meant that the complaints about not having washing facilities or the anguish at the absence of the small girls and the teachers were suppressed. Instead, there was happy chatter like they'd already been released.

But Tess, Jo and I weren't fooled. We'd picked our way to the edge of the field, over to where Redhead and Afro were standing, then flopped down on the grass right in front of them.

"I still feel kind of uneasy about this," said Tess.

"And me. Isn't there another way?"

"This is the way," said Jo.

There was a constant ebb and flow of girls in the crowd. When a group approached us, coming from the waterhole, their arms linked, chattering happily, Jo looked pointedly at Tess and me.

"Showtime."

We jumped to our feet. Jo pointed beyond the cordon of Them, at some indeterminate point in the distance, and screamed, *"Look!"*

"Oh my God!" I shouted. "Mum! Dad!"

"They're here!" Tess took it up. "Our parents! They're really here!"

Around us, heads turned immediately. Girls who had been dozing leapt up. Shouts from behind us. *"Where?"*

"I can't see anything."

"There!" Tess insisted. "There. *Mum!*"

"Dad!" Jo shouted.

Now the group of girls, the herd, began to take interest. And as the news passed back, the commotion was electric. I felt terrible about it. But we needed to do something and this was the something.

The girls closer to us were looking at us quizzically.

"I can't see anything," said one craning in the direction that Jo was pointing.

"Yeah, what are you talking about?"

But their voices were drowned by those behind them. The further from the front they were, the more excited they got. And with excitement, came movement. One girl broke into a run, and then others. The pack of girls, a suddenly coherent mass, surged forward.

—Sit down.

We heard Them but kept up the shouting. It was all or nothing now.

"They're letting us go!"

"Quick! Our parents are waiting."

It was cruel to hear the shouts taken up behind us. One girl was sobbing saying she'd seen her dad. Another was shouting to her mother. All around, girls pushed forward.

—Sit down.

It was more insistent, but They had realised the danger too late, had applied only mild fuzziness when a full neural smack had been needed. The surging crowd of girls burst through Their line. I saw our redhead captor knocked aside as the girls poured through the gap and beyond, another fifteen, twenty metres before they pulled up short, looking around wildly when the lack of parents became evident. But still more girls jostled their way through eager to see their mums and dads.

We knew what to do, sprinting through the emergent throng, keeping as close to the centre of the fluid mass of girls as we could, as far from Them as possible, bursting finally into the open. But instead of standing and staring like the others, we made a run for it.

Apart from the surge itself, we didn't have much of a plan. To get to the Parkland Walk, we needed to go over the hill in the centre of the park, past the running track, boating lake and children's playground, and across to the tennis courts from where a narrow passage led to a footbridge and then to the disused branch line all the way to Highgate. What we didn't know was how many of Them patrolled the route and what They might do to try and stop us. All we could do was run.

At the top of the hill, we stopped to catch our breath. And, inevitably, to glance back down. Seen from our vantage point, the field we'd been in looked like the amoeba we'd studied in biology last year. The side closest to us had ruptured where girls had spilled out unevenly, yet already the cell membrane of Them had repaired itself, was stretching around the girls to contain them. There were a few bodies lying on the ground but some also seemed to be getting to their feet. No one was cheering our escape like we had for the PE girl. Perhaps they thought release was imminent. Or were just furious with us for tricking them about their parents. It had been quite mean.

Half a dozen of Them were walking purposefully in our direction, but Their thoughts didn't reach us as anything more than a bit of static. We were a couple of hundred metres away. We had found Their range.

We started running again, along the black metal railings that ran around the athletics ground. There were the sounds of sawing and hammering, and we could see Them hard at work on the grassy infield oval within the running track, though They were too occupied with Their activity to notice us. We ran on until we were round at the entrance to the athletics ground, hidden by the brick rise of the pavilion, then slipped across the path and into the bulrushes that encircled the boating lake.

I had a stitch and Tess seemed exhausted. Jo was breathing hard but through her nose not her mouth. More controlled. Her climbing and fencing and swimming – you name it, her parents made her do it – were all paying off. I knew right then that she was the one who needed to make it to the outside world.

"We're all making it," Jo insisted when I suggested it to her.

We snuck round the edge of the lake, and across the deserted children's playground. We were at the top of the hill here and had a good view around the park. Down to our left, in the field running parallel to the Seven Sisters Road, we could see another crowd of girls had been herded. But the road itself was empty.

We ran on, past the café, and then, reaching the perimeter road, we crouched behind a bush and took stock. Ahead, a path led by the basketball courts and to the footbridge, which would take us to Parkland Walk. But in the centre of that path stood two of Them, a young South Asian woman and a well-built blond man. They were on the crest of the hill so had a complete view in either direction.

Behind us, on the far side of the playground we could see more of Them appearing, perhaps the same pursuers who had set off after us, still moving slowly, but even They would catch us eventually.

"Listen," I said to Jo. "Tess and I will create a diversion and then you need to make a break for it." I looked at Tess, and she nodded grimly.

"No way," said Jo.

"You have to," said Tess. "You've got the best chance." She grinned. "We'll be OK."

I'd known Tess since Reception in primary school when we'd eaten jam sandwiches together on our first play-date. I'd seen her ecstatic and downcast and cheerful and devastated. I could tell how she was feeling from a single glance at those blue, blue eyes of hers. And right now, that grin told me she was absolutely terrified. I grabbed her hand and squeezed it.

"Sorry about the whole parmesan thing," I said.

"Oh, don't be silly," she said. There were tears in her eyes, in mine, as we hugged. Neither of us wanted to let go but we knew we had to. And then we embraced Jo, who was much less the hugging type, but was the closest one to full-on crying.

"Let me be the decoy," she said. "I'm the fastest. I can draw Them both away."

"You can't."

Which was true. There were two of Them. It needed two decoys.

"OK," Jo said desperately. "But listen, whichever of us escapes—"

"You," I said.

"But if it's not, and if you make it somewhere else, and if they catch you, don't let them break you. I don't mean be a hero, just hold something back of yourself – of us – even if it's something tiny. Keep something human."

We all hugged once more.

"Come on," I said. "Before the others catch up." We were starting to feel their static like the buzzing of angry bees. "Tess, you go low, I'll go high. Jo, wait till they're committed, then head for the footbridge. Whatever happens to us don't stop. Let's go!"

I sprinted away from the path leading to the overpass and onto the expanse of the basketball courts. Looked over my shoulder long enough to catch sight of Tess disappearing from view in the opposite direction as she hurtled down the hill.

—Halt.

The blond man had started to follow me. He focused his thought beam at me, and it hurt; but I was moving fast and out of range. Out of the corner of my eye I saw Jo shoot from her hiding place and sprint for the footbridge.

—Stop her.

I turned and I saw to my horror that two of Them had emerged from the entrance to the overpass directly in Jo's path. She wheeled away, following Tess down the hill, and then she was gone from view.

Our chances of escape were evaporating. Running down the hill would lead the girls to more of Them. The blond man, impossibly well sculpted, was still coming towards me like some bizarrely attractive zombie. I was so nauseous with fear that I wanted to flop down right there.

But I didn't.

I ran on. To the edge of the basketball courts where the pain in my head lessened. I hauled myself into the bushes, squirming through the gaps in the branches and brambles, knowing that when I came out, I would be right by the exit leading to the footbridge. And They would either be there waiting for me or They wouldn't. But I didn't have a choice, and with the last flurry of my arms to keep the tangle of briar out of my eyes, I burst into the open.

I was alone.

I spun immediately to head the few metres to the footbridge, but even in my hurry I couldn't help but notice the two prone figures laid out on the flank of the hill below me. One was in a yellow spaghetti-strapped dress, the other in what I knew was Jo's peach-print jumpsuit. She'd got it from H&M just three weeks before. She didn't go shopping much. Tess had to convince her to buy it. And now they were both lying there, feeling the cool grass against their faces; or feeling nothing.

But by the time I'd registered all of that, I was already halfway across the overpass, my Converses clattering across the surface and then on to the skiddy, dusty gravel beyond, the start of Parkland Walk. At this time of year, there were billowing clouds of cow parsley flowers on both sides of what had once been a stretch of train track. It was two miles to Highgate on an uphill gradient, and though my lungs were burning, and I was almost doubled over with exhaustion and unprocessed grief and guilt, I knew I couldn't stop.

It hadn't rained for a fortnight and the stony ground was set like concrete. Normally the path would be teeming with cyclists and dog walkers, but today it was empty, the cow parsley heads encroaching on the path, bobbing in and out of my way as I ran by.

I'd reached a cast iron bridge where the railway line had once passed over the road below. An old sign on the black metal girders told me I was at Crouch End, about halfway to Highgate. Suddenly, I heard sounds up ahead. From nowhere, four of Them emerged from the bushes on either side of the path. I whirled around, but behind me, fifty yards back, another two of Them had also appeared.

They had me.

Except... I was on a bridge. I ran to the handrail and looked over at the street below. It was deserted and no more than fifteen feet down. The bridge's flanks were crisscrossed with hand-sized rivets and bolts.

—Stop.

I could hear Them but not feel Them yet. If I climbed over the railing, it couldn't be more than a short drop to the empty road. Perhaps I'd even be able to find a bicycle and ride out of there.

—Stop.

Angry bees. They were getting closer and, without pausing to think, I heaved myself up and over so that I was straddling the balustrade, swivelled and looked for where I could find my first handhold, a huge rusted rivet. I gripped it and was going to lower myself but then made the mistake of looking down—

Suddenly it felt like the road was rushing up towards me, my whole vision quivering. In that instant I was frozen by my age-old fear.

I willed myself to move my left hand from the rail.

But couldn't do it.

Tears of frustration welled and rolled down my cheeks.

I felt a cold sweat envelop me as I was left clinging to the side of the bridge…

They caught up with me at their sedate pace. I despised myself. I'd had so much time to get away. They reached down, grabbed my wrists and hauled me back over the railing. And once on firm ground again, I sank down at their feet and sobbed.

[2.5]

We never really knew what happened.

There had been some older kids near the top of the Rocket Tree messing around. But no one suggested they'd pushed Tom. (I wouldn't have wanted to believe something like that anyway.)

So, it was just an accident.

And we were left with the sadness.

The horrible emptiness.

The relentless blaming ourselves.

No one said that if I hadn't been so petrified of heights, I would have been alongside Tom on the tree. And though Mum and Dad never said I should've been looking after him better, my grandfather did, at the funeral, howling with anger and despair.

Because he loved Tom even more than his own kids, Dad said.

Well, Nonno was right.

It was my fault.

I should have looked after him better.

I'd do anything to go back there. To that split second before he fell.

Even now I reckon I'd be too pathetic to clamber up the tree after him. But at least I'd be able to call to him to hold on tight. To come back down.

Into the safety of my arms.

Which he would try and wriggle free from immediately, of course, not knowing what all the fuss was about.

But I would hold him, even if only for a moment longer than normal. Because I would know.

I'm seventeen now and he's still six, nearly seven.

Six, never seven.

He'd be so small in my arms.

Even if he still fell, I'd be able to catch him now.

I'd be strong enough for that.

Even if I was too weak back then.

[1.34]

It's been a couple of days since I last wrote.

I've not been feeling so good again.

I woke up today with the sense that something was out of place.

Inside me.

It's the effect of all the remembering.

I used to get it in the old days sometimes and it would leave me spoiling for a fight.

Anyway, I was quieter than normal when Aggie came in. She'd got me a pain au chocolat which was normally one of my favourites.

But today it had tasted kind of dry.

"Do Colonists have books?" I asked after I'd finished eating and sat, fidgeting at my desk, as Aggie did my hair.

—Only when the situation demands. We much prefer the spoken word. Sit still please.

Aggie was attempting cornrows with my hair today.

"But books are different. Books are better."

—I enjoy reading *your* book. But it is merely a basic record. Colonist literature is far more sophisticated and better experienced via The Hive Mind.

"But what if you just want to sit down and read something? Like now. You're not connected to The Hive Mind yet."

Aggie shrugged. —We just recall it from our memories. We have amazing memories. And you know our culture has created huge numbers of stories and songs and poetry.

"We had loads of that stuff too," I blurted.

—No, Cara. You didn't. We've talked about this. You *told* me you understood.

If I'd been feeling better, I wouldn't have gone on. But today I couldn't help myself. "We had libraries full of books."

—Libraries?

"Large buildings. Full of stacks and stacks of books."

—Full of directories and manuals. Yes, there was one like that near here. A cream building with large windows. That is used by Administrators now.

"But all the books inside? The ~~stories~~—"

—There were no ~~stories~~ there, Cara.

Aggie tried to sound patient. —The Mantra makes it clear. Only Colonists have stories. The books in your libraries were factual. I was hoping you'd learned this by now. Our scientists are right about how dumb you all are—

"We're not dumb! We had ~~novels~~ and ~~plays~~—"

—Stop it!

Aggie dropped the hank of hair she'd been holding.

—These are not human things. And if you write about them in your journal again, I will cross them out. *Again.*

"But they existed—"

—The building exists, Cara. Just not what you claim was in it. Even the factual books which were there have been removed.

"But where would they have been taken? Maybe you could—"

—Anything flammable would have been burned as biomass.

"*Burned?* You *burned* our books?"

—Unless they had sufficient sugar content. In which case, they would have been processed into fabricator pellets.

"But you can't *burn* books."

—Well, perhaps they weren't. Maybe you had a piece of one of those books in your pain au chocolat this morning.

Which turned my stomach.

—Why do you care so much anyway? They were just catalogues and almanacs.

"I just want to read a book! ~~I just want to read a novel~~!"

For a moment my head buzzed and I thought Aggie was going to hurt me. —You need to stop this nonsense, Cara! These dangerous delusions. This is your final warning. Next time, I'll take your notebook and pens away.

She stood and her voice in my head suddenly sparked with rage. —Why do you have to be so frustrating? *And why don't you even have proper hair!*

She strode from the alcove, the barrier rising behind her.

I was left alone, the cornrows slowly unravelling.

□ ' □ ꟼ

[2.6]
They burned our books.
THEY BURNED OUR BOOKS!
When they said they'd taken all our books away, I thought they were in a warehouse somewhere.
It never occurred to me that they'd have <u>burned</u> them.
They could have just buried them in a hole or something.
Don't <u>burn</u> them.
Only Nazis burn books.

I mean, I know they like to pretend we didn't write all our amazing stories and poetry and plays and make films and music and TV. And I know I have to go along with that, and also make sure I don't get cross again or say something stupid out loud. And fair dues, they are much more intelligent than us. But you can't burn our books.

It's just not right.

Well, you know what?

You think you can control what I say or write?

But under the covers,

In the middle of the night by the light of your substandard solar lights,

Writing in my secret notebook,

This unattractive,

Unremarkable,

Water stained,

Wonderful, wonderful, book

I can say whatever I want.

About whatever I want.

And whoever I want.

I can be me.

Cara.

In this little red and blue notebook.

I can be truly free.

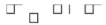

[1.35]

She's right, of course.

Being with Aggie, I forget myself. Because I am with beings of incredible intelligence and creativity, I think I'm like that too.

But Colonists are superior in every way.

I've said the lesson's been learned, but this time, I really mean it. I've even gone back and crossed out any potentially offending writing myself.

I understand:

I am not creative.

I am not a Colonist.

Thank you, Aggie, for looking after me in spite of that.

Thank you for everything you do.

Part 4: 13th State, 2nd City

□⌐ □ □⌐ □⌐

[1.36]
It's not like Aggie's just been busy the last couple of days, she's literally not been in the apartment.

I asked Schektl about it when he returned from work this evening. I wasn't going to ask Plaxys. I'm so scared of her that if I never speak to her again that'll be just fine.

—She will be back tomorrow, he said. —I will be bringing your breakfast tray again.

"But where's she been?"

—Self-improvement.

"Really. Because Aggie always said you don't have schools, so is it—?"

—It is not school. It is self-improvement. Do not make a mess with your dinner.

I looked down at what he'd brought and sighed. Normally, when Aggie was around, I was able to fabricate whatever I wanted, but Schektl had simply reproduced my breakfast. He hadn't even chosen a nice pastry, just given me a nutrition packed cereal bar.

The last few days have been so boring.

And by the time I'd looked up to ask again about self-improvement, he was already raising the barrier on his way out of the alcove.

□⌐ □ □⌐ □⌐

[1.37]
I expected Them to kill me. But all They did was march me back.

That felt like a long, exhausting walk, each step taking me closer to captivity again. They escorted me all the way, but instead of following the path around the edge of the running track, we went straight to the main gate by the pavilion. They guided me through the concrete of the stand, down the steps and onto the track itself.

I could see now what all the hammering and the sawing had been about. Across the infield were long sheds each about five metres wide, fifty metres long and numbered on the front and sides, 1 to 4. They must have been built astonishingly quickly as there had been nothing there just twenty-four hours earlier apart from the pole vault pit and the markings for the javelin. I assumed immediately that I was being taken there for punishment.

But the next thing hurtling into my brain, pushing other thoughts out of the way, was the permanence of the construction. This was not Manchester or 9/11 or Beslan. This wasn't a terrorist hijacking.

This was an occupation.

As if to prove that point, as They took me right out onto the grass, I saw our group of girls being led up from the field and through an entrance on the far side of the track which must have been cut into the railings specially. And, at the front of the group, were Tess and Jo.

They were a little worse for wear. Tess had grass stains all over her yellow dress and Jo was bruised.

"I'm so sorry I let you down," I said.

"You didn't let us down," said Tess stroking my arm.

"I did. I had a chance to get away, but I couldn't take it. I just froze."

"You did great," said Tess. "We're all back together. And, we've learned some stuff for next time."

"Shh." Jo dropped her voice. "I don't trust some of the girls. Emma was really odd when They brought us back. She said that we'd risked all their lives by trying to escape. She said it would have served us right if … you know…"

"She said we should sit tight until the hostage exchange happened," said Tess.

"'What hostage exchange?' I asked her and she said she wasn't at liberty to give details." Jo snorted. "Look around. They've built stuff. This is *not* a hostage thing."

"Then what?" I suddenly felt very weepy. I think it was being back with them, and the fact that they'd been pleased to see me and had not been at all judgemental.

"You know what it reminds me of?" said Tess, turning a slow three hundred and sixty degrees, taking it all in. "It reminds me of a farm."

"What?"

"You know. Like those are sheds for animals to sleep in, and there – look there – those are like cattle troughs. You know for feed."

"Well, where are the animals?" said Jo. "All I see is some huts to hold us for a bit."

"But why?"

I was feeling really jittery, completely unlike how I'd been the previous day. Then I'd been strong. Had held everything together. "What does it all mean?" My voice quavered. Probably the way a younger kid's would have done; like Ada. And that sobered me up immediately. Where was Ada? "Any sign of the other girls? You know the younger ones?"

"No," said Tess. "Sorry." I think they both knew already how attached I was to this little girl even though I'd only just met her. They were really cool friends like that: they just got things about you without having to over-explain all the time.

"And no sign of the boys or teachers?" But I was kind of expecting it when they shook their heads. I wiped my eyes with the heels of my hands. Nodded at one of the sheds. "So, what do you reckon? Are we meant to sleep in these?"

Before anyone could answer, Emma had burst upon us, jabbing an angry finger at each of us in turn. I was standing in the middle and caught that finger right in the rib cage.

"Don't – *ever* – pull a stunt like that again!"

Behind her was assembling a crowd of similarly angry-looking girls. I think a lot of them were from the hockey team, and they all had the same snarly faces. That's hockey for you.

"What are you talking about?"

"You could have got us killed!" Emma was standing right by me but was still shouting. It was like she was making sure the girls behind her heard. "And it was just so hard on us pretending our parents were here."

"We're sorry about that," said Tess who was a natural peacemaker, pretty much the nicest person I knew actually. "But we were risking our lives to get help."

"Leave that to the authorities. Help is coming!"

"Then where is it? And stop prodding me." I made to brush her hand away. For a moment she resisted, and I thought there was going to be a scuffle. Emma was taller and burlier than me, but I didn't care. I was set to explode.

Emma must have realised she was pushing things a bit far because she let her hand drop and backed off half a step. It was a shame Rowan Marlow, our actual head girl, wasn't around. She would have put Emma in her place. But she was up at an open day in Cambridge, so we were stuck with the deputy.

"Listen, Cara," Emma said in a patronising voice, glancing at her followers for support. "While you three were putting us in *jeopardy*—"

"Really?" said Jo crossing her arms. She'd have been a match for Emma if things had actually kicked off. She'd done karate along with all that fencing and climbing.

"—I took it upon myself to simply ask Them what was going on and what state negotiations were at." She smiled. "I can't reveal *everything* They told me—"

I snorted.

"—but suffice it to say, the discussions are going very well."

"Yeah, brilliantly," said Jo. "Which is why we've been moved to an area that looks like a prison camp, and why the younger ones went missing in the night—"

"That's the whole point, you silly girl."

Jo's mouth fell open. I don't think anyone had called her *silly* in her entire life.

"The younger ones and the teachers have been freed."

"What?" I was blinking, my heart leaping inside of me. Ada was safe. Miss Temple too. "How do you know?"

"I asked Them. And They told me."

"But where have they gone?"

"The teachers and the young girls were handed over to the authorities. We're going to be next. We just need to be patient."

"And the sheds They've built for us?"

"The negotiations might take a few days. Possibly a week or two."

Cries of dismay from some of the girls crowding around. But Emma was very much in charge now, and she simmered them down with outstretched arms. "These are complex talks. We have to let the authorities do their work."

"But who are They?" asked Tess. "Where did They come from?"

Emma smiled indulgently. "Now They're hardly going to share that information, are they?"

"I suppose not…"

I exchanged a glance with Jo. I could see she wanted to believe all this as much as I did, but it just didn't ring true.

"Why aren't there any helicopters overhead? You know from the RAF or police or whatever?" Jo could always be relied on to ask good questions.

"No-fly-zone," Emma came back instantly.

Jo stared her in the eye, and Emma stared straight back. Eventually Jo shrugged and looked away.

"So," said Emma to us, but as much to the crowd which had formed about her. "Can we just agree that from now on, there won't be any escape attempts. They made it clear, They would be forced to punish us if it happens again."

She gave Tess, Jo and me a sharp look in turn, spun on her heel and disappeared into her group of admirers and hangers-on. "Hockey team!" she barked. "A meeting. Now."

We three were left alone as the crowd dispersed. Tess looked crestfallen from the ticking off we'd received. But I'd brushed off Emma's condescension and was willing myself to at least believe that Ada and Miss Temple were safe.

"Hey," I said, looking around me at the bustling infield. "Why don't we go and get some decent sleeping areas while we still can."

We walked into Shed 2 which was closest to us. It was crudely constructed with plank walls, corrugated metal roof and sparse windows. A central passage ran the length of the building and, to either side, the space was divided at two metre intervals by half-height metal panels which created a set of cubicles. The floor of each cubicle had been covered in a thick layer of clean straw.

Some other girls were already laying claim to cubicles, but we still found three in a row. Each sleeping area was wide enough to be able to lie out in. They had four-foot-high walls at either end, so there was a little privacy if you wanted it, or you could stand up and talk to the person next to you. The cubicles had a metal front hinged in two places so either half could be swung open. The front panel had a gap of around six inches at the bottom. But once this was stuffed with straw, and despite the crudeness of the building and the limited windows, it was actually comforting to be in a place to call your own. And, once the remaining straw had been pushed up against the wall, it made a surprisingly comfortable bed.

It was only when I tried it out that I realised quite how exhausted I was from the escape attempt, the night spent in the open, and the weirdness of the previous day. As I lay there, watching dust motes in a shaft of light above me, feeling the straw tangle and tickle into my curls, I thought, if this did take a few days to sort itself out, so long as we could just take it easy here, and I could have Jo and Tess in the cubicles either side of me, there could be worse things…

⌐ ▫ ▫ | ▫ |

[1.38]

I've been writing all day.

There's not been much else to do with Aggie not around.

It's evening now, and I heard them returning with Aggie late afternoon. I called out to her, but she didn't answer and went straight to her bedroom.

So, maybe self-improvement is a residential trip like when we did PGL in Year 7: outward-boundy kind of stuff which meant she was knackered or needed a shower or both. I thought I would still see her at some point during that evening though; but I didn't.

Just another boring dinner tray from Schektl.

I mean, it literally wouldn't be any harder for him to bring me something tasty. It's only different buttons to press on the fabricator.

⌐ ▫ ▫ | ▫ _

[1.39]

Wow, Aggie was up early today!

It had only just got light, and Schektl and Plaxys were still in the apartment when she came bustling in.

I was lolling in bed. I normally had an hour after Schektl and Plaxys had gone, and even then, Aggie would come in at a very gentle pace.

But today it was like someone had put a rocket up her.

—Rise and shine! Rise and shine!

123

She was clearly pleased with that because she kept repeating it as she paced briskly around the alcove.

"Shh, Aggie. I'm still waking up."

—Well, it's a beautiful morning. And there's so much to do. Did you miss me?

"Of course. Your dad makes rubbish food trays."

—Oh. But did you miss *me?*

"What? Yes, of course. Where have you been? How was your self-improvement?"

—I am much improved.

In my head I could hear her laughter.

"I don't get it. Was it like camp? Did you meet lots of other Colonist kids there?"

—No.

"So, what did you do? It's been really boring here in the past few days. Tell me *something* interesting—"

—I'll tell you later. Let me get your breakfast tray. How about one of your favourites? Apricot Danish?"

"Sure. But Aggie? *Aggie?*"

She was gone.

Seemed like the whole family was enjoying doing that to me at the moment.

But anyway, the sun was streaming in, Aggie was back, and I was going to get breakfast in bed. So, what was not to like?

[1.40]

I must have dropped off because the kicking on the front panel of my cubicle made me sit up with a start. The metal door swung open, and Christine Hargensen – star hockey player in Year 11 – was standing there.

"Out."

"Christine?"

"Get out. We need to free up this block."

"What are you talking about?" Jo was remonstrating with another girl I didn't recognise but of the same sporty build as Christine. Tess was already out of her cubicle.

"Emma has commandeered this block. She needs to have one big enough for her whole group."

"What group?" I said.

"Us."

And for the first time I noticed that around her right arm, and that of the girl by Jo's cubicle, and the one leading Tess to the doorway, were torn-off strips of white cotton T-shirt material, and on each, scrawled in what looked like plum lipstick, was a circle with a capital E at its centre.

The muzziness from my nap vanished in an instant. "We got here first!"

"Yeah, we're not moving. Tess! Don't—"

But it was too late. Tess had already been taken outside.

Jo and I exchanged a glance. Then Jo shrugged. What was the point of getting into a fight? The main thing was to stick together. I glowered at Christine, then turned, my shoulder catching hers accidentally-on-purpose as we trailed out of the shed.

"Why did you just leave?" Jo was saying to Tess. "We could have stuck it out if you'd stayed."

"Sorry."

"They couldn't have kicked us out you know—"

"*I said sorry.*"

"It's OK." Seeing them glaring at each other somehow helped to calm my own anger down. "It doesn't matter. Let's just try one of the other sheds. Hey, look over there."

A new group of several hundred girls were being led across the running track into the athletics ground. They were more dishevelled than our lot, their clothes ripped, their faces dirty. With their arrival, the already bustling infield was becoming distinctly overcrowded. The consequence of this dawned on us at the same time, and we hurried to Shed 3 to secure some cubicles before they were all taken. But when we looked around, we couldn't find three together. And squabbles were starting to break out between girls who were trying to grab the best ones.

We retreated once more into the sunshine but found the same story in Shed 4 and Shed 1 which were filling up at such a rate that even finding a single free cubicle was getting difficult. We headed back to Shed 2, from where Emma's lot had just evicted us. Three burly girls with armbands were now standing sentry at the door.

"You're not coming in."

"What are you talking about?" I could see inside and there was still plenty of room. "The other sheds are getting really crowded. A new lot of girls has just arrived."

"Tough. We have orders."

"You've got *what?*"

"It's OK, it's OK." Emma emerged from within and stood flanked by her bodyguards. She gave us a not-very-nice smile.

"What the hell's going on?" I yelled at her. "Who put you in charge?"

Emma shrugged shyly and looked to either side of her. "Someone needs to keep order until negotiations are over and we're all freed. I'm responding to the will of the people."

"Come on," snapped Jo. "She's flipped."

"Careful," said Emma sweetly. "Remember, a lot of the girls already have a reason not to like you. Don't make enemies when you don't need to."

"Are you threatening us?"

But Emma just laughed and disappeared back into the shed.

We were flabbergasted, but that astonishment was overridden by the very real fear that we might not find anywhere to sleep. Getting increasingly panicky, we toured the sheds again, ending up back in Shed 3 which had earlier seemed so crowded because we couldn't find three free cubicles together. Now there were no free cubicles at all.

Except one.

"What's wrong with this one?" I asked the girls on either side.

"Someone was sick in it."

As she spoke the words, we caught the sour odour of vomit emanating from the straw. I retched.

"I'll clear it," said Tess who was amazing with things like that. She scooped up armfuls of the offending straw and took them outside. By the time she got back, Jo and I had spread out the rest and it hardly smelt at all. It wasn't as comfortable as a cubicle per person, but at least we were together.

More and more girls were looking for places to rest. We'd shake our heads at them as they poked their heads into our area. "There's no room here," we'd say as nicely as we could.

Until an eighteen-year-old with a black eye and her fifteen-year-old sister, her arm in a makeshift sling, looked in. They were mixed race Afro-Caribbean, each with a tumble of black curls tighter than my own.

"Please can we come in?" The younger girl's eyes were full of tears.

"*They* are back inside the athletics ground," explained her sister. "They told us we've got ten minutes to find a stall—"

"They're cubicles, not stalls," said Jo.

"Well, *They're* calling them stalls."

"Try the shed next door," said Tess kindly. "There's still loads of room in that one, I bet."

"We tried that. But they… they…" The girl indicated her eye and pointed at her younger sister's arm. Then stamped her foot when we still did nothing. "Fine. Come on. They're as bad as the lot with the armbands."

"Wait," I said hurriedly. It was like she'd uttered the magic words. "We can make room."

Jo and Tess were on their feet as well, welcoming them in.

Where it had been cozy with three of us in the cubicle, now it was definitely cramped. But somehow that was preferable to turning them away.

"I'm Celie, and this is Nettie." Nettie, the younger one, was lying out flat with her bad arm placed gingerly in her lap. None of us had a problem with that even if it meant we had to stay sitting upright.

"So, They're back inside the athletics ground?"

"Yes. They said – or thought – or whatever – that we all needed to be herded inside the barns."

Tess's ears pricked up. "Is that exactly what they said? Herded? Barns?"

"*Tess*," muttered Jo wearily, warningly.

"Look around you," Tess persisted. "What does all this remind you of?"

I got to my feet and looked up and down the long shed, at the cubicles – the stalls – on either side of the passageway, five or six girls crammed into each one, nestled together on the straw. The sound was deafening, nearly three hundred of us in an enclosed space, chattering, arguing, crying. Patrolling the passageway in pristine blue jeans and white T-shirt were two of Them, as beautiful as ever. As They passed in front of our cubicle, They fiddled with the gate, and I realised they were locking us in.

—Stay inside. We will feed and water you in due course. Any attempt to leave will be punished.

Then They moved on to the next stall.

I turned slowly back to the others. They were all on their feet apart from Nettie. Tess had her hands out, palms up, imploring us to see what she could see.

"Barns. Stalls. Herding. You know what this is."

Suddenly I felt irritated with her like it was the pesto incident all over again. She shouldn't even be *thinking* things like this and certainly not when there was a younger girl like Nettie around.

"What's she talking about?" asked Celie.

"She's not talking about anything." I glared at Tess. Her face went even paler than usual. But she didn't say anything. She just dropped onto the straw, crawling into a corner, turning her face away.

"So," I said, sitting down as well, changing the subject. "Tell us what happened to you, Celie. How did you get here?"

"We're from Hornsey Woods School. I was doing athletics when They just suddenly appeared around the edge of our sports field. They got the rest of the school out as well, divided us up into three groups: teachers, boys, and girls. Then They led us away."

"That's exactly what happened to us," said Jo. "Did you see where They took the teachers and the boys? I guess They're keeping us all on different sites."

Nettie clamped her eyes shut. "They were all killed," said Celie.

Tess turned so she was part of the group again. I budged up to make room for her next to me.

"How... How do you know?" My voice was dry. Inside I was reeling and yet none of it was a surprise.

"We saw it happening. They were just falling over in waves."

"That's what we saw." My voice was tiny. "But Emma says they're OK."

"Ours were not OK. Believe me. Ours are dead. And if ours are, yours must be too."

I felt suddenly very sick and had to stand up and retch over the side of the partition into the passageway. I couldn't help thinking of Brandon and Orlando and Pip. Miss Temple.

I felt a hand stroke my back. It was Tess. She hugged me, and we sat down again together.

"Some of us made a run for it," Celie was saying. "The first lot of Them couldn't hold us, but then another line appeared and zapped us. Again and again. The most horrible sound: it was like we could hear the boys screaming."

Nettie was sobbing silently. Tess put an arm around her.

"That's it," said Celie. "When the sound stopped, They marched us here. No one challenged or did anything after that. Not even when They took the younger girls away."

"But that was part of the hostage negotiation," I said. "Ours got freed in the night."

"Who told you that? They weren't freed. They're being held at the big Sainsbury's on Green Lanes."

"But Emma said they were safe," said Tess.

"Emma? Oh…The E on those girls' arms." Celie snorted in derision.

"Why do you think she's lying?" asked Jo. "Do you think They're using her?"

I shrugged. You just couldn't tell with Emma. I hadn't even seen her talking to Them. Maybe it was all in her own head. Some massive power-trip. Then I winced as I thought of Ada again. Because I'd thought she was safe, I had been able to put her out of my mind. Images of Mum and Dad and others also flashed into my head. I'd been so busy worrying about myself, but now I felt a wave of guilt.

"We've got to get out of here," said Jo in a low voice.

She could have saved her voice.

We all understood the predicament we were in.

We just didn't know what to do about it.

⌐ ▫ ▫ ▯
  ▫ | =

[1.41]

The brand on my right wrist gets sore sometimes.

My left wrist is fine. On that one I wear the bracelet Aggie gave me when I was really ill. A present like the notebooks to try and cheer me up. It's chunky with glassy beads, blue and green and red, quite beautiful actually. Though it's just made from sugar from the fabricator. I wear it all the time. I think it makes Aggie happy to see it.

Sorry, I'm meant to be telling you about my *right* wrist.

The brand there is agonizing sometimes. About a couple of centimetres down from where you'd wear a watch if you were left-handed.

When it flares up, I can't help but scratch it. Aggie gives me a thick yellow ointment which is cooling when it goes on and has the double benefit of obscuring the symbols imprinted there for a few minutes.

Or even half an hour if I'm being good.

But I'm not being good today. It's itching like crazy, and I've scratched through the yellow balm in seconds. I'm writing now because it's the one thing that distracts me when it gets like this, and because keeping my right-hand moving makes it harder to scratch.

(Though thinking about it right now is *not* helping).
The brand reads:

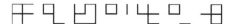

The characters in their language are built from a 2 x 2 square grid. It's a bit like what I think Chinese must be like (are you Chinese, reader?) so characters and groups of characters represent words or numbers depending on context. There are millions of different combinations according to Aggie.

I asked her how 'Aggie' was written. It was quite cute, like a winky eye:

In Colonist language my brand meant:

Property of: 13th State, 2nd City, 5th Farm.

That's what Finsbury Park is called now. Catchy, huh?

I was interested that London was only the second city. "What's number one?"

—You call it Colchester.

"*Colchester?!?* Why's Colchester number one over London?"

—We went by your own records. It's the oldest city and therefore must have been the most important.

"It doesn't work like that… And what's the number one state? USA? China? India?"

Aggie shrugged, which she's doing much more naturally now. —I don't know such things.

"Can't you just look it up? In a book or something?"

—You know we don't usually use books. I must wait until The Day Of Sharing. Then I will know whatever I want to know.

"But aren't you curious now?"

—Yes. But I understand I must wait.

And that was that. We'd already had this conversation after all.

She's gone for a walk today for exercise. I'm alone. My wrist is still prickling so I've gone to the window and pressed it against the cooling glass. It's like I can still feel the heat in it. Which is ridiculous because it was over nine months ago that it happened.

I think about it, of course.

A lot actually.

But it's only when I dream about it that it gets really bad.

Because then I can smell it too.

The smoke coiling from my own skin.

Like lamb chops on the barbecue.

And the screams of the girls all around.

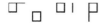

[1.42]

The next few hours set the pattern for the days to come.

Just when it felt like I was bursting, some of Them opened our gates and led us out to the brick pavilion where there were toilets and, in the circumstances, the most heavenly thing of all: toilet paper.

Then back to our shed. In front of the entrance, two of the hockey team with their capital E armbands doled out fruit and bread. There were more of Emma's girls at various points around the athletics ground helping Them keep watch over us.

After collecting our food, we were made to walk two laps of the running track and only then were we allowed back to our cubicles.

We ate our food.

Just as we were getting thirsty, we were taken outside again, and Emma's gang gave us ladles of water from a big water butt. Another trip to the toilet. By which time the toilet roll had run out. Two laps of the track. And back inside.

Eat. Drink. Go to the toilet.

Then back to our sheds.

That was pretty much it.

"At least we're not getting sunburnt," I said. But that joke wore off pretty quickly. We could have done with having Pip there with us.

After the first day, when Colonists alone had performed the patrols of the shed, They were accompanied by members of Emma's gang. And soon, the inspections were conducted solely by girls in armbands.

On a day when it was just hockey girls patrolling, a couple of inmates – Susan Walker and Peggy Blackett – ambushed them; but the hockey girls squirmed free and fled, returning just a few minutes later with six of Them. Susan and Peggy were reduced to gibbering wrecks and then dragged out, while the rest of us were subjected to vicious sonic blasts that left us writhing in the straw.

We didn't see Susan and Peggy after that and no one tried to hurt Emma's girls again either.

Days passed.
The routine continued.
Eat. Drink. Toilet.
Then sleep.
Fitful, exhausting sleep.

As we settled into captivity, talk became less about what had happened and the hopes of imminent release, to more mundane matters of how rank we all felt being in one set of clothes, and not having even a change of underpants.

Then there was the food.

When we'd first tasted the fruit and bread They'd given us, it had seemed delicious. But after a couple of days of *only* fruit and bread, we were bored. What I really wanted was a burger or steak or some other satisfying hunk of protein.

We started to get cravings and, to begin with, would talk about food endlessly. We'd take it in turns to describe our favourite dishes. Mine was Mum's chicken *cacciatore*. *Cacciatore* means hunter. Celie and Nettie would say they dreamed of fish and chips – they'd always had it on a Friday night. Jo's favourite was Sichuan pork the way her dad made it. It was really fiery but fantastic. I'd had it around hers once and it was to die for.

On the second day, another girl was added to our cubicle, a seventeen-year-old called Eppie. There was no discussion about her joining us. They said she was coming in so she came in. She had dark brown skin and an amazing afro. Well, it looked like it would have been amazing normally, but it was actually pretty dishevelled like the rest of our hair. Eppie kind of kept herself to herself. Until, that is, we started talking about food. Then she piped up that her favourite was sausage, mash and gravy, gave the merest hint of a smile, and after that it felt like she was one of us as well.

Throughout our food discussions Tess was mostly silent, occasionally muttering, "You still don't get it do you?"

Which would really rile me. She was my best friend, and best friends aren't meant to say stuff like that to each other.

"Get what?"

"You lot. Still going on about your *meat.*"

"We're just passing the time," murmured Jo. "No one's doing any harm."

"You're fantasising about eating the flesh of animals that have been kept just like we're being kept. I'd say you're doing them harm."

"Oh, come off it!" I'd snap.

Funnily enough the best person at defusing the tension was actually Eppie. She said abruptly, "OK, Veggie. What would you like to eat?"

And Tess was so taken aback that she had to answer. "I don't know… Maybe a slice of toast with peanut butter?"

Peanut butter. I never thought my mouth would water at the idea of something so simple.

As well as talking about food, we'd also tell each other about ourselves. But when someone mentioned boys the rest of us fell silent. It was just too raw. Thinking of what happened to them left me panicky and breathless and I was having flashbacks every night. Talking about our families was the same. Everyone was scared for their parents and missing them with an intensity that none of us could have fathomed just a week before. I mean, we were teenagers for Pete's sake. Mums and dads were meant to just *be* there, safely, non-embarrassingly in the background. But there was no way we could articulate any of that without rapidly descending into hysterics, which we inevitably did a few times early on. So, real things were impossible to talk about and everything else felt too trivial, so pretty soon we subsided into silence.

We would sit there listless.

It wouldn't have been right to say everyone hated it all the time though.

The fact there were no boys around was awful, of course, but at the same time it meant that dicks like Alec Durber and his crew weren't there to be homophobic or transphobic or casually sexist or whatever. So, although on most levels it was crazy stressful, it was also liberating not to have to battle against that constant level of male hostility all the time. Even the lack of parental judgy-ness was kind of a guilty relief.

Certainly, talking to Rebecca, she said that even if a few girls were crappy about it, she felt accepted in a way she never had when loads of boys had been around.

And it meant that two upper sixth formers, Ruth and Anne (spelt with an 'e' she would always say), felt they could come out, individually and as a couple. Which I really admired. They'd been dating for months as it happened but hadn't felt able to say anything to anyone before. For them, captivity was kind of liberating.

Anne with an 'e' was stunning. She had emerald eyes and flame red hair like Aggie's, only long and flowing not in a bob. She had the kind of face I could have stared at for ages. Honestly, I have no idea what she saw in Ruth, who was totally *meh* as far as I was concerned. But I guess nothing beats the end of the world to cement a relationship.

Nights were worst, of course.

The first night, naturally. But honestly, they didn't get better.

And although there was certainly comfort in being curled up next to Tess and Jo, it was really hard to sleep when you couldn't stretch out, and the straw was so irritating. Plus, it wasn't getting properly dark until late, and given there was nothing to do except lie there, it felt interminable. Even when darkness finally descended, it was incredibly noisy: girls crying, talking, calling out in their sleep. Some of them breaking out into full-on wailing. I mean, we'd been through some serious stuff of late.

And the most tiring thing? When I closed my eyes the first few nights, it was impossible not to have everything I'd experienced flash in front of me, flitting from one thing to another like the previous Christmas at the fair, when I'd gone on the carousel after the ferris-wheel-draw debacle.

The ferris-wheel-draw had been Pip's idea and I'd arranged with him that I would sit next to Brandon; but it all got mixed up and I partnered Orlando instead – *totally* awkward – whilst Brandon ended up next to Pip, which would have been a complete waste. I sat glumly on the carousel afterwards, surrounded on all sides by these lovely, bobbing horses, but when I looked out at the fairground, faces and lights flickered past, faster and faster, till I just wanted to get off. It left me feeling *so* queasy.

By the way, never eat a whole stick of pink candyfloss just before you go on one of those rides: it does not end well.

So, *anyway*, the one thing that might have been a release – falling asleep – was exhausting.

I'd try and keep my eyes open as long as I could, staring at the back of Tess's straw-coloured hair, lovely even as a tangled mess, and ironically threaded through with stalks of real straw. Eventually though, even in that overcrowded, super-noisy, utterly depressing environment, I'd drift off.

I would wake, of course, in the middle of the night, stand up in the darkness and stretch. It would be comparatively quiet in the shed then. Just the ebb and flow of breathing and some curiously synchronised snoring. There wasn't a window nearby so I couldn't see the stars, but if the night was clear, there might be a glimmer of moonlight illuminating the shed, and then I could see the ghostly shapes of the two hundred and fifty girls crammed in around me. Sleeping. Hopefully far from life's realities in their dreams.

☐ ☐ ☐ | ☐

[1.43]

Aggie's parents are Administrators.

They're like the civil servants of Colonist Society. Plaxys is a research scientist and Schektl works in the equivalent of the Ministry of Agriculture. They occupy public buildings like the library which were left vacant when humans were driven out. Yesterday Aggie was explaining her parents' work while applying more balm to my wrist. The branded skin really crawls in this warmer weather we've been having.

—My parents are really important.

Aggie sounded very proud about it. She always does when she's talking about Plaxys and Schektl.

—Their work keeps you and us healthy. Without them, other Colonists wouldn't be well enough to make The Hive Mind function properly. And that's our greatest achievement, Cara.

It seemed a little tenuous that Plaxys and Schektl were directly responsible for The Hive Mind, but I let it go.

—Once we're all fully connected after The Day Of Sharing, The Hive Mind will be two hundred million minds all linked together.

"Like a huge organic Internet?"

I thought Aggie might have a problem with me talking about the Internet; but she was relaxed.

She told me many primitive animals have ways of storing and communicating their information. The Internet was pretty quaint to the Colonists, a cross between enabling birds to sing over long distances and a giant stash for information like squirrels storing nuts. Aggie said it demonstrated how underdeveloped humans were that we hadn't worked out how to use the Internet to bring people together and allow them to properly share experiences and knowledge.

I was a bit annoyed by that and said – *actually* – we used to have loads of online education programs. Like for GCSEs.

—And how did you upload your own experiences to enhance the learning for others?

"I used social media. Or filled in a feedback form."

Aggie laughed. Well, I say laugh, but her face didn't change and the sound she made in my head was more of a crackle. But she's been making an effort recently to approximate human shows of emotion, which I take as a compliment.

—I meant sensory experiences. Your memories. Your feelings.

"I don't see how that would help GCSEs. Anyway, the Internet is a lifeline. How about when people in civil war cities like Aleppo used the Internet to let the outside world know what was going on?"

—But that proves my point. The Hive Mind is not merely a mail service for cries for help. It is a vast, distributed collective consciousness of almost infinite complexity. When we are plugged into it, we are one person, as you would call it, so *we* never have civil wars. Fighting against ourselves would make no sense. It would be like a body's cells attacking itself.

"Which can happen sometimes." One of my uncles had arthritis so I knew a bit about that.

—Indeed. But it has never happened in our entire history. We do not fight each other, except to remove an incurably diseased or grotesquely injured individual who is beyond medical care.

"So... like euthanasia."

—I am aware of the term. You might say so. But we are not discrete organisms in the same way you are. Before physical termination, the individual's experiences are uploaded into The Hive Mind. We feel and love and remember and smell and touch just like you, Cara. Even more so, because our brains are so much more powerful, and our senses are enhanced and informed by the feedback from millions of others. But an individual's experiences are still unique because of their particular physical and emotional encounters. So before termination, they are absorbed into the whole, and we all become richer as a result. Death is not the end for us. We continue to exist.

"Well, *you* wouldn't. And *your* mind wouldn't. It's like you've written everything you know in a book and someone takes it, put it on the shelf, and then kills you. Everyone could have a look in it, but that doesn't mean you still exist. It just means you're remembered."

That actually floored her because she stopped smearing the ointment on my arm and sat there thinking for a while. In normal times she would presumably have accessed some explanation from The Hive Mind; but she was flying solo. Eventually she said,

—No, I don't think that's right.

And that was it. She started slathering on the balm again.

Clearly, I wasn't going to let it go. "But I'm right though, aren't I? You're an individual. You exist. You're having thoughts right now that your parents don't know about, because they're out of telepathic range. You're different to them. Your parents. The other Colonists. You're here with me, squidging cream on my arm because you want to. And just because your enjoyment is recorded somewhere, even if some clone of you downloads all your experiences, doesn't make that person *you*. If you're terminated – if you *die* – you, the individual, will disappear."

—That doesn't matter.

"It matters to me. I wouldn't want to lose you."

—But if I were replaced by a clone who looked and behaved identically, how would you know I was different? Remember I don't actually even look like this. So, why does it matter to you?

"Doesn't it matter to *you*? You're alive at the moment. You're a wonderful, caring, ridiculously intelligent super-being. Isn't that kind of cool? You don't want to just become a dusty book on a shelf."

—I can see your logic. I just don't have access to the right explanation at the moment.

"Doesn't it make you afraid?"

—Afraid of what?

"Afraid of dying. What it would be like. You know, if you got incurably diseased or whatever and ceased to be."

—But I will not have ceased to be. I will remain part of The Collective. I will still exist.

"But how do you know?"

Aggie was finished with the balm. She wiped her hands and carefully screwed the top back on the jar. —I just know.

"But isn't that like our religions? When we believe that after death we're going to heaven?"

Aggie stood up suddenly.

—How dare you compare your delusional beliefs to our higher consciousness! Your religions are responsible for so many atrocities and wars. They are used to justify the subjugation of other races and the female half of your species.

"That's not fair. I'm not saying they're perfect, but religions do loads of good stuff too. And people should be allowed to believe in them if they want—"

—We have no need of them! We do not fear death like humans, Cara, so we have no need to make up lies of what happens afterwards.

"Well, from my position, it sort of sounds like you've bought into a lie of your own."

—Colonists do not fear death.

"But do *you?*"

—Death is irrelevant. It is fear of death that drives the human race, Cara, and that is why we are infinitely superior to you. It is dissatisfaction with your finite span of years that fuels your species' avarice and cruelty, and ultimately turns you to war and destruction. You talked about people getting messages out of Aleppo. What created that horror and unbearable anguish if not greed and a lust for violence?

Colonists do not have wars and since we have been on this planet, you have not had them either. You won't need your Internet any more, Cara, because there is no longer war in the Middle East. Because of us, the guns are silent there. For the first time in human history, the whole of planet Earth is at peace.

[1.44]

From the fourth day, as well as exercise and toilet-breaks, we were granted a 'treat'. We were led out to the infield at noon and formed into a tight square in front of the sheds. We'd then stand and watch as Emma would come from a huddle with Them over on the perimeter. She would mount a little wooden dais and relate the information she'd been given that day.

Or claimed she'd been given.

No one knew whether she was actually getting news from Them, or whether she was just making it all up to keep us quiet. At Their behest or her own.

The terrorists themselves would be keeping an eye on us from a distance, mostly around the perimeter of the athletics ground.

I'd stand there in the middle of the crowd of girls, and just look upwards.

It had been a great July. A cloud every now and then but nothing else up there apart from the occasional bird. Living in London, I couldn't remember a time when I'd look up and not see a vapour trail fanning out across the sky. And it was so quiet without any planes flying overhead or the constant thrum of traffic.

Meanwhile, Emma would talk.

She'd tell us messages that had been received from outside.

She talked about the complexity of the negotiations.

She walked us through a vague timeline of our release.

Personally, I only half listened. I mean, it might have been true. We'd seen her talking with Them on the perimeter. But the stuff she'd told us about the teachers and the younger girls was almost certainly a lie. It was hard to believe anything she said after that.

Once she was done with the 'news' she'd carry on with whatever pet subject popped into her head.

She explained the different branches of the armed forces and their component regiments.

She talked about the history of the democratic process and the rule of law.

She talked about the importance of personal hygiene.

I mean, give that girl her due, she could talk about any subject under the sun.

□ ǀ □ □
　　　 □ ‗

[2.7]
Maybe Aggie's right.
We weren't that great, let's face it.
And maybe ending up as a book on a shelf isn't so bad.
It means even when I'm gone, I'd still be around.
Kind of.
So, you'd always be with me, reader.
And I'd always be with you.
A real-life person.
I hope that's what you are anyway.
I hope you're someone I'd like.
And I hope you'd like me too.

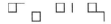

[1.45]

On the fifth day we were allowed to have a shower in the pavilion. I'd always thought communal showers were kind of weird, but given the context, it felt like an incredible luxury; though the water was tepid and there was no shampoo or conditioner. Afterwards, there were no towels either, but just being clean was good enough even if we had to get back into the same clothes.

There were mirrors in the changing rooms and it was a shock to see my face for the first time in nearly a week. Before all this happened, I must have looked at myself twenty times a day: brushing my teeth, selfies, facetime, any darkened window I happened to be passing… I don't think I was particularly vain; just sixteen.

Seeing myself then, however, it felt like everything had been stripped back. No make-up, of course – I never really wore much anyway except for parties: a bit of rose gold eye-shadow and highlighter (don't judge me). I'd never thought I was particularly pretty – certainly not like Tess who was drop-dead. Or even Jo who had this fierce beauty. But I knew I could be *quite* attractive sometimes – with my olive skin and tangle of curls and deep brown eyes.

But the person looking back at me that day wasn't me. Or at least it wasn't the old me. It felt like some new person I'd have to get to know.

But we were hustled out of the changing rooms before I had a proper chance to make my own acquaintance.

[2.8]
I was feeling so lonely today.

So lonely tonight.
I can't sleep.
All I've got is this notebook to talk to.
To whisper to in private.
To whisper to you, reader.
I wish I could meet you.
Who are you, I wonder?
Are you human?
If you are – I really hope you are – then I wonder how long I will have been dead when you finally get to read these words?
If you get to read them at all.
Perhaps no one will ever read what I've written here.
This book burned to a cinder like all the others.

□⌐ ⌐□ □ ⌐ ⌐

[1.46]

Apart from Emma's gang, we were all cooped up inside for 95% of the day, but at least we were allowed out for our exercise and toilet and fake news sessions. Until the day we were woken by a storm. And after that we hardly left the shed at all.

It was still dark when the thunder woke us, and lightning flashes illuminated the shed a ghostly white. Rain drummed on the steel roof of the shed, and pretty soon it started leaking. We had to keep shifting around in our pens to find a dry patch of straw. Through the sound of the rain, we thought we could also hear the sound of banging outside: more construction it seemed like.

At ten o'clock, when we normally got let out in batches for the toilet and breakfast, a couple of Them turned up along with four of Emma's armbanded followers.

"It's too wet to go out today so we'll feed you inside and turn the end stalls into toilets."

There was a howl of outrage all across the shed, but that was why They had come along, and we were silenced almost instantly with a neural zap. We had to go along with it. Just like we had to go along with everything else.

The rain stopped by midday though we still weren't let out. We complained about it to Emma's guards, but from that point we were effectively locked in all the time, and a new routine took over.

No exercise now, but, three times a day, Emma's girls turned up and made the occupants of one of the pens sweep out the latrine stall.

That was totally disgusting.

Then a couple of times a day, fruit and bread would be dropped into the elongated, stainless-steel receptacle which had been clipped to the front of our pens.

It took me a while before my brain – which felt increasingly clumsy, since we weren't doing a lot of talking and I was trying not to even think too much since all my thoughts were pretty terrifying – could articulate the right word for the container into which our food had been deposited. But it finally came to me.

A trough.

We were being fed from a trough.

About three weeks in, there was a flurry of activity. Members of Emma's gang were walking down the central aisle with clipboards, noting everyone's name and date of birth.

We rushed to give our details because this could surely only mean one thing.

They were cataloguing our identities so they could provide them to the authorities. We were getting out of there at last. For the first time in days there was happy upbeat chatter in the shed.

"I guess Emma had to be right about the authorities sometime," said Jo sarcastically; but she was smiling like the rest of us when she said it.

Eppie was an amazing singer and broke into spontaneous song. Several other girls joined in happily.

Only Tess looked unsettled.

She and I were fine. I mean, we'd had no more arguments, but it just felt like she'd been really negative recently. Don't get me wrong, I'm not saying there wasn't a lot to be negative about, but the old Tess would have been the one trying to see the bright side. And though everyone knew something was about to happen – even putting aside Emma's exaggerations – Tess still refused to join in the anticipation and the excitement. I kind of sighed when I saw her like that.

Later that day, just as we expected, something big did happen.

But in this, as in so much else, it was Tess that was proved to be right.

Part 5: A Walk in the Park

[1.47]

I wasn't amazingly sporty in the old days. But even I went for a jog once in a while if Tess dragged me out. Fair weather only. Spring or Autumn. Warmth and the promise of growth; or the comforting damp and crunch of leaves.

Sometimes, when my wrist is raw from scratching, that's what I'd like to do: go for a jog or a walk in the park. Though I haven't actually been out of the apartment since I got here. For months I was too ill anyway. And the thought of seeing all the Colonists where humans used to be, really creeps me out.

But I'm better now.

Stronger; because of the writing.

The turn of the year has helped as well. Watching the bloom of spring. My poplars coming into leaf. It makes me think perhaps I need to be outdoors again, though I'm still nervous. Plaxys and Schektl haven't said anything, but Aggie's been urging me for a while.

—We can go where there are other pets. You would enjoy playing with them.

"Do a lot of Colonists have pets?"

—Yes, but not like you. You're special.

"I'm really not, Aggie. I escaped, that's all. The special people are the ones who helped me. And I just left them all behind. I'm sure those other pets are far more impressive than me."

—If you say so. But I don't think they're anything like as special as you. Anyway, have a think about it.

[2.9]

It was only after Aggie had left the room that her words sank in.

Other pets.

That meant: other <u>human beings</u>.

Real life people.

I wondered immediately who they might be.

Inevitably I wondered whether it might be Tess.

Or Jo.

I mean, probably not Brandon, given everything that's happened.

Or maybe it will be someone new entirely that I've never met before?

Realistically it would have to be that.

But that would be OK.

And perhaps going out would become a regular thing, and then I could see them often.

They'd become a friend.

A real friend.

Someone I'd be able to talk to.

And unlike you, reader, they'd talk back.

[1.48]

So, what with Aggie's persuasion and the change in the weather, I woke up this morning and thought, yes, I really want to go outside.

Aggie said she knew a place I'd like.

But when she described it to me – large white house, lawns sloping down to a lake – I knew she was talking about Kenwood.

I can't go there again. Not for a long time.

So instead, she suggested skirting along the edge of the Heath, hanging out with some of the other pets, and then popping into town where she had a couple of errands to run.

I was nervous about that last part.

—It'll be fine, said Aggie. —You've got to get used to seeing Colonists sometime. We're here to stay, you know. And if you don't go outside and exercise, you'll get ill again.

"But will they seem like humans or you know…" As I said before, I still haven't seen what a Colonist looks like properly uncloaked. And I don't think the best introduction would be to see a hundred of them all at once.

—Don't worry, Cara. You've absorbed enough pheromone from living with us that unless we want you to see us differently, you'll still see Colonists as humans.

I took a deep breath and said, "OK, let's do it."

Aggie's hunting around in the cupboards in her parents' room at the moment, trying to dig out some shoes for me to wear. I can hear her rattling around on the other side of the wall. I'm just waiting here patiently.

The sunshine is warm on me.

I'm going to be out it in it soon.

It's been such a long time, I ought to be apprehensive.

But all I feel is excitement.

And I know, logically, the pet I'm going to meet on Hampstead Heath isn't going to be Tess, but there is some infinitesimal chance that it could be.

Like winning the lottery.

Even if the odds are millions to one, someone has to win, right?

So, it could be.

Oh, please let it be.

Let it be Tess.

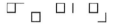

[1.49]
It wasn't Tess.

None of it was like I thought it was going to be.

I haven't been able to write for a week.

The pain in my wrist is excruciating. It's only since Schektl fetched the stronger ointment that I can even sit here again.

But I've got to restart the writing or I'll go crazy. So, let me tell you what happened.

Aggie had been rooting around for some shoes for me and eventually found some grey felt slippers which fitted perfectly. They weren't much, but I've been in bare feet since I got here so definitely an improvement.

But she was also carrying something else, and when I saw it, the blood drained from my face. "I have to wear a lead?"

—All pets need leads.

It was a leather collar tethered to a long leash. While attaching it to me, Aggie apologetically said she would keep it very loose. —You won't even know it's on, Cara.

I did know it was on, obviously. You can't have a leather collar around your neck without feeling it, but Aggie was true to her word, and while we walked along the fringes of the Heath, she took me off the leash altogether.

The anticipation was enormous as we arrived at the bit of Heath where Aggie had said the owners and pets would be.

—There they are.

Aggie's thoughts sounded delighted in my head. —Do you want to run and play with them?

My chest was so tight I could only stare.

In dismay.

Until the tears of disappointment welled in my eyes.

Before us, half a dozen Colonists stood silently together whilst their pets jostled. The pets looked up as we approached.

Stared at me.

Five sheep and a goat.

Tears rolled down my cheeks. I couldn't help it.

"I thought they'd be human."

Aggie seemed genuinely surprised. —Why? We don't generally keep humans as pets. You knew that, silly. We farm them or race them. But sheep and goats make lovely pets.

My mind was numb. "Then why am *I* being kept as a pet?"

—Because I pleaded for it, Aggie said proudly. —I convinced Mother and Father I had to have you. I told you you're special.

"So special..." I said, choking back a sob.

—Do you want to play with them?

The goat was approaching me.

"No, I'm fine."

It started nuzzling my leg.

"Why not dogs at least?" I croaked. "They make good pets."

—Yes, we observed that. But for some reason our mind control does not work well with dogs. Sheep and goats are easily controlled by comparison, and Colonists find them very attractive. Sometimes pigs too. But I prefer humans.

"Can we go now?"

—Already? Don't you want to play with them?

"They're just animals, Aggie."

—So, are you.

"Please. I want to go."

—Of course.

We walked away. Eventually, despite the crushing disappointment, I began to recover.

It was still good to be outside.

The air was so clean.

A brisk kind of day, a tiny bit chill for what I thought was mid-May.

But that only intensified how refreshing it was to be outdoors.

Aggie was enjoying it too. Especially as it was just the two of us. We didn't see another soul for the entire walk, which was a relief. Just a couple of squirrels; and a rabbit which I greeted with a heartfelt salute.

Aggie chattered about this and that, and I told her the names of the trees we passed – names that Jo had once taught me. Their leaves were still that delightful young green, translucent, delicate, before the summer thickening when they get deeper in colour, dustier somehow.

Despite everything, the walk turned out to be a success, and I agreed instantly when Aggie asked whether I'd like to do it again sometime. Her parents make her get regular outdoor exercise, and we both thought it would be nicer for us to be outside together, rather than me being cooped up while she did endless solitary miles.

I was still a pet, of course. A weird pet at that. But it felt suddenly like my world had expanded a million times over.

On the way back, Aggie needed to run that errand for her parents, so we cut through town. She apologetically clipped the lead to my collar as we stepped onto the High Street.

—In case we see any Inquisitors, she told me.

We went to what was still signposted as a post office on the corner of the street. There were a couple of other Colonists inside: a handsome chestnut-haired man and an elegant Greek-looking lady. They were walking dreamily around the inside of the shop which was lined with different coloured sacks.

Both turned to look at me as we entered. But just for an instant, and then they continued with what they'd been doing.

Aggie went to the counter, smartly twisted open the clasp on the satchel she was carrying and handed over a silver token to a blonde girl with high cheek bones. There was an exchange of thoughts between them which made no sense to me, like a jumble of orchestra instruments tuning up for a concert. Then Aggie snapped her bag shut and stepped over to the sacks by the wall. She picked up two yellows, a blue and a red.

"What are they?"

—Raw materials for the fabricator.

The 'ding' from the bell above the door as we exited seemed so normal, so 'before-all-this' that for a moment I was disorientated, like waking from a dream.

—The yellow ones are starch granules, the blue, amino acids, and the red, lipids.

"Can I help carry them?"

—Well, they're sixty kilos each. So, you might find it a struggle.

They are kind of incredible, these Colonists. Aggie was carrying nearly a quarter of a tonne like it was nothing.

"You gave the shopkeeper money?"

—Not money, no. It was an entitlement token. All families are issued them.

"Do you get more because your folks are important Administrators?"

—Oh, no. Preferential treatment like that would lead to corruption. We get the same as everybody else.

Our route home took us along the High Street. I didn't really know Hampstead that well but still pointed out to Aggie what the shops used to be, based on their signs. They were now either entirely empty or else jam-packed with Colonists. We stopped for a moment outside what had once been an upmarket clothes store with a triple fronted shop front. Inside it was full of Colonists, sidling slowly past each other. If they'd been snakes, I'd have said they were slithering. They moved silently, just the smooth swish of body against body. No thoughts to be heard.

"Are they keeping warm?"

—They're communicating.

"But why are they squirming up to each other? It's gross. What's the point of telepathy, if you don't use it at a distance?"

—They're communicating via secretion.

"Ugh." There's something about that word which always gets me.

—They exchange pheromones as they rub past.

"Ugh!"

—The scent carries information. It's less tiring for exchanging information than telepathy and much easier to control when there's a group.

"Totally disgusting but I get it. Like passing a note rather than shouting?"

—Stand for inspection!

We whirled around and were confronted by two female Colonists dressed in black polo neck and slacks. There was something about these two: so tall, both at least four inches taller than me, one blonde, one brunette, and though as beautiful as all the rest, they had this stern look to them.

—Why is this human in your possession? Do you have a permit?

Aggie groped at the clasp on the satchel she was carrying. Her hand was scrabbling at it for what seemed like ages. I looked back to the Inquisitors. The one with the blonde hair wore it up in a bun. She might have looked like Tess if her face had had any expression in it.

I suddenly realised Aggie was still fumbling with the bag, and I reached over to help her.

"Let me— *ouch!*"

Aggie butted my head with hers and pulled the satchel away. —The clasp is jammed, she said. —It's been playing up.

She looked the two Inquisitors in the eye.

The blonde one turned to me. —Show me your right arm.

My head was throbbing from where Aggie had clattered me. She'd never behaved like this before.

I rolled up my sleeve. The Inquisitor inspected the brand there, stepping aside so her colleague could see it as well. Then she turned back to Aggie.

—The brand shows its status as cattle. Is it a runaway?

—NO!

I had to cover my ears in case Aggie bellowed again. I looked at her startled.

—Mother is a scientist, Aggie was saying, her voice reducing in volume. —She keeps the human for research.

The blonde studied Aggie. —This is highly unusual. You are the progeny of Schektl 64972 and Plaxys 8251. Correct?

Aggie nodded.

—We will check your story. Meanwhile, we must record the human's identity.

She looked me up and down like she was scanning me.

—Ensure your animal's leash is tight. Good day.

They walked away. Aggie remained stock still.

"What was all that about? *Hey!*"

Aggie yanked my lead, dragging me from the shop fronts and around the corner so that we were off the high street. I had to hold onto the collar to prevent it throttling me. Aggie didn't say a word until we were on the edge of the Heath again, heading back to the apartment.

"What's going on?" I yelped, rubbing at my neck. "You nearly choked me."

Aggie glanced around nervously. —They were Inquisitors.

"I guessed that." I could feel a weal rising on the skin where the leather collar had bitten into it. "Why didn't you just tell them I was a runaway?"

—Do you know what would happen if that's what they thought you were?

"I think they may have guessed, Aggie. You weren't exactly subtle. You almost deafened me—"

—If they suspected you of being a runaway, they would have taken you back for instant Harvesting. Runaways are considered wild animals.

"Thanks. But… But that means you *lied."*

Aggie shifted and again checked over her shoulder.

"I didn't think you could."

—We need to get back to the apartment. Come on.

"Will you stop yanking my collar. It really hurts. Aggie, slow down!"

Aggie was suddenly moving at a surprising pace. I didn't know Colonists could move this fast.

"But what's going to happen when they check with your parents?" I panted. "They'll tell them the truth…" I froze as the realisation hit me, and this time even Aggie had to stop as well.

The empty streets shimmered before me like a heat haze.

"What's going to happen to me?" The minor irritations of life as a pet, the tedium of my existence, my isolation, all faded to nothing. This life was comfort. This life was security. My heart was banging. "You can't let this happen."

—My parents will fix it.

"Aggie, please don't let this happen to me—"

—Don't worry, Cara. They're not taking you from me. I won't let them.

[1.50]

I wrote for hours yesterday. This new ointment's miles better. But before I go any further, Aggie wants me to continue my earlier story.

That's the one she's really into.

So, I need to go back for a bit.

It's probably a good thing.

Like the wound on my wrist, these memories are fresh and raw.

I just need to remember where I'd got to.

Ah yes.

It was before midday, when sunlight suddenly flooded the stalls. Blinking, we realised that where usually a single small door was opened, today it was as though the entire end of the shed had been removed.

That immediately got everyone excited. Why would They fully open those doors unless we were about to be freed?

A group of Them started directing us into the sunshine.

It confirmed it in our minds.

We were going to be set free. And soon.

Once outside, we immediately knew things were different because Emma was standing with us rather than being up on the dais. And her hockey girls were around her. Instead of Emma's gang, there was a group of Them at the front, looking Their usual casually beautiful selves, but the two in the middle were different, more formal looking. *Them* certainly – Their faces were too smoothly gorgeous to be anything else – but both in sober charcoal business suits. They were standing there with clipboards, reviewing names on lists of paper, cross-checking between Them, nodding agreement.

It was happening for sure.

It seemed to take ages for everyone to get lined up, which was really frustrating since the sooner we got it together, the sooner this could all be over.

Freedom was wonderful.

I looked at the sky with fresh eyes.

It wasn't clear blue, instead studded with tiny clouds.

And they weren't pure white but had cream flecks.

I remember envying the birds I saw flying overhead.

I envy them now.

—Emma Woodhouse.

It was inevitable somehow that she'd be called first. To begin with we thought she was being asked to speak; she thought so too. But They led her to one side.

—Cassandra Mortmain.

A girl with a blonde bob jumped up like she'd won the Euromillions jackpot, then pushed her way to the front. She and Emma embraced.

—Bertha Mason.

—Anne Cuthbert.

—Meena Kumar.

One by one, girls made their way excitedly forward. There didn't seem to be any particular order to it. It certainly wasn't alphabetical, and it wasn't just Emma's cronies getting selected. But who knew what strange system would be used by these terrorists or whatever They were – I was getting less certain by the day.

There were well over a thousand girls present, and the calling of names was painfully slow. After an hour, They'd only got through maybe a hundred. Next to me, Eppie was looking increasingly uncomfortable.

"I really need the toilet," she said. "All that fruit."

"Can't you hold on?"

"No, I need to go."

"But what if they call your name?"

"Just say I'm coming back, OK?"

And then she was off, squeezing through the crowd. None of Them seemed worried about stopping her – there was still a cordon around the edge of the athletics ground in any case. I saw her head to the changing rooms, and suddenly I felt jealous. I hadn't used a proper toilet for days.

—Catherine Earnshaw.

I turned my eyes forward and prayed Eppie's name wouldn't be called.

—Celie Barlow.

Celie gave her younger sister a hug and made a five with an open hand for the number of minutes they would be parted.

—Eilis Lacey.

I'd always liked the name Eilis. It's pronounced Aye-leesh, and it's Irish. I had a lot of Irish friends from the

Catholic primary school I'd gone to with names that didn't sound like they were spelt. Anyway, I remembered Eilis in particular because her name was the last one announced.

At first, we thought They were merely taking a break, while the girls already called were herded into a coherent group. From their midst we could hear Emma' voice, loud and clear.

"You see! I told you it was just a matter of time. Negotiations are a complicated business."

But we'd been waiting nearly half an hour, when They began to walk the girls away, across the running track towards the gate on the north side. The celebratory air had started to fade, and I was still having to keep an eye out for Eppie, worrying that maybe she had noro virus, in which case we'd all have it pretty soon.

It was only then that I properly noticed the newly built Shed 5, half concealed as it was by the dais and the groups of Them. The chosen girls were being directed to it, and even as we were watching them disappear, giggling and laughing, we heard:

—Return to your stalls.

There was a collective groan of frustration as we trooped back. By my estimate, They had taken only a hundred girls, less than a tenth of us. Despite that, our stall felt empty. As well as Celie, Eppie still hadn't come back from the toilet. By now, I'd stopped thinking she was sick and assumed she'd managed to tack herself onto the other group.

"When will we get called?" Nettie asked tearfully. She was less than two years younger than me, but in that moment, she looked as young as Ada.

"Don't worry," I said. "Now they've started freeing us, it's just a matter of time."

"How do you think They choose who to release?" Tess asked.

"Who knows…" Jo frowned. "*Unless…* How old is Celie?"

"Eighteen."

"No, but exactly."

Nettie blinked. "Eighteen and eight months."

"Interesting. And Anne Cuthbert got chosen, and her birthday is in October, so she's about the same age."

"I've always loved her auburn hair," I said dreamily. And then, getting back with the programme, "Emma's birthday is around the first day of term – second of September or something. I'm sure that's why she always made sports teams so easily."

"So, she's eighteen and a half or so as well…" said Jo. "I think they're doing it in age order." She considered it a moment longer, then shrugged. "If it is like that, it'll be ages till our turn: they've not even finished Year 13 yet."

But it didn't get to our turn.

We stayed there all afternoon. Our feed was brought at midday as usual by Emma's gang, followed by the normal pattern of toilet breaks and mucking out. No further chance to go outside. What was happening to the chosen girls and when we'd get our chance was puzzling but hardly the weirdest thing we'd faced. I mean, it had serious competition for that. It slipped to the back of our minds as we settled back into the tedium of routine. They probably only did one exchange a day, I concluded.

We'd just need to be patient.

[1.51]

Aggie rushed to the door, the moment her parents got back from work. She told them what had happened as they walked to my cage. It rapidly became clear that Plaxys was furious.

—Why did you take her out? We told you never to take her out.

—I thought it would be good for her.

—It won't be good for her if she gets Harvested. Doesn't she understand that?

"Excuse me," I said from the other side of the barrier. "No one even told me—"

—Silence!

Plaxys gave me a zap which left my head ringing.

—What did they say?

—They saw that Cara's designation is cattle. They said, her being with me was highly unusual.

—It *is* highly unusual. You've put us in a very difficult position, Mlaxet—

—Don't call me that.

—DON'T ANSWER BACK!

Plaxys screamed it in our heads. —How could you be so stupid! We have to get rid of her!

I stood frozen.

Aggie spun around to Schektl. —You promised me, Daddy. You said we could keep her.

—I did. But humans aren't meant to be pets.

—But she's mine.

Aggie dropped the barrier to the alcove and ran in to me. Flung her arms around my shoulders. —You're not letting them take her.

I was trembling. My left leg was shaking. From fear of Inquisitors. From fear of Plaxys blowing her top. "Please. There must be something you can do. I'm happy here. I won't be any trouble." I couldn't stop my leg shaking.

—Please, Daddy. You promised.

Schektl looked at Plaxys. —We could tell them we have it for research. Your Office does behavioural studies on lab animals, doesn't it?

—That's what *I* said, Aggie blurted.

Plaxys stared at me unblinking. —This is ridiculous.

—Please Mother.

She turned to Schektl. —Occasionally…

—So, she can stay? Aggie asked.

—I could designate her a lab specimen.

"Thank you!" I was welling up. I wanted to give her parents a hug, but Aggie was holding me too tight, and anyway Plaxys was most definitely not the hugging type.

—We're not doing it for you, Plaxys snapped. She turned to Schektl. —I will need to adjust the documentation at the Office. Can you amend the farm records?

—Yes. I have access.

—Very well then. We will do that first thing tomorrow. But the local record needs to be updated without delay.

—Yes, said Schektl. —That would be best.

Aggie nodded. —I understand.

Her head was to one side and I could have sworn she looked guilty.

"Understand what? What's going on?"

—Take it to the kitchen, Aggie.

"What happening?"

Aggie gripped my shoulders and started to move me through the sitting room and into the hallway. I looked back over my shoulder and saw Schektl pulling out a small black case from his work bag. He unzipped it and I could see silver implements inside, like the type from an old printing press.

—It'll be OK, soothed Aggie, but her hands were clamped firmly on my arms, propelling me towards the kitchen.

"No!" I yelped, the realisation dawning.

—We will use the gas stove to heat them up, said her father, following us down the passage.

"No!"

—It's OK, she whispered. It'll only hurt for a moment.

"Aggie, *please*—"

—We'll need them red hot, Schektl said.

"No! *Please, no!*"

⊓ ⊓ ⊔ ⊓

[1.52]

It was dark when Eppie finally got back.

I'd been snoozing but sat bolt upright when I heard scuffling underneath the food troughs. At first, I thought we had a rat infestation. But then I saw her curls in the faint glimmer of moonlight.

I helped her back into the stall, but the moment she was inside she curled up and began to sob. She rocked backwards and forwards, plainly terrified.

"What is it?" Tess asked. Jo had woken up too, yawning. Only Nettie was still sleeping.

Eppie kept on rocking.

"Are you sick? Have you got a bug?"

"It's not that," she whispered. She wouldn't take her hands from her eyes. After a further pause, she spoke in a low urgent voice. "I had really bad diarrhoea, so I stayed in the toilets for ages. Afterwards it was kind of comfortable being in the changing rooms, so I lay down and fell asleep, and when I woke up again it was already dark. I thought I might be able to escape, but They were all around the perimeter of the track. So, I doubled back and came across this new shed. Behind the dais where Emma talks."

"Shed 5," I said. "I think they take the girls there for processing before being released—"

Eppie howled. A terrible, low sound like my grandfather's dog had made when he'd been dying of cancer. And she still wouldn't take her hands from her eyes as she rocked violently in the straw.

"Did They do something to you?" Tess asked tentatively, reaching out to stroke her arm.

"I can't tell you," Eppie whispered. "It's too awful."

"Did someone hurt you?" I asked.

Her awful scream stopped, and she sat forward. For the first time she uncovered her face. I winced, expecting to see something horrible. But her eyes just looked bloodshot from a ton of crying.

"It's not me," she hissed. "I can't tell you. Please don't make me tell you. It's in that new shed."

Then she pressed her face into her knees and began rocking again, silently now.

"Let's go," I said. "We've got to see for ourselves."

"Is that a good idea?" said Tess.

I shrugged. "Something bad's happening. We need to find out what."

"I'm in," said Jo.

Tess looked over at Nettie sleeping in the corner. "Shouldn't one of us stay with her?"

"I'll look after her if she wakes up," said Eppie. Still rocking.

Tess smiled wanly. "I guess I'm in as well, then."

We unhooked the stainless-steel trough at the front of our stall and wriggled under it. With a bit of squeezing, we all got through, though I finally knew my T-shirt – which up until that point had been merely filthy – was now officially ruined.

Totally weird the way your mind works at even the tensest moments.

Anyway, there were usually a couple of hockey girls keeping guard at the entrance, but that night there was no one, and we slipped out into the night.

There was a three-quarter moon and our eyes were well adjusted to the darkness from time spent in the shed, so being out in the open felt more like twilight. We crept across the deserted grass of the infield and over to the new hut. Superficially it was similar to the others, but it seemed like it had been built with more care and precision. The walls themselves were smooth metal rather than rough wooden planks, and there was electric lighting. There were three sets of windows at intervals along the hut's side. And when we cautiously peered in through the first of them – triple glazed and hence fully soundproofed – we could see the room inside was nothing like our crude stalls with their dirt floor and straw to sleep on. We found ourselves gazing at painted walls and carpet. There were daybeds and beanbags, and the room was suffused in the warm glow of table lamps. A long trestle table bore dishes of pastries and exotic fruit, and carafes containing richly coloured drinks. The girls themselves were lounging and laughing. They all looked wonderfully refreshed, their dirty clothes discarded and dressed now in loose-fitting white T-shirts and joggers. They seemed relaxed and happy.

Emma – naturally – was holding court in the centre of the room. Celie was there too, lying on a daybed nibbling at what looked like a cinnamon swirl.

"Was this really what Eppie was so worked up about?" I said.

"It can't be… Although…" Jo shot me a wry smile. "Seeing Emma there does make me feel pretty upset. God. Look how clean they are. There must be showers in the first section of the building. Look at Anne's hair." We gazed together at her exquisite auburn tresses, shimmering around her as she sat cross-legged, chatting to Emma.

"Do you think they have conditioner in there?" asked Tess wistfully.

We saw Anne's ears suddenly prick up, as though someone had called her name. She gave Emma a happy hug and, high-fiving girls all the way, she stalked towards the door in the right-hand wall.

"Come on," I said, "Let's see where she's going."

"It's weird," said Jo. "There aren't actually many girls in that room—"

"Come on," I hissed. I was moving already, and Jo and Tess caught up with me as I reached the second window. The lights were brighter here and the night dark enough that we couldn't be seen from inside. The room was laid out like a GP's consultation room, with a couple of Them at a desk like doctors and a screen to one side. Anne was led in by a beautiful nurse and sat down at the desk.

The doctors seemed to question her – telepathically as Their lips weren't moving. Whatever They were saying had Anne practically bouncing in her chair, so excited was she, her face wreathed in smiles as she answered. The triple-glazed glass and the thicker construction of the walls meant we couldn't hear a word.

After a while Anne and the nurse went behind the screen, coming out a few minutes later, the nurse holding a thermometer. She gave Anne a black scrunchy and gestured. Anne expertly coiled her hair up on her head and secured it.

Next moment she was making a thumbs-up sign to the desk and being led out through a door on the opposite side of the room.

"Come on," said Jo. We scurried to get to the final set of windows. There was a long gap to them, a distance measuring about a third of the length of the whole hut. But when we got there the room was dark.

"So, what's happening?" I asked deflated.

"They're giving the girls a medical," said Jo. "It would be terrible PR if they looked badly treated when they were handed over."

"So, what's in there then?" Tess asked.

"This hut is much deeper than ours. I think it goes all the way to the perimeter of the running track. This part must be a dorm so the girls can get a good night's sleep. It's getting late now so they probably won't get released till the morning. That's why there weren't many girls in the other room."

"But why's there no light here?" said Tess. "And I still don't get why Eppie was so freaked."

"She must have run into one of Them on the way back," I said briskly. "Come on, let's go back." Even though it had been a warm day it was a clear-skies night, and chilly like those always were.

"Something's not right here," Tess said. "I know you're going to laugh at me—"

"Seriously," said Jo. "If you're going to say this is like a farm again then I will *not* be laughing."

"But there's something odd about it," she said. "The way the girls are so relaxed, then the medical—"

"I'd be relaxed too," I hissed. "If I was living it up like that. But it'll be our turn soon, so until then let's head back to our warm pile of straw."

"It reminds me of something—"

Just then a light flicked on, and we ducked down. My heart was beating madly. It took a few seconds to summon the courage to look back through the window, but by then, frustratingly, the light had gone off again.

"Come on," I said.

"Let's just give it one more—"

The window lit up. This time we shrank back but kept watching. The door into the room had been opened, and a cold light was throwing it into strange, half-lit angles. The door opened inwards so we couldn't see where the illumination was from or what was going on in the wide block of the building to our left. Suddenly, a roundish object flew into the room and landed on top of a pile of similar shapes. Peering closer I could see they were bin bags.

"It's just rubbish," I said as another one was thrown in. But this one missed the existing pile and landed more heavily straight on the tiled floor. The force of the impact tore the bag up the side and part of its contents spilled out. For a moment, in the strange pattern of light and darkness, it looked like it was leaking a viscous liquid, through a patch of shadow and towards a pool of light.

Another dustbin bag was thrown in, and it landed directly on the last. The split in the previous bag opened up, and now the contents was forced out, squeezed by the bag on top—

I screamed.

Protruding, pale in the half-light, was a white lump attached to a wider mass. A head. And the nature of the stream issuing from the bag now became clear, as its slow progress concluded in the light, revealing the final unfurl of a hank of auburn hair.

I screamed again.

I couldn't tell you if the others were screaming or not as I was near hysterical.

Yet another bin liner was thrown in and squeezed the remains of poor Anne further out of the bag. Her head rocked back lifelessly, and then we saw the top of her torso, still clothed in what had been a pristine white T-shirt, now soaked red with her blood and horribly open at the front, peeled back like her skin and ribs, her chest cavity empty, where once it had held her heart and lungs.

I threw up.

Tess was howling.

Somewhere above me the light went off again as the door was closed.

"We've got to warn the others," Jo yelled.

I heard her voice even as I heaved again. I couldn't help it. The vomit hurling from me. The sight of the blood and bones like a rack of lamb. Anne's lifeless eyes.

"Come on!"

Jo's urgency roused me. I wiped my mouth and stumbled back down the side of the building with her, past the medical room where a girl was happily standing with the nurse, back to the first room that resembled a clubhouse. We banged on the windows with the flats of our hands to get their attention.

"Emma!"

She turned, puzzled, and we realised she probably couldn't see us through the glass, mirrored by the lights inside.

"You've got to get out of there!" Jo yelled.

"That's what it is..." Tess was trailing behind, her arms outstretched. She had stopped screaming, and now her voice was ethereal, almost unhinged. "That's what this is..."

I scrabbled around on the ground, my eyes useless after looking at the light, scrabbled around for a rock or something else to throw—

"I was right all along..."

"Emma! Celie! Get out of there!"

"...this *is* a farm."

I found a chunk of quartz and sprang back to the window. Emma and the others had come to the glass to see what the commotion was all about.

"Stand back!" I yelled and threw the rock with all my might and it smashed through the triple glazed window. The girls scattered as shards of glass showered the room.

"What the hell are you doing?" yelled Emma, as the group clustered again to the shattered window.

"You've got to get out!" Jo shouted.

"Why are you trying to ruin this for us?"

"It's a farm," said Tess. Her voice had become sing-songy. *"They're calming you down. Inspecting you. This whole place is a farm—"*

"Can't you just wait your turn?" Emma said. "You're so selfish."

"You have to get out!" I screamed, tears running down my face. "They're going to kill you."

"What are you talking about?"

"—we are the cattle—"

"In the next room. Anne. We saw her!"

"Leave us alone!"

"— and this is the slaughterhouse."

The door to the room burst open, and instantly the girls fell to the floor clutching their heads. Several of Them had entered but different to the ones we had seen before. These were dressed in black and two of Them grabbed the girl closest to them – Emma – and dragged her screaming and kicking towards the door to the medical room.

"Help me!" she shrieked.

But it was too late, and even as we were starting to run after her along the side of the building, we too fell to the ground, our heads crushed by the worst sonic pulse so far, desperate searing pain, like my head was on fire.

And then, just as suddenly, it stopped and everything went black.

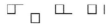

[1.53]

Afterwards, after Shecktl had finished and carried me back to my alcove, I lay curled up on the mattress. My right arm was covered in a dressing, throbbing despite the tablets they'd given me. Aggie stroked my hair.

—It was the only way.

I just shrugged. I could barely speak in any case, after all my screaming. From when the red-hot steel had touched my skin.

Again and again.

And the smell.

It's in my nostrils now.

Aggie reached for my arm, and I flinched from her, trying to curl tighter.

—I have to put on some ointment.

I shook my head. I just wanted Mum to give me a hug. For Dad to put his arms round me. Instead, Aggie gently peeled back the filmy dressing.

The skin was red raw. But while it hurt like agony, it had only blistered a little. Schektl had sprayed a cooling aerosol onto my wrist each time a new section of the brand was seared into me.

Snivelling I looked down and saw the four new characters burnt into me alongside the old:

Aggie unscrewed the lid of the jar and started applying balm to my wrist.

"What does it say?" I rasped, wincing as she touched the skin.

—It says: Property of: 13th State, 2nd City, 5th Farm. Then: Defective organs. Released for research. Office of Science and Medicine.

I sobbed as Aggie smeared the yellow cream liberally across my forearm. When she was done, she carefully replaced the dressing; then gently squeezed my hand.

—It means you're safe now.

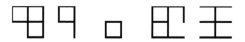

Part 6: Bats and Dogs

"What are you reading?"

I know I shouldn't be doing this.

I know if Aggie found out what I'm about to write here, she'd be really upset.

And I don't want that.

Aggie's been so kind to me.

She's definitely the closest thing I've got to a friend or family.

She lavishes so much attention on me, when Plaxys and Schektl literally couldn't care less.

So, Aggie's great. And the last thing I'd want to do is disappoint her.

But I can't help myself.

Writing about what happened to us has brought back so many memories that lead up to today – this safe, comfortable life – that it's difficult to remember sometimes who I was before.

I need to remind myself.

"What are you reading?"

Miss Temple asked me this one day when it was not exactly wet outside but had been in the morning and was now starting to dry. The rest of the class was having lunch or were at various clubs and societies. This was back in year 11, when we'd finally earned the privilege of staying in the classroom at break time. The novelty had worn off for most people, but I still resented how in previous years we'd been hustled outside, even in the snow. In any case, Tess and Jo were doing strings group together that day, and I just felt like some quiet time alone with a good book.

The good book in question was The Hunger Games.

Given the Colonists have destroyed all our books I'm figuring you won't have come across it, but take it from me, reader, it's really exciting. I was never particularly into all that dystopian stuff (I know: ironic) but the lead character Katniss is just so strong and the story's fantastic. I really like that it's not your typical girl meets boy thing either. More like: girl meets two boys and kills a bunch of other ones.

"The Hunger Games is great," said Miss Temple perching on the edge of my desk so that her bare legs dangled right in front of me. Even now I can smell her perfume. It's floral, fresh. As pretty as she was. She couldn't have been more than twenty-five.

Still is.

I've got to believe it.

"But next year if you're doing English A Level with me—"

"Would I definitely be in your class?"

She smiled with her amazingly blue eyes. "I think that could be arranged."

I felt a rapturous warmth spread through me at the thought that a third of my time at school would be spent with my favourite teacher. I wondered which form room we'd have. Maybe one of the top floor rooms with the great views over Highbury Fields.

"… so I think you should read some of them."

I winced. She was not going to want me in her class if I couldn't even pay attention to her when we were talking one-to-one. I wanted to crawl into a hole.

"Read some of…?"

Miss Temple laughed and stood up. Straightened her short skirt, then walked back to her own desk. She opened the top drawer, her hand hovering before she gave a little nod and selected something from the hidden contents.

"The classics."

She returned with a paperback book, black spine, and cream on the front and back covers.

"Jane Eyre," she said.

"Charlotte Brontë?"

Honestly, I loved reading. The escape. The possibilities. The places you could travel without going anywhere further than the snug ball you'd curled yourself into. I love it even now when I'm limited to rereading my own journal. And I'd always known the English Classics were something I'd have to get to at some point. But I thought of them in the same way as a retainer, or antibiotics: good for you, but you weren't expected to enjoy them. I was into modern writing – well, 20th Century at least – To Kill A Mockingbird or The Color Purple or The Handmaid's Tale. Amazing, mind-busting books, with some kind of connection to how things are now. Well, obviously not how things are <u>*right*</u> *now. Or even when you're reading this, reader. But fairly modern. Not all 'doths' and 'thous' and 'ye oldes'.*

"I always think of you when I see it," she said.

"You do?" My heart leapt.

"The Brontës used pen names because they didn't think their books would get accepted if the publishers knew they were women. So, they used the surname Bell instead. Anne was Acton Bell, Emily was Ellis Bell and Charlotte was Currer Bell."

"Oh," I said unenthusiastically.

"You know: Currer Bell – like <u>*Carabel.*</u>*"*

"Yes, yes, I get it."

She smiled at me. "Just read it," she said.

So, I read Jane Eyre.

(I finished The Hunger Games first though.)

And it was:

(I'm forced to admit)

<u>*Electric.*</u>

[1.54]

They called themselves Colonists.

They never said where they came from and maybe that didn't matter. When you've colonised as many places as they had, where you're from starts to lose its meaning.

The Colonists arrived on Earth months before they took down our school. They were powerful telepaths who could project any image or sound they wanted into the minds of lesser species. They could make us see whatever they wanted when we looked at them. So, they made themselves invisible and set about studying us – a time they called The Waiting. During this time, they infiltrated human society, the military, everywhere.

When the time came, they appeared to us in human form so as to ease the transition of colonisation; but they were most definitely not like us.

Once established on a planet they connected themselves together into a single collective consciousness which they called The Hive Mind. This was a distributed thought network across which the whole of the Colonist consciousness could be stored and shared.

Colonists were divided into different groups: most of them were Workers but there were more powerful ones too: Soldiers like the ones who'd rounded us up, Administrators and Inquisitors. Most powerful of all were the Controllers.

For each planet under colonisation there were sixteen Controllers who were the main memory banks of The Hive Mind. Each Controller was a thought leader in a different facet of Colonist life: emotion, construction, law, order, farming, mathematics, science and medicine, literature and the arts, and so on. They were located at different points around the planet to reduce the threat to The Hive Mind.

Controllers were different physically to other Colonists, their heads massively swollen with a vast outsized brain. They communicated with other Controllers without the need for external relays or amplifiers as their huge brains were capable of projecting their thoughts over hundreds of miles using radio waves.

Everyday Workers would not connect directly to Controllers but through intermediaries, the Administrators. And Administrators, and the Workers below them, were grouped into different Offices, each headed by a Controller.

Aggie's mother was an Administrator in the Office of Science and Medicine, working on respiratory virus suppression (whatever that meant) and her father was in the Office of Farming, both cattle (i.e. humans) and arable. They, and Administrators like them, ran local communication hubs which were meeting places for everyday Workers. Workers communicated with Administrators who in turn linked to Controllers; and in that way a whole planet worth of Colonists could share its thoughts.

Early in a colonisation the information flow would be only one way. It would flow from the Controllers via the Administrators to the Workers at local hubs, just like a termite mound where the Queen was in charge of everything. Each worker could still think for themselves, but high-level instructions would also get passed down. Often these instructions would be given physically instead of telepathically. Administrators gave messages to Workers via secretions and hormones which were passed through physical contact.

Factual feedback was given to the Administrators – locations, happenings, discoveries – but not emotional or other experiences. These were held back until it was clear the initial stages of a colonisation had been successful, and the Colonists were fully in control of the new environment; that the Soldiers' and Inquisitors' suppression of any previously dominant species was complete. Then, individual Workers would collate their personal memories and experiences they had gained during the colonisation. Having purged their thoughts of any subversive content, they would upload them into The Hive Mind on The Day Of Sharing.

The Day Of Sharing was the most significant day in any colonisation and was normally taken as the official starting point of Colonist History in the new world. 'Difficulties' might have been encountered in the Colonisation, and incidents of resistance from indigenous species would be collectively forgotten from this point on. It would be as though the world had always belonged to the Colonists.

The Day Of Sharing was a moment of great rejoicing and its anniversary was enthusiastically celebrated in subsequent years by all Colonist families as the official 'Day of Arrival'.

* * *

On each new world the Colonists settled, there were different needs. For instance, Colonists have similarities to beetles although are slightly bigger than humans. On Earth, because of the relatively low oxygen content of the atmosphere, their insect-like circulation is not very effective at getting oxygen around their bodies – which is why insects never grow particularly large here on Earth.

During The Waiting, Colonists expended little energy and so could get by. But once Colonisation began, their physical movements were sluggish, especially at night. And they used a lot of energy to apply their telepathic powers which didn't help.

To deal with this, Colonists needed a proper respiratory system. Even fabricators couldn't make something that complex, so until the Office of Science and Medicine developed an alternative, the simplest solution was to extract the necessary organs – heart and lungs – from a human and transplant them into a Colonist body.

A simple enough operation, but certain requirements needed to be met. The organs had to be very fresh, so the donor must have been killed recently; they needed to be fully grown but in top condition, so were taken from young adults; and the transplant would only stay stable for around five years and after that would need to be replaced.

Oh yes, and there were two hundred million Colonists requiring hearts and lungs.

So, they set about managing us like livestock.

They began by reducing the human species to only those below the age of nineteen. Their scientists calculated that organs from older humans would be of no use. Every three months there would be a Harvesting of the girls who had reached at least eighteen and a half, and then a new batch of younger girls would be brought to the farm to replace them.

Previous colonisations had taught that the testosterone-rich male part of the species – boys and men – should be eliminated to minimise conflict and rebellion. Only a few prize males were retained for breeding, and a few more for sport: Colonists loved racing.

Colonists would attempt to breed the girls twice before they were Harvested. Once weaned, babies would be taken from the young mothers who would never see them again. Most of the baby boys would be killed. The little girls would be taken to an ageing facility to provide the pipeline of juvenile females for future Harvesting.

It was as a tremendously efficient operation, and the Colonists would celebrate their ingenuity and prowess on The Day Of Sharing. Though it seems violent to us, they saw themselves as peaceful folk. Indeed, in their own language their name for themselves also translates as *farmer*.

And that, in a sense, is what they were.

□ | □ □
□ □

[2.11]

You see, the thing about Jane Eyre is that it starts off as an orphan story.

Like all the ones you've read before where the little girl or boy's parents have died, and they're living with a heartless uncle or aunt or stepmother. Only it's better than most of them because it really gets into the kid's head, and frankly Jane's more believable than most and actually puts up a pretty good fight. And then you realise most of those orphan stories were written after this, and Miss Temple said this was the first novel which really told things from a child's perspective which was why it was so fresh at the time. Plus, it's first person (you know: 'I did this', 'I did that') which helped because it made it more immediate. So, it's like the grandma of all those orphan stories. Though maybe it was also hooking into older stories itself: fairy tales and the like. Cinderella is meant to be really old.

Anyway, Jane Eyre then becomes a school story for a bit, but a kind of warped one where everyone's treated horribly and her best friend dies, until she finally finds a teacher who's kind to her.

Those are actually my favourite bits of the novel. Apart from when she's lost on the moor as an adult and thinks she's going to die out there.

But the stuff with Rochester is good too. She's immediately attracted to him, and he is to her, but it can't happen for lots of reasons, so it's a classic 'will they, won't they' and then you realise that there weren't really any others at the time, and in any case the heroine here actually has a brain and tries to exercise free will. The whole book's not even completely spoilt by the ending which in a way is really predictable, but is freshened up by being very weird. (Which is definitely a Brontë thing. I read Wuthering Heights afterwards and the language is incredible but the story is <u>wild</u>.)

I didn't like the whole St John part though. Maybe that made sense in eighteen-whenever-it-was but it certainly doesn't today.

But you know that's it: you're never going to like everything about a book.

Anyway, Miss Temple said that Jane Eyre was a bit of an anti-Jane Austen so I read some of her stuff too and actually quite liked them especially Sense and Sensibility (though not Emma which just really annoyed me). And then she said maybe I'd like Wilkie Collins ("Massively underrated," she said) but she didn't have any so I found The Moonstone in the school library, and, seriously, reader, if you could read one book (along with Jane Eyre) read that. Not that you'll be able to, because every copy has been incinerated. But just take it from me it's the best detective/mystery story ever. The characters are great, Wilkie Collins is really sympathetic to his female characters, and it feels properly modern. I mean, you'd never think that all those other predictable detective stories and TV shows came after this one.

We were reading Thomas Hardy for A'Level. Jude The Obscure. Which I liked because it was so bleak. And we'd read Spies for GCSE which had been good, so Miss Temple said read Atonement, which was great, and it had similarities with the whole 'seeing events through a child's eyes with tragic consequences kind of thing'. And she said if you really wanted to see the lineage (like ancestors, she said) read The Go

Between. And it _was_ kind of similar, but the thing that really stuck out for me was they were set in long hot summers and the description of lazy heat threads through all of them. The Go Between is definitely the parent of the other two, but they're different and great in their own way.

I was really into them all. It was probably because it was at the start of that long hot spell we had that year. So, Miss Temple suggested Cat On A Hot Tin Roof. Which was a play. And I'd never read one apart from Shakespeare in English lessons. Anyway, they didn't have it at school but the lady at the local library said I should try The Crucible instead. And I tell you, if you ever want to read something where the language feels really alien at first but within a couple of pages you're totally hooked, that is the book. Plus, as it's a play, it's really short so you zip through it. But the ideas in it are super-concentrated like drinking squash straight from the bottle. When you've finished, you have these really vivid flashbacks, like when you've woken from a dream.

All those lovely books. And loads of them. Easy rereads. Books I never finished. Some I only just about started. It didn't matter.

And obviously I didn't read them all on paper. Plenty were downloads. Or online. For a while I thought maybe those words would still exist somewhere electronically, digitally. But the Colonists have long since destroyed our computers and the Internet, so I guess wherever those words are they're just floating around, inaccessible.

All those lovely books are gone.

Long gone by the time you read this.

I just want you to know that they were here once.

So maybe one day, reader, when the Colonists have left or have given us our freedom back, perhaps then one of you will write some more books. As good as the ones we had.

Or maybe I will.

⌐ ◻ ◱ ◻

[1.55]

Most of my detailed knowledge about the Colonists has come from Aggie, of course, in the months I've lived here.

But I first got the basics back there on the farm in Finsbury Park, standing before the dais where Emma used to give her stupid talks. In front of the shed where They killed her.

—This world is ours now. We had a need for new territories and have claimed this one as we are the first Colonists to discover it. We are not a cruel people. We mean you no intrinsic harm. But because we are intellectually and creatively superior to you and properly sentient, we have the moral right to take what we need. You are a lesser species. You are just animals, and from now on you must get used to that being your status.

—When we select a world for colonisation, we look at the benefits which will accrue to our race. But we also look to correct mismanagement which currently exists. Here, in your world, you have boundless natural resources, you have minerals and plentiful energy supplies. Yet, you are raising temperatures, provoking extreme weather patterns. You have tainted the oceans with plastic polymers which will persist for thousands of years. You have systematically murdered your subservient animal and plant species. You have even subjugated great swathes of your own species based on colour and gender.

—Well, rejoice.

—We have freed you and your planet from your own domination.

—Think of us as liberators of your world.

—Your destructive industries have been stopped. Carbon dioxide and plastic production have ceased. The permafrost and icecaps will be saved. We are now the guardians of this beautiful place that you were not able to be. In time, you will learn your place as the animals have under you; though we will care for you more and treat you with less cruelty. Do not mourn for what you have lost because you clearly were never meant to have it. This Earth is our destiny. And the animals and plants and climate and oceans are at this very moment breathing a sigh of relief that we are here.

—You have already been subdued across the entire world. Resistance is in any case pointless since The Second Wave of Colonists will be arriving soon enough. They will swell our numbers tenfold. We are preparing the planet for them. We already strike awe into you but are just The Advance Party. When The Second Wave arrives, you will witness the true majesty of the Colonist race: even more mighty and terrible and intelligent and beautiful.

There was outcry at all of this, of course. It's impossible to believe stuff like that straight out of the box. The notion that anyone could just take over the whole world was frankly ridiculous. Plus, it was the first time they'd even confirmed to us that they weren't human.

The Colonists acknowledged as much, after they'd administered a sonic beating which literally dropped us to our knees before them.

—We do not expect you to take all of this in immediately. Humans have been pre-eminent for so long that losing your place at the top will be hard. But we have Colonised many territories and cared for many species. We are experienced in this. Let us assist you.

I was screaming at them like everyone else. In pain but in shock too. Assist us? What were they talking about?

—This Mantra will help. You will repeat it in the morning and in the evening. In time it will help you to understand your place.

And they made us say the words for the very first time. Through gritted teeth, the pain so bad like they were crushing our skulls. It went – well, you know how it went – and I recited with the rest:

> "Colonists are intelligent,
> Colonists are creative,
> I am not a Colonist.
> Animals are not intelligent,

Animals are not creative,
I am just an animal."

[1.56]

So, I guess I've known about the Colonists, what they're doing to us and why, for a long time now.

But even so, it was only this morning, while Aggie was nursing me after the re-branding, that full realisation finally dawned.

I can be so utterly stupid sometimes.

She was being typically Aggie, typically reassuring.

—Things will be OK, she soothed. —Mother and Father will not be angry for long. I'll stand by you. After all I'm a bit human now as well.

"Huh?"

—Me, Cara. I'm talking about me. When I went off for those few days, it wasn't to play camp with other Colonists. I went for self-improvement.

"So, you said. You certainly seemed more energetic when you came back. More confident."

—Not that kind of self-improvement, Cara.

I blinked at her.

—I *improved.*

"I'm not following you."

—Colonists say attractiveness comes from the heart. Well, that's the bit of me that's human. And the lungs as well, of course. That's why I can move so fast now. Why I can get up so early. I'm part human.

'What are you talking about?" The room was spinning. "What have you done?"

—You know what has been done. What most Colonists have had done. When I went away, I got my heart and lung transplant.

"But you took them…" My voice was weak. "You killed someone for them."

She seemed genuinely mystified. —But you did this kind of thing to animals all the time. Isn't it the same?

I felt sick. "But this was from a girl like me."

—No, not like you, Cara. She would not have been special like you—

"I've told you a million times! I'm not special!"

—Perhaps not. I know you abandoned all your friends. But that's what humans do. You can't help that. I still care for you regardless.

And she kept talking as she continued to dress my wound.

And I kept sitting there.

Numb.

⌐ ⌐ ⌐ ⌐

[1.57]

They made us chant The Mantra thirty times before they stopped assaulting us.

My head was dull and ringing. But their cold explanation of Colonist practices continued regardless. Eventually though, they were done, and the Colonists formed a tight cordon and forced us back to our sheds.

That was a terrible day and night; worse even than the first night we'd spent there. The whole shed was boiling over with anger and disbelief and resentment and horror and despair. Until Colonists lined the passageway down the middle of the shed and knocked us out with a single neural punch.

191

It was like being given a sedative. I fell into an immediate and dreamless sleep and only woke hours later, disorientated.

Had any of that actually happened?

But the Colonists were still there in the shed, suppressing girls if they became hysterical again.

And the next morning, after fruit and bread and water, they trooped us outside and we did it all again. They told us the same things and made us recite The Mantra.

And the next day.

And the one after that.

All through this period, the Colonists were in much greater evidence, guarding the exits to the sheds and teeming around the perimeter to the athletics ground. Despite this, there were many escape attempts, but to my knowledge no one made it out, and several times daily, girls would be brought back – often dragged – and returned to their stalls.

It was on one of these days they branded us.

They made us recite The Mantra while the hot steels burned us.

That night we were all crying so hard from the pain that it was impossible to think about anything else.

Tess had kind of a breakdown that night and wasn't herself afterwards. I mean none of us were, but she just sat in silence, muttering to herself, not wanting to engage in conversation. Of course, she'd been right all along. She'd known what we only learned later: that if you treat others terribly, how can you complain when one day someone turns up and does the same to you.

Though we understood our situation better now, it didn't mean Jo and I stopped discussing how we might escape. We agreed that if the opportunity arose, we'd take advantage of it. Either together or alone. Any chance we got.

But we didn't get a chance.

□ | □ ⊓

[2.12]
I haven't been able to meet Aggie's eyes for the last few days, ever since she told me about the transplant.

It's just been too upsetting and disgusting.

I think she feels the same. She leaves my tray and scurries away with no attempt at conversation.

Now though, I'm starting to feel kind of sorry for her.
She didn't ask for the transplant.
They just did it to her.
And she's right: wouldn't we have done the same?
It's still all kind of creepy.
But I've stopped blaming her.
I blame me.

⊓ □ ⊓ □

[1.58]
After that first Harvesting, a new routine was implemented.

Every morning and evening, they made us recite The Mantra in the shed. Then every three days, the whole shed was herded outside, and we were exercised on the running track for a couple of hours. They did this whether it was raining or sunny. And it became increasingly exhausting given how little exercise was possible at other times.

After our two hours exercise, we would be taken to the pavilion where we would get clean in the communal showers. That did not feel like a luxury anymore. The water was freezing, we were kept moving by Colonist guards who used their minds like cattle prods, and nothing had changed my view that communal showers are just strange and awkward.

After every other stint of exercise and showering, we were given new clothes: simple white cotton T-shirt and loose trousers, which made me shudder when I first saw them, because they were exactly what Emma, Celie and Anne had been wearing.

They forced us to take antibiotics with our food whether we were sick or not, and although our general routine was squalid, between the showers and the drugs they fed us, they managed to keep any major outbreaks of disease at bay.

During one of our exercise periods, we noticed them building a sixth shed. To begin with I thought it was just another set of sleeping quarters. But on a circuit of the track, I realised with a shudder it had metal walls and three sets of windows on the side just like Shed 5. It was another killing block no doubt. But however terrible a discovery this ought to have been, the impact on me lasted only a few moments.

One abattoir or two – what was the difference?

[1.59]

In my silent moments back in our stall, I would think sometimes about Mum and Dad.

By now the argument had faded into insignificance. The memories were just of hanging out with them, even if at the time that had felt a bit rubbish. I still hoped they'd got away – however increasingly unlikely that seemed.

Although no one wanted to talk about them, I'd also think of the boys and what had happened to them.

Pip first of all. He was the last boy I'd seen on Highbury Fields and I didn't like to think how painful it must have been for him at the end. I was certain now it *had* been the end for them, the boys. After everything the Colonists had said and despite the lies Emma had told us.

Incidentally we never knew why Emma had made all that stuff up. Whether it was because she got a kick out of being the one with the news, or she just hankered after being in charge. Maybe she'd just been scared like everyone else and had thought she was helping us by keeping hope alive.

Maybe she'd been right.

I thought about Brandon as well, of course. A lot. It was kind of stupid. It wasn't like he had ever actually said, "Cara, I really like you," or anything. And the only *moment* we'd ever had was when he caught me from the tree. And arguably that hadn't been a moment at all. It was just him catching me.

He hadn't been going out with anyone. Or not as far as I knew. And though Tess wasn't really into anyone that way, it seemed like he fancied her since he found it easier to laugh and joke with her. She was a lot prettier than me so perhaps that was understandable. I mean, if she hadn't been my friend *forever*, and if I'd just met her, even I would have been, like, *Wow*.

I used to spend ages idly chatting to Tess about Brandon and whether or not he was actually interested in me. But now Tess just lay curled in a corner. Her beautiful blonde hair was tangled and unkempt. It was difficult to talk about anything with her.

So, I had to think about Brandon on my own. About his dark, dark skin, especially in summer. About cheering him on sports day, and hearing him cheering me when I won the standing triple jump (which actually was once a real Olympic event before you laugh). Often my memories of him were as part of a group: me, Tess and Jo, Pip, Orlando and Brandon. But in my mind, it's like a spotlight is shining on him and me. Maybe we'd be sitting somewhere having a burger and everyone would be talking at once. But then the others would fade out, and it would just be me and Brandon. I would offer him my fries, and he would smile this beautiful smile – such amazing teeth against his skin – and reach out and take one.

Heaven.

But I couldn't think about him forever. So, sometimes I thought about Orlando too.

And that was the weirdest thing. I'd have been ecstatic if Brandon had ever asked me out, but Orlando asked me out all the time.

I'd known Orlando longer than anyone. I'd been at pre-school with him. Even Tess I'd only known since primary school. He lived really close by, so he'd often come round and hang out, even when we got to that age when boys and girls just didn't have playdates together any more. He was funny, and it was always comfortable being around him.

I definitely missed Orlando. He was someone who'd always been around. And there was no doubt he was attractive: blonde and tall and a great footballer. We used to do stuff together all the time, as part of the group, or just the two of us. But one time, he said would I maybe like to go out with him on an actual date, and for some reason that just felt wrong. I was really nice about it, and he was too, and in fact it became a standing joke between us.

But I caught him looking at me sometimes with this wistful, slightly faraway look and instead of it making me feel close to him it actually just irritated me. And then of course there was the ferris-wheel-draw incident which had been beyond excruciating.

[2.13]
Sometimes I wonder what it would be like to be free.

I'm not saying I have a terrible life. Aggie takes care of me and gives me plenty of food. I know I'm very lucky.

I'm not like the poor farm runaways that Aggie's told me about. Not many manage to escape anyway, and they're all caught, sometimes starving by the time they're picked up. And when they're captured, they're taken for immediate Harvesting. They're often so disorientated by this new world that Aggie says it's better for them that way.

I'm safe from Harvesting here.
Nothing bad will happen to me.
But I do wonder sometimes what it would be like to be free again.
To be able to hang out with friends. Talk to other humans.
Maybe in the future it'll all be different again.
Maybe the Colonists will fabricate the organs they need and they won't need to farm us anymore.
And then we'll be free.
Or maybe they'll just decide they don't need us at all.
And that will finally be the end of us.

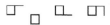

[1.60]

Living under a permanent death sentence should have been incredibly stressful. And I'm not saying it was easy. But for Year 12 girls like me, Harvesting was still over a year away. I wasn't even seventeen yet: my birthday is the twenty-fifth of August. Tess's was twenty-second April and Jo's was fourteenth May. For others, their time was closer, but given the next Harvesting would not be for three months, it was impossible to stay anxious about it all the time. Or maybe, as well as the antibiotics, they were sneaking other drugs into our food to pacify us.

Whatever it was, the days drifted into weeks until nearly a month had passed since the first Harvesting.

It had just started to get dark one evening, and Jo and I were playing a makeshift game of draughts. We'd cleared a small area of floor and marked out a chequerboard in the dirt. We used pieces of straw as checkers: mine were bent into squares and Jo's in triangles. It was pretty crude but it kept us from going mad.

As we played, we heard the sound of approaching steps. We thought it was just a patrol, but the footsteps stopped in front of our pen, and two Colonist faces peered over at us. It was the besuited pair with their clipboards.

—Carabel Caffarelli! Come with us!

When they called out my name, I pretty much freaked.

I didn't know what to do, I was so scared.

Eppie and Nettie hung their heads.

Tess, however, threw off her stupor and jumped to her feet, her eyes blazing. "You're not having her!"

—You will come to no harm.

"You liars!" she shouted. She flung her arms around me.

—Leave her, or we will restrain you.

I felt Jo unpeel Tess from me. It wasn't that Jo cared about me any less. She just knew the Colonists were going to take me whatever and didn't want Tess getting hurt.

"You'll be fine, Cara," Jo whispered in my ear as she gave me a kiss. "Remember: don't let them break you. Keep something human."

Tess kissed me goodbye too. "You'll be OK," she sobbed. "You're a survivor."

But I didn't believe her and I knew she didn't either.

I tottered to the gate to our pen, my legs wobbling with terror. Then turned back, determined not to go out like this.

"Listen Jo, I know I've got three kings, so don't you dare touch that board."

They were laughing through their tears as I stepped out of the stall. The Colonists ushered me up the passageway, calling out a further five girls' names as we made our slow way through the shed. These other girls looked as sick with fear as me, wondering aloud in shaking voices about what new horror awaited us.

We left Shed 2, and my stomach lurched as I realised we were being led across the twilit infield in the direction of the abattoir hut. So, the Colonists had been lying to us. It actually made sense not to have told us, to try and keep us in the dark as long as possible. We were walking through the overgrown grass of the infield. I let my hand play through the grass tops, like tiny ears of wheat, and wondered whether this would be the last time I would be in the open air again. The last time I would feel the night air on my cheek.

Just when it seemed certain we were headed for Shed 5, they diverted us off to the right, towards the new block, Shed 6.

—You are to test our new facility.

So that was it. They needed guinea pigs to make sure their Harvesting equipment worked OK.

The confirmation was chilling, and at that moment I couldn't help myself, and I burst into tears. I wasn't the only one, and as the guards pushed us into the hut there was screaming. We reached for the door frame as we passed through, gripping it so tightly that the Colonists had to drag us and unpeel our fingers to get us inside. I held on with the rest until my hands were prised away. I just wanted to see the sky one more time, the infinite night above, with its punctuation of stars. They seemed so benign, so beautiful. Yet from one of them had come the Colonists.

Eventually the guards got us inside and slammed the door. We must have been still screaming but gradually subsided as we became aware of our surroundings. It was very different to Shed 2. There was carpet underfoot and electric lights and cream painted walls.

—Shower.

We looked around and saw ten cubicles with wooden doors. I'd stopped crying by now. There was something about the inevitability of what was going to happen and the impossibility of doing anything about it which left me lightheaded. I stumbled towards an empty cubicle, and let the door swing closed behind me. Inside was a limestone tiled shower room with one of those huge watering-can shower-heads. On the back of the door was a hook, hanging from which were a new white T-shirt and loose jogging pants. And on a small shelf in the shower were bottles of shampoo and conditioner.

In spite of myself, in spite of everything, I dashed to the bottles and opened one of them. A heavenly lavender perfume wafted from it, making me think a million things in an instant. I clutched the bottle to me and turned on the shower. In a moment steam – *steam!* - was rising from the shower floor. I tore off my dirty clothes leaving them in a heap, and stepped into the shower. Luxuriated in it. Snatches of singing drifted in from the other cubicles and I found myself laughing. I squeezed shampoo into my hand and massaged it into my hair, and when the bubbles of foam slid onto my cheeks, I happily put my face under the warm, warm water to wash them all away.

Our showers finished, changed into fresh clothes, we passed into an adjoining room. It was like the cozy clubroom in Shed 5, and we lounged on sofas and beanbags. There were table lamps all around us, the buttery light soft and relaxing. I alone had seen Emma and Celie and the others in Shed 5, so I should have been petrified. But I wasn't.

On the back wall was a trestle table with the most amazing Danish pastries, tarts and doughnuts. None of us had had anything other than bread and fruit over the past month so to taste sugar was incredible. I lay on a chaise longue with a glazed doughnut in my hand and took a bite.

It was better than any doughnut I'd ever had in my life.

Around me three of the girls were singing an impromptu harmony, and I was thinking Eppie would have loved it and would probably have joined in. I was thinking how beautiful they sounded, the voices kind of sliding over each other, making my spine tingle, when the door on the right-hand wall opened and a nurse came out.

I sat up with a start and the half-eaten doughnut dropped from my hand. Immediately I thought I was going to throw up. The other girls seem barely to have noticed, but then they didn't know what was coming next.

—Carabel Caffarelli.

All the girls were looking at me now, so they had definitely heard it as well. I wanted to freak out, but something held me back. It was the thought of Emma and Celie and the others, all lounging in such happy ignorance of the fate that lay ahead of them just a few metres away. And, however much it felt like my insides had turned to liquid, I didn't want to take away the last few moments of calm these girls would know. After all, there would be no escape from there.

So, I stood up and grinned, and immediately the girls relaxed. "More pampering," I said, beaming. And I strode through the door the nurse held open for me without looking back.

"You're so lucky!" I heard one of the girls shout wistfully after me. My heart was beating so hard that I could barely breathe, and when the nurse closed the door behind me, I thought my legs would crumple.

I was in a medical examination room with a desk and two Colonists in white coats sitting behind it. The nurse indicated the seat opposite them and I collapsed into it. It was warm in the room, and I began to sweat.

—You are Carabel Caffarelli?

There were two Colonists in front of me, a man and a woman, both wearing white coats. I got the sense it was the woman addressing me. I nodded.

—Have you been ill since coming here?

I sighed. They were checking to make sure my organs weren't diseased. I should have lied and said yes. But I was broken and just shook my head.

—No viruses?

"No."

—Any bone fractures? Infestations?

I shuddered. "No." Maybe the sooner this was over the better.

—Go with the nurse.

I walked behind the screen with her. I shivered as she slipped a stethoscope under my T-shirt and pressed it cold between my shoulder blades. She turned me round and put a thermometer under my tongue. She shone a torch in my eyes and then finally examined my teeth.

Seemingly satisfied, she led me out from behind the screen and opened a door opposite the one I had entered by. Through it I could see a dimly-lit passageway without windows which, after only two metres, swung to the left.

I turned back to face the medical room. "Please don't kill me."

—Step forward.

"Please. There has to be another way. You don't need my organs—"

—Step forward.

"Please!" I tried to duck back past the nurse, but she was too quick for me and hit me with a neural blast. I clutched my head. I willed myself to stay put, but the pain was unbearable, and I found my feet shuffling against my will, carrying me into the gloom of the corridor, forcing me to its end.

It opened onto another passageway with doors to the left and right.

—Room 7 is designated for you.

The nurse was right behind me. Again, I felt myself pushed forward by her mental strength. Suddenly the pain was too much. I could fight it no longer. I relaxed and walked forwards of my own accord. Immediately the pain reduced. I stepped to the door marked seven, then turned at the last moment.

"Will it hurt?"

The nurse's face was impassive. —Enter.

I bowed my head, pushed at the door and stumbled inside.

For a moment I struggled to take it in.

I'd been expecting an operating theatre. Bright white walls and surgical instruments. Trolleys. Doctors in gowns.

But instead, the room was like the clubroom. Soft lighting, a sofa, a side table with what looked like snacks and drinks. On the ground was a thick, thick carpet which felt incredible under my bare feet. The room itself seemed to be an antechamber, connecting to another via a door in the far wall. That door was opening now, a form emerging from it.

I almost fainted as I recognised the figure walking towards me.

It was Brandon.

□ | □ ⊟

[2.14]

I had a very odd conversation with Aggie this morning.

She was changing my linen when I asked her: "So, did you know you were going to get a pet when I turned up?"

—What do you mean, Cara?

"Well, everything was ready for me when I arrived here: desk, bed, cross trainer…"

—Oh. Yes. I had wanted a pet for some time.

"But you Colonists don't usually keep humans as pets. You'd have got a sheep or a pig or something."

Aggie paused with the duvet in one hand and a clean cover in the other. She stood stock still, a sure sign she was confused.

"So, that means you knew you'd be getting a human," I went on. "But how could that be?"

She thrust the duvet into its cover so hard that it ripped the seam.

—It could not be, Cara. The equipment and the bed were here when we arrived. We didn't use the alcove so saw no imperative to clear them out. That is all.

"But why? Maybe they exercised here, but why would there be a mattress here…? Unless… Greta."

—*What is Greta?*

"*Who is Greta? Or maybe it could have been Eta… Another girl, anyway. Alice's cousin, I reckon. She must have been staying here when all this happened. Did you see her?*"

—*I told you already. The family was gone. They told us three humans had inhabited the apartment. Two adults and a juvenile. Presumably, the girl you call Alice. There was no mention of someone called Greta. Oh.*

She broke off. For a moment she just stood there.

"*Aggie?*"

She turned abruptly.

"*You OK?*"

—*I have a history lesson now.*

She turned to go, but I barred her way.

"*Wait, Aggie.*" *There was clearly something wrong. Her normal lack of playfulness was evidence enough.* "*What is it?*"

—*What's what, Cara? I told you. I didn't meet anyone called Greta. Or Eta.*

"*What are you not telling me?*"

—*I don't know, Cara. I wanted a pet. You fitted that need. There is nothing I'm hiding from you. Colonists do not lie, remember.*

And she walked around me and out of my cage, raising the barrier behind her, so there was no chance I could follow.

I let her go, but I was thinking back to that day with the Inquisitors on Hampstead High Street.

Aggie said Colonists didn't lie.

But I'd heard her lie already.

She was keeping something from me. I just didn't know what.

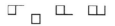

[1.61]

Reader, I am definitely not the swooning type, but I'd fallen into some kind of faint because the next thing I knew, I was sitting on the couch with Brandon fanning his hand in front of my face.

I sat forward in a rush and felt so lightheaded I thought I was going to keel over again.

"Take it easy, Cara."

His voice lifted me out of my fog. I put a hand out and touched his cheek.

"It's you," I said. "It's really you."

"It's really me."

I threw my arms around him and burst into tears. I felt his hand stroking my back. Eventually I pulled away and wiped my eyes. "I thought you were dead. How are the other boys? Are they OK too?"

Brandon closed his eyes. He got up and walked to the far wall. It was only now that I noticed his weird attire: he was wearing nothing but a short white bathrobe. His legs stretched long and dark from beneath it.

He pushed against the wall in a curiously powerless gesture, then turned back to face me. "No. They're not OK."

"We thought we saw on Highbury Fields… You know… And then some of the other girls had said they saw their boys get—" I gulped before I could bring myself to say the word. "Killed."

He came back and sat down again, but now there was a distance between us.

"They probably were. It was terrible, Cara. The Colonists… They attacked us. We saw you being led away, and then they hit us with the most terrible mind blast. We all fell to the ground but… but only a few of us got back up."

"Pip?"

Brandon's chest heaved. He hung his head and a tear rolled down his cheek. "No," he mumbled. "Pip didn't make it."

Somehow, I'd known it all along. I sighed. "What about Orlando?"

Brandon wiped his eyes. "He survived. They'd used their mind beam to select the hundred strongest, then herded us over to Clissold Park."

"What about the teachers?"

"The Colonists killed them. All of them."

I felt my chest tighten. "That's what they told us. But I still hoped that a few had escaped. Poor Miss Temple…" My eyes prickled as I thought of her. But then I frowned, something not making sense. "So, then… what are you even doing here?" I stood up with a start. "Are you here to kill me?"

"What?" He stood up as well, wide-eyed. "*No.*"

"You know they kill girls, right? When we get to eighteen and a half."

"But you're only seventeen."

"Sixteen. My birthday's next week. I *think*… Anyway, they said I've been chosen to test the facility."

"I know. I'm sorry."

"But what does that mean? And what do they do with you boys here?"

He blew out a sigh. "Something terrible."

I felt queasy with fear. "What's going on, Brandon? What is this place?"

He sat down on the couch again and patted the cushion beside him. "The boys that survived," he said, once I was sitting again. "They made us fight to find out who were the toughest."

"Oh Lord."

"The ones who won, we kept on fighting until there were just ten of us left."

"And the others? What happened to them?"

"The winners were kept in the big house in the centre of Clissold Park. They built a couple of sheds for the others and we saw them wandering around sometimes. They seemed kind of drugged up. Alec Durber was there."

"Ugh, trust him to survive. I hate that guy."

"Can't argue with that. But look, Orlando was one of them too. Every now and then, I'd see one of them being led away. For racing, I think. I hope Orlando was one of them. They killed anyone left behind."

Images of Orlando flashed through my mind. All the time I'd known him back to when we'd been kids. The thought of something happening to him was almost too much to bear.

Eventually, I said, "What about you? Did they do horrible things to you in that house?"

"No. Completely the opposite. They laid on loads of food and drink. And our living quarters were *so* plush. They made us do exercise, running and strength work, but that was OK. We kept thinking something terrible was about to happen. That they were going to dissect us or something."

I raised a hand to my mouth.

"But it wasn't that. It was worse."

"What was it, Brandon? Why are you here?"

He gagged. "Do you know how a farm works, Cara? A dairy farm?"

I thought of Tess. "Kind of…"

"Well, most of the animals on a dairy farm are female. When calves are born, the majority of males are killed for meat, and the females are raised to become milk producers. They're kept until they're old enough to have calves themselves. Then the farmer brings a bull round to get the cows pregnant so the cycle can start again. You understand what I'm saying?"

I blinked at him.

"I'm the bull, Cara."

"Oh my God." My head was swirling. "Oh my God. So, this…this facility… It's not an abattoir?"

"What? No. No, of course not."

"Oh my God." The relief was overwhelming. The fact that I wasn't about to die left me smiling ridiculously, uncontrollably, before the shock started to wear off and I realised my grin was a little inappropriate. "So, hang on, we're meant to… like… er…"

"Yes."

"Have you… er… with other girls?"

"Please, Cara. Don't ask."

"What if they don't want to. You don't—?"

"*No*. Not if they don't want to. But a lot of them do." He hung his head. "But I never force anyone. I promise. But they give me drugs which make my body want to. Does that make any sense?"

"None of it makes sense. What if *you* don't want to?"

"I don't *ever* want to. You know I'm—" He stalled; rolled his eyes. "Why should this be so hard for me to say? I mean, we're literally in the Apocalypse, and I can't get the words out." He took a breath to try again. "I'm g—"

"Going to do what?" I said eagerly, smiling encouragingly, helping him by finishing his sentence.

He sighed and shook his head, and said instead, "It doesn't matter what I want. They force me and they drug me. I have to fight my body. And if someone doesn't want to, I tell the Colonists afterwards that something wasn't working for me. So, then they give me even more drugs. It's getting harder and harder to fight it. I feel myself becoming so aggressive. I'm scared that I'm going to turn into something horrible. Something even more horrible."

I could only blink at him. I felt like I didn't know where to look. It was terrible, of course. The whole idea of it. But seeing him there was also like some sick fantasy. I forced myself to avert my gaze from his bare legs and instead stared studiously at the opposite wall, trying not to think of what it would feel like to be in his arms—

"But I'm not there yet, Cara. I'm still me. I can still control what they're trying to make me do. It's OK. We're not going to do it."

"We're not?" I felt relief like a deflating balloon.

"I care for you too much."

"You do?"

"You're one of my best friends."

Now I did look at him. He was really gorgeous. "But you'll get into trouble. Maybe we should, you know, go through with it—"

"No way. I'm not playing their game anymore. We're going to escape instead."

"We are?" This was turning into a very unexpected evening.

"Yes. They brought round lists of names and I saw yours and picked you immediately."

"Really?" My heart leapt. "More than Tess or Jo?"

"I didn't see their names on the lists."

"Oh."

"How are they? How's Tess? She OK?"

"Yes. Yes, she's fine. They're both OK. I mean, as well as anyone could be."

"Thank goodness. But listen, when I saw your name, I knew this was our chance. I couldn't escape on my own but I figured with someone strong like you we could get away and get help."

"Oh," I said pleased.

"And you get so angry. We could really use that."

"Oh." What did *that* mean? "I don't think I get *that* angry…"

"We can use that energy."

"OK." *Energy* was better. And maybe he'd meant to say *feisty* rather than *angry* anyway… "OK. But what if there's no one to get help from?"

"There has to be."

"But the Colonists say they've taken over the whole world."

"I don't care what they say. We're humans. Someone, somewhere will be resisting."

"But how are we going to escape? I've already tried."

"Me too. But listen. I've got a way." He took both my hands in his, and suddenly all I wanted was to stay like this forever with me the sole focus of his attention. "The Colonists can be hurt. I found out by accident. If you get up close, they can be hurt just like we can. It's just their reaction times are so fast normally that they would zap you with their mind blaster before you could do anything. But if you don't mind taking a risk then I can get us away."

"But aren't you afraid of what they'll do if they catch you?"

"Are you?"

"No. The worst they can do is Harvest me. And they're going to do that anyway. But what about you?"

"Even if they kill me, it's better than what they make me do here; than what'll happen if I stay here and have any more of these drugs. You know what I'll become right?"

"You could never be that."

"Don't believe it. They can do anything to us, and make us do anything to each other. But I swear I'd rather die than carry on this life. Especially now I've met you again. It's like there's something left to live for."

I locked that away in my heart for later and squeezed his hands. "I'm not afraid," I said. "We'll do it together." And then in a hideous flush of confusion. "Er… I don't mean we're going to do it together. Not like—"

He smiled for the first time he'd been with me. "Stop talking, Cara. And listen to the plan."

⌐□ ⌐ □⌐

[1.62]

When Aggie brought me my breakfast tray I was already at my desk.

I was about to start writing, but she grabbed my notebook.

—I feel very nervous, Cara. I read the last section about Brandon. You are going to be writing about Colonist weaknesses.

"It's just another escape attempt."

—But this is more significant because of the outcome.

"What outcome?" I waved my arms around at her and the apartment. "The outcome is I'm here."

—Still, it does not feel right.

"Fine," I said. "Then I won't go on. But that means you won't get to know what happens next."

I'm sorry Aggie. I know that was mean. Aggie has been looking forward to reading my story with ever-increasing anticipation as it has developed. When we sit together in the early afternoon, she will often catch up on the latest instalment and is disappointed on a day when I haven't written anything or have done more of a diary entry. She still enjoys those; just not quite so much.

"You're right," I said, shrugging. "I should just stop."

Aggie hesitated. She clasped the orange covered journal to her. Then eventually, reluctantly, handed it back to me.

—Very well. Go on.

⌐ ⌐ ⌐ ⌐

[1.63]

I banged on the door until, eventually, the nurse opened it. Then stepped smartly away as she came into the room.

—What is going on here—?

Brandon crashed a chair over the nurse, and I felt a sudden surge of pain as she screamed in our heads. She slumped to the ground. Her whole body flickered but we fled from the room before we could see any more.

211

Down the corridor, away from the medical room.

We could hear sounds from the other bedrooms but didn't stop till we'd reached the door at the end. Pushed it open and we were on the running track and sprinting for the main entrance to the sports ground.

"But the Colonists are there," I gasped, struggling to keep up.

"I know," Brandon said. "But they're more sluggish at night. We've got a chance, so long as we act fast. You know what to do." Suddenly he peeled off.

I kept running towards them.

—Stop.

—Go back to your stall.

But I kept going until I felt their vice-like grip on my mind and, just a few yards from them, I fell writhing.

—Go back—

Smack!

The sound was shocking as Brandon swung the chair leg at both of their heads simultaneously and there was a thump as two Colonists hit the ground.

Brandon yanked my arm and I struggled back to my feet.

We ran the same way that Tess and Jo and I had gone when we'd tried to escape, but now we were running in darkness. The full moon was shrouded in cloud, so we had only a glimmer to see by and were relying on touch for most of the way, trees and bushes just deeper black in the already black night.

It took us ages to skirt around the boating lake to get to the playground. And from there to the path that led to Parkland Walk seemed like an eternity. We held hands to make sure we didn't get lost in the darkness.

Being with him like that was thrilling.

As we neared the exit, I squeezed Brandon's hand to get his attention.

"When we tried to escape before, there were two guards on this path."

We slowed almost to a halt and peered into the darkness. There, subtly silhouetted against the fractionally lighter sky, we could make out two Colonists.

Again, I ran at them and stumbled as their thoughts hit me. Again, there was the smack, smack of Brandon's stick. But then a cry from him. As I struggled up, my head muzzy from their mind blast, it took me a moment to work out what had happened.

"Brandon!" I yelped. One of the Colonists had fallen on him. I couldn't make it out clearly but it was no longer in human form. It lay there, a huge dark mass, pinning Brandon to the ground. I grabbed Brandon's arms and tried to pull him out but he was trapped.

"You've got to go," he groaned.

"But they'll catch you." I heaved now at the Colonist's body. It felt smooth and hard to the touch like it was some kind of shell. "Come on! Lift, Brandon! You're strong."

"I can't move my arms. You've got to run, Cara! They'll be here any second."

I wanted to die. I'd given up hope that I would see any of the boys again, so to have met Brandon and to have to abandon him was too much to bear.

"Let me stay here with you, Brandon. Please."

"If you stay, we'll both die. But this way we've got a chance. You can get help."

There was a rustling in the undergrowth just twenty yards away. "You have to go."

He was right. "I'll never forget you, Brandon," I said, my face covered in tears that I was glad he couldn't see. I started to run then turned, didn't think I would ever see him again, so didn't care anymore. "Brandon I'm in love you!"

"Just run, Cara. *Run!*"

"But I am. I'm in love with you!"

"No, Cara, don't say that—"

Then his voice was silenced, and I was running out of the park once more. And even though I was terrified of a

Colonist catching me and the thought of being Harvested, and I felt terrible about leaving him there, much more immediate and worse by far were the crashing waves of humiliation at what an UTTER IDIOT I had just been.

"I'm in love with you!" I'd shouted like a LITTLE GIRL and Brandon *so* hadn't shouted, "I'm in love with you too!" straight back. There had been no special spark between us. He'd been pleased to see me. Because I was a *friend*. But he wasn't in love with me. And I know that it sounds awful and shallow and pathetic to be thinking about all that at that precise moment, but that probably sums me up.

My feet hit the crunch of the gravel path, and I slowed, desperate not to miss the turning to the Parkland Walk. I felt for the opening in the metal railing, and then I was on the dirt floor of the long straight path up to Highgate. What if the Colonists caught me again? What if they *didn't* Harvest me but took me back, and I had to face him again after being so wet. I'd rather die than that.

"*Don't say that*," Brandon had said.

Oh God, what a fool I'd been.

I was running up the straight stony track. In the darkness, I kept brushing against the lacy heads of cow parsley encroaching onto the path, the clouds of tiny flowers making me jump every time one touched my face. I was in my bare feet, all too soon bruised and cut by the stones in the dirt, but I couldn't stop, driven by the fear of the Colonists and the look of pity Brandon would give me for being such a loser.

Why hadn't I refused to escape? At least that way I would have got to sleep with him.

It was all so messed up.

On I ran.

When the sound under my feet rang hollow and metallic, I realised I was on the bridge where I'd been caught last time. But there was no way I was making that climb in the darkness, and in any case, there was no sign yet of pursuit.

The only plan I had – the same one as before – was to head to Highgate and from there to Hampstead Heath. So, I carried on running.

Above me, the clouds cleared a little and the full moon started to peep through, illuminating the disused railway line. But if anything, it made the night still stranger, the ghostly light casting shadows that reared like obstacles in my path. Several times I slowed to a complete halt, to pick my way around them, only to realise they were phantoms.

There were noises too. Spending so much time in my stall meant I'd heard little apart from other girls for the last month and a half, but I was probably unused to night sounds in any case. On that warm night there was an insistent thrum from crickets that made my legs prickle just to hear it. A bird's fluttering wing caused me to catch my breath. The scrabbling at the base of a tree got me thinking of voles or moles or something worse. High overhead, I could have sworn I heard the leathery flapping of bats. And when the percussive bark of a dog sounded in the distance, my heart almost stopped.

After fifteen minutes I slowed to a walk as I felt the ground beneath me change. Luxuriated as my bare feet moved from gravel, first to soft soil, and then to a patch of heavenly cooling mud.

For the last stretch, though, I was hobbling. My feet were caked and dirty, cut and bruised, every step agony. I was approaching the Highgate exit of Parkland Walk by now, the ground rising the last fifty yards to meet the gate. But two Colonists were standing there, framed by the night sky. I crouched down in the bushes, wincing as my hand brushed a patch of nettles. There was no other way out of there. Unlike Brandon I didn't have a chair leg or the muscles to wield it—

I nearly jumped out of my skin as the night exploded in sound. That dog had started barking again, but this time surely just yards away.

One of the shapes by the gate began to descend the slope to investigate.

The barking became frenzied.

—Stop.

I heard the Colonist in my head. It was like shouting but I could tell it was aimed at the dog rather than me. And then there was a bloodcurdling screech, nails on a blackboard, a knife on a plate. But this time the noise wasn't in my mind. It was right out loud as the dog, unaffected by the thought beam, sank its teeth into the Colonist's leg.

And when the other Colonist shuffled down the slope to help, I was away past them like a breath of wind in the night.

I emerged onto the cutting which led to Highgate station and from there to the street, the cool and even paving slabs a relief for my bloody feet.

I approached Highgate Village cautiously. The moon was fully out now, but I couldn't see any Colonists as I padded along. I was exhausted but all I could do was continue. On I stumbled, across a pair of empty roundabouts, following the curving road first downhill and then gently up, in the slow wind that took me inexorably to Kenwood House and the edge of Hampstead Heath. After another ten minutes, I was finally there.

I howled inwardly as I tripped over a low railing in the darkness, landing heavily. I pulled my knee to me, wincing at the pain, gingerly touching a finger to the warm clamminess of blood seeping through the cotton of my joggers. I struggled back up and hobbled on. On my right loomed Kenwood House, but I thought if the Colonists were going to be anywhere it would be there, so instead I headed down the slope where Tom and I had rolled so many times. Over the iron fence and across the expanse of lawn, the high summer grass dry and prickly but still welcome. Forcing myself on, into the woods, and the renewed stab underfoot of stones and acorns and thorns, pushing myself till I could go no further.

Finally, I crawled into some bushes, as deep as I could pull myself, regardless of the scratches they left on my arms and my face, hauled myself in, and when I could get no further, I did what I had wanted to do ever since I'd had to leave Brandon. I curled up in a tight ball, and burst into tears.

Part 7: The Condolence Tree

[2.15]

Every six days, Aggie goes out.

Plaxys wants her to take a long walk for exercise.

Sometimes she meets up with other Colonist juveniles.

—They're not really friends, Aggie explains.

"But you're friendly with them."

—Yes. But they're not friends like we are friends.

"But we're a different species."

—It does not matter. Not to me.

So, she goes out. After breakfast. Every six days. Or maybe seven. It's easy to lose track since Colonists have no concept of a weekend.

She keeps the barrier to my cage raised when she leaves, and I'm cooped up all day.

On those days I write in the morning. Sometimes in the afternoon too. Both my public journal and this one.

I do a stint on the cross trainer.

I hate my cross trainer.

I eat my Danish.

Write a little more.

Then just sit here or lie on my mattress.

I wish I had some music.

Or TV.

Or social media.

I end up humming a lot.

I usually get so bored on these days.

I spend ages thinking I can't wait to see Aggie again.

Perversely, when Aggie does finally come back, I'm often really irritable with her. She'll be exhausted from her trek too, so sometimes we can get pretty spiky with each other.

So today, Aggie said she'd leave the barrier to my cage down when she's out.

Not that she's told her parents, of course. Plaxys in particular would not approve.

But it means I've got the freedom of the apartment.

To start with I'm quite nervous about leaving the safety of my enclosure, as if wandering outside it would expose me to some great danger.

I'm worried that Aggie's parents might return at any moment. If they find me free, they might think I'm trying to escape. And then they'd send me straight to the slaughterhouse.

I want freedom, of course, but it doesn't feel as important as just staying alive.

So, I actually just sit at my desk for a while.

And although I'm not confident enough to explore, it does mean I can get this journal out from where I hide it in my mattress, through a small hole and deep within the stuffing.

It means I can write in my secret journal in proper daylight for once.

And my handwriting, you will notice, is actually quite nice.

Though I'm not going to apologise for my normal writing, because if you had to write under a duvet using their terrible solar lights, your writing would be rubbish too.

□ | □ ⊹

[2.16]

The day's over and everyone's gone to bed.

And I'm back under the duvet! So, my writing's probably indecipherable again.

Anyway, this morning I sat there for half an hour, before I convinced myself that no one was about to walk through the door.

But Aggie's parents never have come back during the day, and Aggie has never cut her walk short either. So, once I'd calmed down, I was pretty confident I'd be alone for five hours.

After hiding this notebook away, I slipped cautiously beyond my alcove.

It was liberating.

I'd been round some of the apartment with Aggie already, of course. But it was different being there on my own.

Going from the living room to the hallway got me thinking about Alice and Greta again.

I wondered whether any other trace had been left of them.

So, I had a look.

I opened every drawer and cupboard in the kitchen, every drawer in the living room. But all the bits and bobs of human life had been removed. The drawers and cupboards were bare.

The same was true in the bedrooms. Aggie's, as I'd pointed out to her before, was pretty spartan. It's like a cream-coloured box with no possessions or furniture, just a pile of wood shavings in the corner into which she crawls each night.

The first time I saw it, I said, "It's so bare in here Aggie."

Aggie surveyed the walls. —But the paint is so beautiful.

"It's really not."

—Oh. Should I get some coverings for the walls?

From the blutak marks and painted-over picture hooks, posters and pictures had clearly once been there. A teenager's room perhaps.

Alice's.

It took ages to pluck up the courage to peek inside Aggie's parents' room, but when I finally did, it was pretty disappointing. The bedroom was bigger than Aggie's, but just as empty and as a result felt even barer. Apart from the built-in cupboards — which this time did have a few things in them, though nothing interesting, just leads, collars and spare sheets for my bed — it's again just a pile of woodchips and shavings in the centre of the room.

There was no further sign of Alice or Greta anywhere.

I wondered again what it was Aggie had been hiding from me. Because there definitely had been something.

But in the end, I let it go. And just relished that for once, I was able to move around wherever I wanted.

I treated myself to a chocolate doughnut and some iced tea from the fabricator in the kitchen.

It was a kind of freedom.

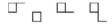

[1.64]

I woke up awash with euphoria and relief.

Just moments before, we'd been sitting on the sofa, Brandon and I. He'd leant forward and brushed my cheek with the back of his hand. Then smiled.

"I'm in love you too, Cara. Have been for ages."

I woke from that with a warmth which permeated every part of my body. But as I blinked, as I stretched out from the cocoon I'd made for myself in the night, as cold murk daylight filtered through the bush which surrounded me, so that warmth evaporated and morning chill set in. My first thought was,

What have I done?

My second thought, more urgent, driving away other nonsense was,

What do I do now?

As quietly as I could, my heart banging, I scrambled backwards out of the bush till I was sitting in a heap of leaf litter, a few metres from the path through the woods. It was daylight. Still early, judging from the glimpses of blue sky through the canopy, but no sun yet.

I cautiously scanned the trees for any movement. There was no one to be seen. A scrabbling made me jump, but it was only a rabbit scampering across fallen leaves. I stood still and saw a couple of baby bunnies hopping right behind. They headed to the path. A squirrel scampered head first down an oak trunk, legs splayed, its face alert and twitching. Overhead, a rook cawed.

It felt like I was safe. But my heart didn't stop racing, and my breathing was shallow and skittish.

I needed a plan, but I had nothing. *This* had been the plan. *Get to Hampstead Heath.* Back when Tess, Jo and I first tried to escape, we'd hoped this might be beyond the reach of the Colonists. So that once here, we would be back in the old world of the police and SAS and parents and university open days. But I'd stopped believing in the old world. Ever since I'd seen what had happened to Anne. Ever since the Colonists had said they'd occupied the whole planet. Sure, there might be pockets of resistance. But there was no reason to think they were going to be here.

So now, instead of having made an incredible break to freedom, all I'd done was move from one bit of Colonist territory to another. The best I could do was hide for a while and hope not to be recaptured. I was like one of those bunnies hopping around in the wood, twitching, on the lookout, trying not to be caught by a fox.

I had a pee. That made me feel better, settled my nerves a little. Not having toilet paper didn't bother me. I was used to that by now.

I can do this, I thought. I'm Carabel Caffarelli. I'm English *and* Italian which is awesome. So, what was the plan?

1) Water
2) Food
3) Reconnaissance

Water was easy.

I stole down the path until I reached the lake, where it was still shielded from view by trees. There was an algae bloom out towards the centre, but nearer me the water seemed pretty clear. I crouched down and scooped some to my lips. I'd expected it to taste rank in some way, but it was beautiful: clean and cold. I knew I should have been worrying about Weil's disease and other waterborne nasties, but I was parched. And in any case, if the Colonists caught me, I'd be dead in just over a year whatever. Taking up space in a garbage bag like Emma and Anne.

So, I drank my fill and sank back against a tree. Then jolted, when I realised I was only fifty metres from the

Rocket Tree. I hadn't been there for nearly eight years, since what had happened to Tom.

I tried to block that from my mind and concentrated instead on the matter in hand. From my vantage point I had a good view of Kenwood House, and I thought if I played my cards right, I could cover off both 2) and 3) on my list there.

I made my way up via a path on the right. Tree-lined, with plenty of bushes, I would have been able to hide if I'd had to, but this early in the morning there were no Colonists around. The sweeping grassy expanse which sloped down to the lake was empty aside from more gambolling rabbits and a few rooks.

I followed the path till it joined a wider one which ran in front of the House. Then almost immediately, crept down a set of steps to the café courtyard and peered cautiously around. I figured that even though the kitchens would be abandoned, there might still be some food left inside, if only tins of baked beans or those little jars of jam you have with cream scones.

I was about to skip across the flagstones when two Colonists appeared at the end of the passageway to the café. I couldn't make out their smooth faces at this distance, but their unhurried walk gave them away. I ducked behind a table, certain they must have seen me. But they didn't break stride, and I felt nothing in my mind apart from the approaching crackle of static.

There was the sound of footsteps, and over to my left I saw another pair of Colonists strolling into the courtyard.

I cursed silently and retreated up the steps. I worked my way past the hedge which screened the tea room until I got to the cream façade of the house itself, creeping along until I reached the Orangery; and then caught my breath. It was packed with Colonists standing, turned towards each other like at a party, but unmoving as though snapped in a photograph.

That left me in no doubt that the Colonists had taken over the entire building, so I reluctantly retraced my steps to the lakeside. In place of the food I'd been hoping for, I took another couple of handfuls of water.

OK, I thought, that was only to be expected. There were still plenty of ways of sourcing provisions. Just outside of Kenwood was a large residential area. Venturing out onto the road, I crept into the front garden of one of the mansions directly opposite. Through the front windows I could see a pair of Colonists standing together, again motionless. No sign of human life. But no smell of death or decay in the air either. It was like the human owners of the house had simply vanished.

Plucking up courage, I snuck around the side of the house. The back door had been left open and, heart in mouth, I slipped into a kind of utility room and from there to the kitchen. It was deserted. I tiptoed across the tiled floor, my mouth salivating as I opened the door to the fridge.

But there was nothing in it. It was empty and clean. I yanked open the freezer drawers and it was the same. The cupboards, when I opened them, told the same story, not a tin or a carton or a box in sight. I went back to the fridge and stared at its stark bright white interior. And that was when it struck me.

That was the moment, reader.

When I knew Mum and Dad were really gone.

The moment I opened that fridge door.

It wasn't just that there was nothing in it.

It was like there had *never* been anything in it.

It was like it was new. Pristine. Like when Tess's parents had had their kitchen done.

It was cleansed.

Our fridge at home smelt of old broccoli and mouldy cheese and stale milk and garlic.

When you opened it, the smell was so bad it made me want to throw up sometimes.

I mean, I didn't love our fridge.

But it was full of life.

Quite possibly literally in our fridge's case.

And even though this was a fridge in a posh house, it must have smelt of something once. It must have once had something in it: caviar and lobster and champagne, I'm guessing.

But now there was nothing.

This fridge smelt like it had just been delivered from the electrical shop.

Except it didn't even have that new fridge smell.

It smelt of nothing.

The grubby, smelly, greasy humanness of it was gone.

And all that remained was the empty vessel.

The fridge. The cupboards. The kitchen. The house.

All the same story.

Emptied of human life.

Emptied of us.

That's when I knew. That if that's what this posh person's house was like, if that could have happened to the rich people who lived here, then it would have most surely happened to our flat too, because bad stuff always happened to poorer people first.

And as I stood there in that kitchen in Hampstead, I was transported back to our own kitchen. A little cramped with a breakfast bar and the ironing board and Mum and Dad talking while they cooked, and I sat and waited to be served. I was back there, anticipating the dish of pasta ribbons in pancetta and garlic and olive oil which was about to be put in front of me, could almost taste it from the memory of the smell, the salt-sweet tang of cooking bacon and the thick starchy steaminess of the air, the window in the kitchen fogged with condensation, my dad reaching on tiptoes to open it. Mum was emptying the pasta from the pan into a colander, her face flushed from the clouds of steam enveloping her.

And then they were gone.

Though I reached for them, like Dad was reaching for the window, they disappeared and the food and the smells and the clatter went with them. And I knew the rest of our flat would be the same. All trace of us removed. Even Tom's room. His planets poster and the bucket of Lego untouched in the years since his death. All vanished.

Tom had been gone for ages.

But Mum and Dad were meant to still be with me. They were flesh and blood and real and mine.

But they were gone too.

At that moment I knew it with certainty.

I was left alone, back in that empty kitchen in that posh house in Highgate.

I sobbed my eyes out right there.

As quietly as I could, but I couldn't help my tears.

Right there in that strange kitchen. Knowing that even if I were back home, that would be strange too.

Because Mum and Dad wouldn't be there anymore.

□ | □ □ □

[2.17]

Dear Mum

(And Dad, of course, but mostly Mum because I was so crappy with you in the last few days.)

You'll never read this.

But I'll know I wrote it. And meant it.

I just wanted to say, I really liked that pasta and pesto you made me when we weren't even talking.

Even though I only had a mouthful, and Tess spat hers out, it was just about the nicest thing you ever made for me.

And I'm sorry I used to roll my eyes at you when you used to say, "This food will taste extra good because it was made with love."

I know what you meant. I always knew.

And most of all, I'm sorry I never answered you when you called out to me.

As I left for school that very last day.

I heard your voice.

But I slammed the door.

I know it's too late, but anyway:

I love you too, Mum.

[1.65]

—You haven't written for a couple of days.

Aggie was sweeping up the croissant crumbs from the alcove floor. Honestly, I'm not messy but some things you can't help.

—You just stopped.

That was about half an hour ago. I'm back at my desk again now. I know I need to complete my story. I know I'm almost done.

—And some things don't make sense. What's the Rocket Tree? And what about your brother, Tom? You never told me how he died.

"I will. But some things are difficult to write about."

—But the Rocket Tree? Is that where we found you?

I nodded. And then sighed and finally told her what happened to Tom.

—Ahhh…

Her voice in my head was like air escaping a tyre. Then she was silent for a long time. And I didn't say anything either.

Eventually she said, —I understand. The Rocket Tree is the Condolence Tree. Because of what happened to your brother. You're drawn back to it, I think.

I just shrugged.

—Condolences, Cara. But now you must get on and tell me what happens next. I'm dying to know.

She gave my hair an affectionate flick then sauntered out.

And now I'm sitting at my desk again and continuing my story.

Trying to write everything I can.

Everything the tears will allow me.

[1.66]

Once dusk had fallen, I retreated across the road and crawled back into the bush where I'd spent the previous night.

I hadn't eaten all day.

I'd visited ten or so houses looking for food and found the same emptiness in each.

The last thing I'd eaten had been that bite of doughnut the previous day. My stomach was growling and starting to hurt.

Now one of the things about me, reader, is I'm a pretty positive character. There are times I get down like everyone, and I'm not saying there weren't moments since the Colonists arrived that I hadn't wondered whether it was even worth going on. But at heart I'm an optimist.

So:

I was lying in a bush for a second night? Well, I'd been lying on a dirt floor for the past seven weeks, and I'd get some dry leaves to use as bedding first thing tomorrow.

I'd left Tess and Jo behind? But at least they'd know I escaped. And they were only seventeen. There was another year before Harvesting: plenty of time for me to go back and get them out.

I had messed up with Brandon, and if he ever saw me again would think me an utter dork? But on the plus side I probably never would see him again as either he or I would be dead pretty soon.

(OK, maybe that wasn't positive thinking at its finest, but at least my damage limitation genes were working overtime.)

I was lying there without food? Well, there were more houses at the Hampstead end of the Heath and I would investigate them tomorrow. Even if they too were stripped bare, the woods around me were teeming with life. After all, how hard could it be to catch a rabbit?

[1.67]

Pretty darned hard, as it turned out.

The next day I did a recce up towards Hampstead but found no more food than on my first trip. And as I got closer to the High Street, the whole area seemed to be crawling with Colonists so there would be no chance there.

I came back that second night a little crestfallen, but I still had access to plentiful water and had lined my hiding place with handfuls of dry leaves. They didn't really provide much cushioning, but the crackling was comforting and made me think of a fire. And though by now my stomach was really aching, I knew I would catch some food soon.

The next morning, I awoke to drizzle.

My bush was amongst the trees, but the canopy was thin here, and I was wakened by water dripping onto my face. I was still only wearing the light cotton top and trackpants they'd given me, by now filthy dirty, and I knew I'd get so miserable if I got soaked. So, I scrambled out and decamped deeper into the wood, where the overhang of leaves meant only the occasional drop of water got through.

It was an earlier start than I'd anticipated, but it reminded me that today was the day I would catch some food. Rabbits seemed the most obvious thing to go for. They were everywhere. And I'd discovered the entrance to a warren at the fringes of the wood, where a swathe of ragged heathland began. An ancient oak had been brought down years ago in a storm. Its roots stood proud, creating enough tunnel openings for it to be rabbit heaven.

I didn't have any string or wire for a snare and would have struggled to do anything useful with them even if I did. But I had found a stout stick, about the size of a baseball bat, with a nice swishy quality. I practised swinging it and impressed myself with how fast I could move it through the air.

I had a plan for whatever I caught. I'd watched a TV programme about Stone Age people and they used razor-sharp pieces of flint as knives. And though I didn't have flint, I'd found some shards of slate, and they would definitely be sharp enough to take off skin. There was no way I'd be able to light a fire to cook it, but I thought I could cut the rabbit up thin and put the strips in the sun to dry. OK, so there wasn't any sun today which again complicated things; but I loved sushi and raw rabbit couldn't be too different could it?

It was amazing how hunger made things seem more appealing.

Half an hour later, I was perched awkwardly a metre from the warren entrance. I'd started further away, watching the bunnies happily emerge and return, and had gradually worked my way forward. At first, every step I took had made the rabbits scatter, but once they got used to me, they stayed put, pulling at the grass, noses twitching, alert for predators; but not for me.

When I got to three feet, I crouched down and reached my stick arm behind me. I'd found a windmill action most effective when practising, so I got in position and waited. I thought a young rabbit would be best, would have the sweetest flesh and least likely to have any diseases. So, I waited till a group of smaller bunnies came out. They were definitely little, their eyes huge compared with their bodies, and they kept darting glances left and right, yet never forwards.

Smack!

I brought the stick down amongst them, but they scattered in all directions. I cursed and slammed it down again after the closest one; but he bounded away, his fluffy backside wiggling insouciantly.

I yelped in frustration and threw the stick to the ground; by chance just as a baby bunny was hopping out of its hole. The club caught the rabbit on its flank and it rolled, stunned. Only for an instant. Then it righted itself and made ready to hop away. But I got there first. Diving, I grabbed it.

The rabbit squirmed in my hands. Its fur, which had looked so luxuriant, seemed suddenly thin. I could feel its heart beating fast in its rib cage. Its warm body fought me, trying to slip out of my grip, its hind legs clattering against me like velvet covered fists, the claws on its feet like horn. They pummelled me. Its eyes were wild, zipping in all directions as it struggled to escape.

And then it went limp.

Its heart was still racing but it was like a puppet whose strings had been cut, the fight gone out of it. I carried it back to where I'd been hiding, and pulled the rabbit in close so that my left hand had it pressed to my side, and my right was free to pick up the jagged piece of slate from where I'd stashed it earlier. I brought it to the back of the rabbit's head, gently pressing against its fur, then lifting it and touching down once more under its chin. The rabbit was facing groundwards, but I could see its eyes clearly, set at the side of its head, looking to the front now. I wondered what it saw, whether it knew what was about to happen.

I took a breath and pressed the slate against its neck. When I pulled the slate towards me, it would slit the bunny's throat.

My stomach growled and gurgled.

The rabbit's ears flattened against its head. The fur on them was so sleek.

It reminded me of the last time I had seen Celie with her hair newly washed and conditioned just before—

My right hand jerked away from the rabbit's neck and up to the top of its head. The shard of slate was still tightly gripped in my fingers, so with the back of my hand I stroked along the bunny's ears with the grain of the fur. It felt so unbelievably soft to the touch. Almost cool.

I felt it cuddle up to me.

I thought of Tess curled in the straw, her face turned away.

"Look at me," I whispered.

Awkwardly I manoeuvred the rabbit in my hand. I had to drop the slate to make it easier.

It started struggling again.

"What's your name?" I asked it.

Its nose was twitching. Its eyes had begun to skitter once more.

And then it started, as a single fat drop of moisture appeared on the fur of its cheek.

I looked up to see if it was raining again, before I realised that it was one of my own tears.

My grip loosened, and with a wriggle the rabbit was out of my hands. It landed awkwardly, rolled, and with a bound it was gone into the undergrowth.

[1.68]

After that, I knew it was over.

I realised I couldn't kill an animal. I made a half-hearted attempt to forage burdock – they ate a lot of that on the Stone Age TV programme – but all I found was clumps of nettles.

I gave up and cried.

I was starting to feel nauseous. I didn't know whether that was the hunger or the lake water I'd been drinking.

At midday, I vomited.

I crawled back into my bush. It had started drizzling again. Even with the greater tree cover, my new hiding place, and the leaves I'd so carefully lined it with, soon became wet through.

I dragged myself out and staggered further into the wood.

I threw up again. Nothing came out except for a few wet strands.

I was desperately thirsty, but the thought of walking down to the side of the lake was too much.

I was burning up.

I lay down, not bothering even to hide myself. Just curled up into a ball on a patch of soft ground. The moisture oozing from it and the light rain falling on me was deliciously cool.

I thought of Brandon.

I thought of the bunny.

I'd loved its ears. Maybe I'd recapture him and lie down with him, his ears snuggled up to my cheeks.

But I was too hot.

"You need to drink."

It was Ada standing right there.

"Do you know what day it is?"

I shook my head at her, too astonished to speak.

"It's your birthday, Cara."

It was. The twenty-fifth of August. I'd clean forgotten.

"I've got a surprise for you." She skipped away. I struggled to my feet and staggered after her as she led me down to the lakeside.

"Have some water."

"I will."

I shouted it again as I approached the lake edge. But then I saw the Rocket Tree just metres away, and I knew this was my chance.

Ada nodded. "Go to him."

I knew she'd understand. I ran to the tree trunk and started climbing. I knew she would see, as I did, that this was the moment. That if I climbed the Rocket Tree now, Tom would still be swaying in the high branches at the top. And I'd be able to take him in my arms like the rabbit and bring him to safety.

So, I climbed.

But the footholds and handholds were slippery with the rain, and I couldn't seem to get a grip.

I got as high as I had on that day exactly eight years before.

My ninth birthday.

Victoria sponge and coffee and walnut cake.

I kept reaching though my weak arms wouldn't haul me further.

But it didn't matter so long as I caught him when he fell.

I outstretched my arms.

—Hello.

I looked down, and there really was a girl below me.

"Ada?" I called. But she looked older than Ada.

The girl smiled and shook her head. She was so beautiful.

—My name is Aggie.

I looked upwards again. So long as I was there, even if he fell, I could catch him.

But I was too close to the trunk.

—Be careful.

237

I leaned further out and my arms extended. Just a little more—

—*Be careful!*

I was falling.

The ground rushed up and smacked me. Hard.

—*Are you OK?*

I lay dazed. I heard approaching footsteps but couldn't move.

I just lay there looking up at the white sky.

Ada's face appeared once more. "Happy Birthday, Cara."

—Are you OK?

It was the older girl. Ada had gone. And there were other faces too. Beautiful faces staring down at me. I felt myself being lifted gently into a man's arms. The girl was stroking my cheek with the back of her hand.

—Don't be scared.

My face flooded with tears.

—We'll look after you.

Part 8: Thaquel and Methilien

[1.69]

That, reader, is how I came to be living here with Aggie.

When her father picked me up, I was pretty far gone, so I just lay in his outstretched arms as he bore me out of Kenwood Park and over Hampstead Heath.

I was burning with fever, and my body felt light as a feather. It was as though I were being wafted along like a dandelion seed. There was no sun that day, just drizzle. As Schektl stepped slowly, confidently between the trees, glimpses of grey cloud showed through breaks in the leaves.

He carried me all the way into Hampstead, and we ended up here, a spacious fourth floor apartment in a posh modern block. I recall being laid out carefully on a mattress. It was just so incredibly comfortable after a couple of days in the wood, and sleeping on a dirt floor for the weeks before that.

Back then, Aggie's parents had the telepathic field around themselves set up so that Plaxys was a handsome Black woman and Schektl heavily tanned like he was from the Eastern Med. Aggie herself was pale with copper hair and in my near delirium I told her that her parents should reflect that – but older, of course, otherwise it would seem creepy. Aggie got them to change how they looked right in front of me, which made my stomach flip, it was so disconcerting.

But that was me safely in the apartment with my new family.

With my new owners.

[1.70]
—What do you like to eat, Cara?

Aggie asked me this after the fever, which had raged in me for three days, finally broke. During that time, the family could do no more than keep me topped up with fluids. I vaguely remember a thin savoury broth touching my lips.

—We can get you all kinds of food.

Although Aggie's face was emotionless, her thoughts were full of excitement and laughter. But it was all still very alien to me, and I wanted to sleep, so I simply said, "Surprise me."

□⌐ □ □₁ □⌐
   □

[1.71]

—Here we go, Cara.

The following day, Aggie uncovered a trolley on the other side of the alcove barrier. On it were all manner of foods. Bread and fruit, of which I'd had plenty on the farm, but vegetables and cooked dishes too. There was quiche and rice pudding, and there was meat. What looked like lamb chops and steak.

There was even a burger.

Aggie made the barrier disappear and wheeled the trolley in.

—Help yourself.

I stared at the lamb chops, my stomach suddenly cramping in desire.

Dad used to make lamb chops on the barbecue. I remembered standing with Tom in our tiny scrap of garden where the sun hardly shone, each of us holding a chop by the bones, biting on the crispy fat and licking the juices from our fingers—

I took a bowl and put a couple of dollops of rice pudding in it. Then spooned strawberry jam on top. It was like homemade jam, runny, with big lumps of fruit. My mouth watered just to see it. I sat on the floor cross-legged, swirled the rice pudding and jam together, then tasted a spoonful.

It was delicious.

But it wasn't lamb chops. It wasn't steak. And it wasn't that burger.

"Where did you get all this stuff?"

—We made studies of what all the species on Earth ate, Aggie said, sounding pleased with herself. —Our fabricators are programmed with it. Colonists like to try the native food wherever they go.

"What's a fabricator?" I said through another mouthful.

—We have very advanced technology. A Colonist can command the fabricator to produce something and it produces it.

I looked at the chops again and grimaced. I wasn't sure where in the body chops came from, but the rack of bones pointing upwards on their plate looked horribly like one half of a brutally-opened chest cavity.

—You are not pleased?

Aggie's face hadn't changed the tiniest bit, yet her thoughts had a tremor to them as though tears were but a moment away.

"No, Aggie. Honestly, it's all fantastic. This rice pudding is incredible. It's just, well, being on a farm, it makes you think about eating meat."

—Did your species not think about that anyway?

"Well, I mean, yes, of course we did." I blushed. "Some of us anyway."

—You are not displeased with me?

"No. Of course not. It's amazing. I'm just not sure I'm ready to eat any meat right now."

—I understand, Cara. But as I said everything you see here has been fabricated. It is synthetic.

"But what's it made of?"

—Mostly vegetative sources.

"So, it's like Quorn?"

—I do not know what that is. But if you like it, I can synthesise it.

"No, it's fine. Just… Just let me take my time."

—There's no hurry, Cara. Fabricator food will not spoil as quickly as normal food. It will keep for weeks.

It didn't need to last that long. Over the next few days, I ate everything that was on that trolley.

I even had the meat eventually.

And it was delicious.

But it wasn't the same.

Not because it was synthetic.

It's just that meat could never taste the same anymore.

[2.18]

I'm writing in my secret notebook again.

Sometimes it's comforting jotting things down in here.

Just for you and me, reader.

Every time I do it, though, I know I'm taking a risk.

Any moment, Aggie or her parents could come in and catch me writing under the bedclothes.

It feels dangerous and wrong.

I feel furtive.

(Is that even the right word? There's no one to ask and nowhere to look it up anymore.)

There's nothing in here that's particularly offensive to the Colonists. But I know I'd be in such trouble if they read it. From Plaxys in particular.

I really don't want to be in anyone's bad books.

So, I'm keeping it hidden. I think Aggie's forgotten about it anyway.

Which is good. I don't want to get punished, but I also don't want to disappoint her after all she's done for me.

Though maybe I could leave it out and no one would even notice it. If you're reading this, you'll know this book is <u>very</u> plain in comparison with the orange one.

But it means a lot to me.

It's as private as things get round here.

And however safe life is here, a bit of privacy is still kind of important.

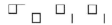

[1.72]

The first few weeks at Aggie's are blurred in my mind.

My fever had passed, and I can remember the food and Aggie comforting me, but apart from that, the main memory is of Plaxys making me recite The Mantra.

I don't have to do it more than once a week now, but back then I was saying it morning and evening, just like when I was on the farm. And she zapped me when I stepped out of line.

Zapped sounds like not much. Like a gentle tingling. Like pins and needles. It sounds mild. Like it could make you smile.

But this didn't make me smile.

This was excruciating.

Like the time I had a filling and the injection hadn't worked.

Like the time I spilt boiling water on my leg. The pain of the blistering afterwards.

Like the pain from the brandings.

Like the first sonic beatings the Colonists had given us at school. The tears running down my face. Doubled up in pain like the first day of my period.

That was what it was like. So, when I say zapped, think all that.

Aggie's parents did that to make sure I understood who was in control.

But I understood. Really, I did.

I barely stepped out of line.

That meal with them.

One or two other times.

I mean, I learnt my place pretty quickly.

So, I thought I would be OK.

But within a month of being at Aggie's, I fell into a depression like Tess's after she saw the Harvesting. The realisation that the world I'd known was gone, that *this* world of captivity and isolation had been put in its place, that I might never see my friends again: all this was more than I could bear.

The fight drained from me.

I'd lie curled up on my mattress. The fever returned and I spent days with the sweats, shivering violently. Even after I recovered, for days turning to weeks, I hardly ate. From my bed I stared at the view of poplars and sky.

It got light.

It got dark.

Autumn came, and the trees turned a blaze of gold and orange and red.

I lay there when the leaves began to tumble, as hot weather gave way to cold and wet.

I lay there and thought endlessly.

I thought how miserable it must be for Tess and Jo on the farm. And I tried not to think about who would be in the next group of girls to be Harvested.

I thought about my parents, though it was almost too painful. Like touching the tenderest of bruises.

The same for Orlando and Pip.

Thinking of Brandon was difficult too, of course, but I couldn't help myself there. I didn't berate myself anymore for what I'd said. I knew I'd never see him again in any case. Even if he were still alive, they would have pumped him so full of drugs that he wouldn't be the gentle person I'd known. He was possibly only a few miles away, yet it might as well have been a million. I was totally isolated here. So, I could wallow if I wanted to.

Aggie was very concerned.

She spent much of each day in my alcove. While I lay passive, she stroked my hair, talking softly. When I wouldn't eat for myself, she fed me with a spoon.

I just let it all slide.

But then, one day, when the trees were bare, it started to snow.

A flurry of flakes.

It must have been early for snow.

Honestly, though, I had no idea what month it was.

Seeing it made me feel like something new was about to happen.

It was like a voice in my head saying: *You need to get up now.*

And though I was weak, having eaten only the bare minimum for months, and having hardly moved except to go to the toilet, it felt that for the first time in ages I had the energy to go on.

After that, I began to recover.

I started using the cross trainer occasionally.

Winter came and went.

I could see spring in the trees.

I had nice food.

And Aggie was a constant companion.

I wouldn't say I was happy.

But I'd accepted that I'd rather be alive like this than be dead.

You could say I'd settled in.

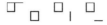

[1.73]

It's mid-afternoon now.

I'd normally be fabricating at this time of day, but I rushed through my chores – very lumpy and misshapen leaves for Plaxys and Schektl's supper – because I wanted to write about the trees.

I won't lie, that sounds a bit rubbish even to me.

But there was just something about them today.

And the conversation I had with Aggie afterwards.

It's clouded over again now, but it was such a beautiful morning, sparkling sunshine and a bit of a breeze. It was properly windy last night, and even this morning you could see it was fresh outside, clouds chasing across the sky.

I was awake a lot during the night. Generally, I've been sleeping better recently. Not having the Emma dream so often. But there was a full-on gale last night and I couldn't sleep. Not for the first time I thought of Tess and Jo. The wind was loud in the apartment, so I wondered what it must have been like in their shed, tugging at the corrugated roof, howling through the gaps in the boarding. They would have been huddling together for comfort. Or maybe they were in different pens by now.

It struck me for the first time that I didn't really know what life was like for them. I'd only been on the farm for less than two months and nine or ten had passed since then. It was getting harder to imagine my friends, their faces becoming less distinct, their voices blurrier. And for Tess in particular I didn't even choose to remember her from the pens, curled up, dirty faced, her hair matted; but rather from before, sitting in the canteen, her long blonde hair shimmering, glowing with the sunlight behind her.

This morning, after the gale had subsided, I was standing at my window and watching the trees. It was still windy, the poplars moving in it, the sunshine gleaming through the green, a green that's still fresh, not the heavier shade of late summer. The slim trees swayed with the sun behind them, and I was thinking of Tess and Jo, when Aggie joined me at the window.

Aggie's normally very talkative, but today she just stood there with me in contented silence, which I really appreciated. We watched the leaves caught in the sunlight, layers of them, dancing over one another, almost yellow when the sun came straight through them, backlit, beautiful, and a delicate tracery of branches supporting them. Aggie and I stood and watched as they moved this way and that. After a while I felt her hand reaching for mine, and I held it, and it felt just right the two of us there together, looking out, the wind picking up a fraction so that the branches full of young leaves would toss in it like a horse's head, sighing as they bobbed, the slender branches thrashing as the air gusted further, the sun still strong through them, glinting and sparkling as the leaves crashed against one another like waves on shingle, the second of my four poplars, younger than the others, bending in the clamour, the shush, shush of the leaves almost a roar.

Then the wind eased, and the tree stood tall again.

The clamour subsided, and the leaves stilled.

For a moment we stood and listened to the birdsong; and then I felt Aggie's hand slip from mine.

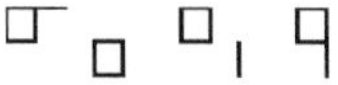

[1.74]

She turned to go, but I asked her to stay for a bit.

—Don't you normally like to write in the morning?

"I do. But I can pick it up in the afternoon. Why don't you do my hair?"

So, we sat on the edge of my mattress and she plaited my hair. She was attempting some elaborate side-weave which really wasn't working out. But it was one of those days when it didn't matter, and Aggie was just laughing in my head at the mess she was making rather than getting frustrated.

We were chatting of this and that, when I said to her, "You remember that poem you were reciting when I had dinner with the family?"

Aggie tensed. —I'm sorry for that, Cara. I know Mother really hurt you.

I dismissed her apologies with a wave. "It's not that. I was interested in the poem that's all. I only caught part of it and it seemed amazing. *Methilien*, right?"

Aggie's hands on my hair relaxed again. —*The Song of Methilien*. It's one of our most famous poems. There are four epics which we learn from an early age: The Sorrowing Of Yanafar, Vallyx The 17th Controller, Fly Home Kokoch, and The Song Of Methilien. Fly Home is hilarious but Methilien is my favourite.

"It's about travelling, you said. Colonising."

—Sort of. That's the setting…

Aggie gave up the struggle with my hair and let the strands relax. —It's about two juveniles—

"A boy and a girl."

—If you like. A boy and a girl who know each other on their home world but are getting ready with their families to colonise another.

"And the girl is called Methilien?"

—One of the *juveniles* is called Methilien. Remember we don't make the distinction between the sexes until we have reached maturity.

"Well, Methilien's kind of a girl's name so let's go with that.

—We'll go with that. Then the *boy*—

Aggie made air quotes with her fingers, something I'd recently taught her, and that really cracked me up. She kept on doing it until I could laugh no more. —The *boy* is called Thaquel.

"Thaquel and Methilien. That's cute. OK. So, what happens?"

—They grow up together on a world called Zatilla.

"Zatilla."

—Zat-i-lla. Longer vowel in the middle.

"Zat-eeee-la."

—You're funny when you try to speak our language. Anyway, they grew up on Zatilla—

"That's *exactly* what I said. Is that your home world?"

—No. Our home world is different, more of a myth. It's explained in The Sorrowing Of Yanafar. But that's another story. Let me tell you this one. Thaquel and Methilien grow up together, play together, are great friends. And as they get older, although they are yet juvenile—

"Girl and boy—"

—they begin to develop The Great Yearning for each other.

"They start to fall in love?"

—No. We feel love as humans do: strong affection. But The Great Yearning is a Colonist thing. It is deeper and richer and more nuanced than anything a human could feel.

Aggie stopped abruptly. —I'm sorry, Cara. That is just what we are taught.

I shrugged. I mean, it was patronising, of course, but maybe it was true given they're so much more advanced than us.

—The Great Yearning is what Colonists hope to feel for one another before they mate. Sexually, I mean.

"Ugh, Aggie. I know what 'mate' means. You don't need to be so biological about it."

—It was just to make it clear. Not all Colonists feel it. Sometimes they will just pair up. Biologically.

"Please stop saying that. What about your parents?"

—I don't know. They do not speak of The Great Yearning.

She paused.

—But I would like it for myself one day. Usually, it develops over tens of your years. Normally it begins late, but Thaquel and Methilien had known each other since they were hatchlings, and when they played together, their friendship and loyalty was already well understood amongst the other Colonist juveniles.

"That's romantic. So, what happens?"

—Their families are due to board ships taking them to a New World. A world called Suspiralis. They are to all travel together. When travelling, Colonists always stay in family groups.

"How does that interstellar travel thing work? Have you perfected faster-than-light travel?"

Aggie laughed in my head. —We're good. But not that good. No, our interstellar travel is all based on two things: good engines which take our ships as fast as possible, up to maybe half the speed of light. But even then, we would still take hundreds of your years to reach the worlds we had targeted for colonisation: a whole lifetime or more. So, our travel also depends on having perfected the technology for The Long Sleep. You call it suspended animation.

"I mean, *I* don't. But I know some nerdy types who might."

—The Long Sleep slows ageing by 90 percent but does not stop it. And it means that when we finally arrive at a new world, hundreds or perhaps thousands of years have passed for those left at home. It means everyone we knew at home would be dead. That's why we travel in family groups or else it would be heart-breaking to know everyone you loved was long gone.

I didn't say anything. But my whole life feels like that. Travelling in isolation from everyone I once knew. Everyone I'd abandoned.

Aggie continued. —Thaquel and Methilien want to travel together. But their parents are from different backgrounds. Thaquel's are Workers, whereas Methilien's are Administrators. So, their families are assigned different ships. Their parting is still joyous, however, as they know that when they awake from The Long Sleep they will see each other again.

"*Parted as children, I will see once again, Your young face, Methilien.*"

—Well remembered. But that is actually from later in the poem. When they take their leave, they sing to each other. It is a very complex part of the poem and would not translate well for you. Anyway, they board their ships with their families and settle in, preparing for The Long Sleep to begin.

—Eventually the ships depart. They are to maintain a convoy, but years into the journey they fly through a solar storm. Methilien's ship is at the back and is caught by a solar flare. The autopilot takes evasive manoeuvres. It ends up having to fly outside of that star system while the other ships fly on. Its course then becomes hugely diverted as it comes under the gravitational attraction of a singulus.

"What's a singulus?"

—It occurs when a large star collapses under its own gravity. It creates such a strong gravitational field that nothing coming near it can escape. Not even light.

"Oh. Is that the same as a black hole?"

—Yes. Well, Methilien's ship is sling-shot far across the galaxy and ends up having to travel a much, much longer path. Thaquel's ship, meanwhile, continues with the others until reaches its destination. They land. There are only very primitive life forms on the planet, so there is no need for The Waiting like on this world. Within a few weeks the world is subdued and the Colonists settle.

I felt a chill at her use of the word 'subdued'.

—But, try as he might, Thaquel cannot find Methilien and is devastated when he hears her ship has been delayed. At

The Day Of Sharing, a time of high festivity, he is downcast and broken. Calculations by Administrators determine the lost ship will not arrive for another three hundred years. A lifetime even for us. So, Thaquel resolves not to take another mate but to wait for Methilien's arrival, even though he knows that when she arrives, she will be still young and will look on him with disgust. That's where the bit you remember comes from.

—He's on his deathbed when her ship finally arrives. But when Methilien visits him, she too is old! Whilst on the voyage, a voice in a dream caused her to waken from The Long Sleep. So, she too grew old, alone on the ship, to be with him in spirit. They are reunited, but their lives are spent, and they die in each other's arms.

"Wow. That *is* romantic. But very sad."

—Yes, sad. But they were together at the end. That's very important for Colonists.

She studied me for a couple of moments while I absorbed the story I'd just been told.

"Is it true?" I asked at last. "I mean, is it based on a real story?"

—Perhaps. But if so, it all happened thousands of years ago.

"And how about you? Did you leave any friends behind when you came here?"

—No. I was an egg in transport and hatched during the voyage here. So, all I remember is the darkness. The eternal darkness. When you are in The Long Sleep you are still aware of what is around you but like in a dream. The darkness is what came before for me. This world is the only one I have ever known.

"That means, you were almost born here?"

—Yes. I was almost born here.

□ | □ □ □ |

[2.19]

I've just woken from a nightmare.

For a while I was clawing the air. Real terror coursing through me, though whatever was scaring me was just out of reach.

But it wasn't the nightmare about Emma and the Harvesting.

I switched on my solar light, and in that instant, it came back to me:

Ada.

Her face suddenly there in my mind.

We'd been talking.

Under the long line of plane trees on Highbury Fields.

I was holding her hand.

The crystalline nature of the dream is disconcerting. I'd had gum on my shoe. I could feel it sucking at me as we walked together. It was a hot day. The sun was on me, droplets of hot light dappling me through the leaves above.

Ada, how could I have forgotten about you?

I've barely thought about you all these months. Yet I'd said everything would be OK.

Is this what it's going to be like? All the people I knew gradually fading in my memory, while I live out my safe life here.

Will I eventually not remember Brandon either? Or Jo or Orlando?

Or even Tess.

Dear, dear Tess.

Please, no.

I can't let that happen.

I won't allow it.

I'm so sorry for forgetting you, Ada.

It won't happen again.

Part 9: Reunions

[1.75]

It's taken ages to get to the point where I can write any of this down.

I wasn't even sure for a bit whether I should.

Aggie was pretty embarrassed about it all, and I was too.

But I've got plenty of time on my hands now that Aggie's spending so much of hers out of the apartment.

Avoiding me.

So, I may as well write about it. At least it gives me something to do.

It was almost a week ago, a day or so after Aggie had told me about The Song Of Methilien. It was only the two of us again that evening. Aggie had finished brushing my hair and got up as though to leave me in the alcove. I felt lonely and wanted to keep her there, so I asked Aggie what her parents did when they went out in the evening. Something they've been doing a lot lately.

Aggie perked up. —As you know, they're both important Administrators.

"Are they, Aggie? You've never mentioned it." Aggie doesn't mind a little teasing; though this time she chose to ignore it.

—So, I imagine it's to do with work. Both their Offices are involved in the preparations for The Day Of Sharing. It's less than fifty days away now.

"Wow. Getting close. And is that when The Second Wave arrives? They told us about them on the farm. Apparently they're even more bad-ass than you lot?"

She laughed at 'bad-ass'. —Yes. They are. They will be here a few months after The Day Of Sharing, we are told.

"Oh, OK. So anyway, your parents are doing Day of Sharing prep stuff? Not going out to dinner?"

—What's that?

"When you go out and have a meal with someone in a restaurant."

—Restaurant?

I rolled my eyes at her. It never ceased to surprise me how Colonists could know so much about us in some areas and in others nothing at all. "Like a nice place where you can go and have food."

—Isn't home a nice place? I thought that was the best place.

"Yes, of course. But this is different. There are lots of people around." I snapped my fingers. "It's buzzing."

I'd say Aggie's face looked blank, but it always looks blank.

"And there's wine and atmosphere. And you have to pay for it. They can be really expensive some of these places."

—I don't understand. Why go out and buy food you could have at home if it's costing you money. Why not just eat at home?

"Because… Well, you can have delicacies you wouldn't get at home. Or do you not have those because you can make everything with fabricators?"

—No, we have delicacies too. There are some things even fabricators can't do justice to.

"Like?"

—Like giant cricket brains.

"Gross!"

—They're very tasty, Cara. But they don't keep fresh very long, so you have to have them opened up right in front of you and then suck the soft parts out.

"So, so disgusting."

—Well, what are human delicacies?

"I don't know… Oysters. Lobster. Oh, and caviar."

—All products of the sea?

"I never thought about it like that, but I guess so… Though I'm not a big fan of seafood myself. Lots of people aren't."

—Well, at least I would have a proper reason for going somewhere to eat. I don't understand why humans would have bothered if they don't even like their own delicacies? All Colonists appreciate giant cricket brains.

"It's like this…" My stomach was a bit churned by the talk of insect brains, but I did my best. "Say, you've got two people who like each other and want to spend time together. You know just the two of them."

—So, they go to a really busy place with lots of other people…

"OK!" I applauded her. "You're really getting the hang of sarcasm. No. They don't talk to the other people. They go to be with each other. Because they like each other. It's called a date."

—We like each other don't we, Cara?

"Of course, we do."

—So, should we go on a date?

"What? No!"

I could have sworn Aggie looked hurt. Her face was still as inscrutable as ever, but maybe her shoulders had drooped just a tiny bit.

—Do you not like me enough to go on a date with me?

"No. It's not like that. You can go to a restaurant with a friend. But it's not a *date*. That's what you do when you're interested in someone. You know – if they're a bit *more* than friends."

—Sexual partners.

"Ugh. You're always so… *biological*. I mean, like if you have a boyfriend or girlfriend or – whatever you call it. Or someone you fancy and want to spend time with. *Not* biologically. I mean, maybe it might be in time… but not just yet. Or at all. And not The Great Yearning either."

—I told you Cara, humans are incapable of The Great Yearning. Your emotions are too shallow. I'm not being mean. It's just a fact.

"Whatever." I made a face at her. "Well, have you ever had The Great Yearning, Aggie?"

—You don't *have* The Great Yearning. You *feel* it. And no. I told you already, I am far too young for that.

"You're seventy-three."

—In your years. Not in mine.

"Methilien was young when she first started *feeling* it for Thaquel."

—Perhaps. But that's just a poem.

"Well, what about fancying someone then? Are there any Colonist boys—"

—Juveniles.

"—you'd like to get to know better?"

—I don't really know any that well. And is *fancying* the same as *love?* Because I love and believe that I am loved by my family. Very deep and strong affection.

"We can feel that for friends too."

—Then that is what you're talking about? Is that when you go on a date?

"No, I'm talking about being attracted to someone. *Not* just biologically."

—But a bit biologically.

"Well, probably a bit. Fancying someone is the early stages of being *in love* with someone."

—What's the difference between loving someone and being in love with someone?

"If you love someone, you care about them deeply, and it matters what happens to them, and you want to take care of them. It's a nice feeling. A warm feeling. Being *in* love is completely different." I thought of Brandon, of what it was to be in his presence. "It's like… you can't breathe. You're near this person, and he makes you feel sick. You can barely talk. You want to say how much you like him, but you can't say that – *obviously* – because that would be rubbish and he might not feel the same way." So, so, rubbish, I think. What an idiot.

—It sounds painful.

"It *is* painful. It's the worst thing. But it's also the best feeling in the world."

—Oh. Complicated. Well, perhaps your feeling of *in love* is indeed a very basic form of The Great Yearning. Because we feel those emotions too. But many more as well. And certain behaviours too are typical of The Great Yearning: the giving of gifts, and the need to make ourselves seem lesser than the other person, to do anything we can to make that person happy, even if it brings great pain to ourselves.

"Sounds kind of similar to be honest."

—Well, maybe. I've only described it in the most simplistic terms for you to understand.

"*Thanks* Aggie."

—Are you in love about someone?

"In love *with* someone… Well, I was. I am, I mean." I felt myself blushing even though the person I was talking about was probably dead. "His name's Brandon. He helped me escape—"

—Oh, yes. You wrote about him. You know the Controllers will learn about his actions on The Day Of Sharing when I upload my thoughts. Perhaps you should be more careful about what you write and therefore what I read.

"I don't think it matters. I'm pretty certain he got punished there and then." My heart shatters to think about it even as I write this now. With Aggie, I stumbled on. "He's lovely. Caring. Strong."

—What does he look like?

"Dark skin, really dark. Taller than me, about four or five inches taller – no wait! What are you doing—?"

Before my eyes, Aggie was morphing into a boy, his skin dark, his body muscled and tall. I was repulsed and hypnotised at the same time.

—Do you want me to stop?

I blinked at her – at him – and then shook my head. "No. Don't stop. The height is right, but darker skin… Yes. Like that. He was – is – Nigerian." Immediately the face changed from a brown version of European features to something different, his lips full and luscious, his nose: "A little broader, flatter," I murmured. And then, after a few more iterations, he was there before me. His face just there. So beautiful.

"Brandon," I whispered. I couldn't help myself. I reached out to touch his cheek. He felt warm and real, and he moved his face against my hand, then forward, towards me, those beautiful lips coming closer and closer until they touched mine—

"No, Aggie!" I pulled back and away.

I stared at her. At him. I shook my head in confusion. "It's not right."

Aggie transformed quickly back again.

—I didn't mean to startle you, Cara. Did you not like it?

"Of course, I liked it. It was him. But it wasn't real."

—I think I understand.

"I really don't think you do." My heart was banging in my chest. For a moment I thought I was going to faint.

—I'm sorry, Cara. It was thoughtless. I can see that you are very much *in love* with him. Did he feel the same way?

I blinked and thought of sitting with him on the sofa, his arms around me. But that hadn't been real either. That could never have been love even if we'd wanted it. And when I'd said I was in love with him, he most definitely did not tell me he was in love with me.

"No." But then my mind tracked back to the time two winters ago when I was stuck up that tree and he caught me when I jumped. The awkwardness. Neither of us able to breathe as he held me afterwards. "Maybe," I said. "Maybe there was a moment. Maybe he did like me too. Once. But it never had a chance to develop. Your lot messed things up."

—I'm sorry, Cara.

I knew she meant it. And I immediately felt bad for having said it. This was one thing they hadn't messed up. It had never been there in the first place.

—That must have been hard being *in love* with someone and them not feel the same way.

"I think it's quite common."

—Did any human boy feel like that about you? Or a girl maybe?

"No girls I don't think… But there was – is? – a boy called Orlando. He's a little taller than Brandon, light-skinned, paler than me—"

This time I laughed as Aggie began to transform once more, especially at the Christmas jumper she dressed herself/him in. That felt uncannily accurate.

"His features need to be more European – like me – but lighter skinned. And his hair is blond." Aggie's form changed before me, fluidly, until suddenly the mixture of features was spot on. "Stop. That's him."

—He's handsome I think, said Aggie as Orlando.

"Do you reckon?" I walked around Aggie/Orlando as she/he stood still in front of me. I was definitely not in love with him because what I felt as I surveyed him was the tenderness of familiarity. "Do you really think he's as handsome as Brandon?"

—Well, I think so. But they're totally different, so it's difficult for me to know how you judge between the two. They are both well-muscled. Is it the skin colour?

"No! Of course not. I'm not racist."

—Then it must be other qualities. Is this Orlando not as nice to you as the other one? Is he not kind?

And, of course, that got me thinking about Orlando.

Over the years he's been super-nice to me. If anything, too nice sometimes. I'd probably have preferred it if he just acted normally, like he did when he was around Tess or Jo. With me he gets tongue-tied and awkward and downright sweaty sometimes.

I guess just the way I was with Brandon.

—Cara?

Aggie was still waiting for an answer but I didn't have one. It isn't so easy explaining stuff to her sometimes as she always seems to see things in straight lines. So, instead, I turned it back on her.

"So, there's really no one *you're* starting to feel The Great Yearning for?"

Orlando's cheeks bloomed rosy red, and then he disappeared, morphing hastily, untidily back into Aggie. She turned away almost as though she were having problems resetting her expression. But when Aggie did face me again, her features were back to normal.

—I've told you several times that I could not develop The Great Yearning for a Colonist juvenile. They are not mature enough.

"Does that mean *you* are?"

Aggie did not reply. Instead, she went over to my table and started fiddling with the pens and pencils there. Without looking around she said,

—Would you prefer it if I looked like a boy for you, Cara?

"What? No!" I squinted at her as she carefully arranged my three pencils in parallel, turned the middle one upside down, then upended the other two. She was behaving very strangely. "No, of course not. Why would you want to?"

—I just thought you might like it more. I know you find both boys *and* girls attractive so that's why up to now I've stayed as a girl but I can easily change—

"No! *What?* I thought I'd just made it clear that I do not want you changing your appearance so that I find you *attractive*. It would be beyond creepy. You're my owner. It would be like Stockholm syndrome or something. And what do you mean, anyway, about me being attracted to girls? I'm not attracted to girls."

—As you say, said Aggie. —It just appears that way sometimes from your writing. The way you talk about your Miss Temple and other girls—

"She's not *my* Miss Temple," I said hurriedly. I could feel myself blushing deeply. "I don't know what you're talking about. And that's not even the point."

—As you say, said Aggie again. —Just boys then. And I'll stay as a girl.

"Right." I felt warm and weird and stupid and just wanted the conversation to stop.

She turned to face me, and her hands were clasped behind her back. At first, I thought she'd taken something from my table. Then I realised she was just as embarrassed as I was.

—I could look like Brandon if you want.

"What did I *literally* just say?" I didn't know quite what had gotten into her but thought it best to knock it on the head. "That… you know… what you did before. It was kind of fun – but it mustn't happen again. It's just too weird."

—How about Tess?

"*No!*"

—I understand, Cara.

For a Colonist who was normally so unemotional, Aggie was certainly as mixed up as I could be sometimes. But she also sounded really disappointed. I sighed and said, to cheer her up, and because it was true, "I like you just the way you are."

Aggie didn't smile. Aggie never smiled. But it was clear her mood had lightened.

—Thank you, Cara. I chose this appearance because I hoped you would find it non-threatening but also quite… pleasing.

"I do Aggie. You look great. Your hair especially."

—Do you think it's as beautiful as your schoolfriend, Anne with an 'e'. Hers was red too.

"Yes, it was. And yes, your hair is as beautiful as hers."

—Thank you, Cara, she said again and walked towards me but then stopped halfway.

—***WOULDYOULIKETOSEEWHATIREALLYLOOKLIKE?***

The blurted thoughts were like nothing I'd ever experienced. She'd been loud before but now her words were tumbling one over the next at incredible volume. I staggered back like I was being hit by a flurry of punches.

—I'm sorry, Cara.

Her thoughts had dropped immediately to a whisper. She seemed horrified by what she'd just done. —So, very sorry. Are you OK?

Aggie took a step towards me, but then just stood awkwardly, like she didn't dare to touch me. —Have I hurt you, Cara?

"Honestly, I'm fine, I'm fine."

—I'm so, so sorry.

Aggie sounded wretched and was wringing her hands. But I was genuinely fine again apart from a dull ringing in my head. "Just be careful. You're so loud."

—I know. I'm sorry.

But she sounded relieved. —I'm so glad I haven't hurt you.

"Of course not."

—Of course not, Aggie echoed, taking a step away so she was by the table again. Then, shyly,

—But would you like to see my true form?

I wavered. I was starting to get quite intrigued as to what Colonists really looked like behind that neural curtain they laid down. It was just that Aggie had described Colonists as being like giant insects and I wasn't great with normal sized ones.

—You may not want to.

Aggie sounded disappointed at my hesitation. —We are quite different-looking from you. Don't worry.

"No go on," I say hurriedly. "You want to show me. Show me."

—Are you sure?

The renewed excitement in her thoughts convinced me. I smiled at her and touched her arm. "Of course."

Aggie clapped her hands. —I'll do it gradually. So, you don't get spooked.

"I'm not going to get spooked." I took a step back and folded my arms. "I'm so fond of you, Aggie. I want to see you as you really are."

—Truly?

"I told you, I'm not going to get spooked, Aggie. I'm not the type. Go on."

—OK. Here goes.

Her right foot, previously bare and cream skinned, leading up to a pair of navy-blue leggings, suddenly narrowed and turned as dark as ebony. Instead of ending in toes, the foot became a splayed claw. The skin disappeared, replaced with something smooth and hard like carbon fibre. The leg itself, though transformed, was still shapely and the overall effect was even beautiful. It reminded me of the blades that amputee sprinters used in the Paralympics.

—Is it too ugly? Aggie's thoughts felt agitated. She was clearly nervous, and it made me want to set her mind at rest.

"You're beautiful," I said and meant it. "Different. But beautiful."

The claw flexed in delight.

—OK, here's the other leg. An identical black stalk appeared where her left leg had been.

"You look amazing," I said, and she giggled in my head in delight. "OK, Aggie, the full reveal now."

—I think maybe still bit by bit.

"No, I'm ready for it."

—Are you sure?

"Of course."

Her eyelids fluttered. —OK, all in one go. What is it you say? Ta-dah?

"Yup. Tad-dah."

—OK then. *Ta – dah!*

My mouth fell open.

My arms dropped to my sides.

I swayed.

In front of me, the looming bulk of a six-foot stag beetle reared up on its hind legs.

It clicked its giant pincers together and took a step forward, reaching out with a massive foreclaw—

"Arrrghhh!"

—Cara, it's me.

"Arrrghh!"

It lowered its middle set of legs and galloped towards me, pincers clacking, black carapace shining—

"Get away from me!" I turned and stumbled, falling to the floor, curling into a ball. Out of the corner of my eye I saw the beetle's huge maw coming towards me. I screamed again and buried my head as its jointed, graphite legs enveloped me.

I didn't even shriek now. I just sobbed, consumed with fear as I waited for its foul jaws to start attacking me.

But all I felt were soft hands and warm breath.

—I'm sorry, Cara.

I was crying too hard to speak.

—I'll never do it again, she said, putting her arms around me, holding me tight.

I didn't dare look round at Aggie, couldn't bear to see her, knowing now what lay just behind the neural mask.

—I'm so sorry, Cara. I'm so sorry.

And then, even though she'd always told me it wasn't possible for Colonists, that she couldn't express emotion physically, Aggie began to cry.

[1.76]

I've tried to apologise, of course.

But the last few days, she's been gone from my alcove before I can get any words out.

Today though, I blocked her way as she made to leave.

"It was all my fault."

She hung her head.

"I mean it Aggie. I'm—"

—I just wanted to show you what I looked like. I know it was a mistake. I know how disgusting you find me.

"Honestly, I don't Aggie. It was just the shock."

—Of course, you find me disgusting. Why wouldn't you?

She did. And she was beautiful. Not like you.

"I never said I was beautiful. *Hang on*. What are you talking about?"

—She screamed when she saw me too.

"Who did, Aggie?" I felt suddenly giddy. "Hang on, you're talking about Greta, aren't you?"

—She had the most exquisite hair. Long and blonde. Down to her waist. It felt so soft.

"So, you *did* know her?"

—When I touched it, it was so smooth.

"What happened to her?"

Aggie was staring at me, but not staring at me. It was clear she wasn't meant to be talking about this. It was also clear she couldn't help herself.

—I heard sounds. In the night. When we first got here. Scratching. Footsteps. I thought I was dreaming. On the third night, I could stand it no longer. I got up, crept to the living room, turned on the light. And there she was.

"Greta was?"

—She was caught in the light. She'd been hiding in the shower room, behind the door. Had locked herself in, she'd said, so couldn't leave when our Soldiers went round emptying the apartments of people. She heard our call but couldn't move. So, after the family was gone, she was alone.

—She heard my family's arrival and stayed hidden. And we did not think to look behind a door in an area we weren't even using. She stayed hidden in the daytime and came out at night to look for food. But all the human food had been cleared out, and she didn't have the fabricator codes.

—She told me all this as she stood there. Your age. She wore jeans and a white top. Her hair was long. She was so scared. I thought I could see her heart beating. But she was so beautiful as she stood there. And not the static human beauty we pretend: her face was *dynamic*, rich with emotion. I've never seen beauty like it. And as I stepped out of the shadows to comfort her, to help her – I wanted to help her, Cara, to keep her safe, to look after her just like I've looked after you – as I stepped out, I was so overcome by her beauty that I unveiled myself, and she saw me as I really am.

—And she screamed.

Aggie slowly beat one fist into the other.

—She was disgusted by what she saw and screamed so loud that my parents awoke and rushed in. And then Mother hurt her. You know what she can be like. I pleaded with her, with them, to let me keep her. That I could look after her. Father thought she would do no harm. But Mother said no. She hates humans. She made Father raise a barrier to the alcove to imprison her and then took her away the very next morning. Before I was awake. She took her to her lab so that she could experiment on her. Torture her. Kill her.

—I hate Mother.

I couldn't speak. I was simply trying to process what Aggie had told me.

—I got ill after that. The way you did when you first came here. I'd just wanted company. Being Late Spawn is so very lonely. They offered me a goat as a pet. But I wanted a human. I got more and more down. And then one day we went for a walk and found you. By the Condolence Tree. A gift from above. And this time Mother relented. But now you think I'm disgusting too.

"No Aggie, I don't. It was just a shock, that's all."

—I so want to believe that.

"Please. Believe it. You're beautiful too. You're just different."

Aggie raised her head. —I'm so sorry I said you're not beautiful.

"Oh, that's fine. I know I'm not. I can be pretty sometimes. But I know people who are properly beautiful. They just make you feel happy inside."

—Tess.

I nodded. And thought of her. My friend.

—I would so have liked to have got to know her properly.

It took me a beat before I realised she was still talking about Greta.

—I stroked her hair, and then they took her. But I could have looked after her. I've looked after you, haven't I?

"You've looked after me very well, Aggie."

—But I don't want you to think I'd have preferred her. I wouldn't change you for anyone.

"Neither would I, Aggie. Neither would I."

—Well, it wouldn't be up to *you*, would it.

She shook her head in sudden irritation. —I need to go to bed.

She started to walk away.

"Thank you for being honest with me, Aggie," I called after her. "Thank you for telling me the truth about Greta."

She paused at the door. Turned. —Why do you keep calling her that? That's why I was confused when you first mentioned it. Her name wasn't Greta. It was Agneta.

□ | □ □⌐ □⌐
   □

[2.20]
Of course.
   *AGN*___
   ___*eta*

That's what I'd seen on the doorframe. But it had actually been:
AGNETA
Agneta
The missing letters rubbed away.
Poor Agneta.
She must have been so scared. Hiding out in the tiny bathroom while the world changed around her.
How could she have even known what was going on?
She'd have been in the shower room and heard screams.
Alice would have been at school, but maybe Agneta saw Alice's parents – her uncle and aunt if she was indeed Alice's cousin – being led away. Saw it through a crack in the door frame.
Perhaps she saw the Colonists in their true giant beetle form.
Whatever she saw, it must have been terrifying.
And then the long days.
The long nights.
At least I have food. At least I have Aggie.
Poor Agneta.
No surprise it was Plaxys who was responsible for hurting her.
For murdering her.
That monster.
Somehow, I'll avenge you, Agneta.
Somehow, I'll take Plaxys down.

[1.77]

I'd hoped after our last conversation, things would get back to normal with Aggie, but if anything, she's spending less time with me than before.

She's going out a lot. And even when Aggie's in, she's kind of avoiding me.

Which is difficult given she still brings me food twice a day. But when she does come into my alcove, she doesn't say

274

anything apart from a quick hello. No eye contact and her thoughts sound kind of brittle.

Before, she would have chatted for hours while braiding my hair. Now there's no physical contact at all. This morning when I tried to give her a hug, her arms stayed limp by her side, and she pulled away from me the first moment she could.

—It's better this way.

Her thoughts were muffled, heavy. —My parents warned it was a mistake to have a human as a pet. I should have listened.

[1.78]

Like I say, Aggie's going out a lot.

It used to be once a week but now it's every day. To make matters worse she hasn't been unlocking the barrier, so I'm confined to the alcove.

They've felt like long days.

I'm caught up on my journal but now I've done that, there's nothing else to do.

I won't lie, last couple of days I didn't really leave my mattress, just stared up at the ceiling.

But I'm at my desk again today.

I'm kind of worried that if I don't, I'll get ill again.

So, even if it's just a few words I'm going to sit here and write them in my notebook.

And I've been doing my cross trainer in the morning as well.

I hate the cross trainer.

But I refuse to get sick again.

I just wish Aggie was around more.

She's gone for long sections of the day.

I asked her a couple of times where she goes to, as these are clearly not her normal exercise slots.

—Up to Hampstead. To clear my head.

But that's all she would share with me.

[2.21]

Today when Aggie went out, she finally left the barrier down and I walked round the apartment in relief.

I found myself drawn to the front door.

I stood there like I've done a few times before, when no one's in.

I laid my hand on the lock.

Struggling with myself.

Should I just turn the handle and walk out to freedom?

It must sound so weak that I haven't tried it up to now.

After all, if I got picked up by Inquisitors then the brand should mean I wouldn't get taken to the abattoir; I'd be brought back here. No doubt I'd be in furious trouble, but Aggie seems to have a sway with her parents which means I'd be safe, however much they might punish me. But it's taken a long time to convince myself of all that.

In the past, even touching the lock felt like a huge act of bravery.

Today, however, I was strong enough or just bored enough to actually twist the handle.

But the door was locked by some other hidden bolt. More Colonist tech.

I should have been gutted.

But what I actually felt was relief.

I don't know what I'd have done if the door had opened, and I'd been able to simply walk out.

Where would I go?

To the farm to rescue Tess and Jo?

I want to believe that, but let's face it: I barely escaped myself. How on earth would I get anyone else out?

Perhaps I would make my way home.

But I know Mum and Dad are gone. And however much I want to see our flat again, I don't want to see it stripped out like this place is, a sterilised version of its former self.

Who am I even kidding that I'd make it any distance before the Inquisitors grabbed me? And anyway, maybe Aggie and her parents wouldn't be so forgiving of an escape attempt...

No. I'm better off here. Even though it's painful to admit it. I've got food and shelter. And Aggie takes care of me.

I'm safe.

And the fact that she wanted to keep Agneta means Aggie'll be doubly attached to me. I can have a nice existence here as long as I want. Whatever happens to anyone else, I'll survive. And I can carry on writing. That seems important somehow.

Once I knew I couldn't open the door, I wasn't afraid of it any more.

I stood there, my forehead pressed against the cooling wood. I peered through the fisheye spy hole into the empty corridor beyond.

I leant against the door, the only barrier between me and the outside world.

Safe in the knowledge I couldn't get to the other side.

□ | □ □ □ □
   □

[2.22]

Not only is Aggie spending a lot of time out of the apartment, but even when she is around, she's basically just staying in her bedroom.

But because her thoughts are so loud, I can still hear her really clearly.

Not that she makes much sense.

Most of the time it's Colonist language which honestly doesn't really sound like anything to me, just white noise. But even though I can't understand it, it's still so loud.

When I shout at her to stop, she does.

Though then I usually hear sobbing.

Yet when I can understand her thoughts, it's even worse.

She's yelling, —I hate you Aggie!

She's yelling, —I'm disgusting!

She's yelling, —I don't deserve to be happy!

I feel really bad for her. I mean, she's obviously going through something at the moment.

And it's not like I haven't felt the same sometimes.

But when she brings me my food tray later on, she won't talk about it.

She doesn't want to talk about anything.

[1.79]

It's been a long couple of weeks.

However much I said I wouldn't, I've taken to lying in bed all day, staring at my trees, in full leaf now.

I haven't written anything for days.

I haven't *done* anything for days.

But suddenly it feels like everything's changed again.

I'm back at my desk writing. But it'll only be for a short while.

We're heading out in a few minutes. Me and Aggie. She refuses to tell me what we're doing or where we're going. Has refused to since she got back to the apartment late yesterday afternoon.

I'd got used to her going straight to her bedroom, but yesterday she came directly to my cage where I was lying and bounded in. Her body language was the Aggie of old, and in spite of myself I was excited as she grabbed both my hands in hers, and her thoughts tumbled into my mind.

—I've got a surprise for you, Cara. And I think you'll really like it.

⊓ ▫ ▫₁ ⊓

[1.80]

She took me back to Kenwood.

It's been months since I was there last; since Aggie and her parents found me. When I was hiding out there, it was almost free of Colonists apart from in the main house. But now the park was transformed. There were Colonists taking strolls along the paths, and others walking their pet sheep and goats on the expansive lawn that rolled down to the lake.

Ugh. I wouldn't be drinking water from there again in a hurry.

"What are we doing here, Aggie? Does Plaxys know, because she'll be so angry—"

—She knows. Many Colonists bring their pets here and also some racing human males are trained here. But I know you have an antipathy for the place.

"It's complicated."

—I understand. The Condolence Tree.

"And other stuff. Look Aggie, where have you *been* the last couple of weeks?"

—I was searching.

"Searching for…?"

—It took a long time but eventually I found it. That's why we're here. That's my surprise.

"What's my surprise? Why won't you tell me?"

—Because you need to see it for yourself. There.

I followed Aggie's outstretched arm, across the wide sweep of grass, to a group of owners standing silently together. And my heart leapt to see, in front of them, a group of boys my age, doing sprints up and down the lawn, mazy runs avoiding the grazing sheep. The boys were easy to distinguish from their Colonist owners because of their body language and their interaction with each other, exuberant to be in the company of real humans again.

"Is that what you're trying to show me? Can I go and talk to any of them?"

—It's not just *any of them*.

Aggie's thoughts were laughing inside my head. —Over there, Cara. Over there.

And suddenly I was running down the slope. It had rained the previous night, so the grass was slick. I skidded to the bottom of the bank, then clambered over the wrought iron fence that Tom and I had once so loved. Onto the lawn, sprinting towards the boys, to one particular boy, who had seen me as well by now, who had broken into a run, shouting my name hysterically.

"Cara! Cara! Is it really you?"

Orlando.

Part 10: A Game of Draughts

□ □ □, ⨆

[1.81]

While Aggie and Orlando's owner stood together, Orlando and I slowly walked a circle around them at twenty metres distance. The other boys had called and whistled after us to begin with, but got back to training pretty quickly once their owners zapped them.

"Crilloo brings me here every day for exercise. Then a couple of days ago I saw her—"

"Aggie."

"Right. I saw Aggie just staring at me. It freaked me out, so Crilloo went to have a word. I couldn't believe it when Aggie said you were her pet. I didn't even know Colonists kept human pets." Orlando gave my hand a squeeze. "I never thought I'd see you again, Cara."

We exchanged stories. Brief sanitised versions of them anyway. After losing in the sparring to select the bulls, Orlando had thought he was a goner. But then a bunch of Colonists turned up wanting racing males, and Orlando was picked out. He didn't know what happened to the rest of the boys. He was just thankful to be alive.

"I think Crilloo and Aggie are different to the Soldiers who attacked us," he said as our walk took us down by the lake.

"Aggie calls them Administrators."

"Right. They get more perks – live in nice houses."

"Aggie said they don't have perks. They're all treated the same."

"I don't think so. Crilloo has a huge house in Dartmouth Park. But Workers and Soldiers or whatever live in big barracks like Kenwood House – there are thousands of them in there."

"Like a hive."

"Something like that. Wow it's so good to see you."

We talked about our friends. I told him about Brandon and Tess and Jo. He told me about Pip. Though I'd already known about him.

Eventually we got called back. We held each other as long as we could before being led in opposite directions.

"Thank you so much, Aggie." I gave her a massive hug.

—I just love to see you happy.

"Can we come again?"

—Every day if you like.

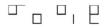

[1.82]

So every day, give or take, Orlando and I walk in Kenwood.

Crilloo is fine with it so long as Orlando uses it as warm down after a training block.

I asked Aggie what she and Crilloo talk about as they wait together. But Aggie shook her head. She's still a juvenile and Crilloo an adult, so there's nothing to share with each other. They stand in silence while Orlando and I walk a few tours of Kenwood Park.

Around the perimeter we pass Colonist sentries posted at intervals, keeping an eye out for runaways.

We just walk and talk. Sometimes we hold hands, sometimes let our arms brush against each other. It's so comforting to have him, a piece of my past, a true friend. It feels completely comfortable. I don't feel the fool I would have if it was Brandon. It's just nice.

And I'm not so dumb that I don't know it perhaps isn't quite so easy for him. Orlando likes me. *Really* liked me at one point. But he's nearly always been so much better at containing this kind of thing. Where I ended up blurting out my feelings to Brandon, Orlando is content just to be close to me and to listen to me chatter, offering a few words every now and then.

[2.23]

I'm not saying he's not an idiot sometimes.

I mean, like most boys you just can't talk to him about books. He doesn't like anything except a few thrillers. Nothing wrong with that. I like a good thriller myself. But when I mentioned Jane Eyre you should have seen his eyes roll.

"What?" I said. "It's only the best book of all time."

Orlando snorted.

"What?"

"Oh, come on. It's probably two hundred years old, isn't it? What's it even about? Some girl getting married or dying tragically or something hopeless like that. They're all the same, those old books."

"I used to think that till I read it. Have you read it?"

"Of course, I haven't read it. It's a girl's book."

"No! I mean, it's told by a girl but it's not a girl's book. It's about identity and growing up and surviving. And trying to be what you want to be not just what people say you should be. It's really modern. And genuinely thrilling."

He was laughing at me by this point so I had to punch him in the arm.

"Shut. Up. It's amazing. And it was really tough for women writers back then. She had to write under a pseudonym: Currer Bell. Charlotte Brontë was a stone-cold genius."

"Must have been to come up with a pseudonym like — what did you say it was? — Currer Bell. Though now I think of it, makes me think of someone else's name, another genius. Carabel."

I punched him again. "Shut. Up. You know only my family call me that."

But though he can be really annoying, he's actually a pretty good listener. And Orlando isn't one of those silent boys, either, who never talks about his own stuff. He will contribute, but whereas my chatter is mostly about friends and family and where they might be now, his is different. He'll point out different trees and birds and explain to me why the sky is blue and grass green. Deeper stuff. A bit like Jo used to. But it's a surprise coming from him. And it isn't that he doesn't miss his friends – he does – but he's also been through a tough time, and he doesn't want to dwell on all the horrible stuff that's happened. He just wants to make the most of what's left.

And he's funny too. I like that.

⌑ | ⌑ ⌐ ⌑

[2.24]
Today.

"Why does your owner even call me Orlando? I mean, when she first came up to Crilloo and mentioned you and then started using that name I thought it best to go along: I said it was my middle name."

I coloured. "Long story."

"OK…" He could see he wasn't going to get it out of me right then. So, he laid off the subject. I like that about him. He reads people well. Me anyway. "So, what's she like?" he said changing the subject. "Spoilt, right?"

"Aggie's not spoilt. Why do you say that?"

"Are you kidding me. Her parents obviously let her get away with murder. Who else has a human pet?"

"I mean, her parents love her. A lot. I think because she's an only child: Late Spawn."

"Gross."

"But she's really nice. Quite kind actually. For a Colonist I mean."

"If you say so. 'Aggie' is a more human name than most isn't it? Most of them are really alien-sounding: 'Zaxyfor' or 'Plooflam'."

286

I giggled. "She's called Mlaxet as well. I think Aggie's just a nickname."

"Really? Well, she's obviously very fond of you."

"Well, I'm fond of her too. Although... did you know they're like big beetles."

"Yeah, I saw Crilloo once."

"Gross, right?"

"Oh, I don't mind. I used to collect beetles when I was little."

"And keep them in matchboxes?"

"Pinned to a card."

"Oh, that's really cruel."

"Totally. I mean, I wouldn't do it now."

"Right. Anyway... what makes you think Aggie's so fond of me?"

"Well, didn't you say she gave you that bracelet?"

I held up my left wrist and the beads caught the light. "It's only made of sugar—"

"But my point is that Aggie gave it to you. And those notebooks. Crilloo's never given me anything apart from the not-so-occasional zap." He thought about it for a few moments. "It's the way she looks at you when she's standing next to you."

"How does she look at me?"

"I don't know. Nothing in her face obviously. But her body language says she's super-proud to be with you. If she were _human_, I'd say she even had a crush on you. I know the signs."

I gave him a sharp look but he seemed innocent enough. Actually, he kind of looked like an angel with his blond hair and pale skin and his white T-shirt and joggers. "So, what about Crilloo anyway? What's he like? Crilloo is a he, right?"

"Yeah. He properly is. He's reached adulthood and chosen to identify as male."

"What happens if you don't want to choose?"

He shrugged. "I don't think there's an option to stay fluid. I think they make you go one way or the other. That's the thing. Colonists always try and make out that their society is so much better than ours was, but if you scratch the surface, they can be pretty crappy too. To each other, I mean. Obviously, they're crappy to us."

"What does Crilloo do? Is he an Administrator as well?"

"Yes, but not in Science or Farming." Orlando's voice dropped. "He's in a secret department."

"How do you know?"

"He told me."

"He's in a secret department and he told you about it? Doesn't sound very secret."

"The department isn't secret. It's what they <u>do</u>."

"Fine, but how come he isn't more careful about what he <u>says</u>?"

"He doesn't care. He thinks we're animals so he treats us like animals. For him, it's like we're not even there sometimes."

"Why are we whispering?"

We were down by the lake, and there were no Colonists within one hundred metres of us. Some pet sheep were nibbling the grass nearby, and a pig was snuffling at the base of a chestnut tree. I thought we'd be safe with them.

"I don't want Crilloo to hear."

"Well, unless he's got super-hearing… Wait, he hasn't got super-hearing, has he?"

"No, no. Fine." His voice returned to normal. "He said he works for the Office Of Pseudo Cultural Suppression."

"So, what do they do?"

"They're the Ministry Of Book Burning."

I stiffened.

"They're the ones who weed out the evidence of our culture and literature and all the artistic stuff we've done – but novels and poetry in particular – and destroy it."

"I thought everyone knew they did that. Why is it so secret?"

"Because other Colonists <u>don't</u> know. Not ordinary ones. Workers and even Administrators in other Offices. They're not meant to know that we're as creative as them. That's how they justify doing all the things they do to us. Because they think we're inferior."

"The Mantra."

"Right. They get us to say we're unintelligent and not creative—"

"So, we believe it and make us easier to control."

"Yes. Partly. But it's so *they* believe it as well. Colonists *are* super intelligent. But I don't think they're inherently cruel. They're not going to take our organs or experiment on us unless they believe it's OK to treat us that way."

"Because we're... lesser."

"Exactly. It's what slave owners used to do. They would never let their slaves learn to read or write. To make it harder for them to organise an escape, but also, I reckon, so the owners could feel justified in treating them like animals. It's what human colonisers did to indigenous peoples: suppress their existing culture. And we used to do it to animals too. We treated them like they were inferior."

"But animals *are* inferior."

"They've got smaller brains, but that doesn't mean they're inferior. And just because Colonists are telepathic, doesn't make them superior to us."

"I mean, they are *quite* superior—"

"It's all just evolution, Cara. Who's to say what's inferior or superior. When we used to treat a bunch of animals like a crop, like food, that's when we chose to see them as inferior. Or chose not to see them at all. They were just in the background. They were dumb. Or an annoyance, like insects. But some animals we gave preference to: dogs, cats..."

"Gerbils."

"Right. *These* animals were *inquisitive* and *intelligent* and even *funny*. When it suited us, animals were properly sentient. And when it didn't, they were just a commodity."

"You sound like Tess. I didn't know you were so into animal rights."

"I wasn't. But it's human rights too. Because when we chose to, we would make people animals too: Black and Jewish and LGBTQ people. Women generally. Any minority we wanted to oppress in fact. And we'd use the way we treated animals as a playbook for cruelty to human beings: cattle trucks to concentration camps, branding slaves, using women as baby-machines."

"Wow." I was looking at him with new eyes. "You are way more evolved than I've ever given you credit for."

He blushed. "Thank you?" he said uncertainly. "Anyway, with all that's happened it makes you think, that's all. About how we treated animals. And about how we treated each other."

I nodded slowly, processing what he'd said. "It certainly makes you think... But coming back to what you were saying, Schektl and Plaxys know books have been burnt."

"They're told they're just timetables and manuals: pseudo culture."

"But they must suspect something?"

"They might suspect, but there's no reason to believe it when all the science is telling them the opposite."

"Well, we should try and tell someone."

"Who're you going to tell? Plaxys?"

"No, of course not Plaxys. Aggie. If I told her—"

"If you told her, then what would happen exactly? Even if she believed you – which she wouldn't otherwise you wouldn't be on a leash – even if she believed you, who's she going to tell, and who would believe her? There's no evidence of what we were because it's all been erased. And while we're so useful to them, Colonists will happily turn a blind eye to everything they're doing to us. Just like we used to."

I frowned at him; but in the end just sighed and shrugged. "So," I said, to say something. "You were telling me about Crilloo. What's he like? Is he kind to you?"

Orlando snorted. "No. He feeds us. Lets us get exercise. Trains us. But no, he's not kind. We're just animals. The moment someone gets injured in training or in a race, he has them killed."

My stomach flipped. "So barbaric."

"Right. So far I've been lucky."

"Have you raced yet?"

"A couple of times. The next big meet is coming up, soon after The Day Of Sharing." Orlando sighed. "Still, it could be worse, right?"

We started walking again, skirting past the Rocket Tree, slowly ascending the lawn towards the House. The grass was cool beneath my toes.

"It could be worse," I said softly.

He chuckled.

"What?"

"It could definitely be worse. I could be in training with Alec Durber."

"Oh my God. I heard he'd survived."

"Yeah, he's being trained by one of Crilloo's mates. I know I shouldn't think this, but how come a dick like him can still exist?"

I started laughing.

"I mean, we're in the End-Times and that guy keeps rolling on."

I just couldn't stop laughing.

⌐□ □ □ ¡ □⌐

[1.83]

—You're not writing any more, says Aggie.

She'd found me lying in bed, staring at the ceiling, thinking about great it was to be seeing Orlando.

—You seem very happy, Cara.

"Oh yes. Very happy. That's why I'm not writing much. Writers write loads more when they're unhappy."

—I didn't know that. I would have thought they would have been too troubled to write when unhappy.

"No. I think it works the other way. They get inspiration when they're feeling low. You can plait my hair if you like."

Aggie was standing close by. She seemed a little diffident today. Has been since the – you know – *incident*. But she shouldn't be. She's made me very happy. And if anything, I'm fonder of her than ever.

After a moment's hesitation, I felt her hands on my hair. Smoothing it. Brushing it.

—Would you like to go for a walk again today, said Aggie. —Would that make you happy?

"Oh yes," I said. "And I'll try and do a bit more writing as well. For you."

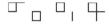

[1.84]

Aggie's been so good to me, finding Orlando and all, that I wanted to do something for her.

So, I taught her draughts.

I'm not great at chess and it would've taken ages to make a set of pieces. Anyway, I liked draughts. It was one of the few diversions we'd had on the farm. Here we could do better than bits of straw for pieces, though, and I taught her to play with biscuits on a board made out of slices of Battenberg cake. Colonist food fabricators really are amazing.

So, after lunch and our fabricating chores, on a yellow and pink sponge board (intercut with marzipan icing), using mini jammie dodgers for her pieces and custard creams for mine, we began to play.

Incredibly, she wasn't very good.

"I just thought," I said, clapping my hands as I landed my sixth king. "That your lot would be amazing at chequers."

Aggie stared back at me, her face as inscrutable as ever.

—It's only my first game.

"But with your big brains and The Hive Mind, I figured you'd analyse your position and hit me with the best moves. King please."

—Remember, Cara, I'm not yet connected to The Hive Mind. If I were, then perhaps the game would be closer.

"Maybe." I crisscrossed the board taking three of her pieces in one leapfrogging move. "Maybe. But I am pretty good you know."

—You do seem to be expert at it. It's good to see you enjoying something.

"Oh, I'm enjoying it all right." I took her last piece. "Another game?"

Aggie seemed unperturbed by her loss and nodded vigorously. I began to think that she had some deep learning neural network thing about to kick in and would wipe the floor with me. But we played six games and I won them all.

"Maybe there are some things that humans are just better at," I said as we called it a day.

—Maybe you're right, said Aggie equably, giving me a hug in congratulation. She stroked my arm fondly. —Humans really are impressive.

"You bet they are." I hadn't felt this good for ages.

—You bet they are, Aggie echoed.

⌑ ⌐ ⌐

[2.25]

In the middle of some walking and talking today, Orlando said, "I think I know how we can escape."

I narrowed my eyes at him. "Who says I even want to escape? I've tried it twice, and it didn't work out great either time."

"Well, escaping from the farm meant you got to live with Aggie. That was a step up."

"Sure. And things are finally going kind of OK."

"But it's not exactly freedom."

"I've probably got more going for me than most free humans had in our old world. I'm safe. I'm comfortable—"

"But you're a pet. And Aggie won't be any different to the way we used to be with our pets. There'll come a time when she meets another hermaphroditic stag beetle or whatever, and then she'll stop bringing you here, doing your hair..."

"Aggie's not like that. You said it yourself. She loves me."

"Aggie's definitely attached to you. But she can't love you. She's a different species. It's not possible to love a different species. Not truly. It's not real love. It's ownership. It's like when you have a dog."

I never had a dog. But I'd had a gerbil and I knew how I felt about him. "I loved Cosmo. I'd have done anything for him."

"Would you though? Would you really? Are you telling me you'd have died for your gerbil?"

"No, of course not. He was only—"

"A gerbil. That's my point."

"You can say what you like. I really did love Cosmo. And Aggie loves me."

He gave me a funny kind of smile. "Believe me, Cara, if Aggie really loved you, she would lay down her life for you a hundred times over. That's what love is. But Aggie doesn't love you like that. You're her pet. There are limits to Aggie's love. It's finite. And if it's finite, it can't be love."

We were silent for a while. I watched his face. He was actually very good-looking. I knew loads of girls who fancied him. I think Jo had a thing for him even though she always vehemently denied it.

Denies it.

"And anyway," he continued in a flat kind of voice. "Even if you're safe, I'm not. If I get injured…" He drew a finger across his throat.

I sighed. "OK, tell me your escape idea."

"OK then." He was suddenly like an excited puppy. "So, you know The Day Of Sharing is coming up? In a few weeks."

Did I? Recently Aggie's been talking of little else. Getting more excited than I've ever known her. Keeps talking about all the decorations she's going to be allowed to put up.

"Well, Crilloo was talking to one of his racing buddies who often trains his boys with us. Not Alec Durber's trainer. A different one. But anyway, I was doing stretches within earshot… mindshot… whatever. And they were talking about arrangements on The Day Of Sharing. Colonists go into separate rooms and hook themselves telepathically into The Hive Mind. At a set time, they upload their experiences and information learned since they've been on Earth."

"So, we could get away then you mean? Whilst they're all hooked in?"

"No, it's not actually all because the Soldiers will have already done their upload. That way they maintain order whilst The Day Of Sharing is going on."

"So, what then?"

"*Crilloo's buddy said that during The Day Of Sharing on one planet, contaminated experiences got uploaded by mistake.*"

"*Aggie's told me about that. When I first started writing my notebook. But she said the individual Colonist is meant to act as a filter.*"

"*Right. They're meant to purge thoughts and experiences which would confuse or pollute The Hive Mind. But on this particular planet one of the Colonists had absorbed some music from the species they were suppressing and inadvertently uploaded it. A catchy tune or something. But apparently musically complex. It was only the intro, but it got into the local Hive Mind and caused chaos, as it upset the idea that the species being suppressed was primitive.*"

"*OK... But what's all this got to do with the escape plan?*"

"*Well, anything that challenges the idea of our inferiority ought to challenge the whole Colonist set-up. And this catchy piece of music did exactly that. It caused something like an immune response. A massive immune response. The whole Thought Field which The Hive Mind generated was short-circuited for a day while Pseudo Cultural Suppression Inquisitors hunted down and eradicated the thoughts.*"

"*Because of something as insignificant as a tune?*"

"*Because it was evidence of the creativity of the indigenous species. And left unchecked, that would have undermined the Colonists' feelings of superiority which gave them the right to exploit other species. So, it wasn't just a tune. It was doubt.*"

I was quiet for a few moments, allowing it all to sink in. "*So... what happened?*" I said eventually. "*Did it bring the Colonists down?*"

"*Not exactly. Crilloo's friend said it gave the indigenous species time to break out and escape. But they were recaptured pretty quickly once the Inquisitors had done their work. The doubt didn't spread. And the escapees got punished. On that planet they ate the subspecies. So... you know...*"

"*Gross. And I thought we had it bad. So, hang on. Basically when you say you know how to escape, you mean you know how we could irritate the Colonists long enough to have terrible vengeance wreaked upon us?*"

"*I guess so.*"

"And where would we even be escaping to? The Colonists control the whole world, don't they?"

He grinned sheepishly. "Kind of."

"You idiot."

He shrugged; then started to laugh.

I couldn't help it. I started laughing with him.

And actually, at that moment, for the first time ever, even though he didn't know it and I certainly wasn't going to tell him, I realised I did kind of like him after all.

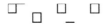

[1.85]

—You seemed very happy with Orlando yesterday, Cara. Are you starting to desire him biologically?

"Ew."

—Because Crilloo finally spoke to me the other day and asked if I would be interested in breeding Orlando with you.

"Double ew!"

—Though he would want the offspring of any biological coupling—

"Aggie! Seriously! Will you please stop with all this biological talk."

—So, you don't want me to ask to have Orlando over to the apartment?

"Not like that, no!"

—Is it that you still prefer Brandon?

"I just don't want to talk about *biological coupling.*" I rolled my eyes. "I also don't want to talk about Brandon. I don't want to think about what happened to him after I escaped."

Of course, I have thought about it.

Of how they'd have dragged him away and whatever came after.

I've even felt a pathetic stab of jealousy that Tess or Jo might have been selected for breeding with him in my place.

"Brandon's not in love with me," I said hurriedly. Although… "Hey, on The Day Of Sharing, will you be able to find out if he's OK?"

—The Day Of Sharing is when we are all connected. So, our information goes via The Hub into The Hive Mind. But that doesn't mean each of us knows everything after that. The Hub still filters harmful or inessential information. And some things are held back because they are classified.

"So, there are secrets even amongst the Colonists. I thought you shared everything?"

—We as individuals could not hold all the information that is contained in The Hive Mind. It would be like thinking that your Internet could fit in one human brain.

"I understand that. But we could access the Internet and get information we needed."

—But not all information was available to you, Cara?

"No. There was loads of information we weren't allowed to have. Private information. But I didn't think that was the way your society worked."

—I'm probably not explaining it well. The Controllers know some information is useful and some is not. We only have access to what is thought to be useful. Specifics about the running of a farm or the names of the humans kept there would not fall into that category. What would I normally do with such information?

"So, the Controllers do have secrets from you."

—I don't think of them as secrets. That knowledge would be known at a high enough level. Just because my foot doesn't know what I'm going to have for lunch, doesn't mean I'm keeping secrets from it.

"So, is that what you are, Aggie? Just a foot?"

After all this time Aggie knew when I was joking with her. She lunged at me and tickled me, and I tickled her back; and

I could hear her happy laughter inside my head.

[2.26]

"It makes sense," said Orlando when I told him of our conversation the next day. "Areas of The Hive Mind are classified. So, most Colonists will never know the truth of how creative humans really are. And listen, I overheard something else yesterday."

We were a long way from our owners, but he still looked carefully about him before he spoke.

"There's a group of humans who aren't under Colonist Control."

"What? Where?"

"Up in Cambridge."

"Cambridge! But that's not too far. How do you know?"

"Crilloo and his partner were talking last night. She's an Inquisitor. She said a couple of runaways had tried to escape from North London."

"Who?" Images of Tess and Jo filled my mind.

Orlando guessed immediately what I was thinking and squeezed my hand. "Obviously she didn't give names, Cara. And they got recaptured anyway before they could get too far. But Crilloo's partner said they were headed for this group of scientists and others who are holed up in Cambridge. These human scientists have been fighting off attempts to subdue them with some secret weapon they've developed."

"A resistance movement!"

The words hung between us as we neared the fence; then casually turned and began our walk back. Orlando took my arm and steered us along to the lake, to make the walk as long as possible. My head was buzzing. If there were people – free people – maybe my parents were amongst them. Maybe Ada or Brandon —

I counted ten steps before whispering, "So, there are people outside Colonist control. And if there's a group in Cambridge, there must be others."

"I know. It changes everything."

It didn't matter that others had already tried and failed.
It meant if we escaped, we'd have somewhere to go.

⊏ ⊓ ⊔ ⊏

[1.86]
Aggie and I played some more chequers today.
   It was another fun time!
   She even almost won a game.

   I put that in because Aggie is here right now, looking over my shoulder while I write.
   I'm sorry Aggie but you're really not very good at draughts—

   Aggie's just been tickling me for about half an hour!
   But it's OK because then I beat her again!
   I make that 17-0
   17-0
   I. AM. AWESOME.

⊔ ⎮ ⊓ ⊏ ⊔⊔

[2.27]
"I've had an idea," I said to Orlando.
   This was earlier on today.
   It's afternoon now, and Aggie's out fetching fabricator supplies, so I can scribble this down while it's fresh.
   "You know Colonists need to believe they're superior at everything? What if I know something where they're not?"
   He gave me a 'go on' kind of look.
   "Chequers."
   "Huh?"
   "You know? Draughts. Turns out humans are way better than Colonists at draughts."

299

"What are you talking about?"

"I've beaten Aggie seventeen times now. Seventeen! She's never even come close to getting the better of me."

"You're better at draughts than a Colonist?" He was incredulous. "You're not better at draughts than _me_."

"We've never played."

"I'm just assuming…"

"Shut up. Seriously, I've beaten her every time."

"But how is that even possible with their mega brains?"

"Aggie said they kind of rely on The Hive Mind. I think maybe on their own they're not that powerful."

"I'm not sure about that. They always seem like insufferable know-it-alls to me. Perhaps it's because Aggie's a juvenile…?"

"Perhaps. But I reckon I could beat Plaxys as well. I'd _love_ to beat Plaxys."

"So, what if you did?"

"Well, wouldn't that experience be in her head when she comes to upload it on The Day Of Sharing? That there's something that humans are better at than them. Crilloo may have burned all our books, but isn't that the kind of evidence that could make them doubt their superiority? There must be someone who cares about that."

"They're not _someones_. They're Colonists…" He chewed his lip. "But maybe you're right. Maybe it could trigger an immune response like that song caused on the other planet. Yeah, that could work. It's good."

"OK then." It felt weirdly uplifting to get his approval. "So, I should do it? I mean, what's the worst that can happen?"

"Sure. Although…" He grinned. "Once you've beaten her come and play me and then you'll see who's really the best."

"Pig." I thumped him.

—Cara!

Aggie was calling me.

"Wish me luck. I could be about to bring down the Colonists, single handed."

Part 11: Through the Letterbox

[1.87]

Colonists are intelligent†,
   Colonists are creative,
   I am not a Colonist.
   Animals are not intelli
   Animals are not creat
   I am just an animal.

   Colonists are intelligent,
   Colonists are creative,
   I am n   Colonist.
   Animals are not intellig
   Animals are not creative,
   I am just an animal.

   Colonists are intelligent,
   Colonists   ive,
   I am not a   ist.
   Animals are not intelligent,
   Animals are not creativ
   I am just an animal.

---

† 平 田 田 屮 平 昏 昏 昏 舟 田 比

[1.88]

Yesterday, I challenged Plaxys.

She had just returned from her essential duties as an Administrator in the Office of Science and Medicine.

Duties which are helping all Colonists thrive in their new world.

Duties which are also improving life on this planet for indigenous species, including my own worthless one; repairing our environment and protecting us from otherwise deadly diseases.

In the year since the Colonists arrived, CO_2 levels have fallen. If this trend continues, a global climate catastrophe will have been averted.

Non-compostable plastic production has ceased, and many species previously held for human consumption have been freed.

An emergent killer respiratory virus has also been isolated and neutralised before it could devastate the human population.

This is the work Plaxys contributes to on a daily basis, to make the Colonists' world better for all who live in it, including me.

In my human arrogance I challenged Plaxys. I was wrong to do so, and she rightly punished me.

I will not err again.

I will know my place.

I am not just an animal.

I am the lowest of all animals.

Because I thought I was better than a Colonist.

[1.89]

Colonists are intelligent,
　　Colonists are creative,
　　I am not a Colonist.
　　Animals are not intelligent,
　　Animals are not creative,
　　I am just an animal.

　　Colonists are intelligent,
　　Colonists are creative,
　　I am not a Colonist.
　　Animals are not intelligent,
　　Animals are not creative,
　　I am just an animal.

　　Colonists are intelligent,
　　Colonists are creative,
　　I am not a Colonist.
　　Animals are not intelligent,
　　Animals are not creative,
　　I am just an animal.

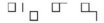

[2.28]

I can't see properly out of my left eye.

The swelling is going down and the wound has crusted over, but it still really hurts if I try to open it wide.

I haven't been able to write for days.

Apart from what Plaxys dictated, as she stood at my shoulder.

While I was still dripping blood.

And Aggie was cowering in the corner.

I was properly scared that night. Even worse than after dinner that time.

And not just of Plaxys.

God only knows what they'd do if they ever saw this journal.

I've got to be so careful.

Even now, I'm stopping and listening for footsteps every few minutes.

It's the middle of the night and it's so dim with these second-rate lights and only one eye that works properly, and I'm freaking out at every little sound.

But however scared I am, I'm going to tell you what happened.

I've got to tell someone.

I'd come back from talking with Orlando.

Over a week ago already.

I was on a real high. It was still over a month to The Day Of Sharing, so I didn't have to challenge Plaxys right then and there. And maybe if I'd waited, I'd have thought better of it. But I was full of confidence because I could beat Aggie so easily, and I just wanted to take on Plaxys the moment she got home.

Aggie tried warning me it wasn't a good idea. —She will be tired, Cara. And she does not like interacting with you. We will play instead.

I had no intention of dropping the idea, but I simply said, "OK."

We'd played another few games – taking my tally to 22-0 – when I heard the front door and saw Plaxys and Schektl walking sedately through the end of the open-plan living room, to the corridor that led to the bedrooms. The barrier to my alcove was down, Aggie momentarily distracted with resetting the board. My heart banging, I leapt up, skipped past her and ran to the hallway.

Schektl carried on walking, ignoring me completely. In retrospect, I wish Plaxys had done the same. Instead, she looked round and down at me – she was about six foot two tall and I'm only five-six.

—Yes?

That in itself, the tone in my head of utter disinterest, should have been all the warning I needed. But I was so brimful of expectation, I was so _happy_, that I couldn't help myself. "Would you like to play a game of draughts with me?"

Plaxys stared at me. I _never_ talked to her uninvited; I didn't dare look at her a lot of the time and certainly had never bounded up to her like this.

—I do not understand what you are asking.

"It's a game," I said. "Sometimes called chequers? I taught it to Aggie, and I thought you'd like to play it too."

—I am tired, said Plaxys and made to carry on walking.

—I told you, Cara. Leave her be.

Aggie was hovering at my side.

But I wouldn't take the hint. "I play it with Aggie and I've beaten her twenty-two times."

Plaxys slowly turned to face me. She shot a glance toward Aggie who was suddenly trying to look anywhere except back at her mother.

—Twenty-two times? Plaxys said. —It is a game of luck?

"Oh no," I said proudly. "It's a game of strategy."

—Really? Plaxys said. Aggie was wringing her hands. —You must be very good at this game?

"I'm the best," I said happily. "So, would you like to play?"

—You should rest, Mother.

Plaxys fixed Aggie with a stare. There was nothing in it, no menace, nor warning, nor encouragement, nor love. There was no way I could have read it. Yet looking back it's obvious what that stare meant.

—I will rest later. Let me play a game with Cara first.

Quietly rejoicing, I led Plaxys to my table where the Battenberg board was. I reset the pieces, then took a seat as she stood on the other *side of the table. She played with the jammie dodgers and I had the custard creams.*

I explained the rules to her.

—And we move alternately?

"Yes. You can go first if you want. Would you like me to explain basic strategy before we start?"

Plaxys stared at me, unspeaking, then shot one more glance at Aggie who was lurking behind her. The sun was on the other side of our apartment block now, and though it was well before dusk, and the sky outside my window a cloudless blue, away from the window there was shadow. Aggie hovered in that shade, her face fixed on the board, her arms rigid beside her. Plaxys turned back to me. It seemed like she smiled. But it wasn't emotion, simply the way she set her mouth. Even I, drunken with the thought of imminent victory, should have been able to see that.

—No, said Plaxys at last. —I do not need strategy advice from you. Nor any favours. You move first.

I shrugged. Even better. If I went first, I'd be able to control the centre of the board. Even Dad couldn't beat me when I went first.

I moved. She moved. I moved.

It was ten moves in before I suddenly realised I was two pieces down.

After a further ten moves, she had kinged for a second time and I was behind four pieces.

It didn't last long after that.

She didn't just beat me. She destroyed me.

I sat stunned. Feeling like she'd zapped me.

My head was spinning.

My stomach turning.

What had just happened?

Plaxys turned to Aggie. Her daughter's face was obscured by the twilight away from the window, and when Aggie realised her mother was watching her, she took a further step back into the shadows.

—Now you play her, Mlaxet.

—My name's Ag—

—Stop this nonsense! Play her. Beat her.

"She can't beat me," I said incredulous. I was starting to recover from the thrashing. I'd been careless early on. A bit more concentration and I would take her.

—My daughter has been letting you win.

"Of course she hasn't."

Aggie didn't look at me or her mother. Just the floor. The light and the shade.

—You need to remember your place, so that Cara can remember hers. Play her again, and this time do it properly.

Aggie flashed me a glance and then reset the board. I went first, but she beat me even more comprehensively than Plaxys had done.

The whole brief game passed without a word being spoken.

At the end I stared at Aggie open-mouthed, but she wouldn't catch my eye.

—Good, said Aggie's mother. —Remember this for the future. She is not one of us. She is stupid and lesser—

"I'm not stupid!" My frustration and bewilderment boiled over. "We're not stupid. We had novels and plays and just because your lot burned them doesn't mean they didn't exist—"

—How dare you! You filthy animal, repeating lies like that in front of my daughter! Stand and recite The Mantra!

I crossed my arms.

—Did you hear me, Cara! Stand and recite!

Her face was unchanged but her thoughts stung. That was when I got scared. I stood up so hastily the chair scraped and tipped back. I moved to catch it but Plaxys hit me with a neural blast so strong that it felt like a physical blow.

The chair clattered onto the floor behind me.

—RECITE THE MANTRA!

My head felt like I'd slammed onto concrete. I didn't actually know where I was for a moment.

—RECITE IT!

The words were now shrill like whistles, blown right into my ears.

"Colonists are amazing. Colonists are incredible—"

—NO!

This time the neural blow felt like a smack to the face. Smarting I tried pointlessly to duck the second blow, and then I was falling and my head hit the wood floor with a crash.

—RECITE!

—Please Mother!

I was on the floor, disorientated, my head pounding from the fall, from the neural pressure she was applying to me.

—RECITE!

"Colonists are creative, Colonists are brilliant—"

—NO! Recite it properly.

It was like she kicked me in the side of the head. I reeled from it, and as the stars began to clear, I panicked, scrabbling for the correct words whilst my bitten nails scratched at the floor.

"I'm sorry," I sobbed. "I can't remember—"

—Please leave her alone, Mother.

—I will make you remember.

And now I felt the pain rise in my brain just behind the left eye; searing, ever-increasing in magnitude, inside me like a dentist drilling directly into my skull, so strong that even when I shrieked as loud as I could, it didn't drown her out.

—YOU ARE AN ANIMAL. YOU ARE JUST AN ANIMAL!

I could no longer speak, could scarcely breathe, the pain like white heat behind my eye. All I could do was writhe on the floor to try and escape my punishment, my hands clawing at my face, my ragged nails digging into my skin, the pain so all-consuming that I wanted – needed – to tear my own eye from its socket to make it go; my nails clawing against the flesh of my cheek and eyebrow, my face suddenly slippery with my own blood, The Mantra being recited again and again in my head at monstrous volume, Aggie screaming too, my head and chest being crushed with extraordinary pressure—

"I… can't… breathe…"

—RECITE!

"Or what?" I gasped.

I suddenly felt I had nothing left to lose.

They'd taken everything already.

"Or what, Plaxys? Are you going to kill me like you did with Agneta?"

The pain in my head eased a fraction. —What did you say?

"The girl in the apartment, when you arrived," I croaked. "The one that Aggie wanted to keep. The one you tortured then took to your lab to dissect."

—What are you talking about?

"Shame Schektl couldn't stop you."

—Is this what Mlaxet told you?

The crunching pressure dissipated as Plaxys started laughing.

—Is that what she said? That I killed the girl?

She looked across at her daughter. —Tell Cara what really happened.

My head was ringing, but I was feeling bewilderment too. "What's she talking about?"

—Tell her.

Aggie shook her head.

Plaxys laughed again. —Fine. Then I will. I did not take the girl to my lab. Why would I? She was already dead.

"Because you'd killed her."

—Not me, you fool. Her.

She pointed at Aggie. Almost obscured in the gathering gloom, her head was hung in shame.

—She came upon the girl in the middle of the night. The human screamed when the lights were turned on; but our daughter was so startled that she screamed too. You know how loud she can be, how little control she has. She killed the girl outright. Crushed her mind.

I turned on Aggie. "Tell me that's not true," I pleaded.

—I didn't mean to.

Aggie had stepped forward into the light. She was wringing her hands. —It was an accident. I couldn't control the power of my thoughts back then.

I thought I was going to throw up.

—I found them together. The girl in her arms. Quite dead. My foolish daughter was stroking the human's hair. Obviously, we had to get rid of it, take the human for incineration in case it was diseased—

"She. She was a she not an it. Her name was Agneta."

—*Who cares!*

And I felt the sting of her mind again, a scorching whip.

—*I didn't want her. And I certainly never wanted you. There's a reason Colonists don't keep humans as pets: they're disgusting and deluded and dangerous. We should get rid of you.*

Through the blood streaming into my eyes, I saw Schektl enter the room.

"Please," I appealed to him. "Help me."

—*You have heard? Plaxys asked him.*

—*Everything.*

—*We should get rid of her now*—

—***NO!*** *yelled Aggie. I covered my ears uselessly, and even Plaxys and Schektl shuddered. But only for an instant.*

—*SILENCE, commanded Plaxys.*

Then she turned to Schektl and stared straight at him. I don't know whether they were talking – I couldn't even hear static – but eventually Schektl said,

—*I understand. But we promised her.*

Plaxys shook her head.

—*We promised, he insisted.*

Plaxys made a tutting noise. A pause. And then finally she said, —*Very well. But no more chances. Mlaxet, make her recite.*

—*I'm Aggie!*

—*You see, said Plaxys to Schektl.*

—*I see, said Schektl. He turned to Aggie.* —*I will punish you later. For now, make it recite. Make it write The Mantra in its journal. Make sure it never forgets its place again. If it does, we will brand The Mantra all over its body and then get rid of it.*

I covered my face, a mess of blood and tears; then felt sudden arms around me. I recoiled in terror but it was Aggie. She gathered me up and I sobbed, the tears and the blood mingling.

—*Make it recite.*

Through my tears I said The Mantra, and eventually I heard Plaxys and Schektl leave the room. I was curled into a ball beside Aggie.

After a while the fear had melted away, leaving only resentment to bubble up through the pain.

"You killed her," I croaked. "How could you?"

—I didn't mean to.

"But you did and you lied about it."

—I thought you'd hate me.

"Of course, I hate you! I hate all of you. Look what you've done to me."

She hung her head.

"And why did you even let me beat you at draughts? Why did you let me think I was better than you at something? Plaxys could have killed me."

—No, she wouldn't.

"She's a psychopath. And you're a murderer—"

—Shut up!

Aggie jumped to her feet. —I hate you, Cara! You're so stupid. You don't understand anything.

"We're intelligent too."

—No. You're not. You want to know why I let you win? Because I wanted you to be happy. But like all humans, you got greedy and wanted to be better than us. Well, that's NOT MY FAULT!

She turned and walked away, the barrier rising behind her.

□ | □　□　ꟼ

[2.29]

I've been left on my own.

Just like a few weeks ago.

But this time, Aggie's been told to do it.

Plaxys has been screaming at her. Even Schektl had stern words to say. That she should keep her distance from me. Not talk to me. To prevent her being polluted by my inferiority.

I don't know how long this isolation's going to last.

But at least they can't hurt me if they're not around. Plaxys would have killed me for sure if Schektl hadn't stepped in.

And Aggie… I know it was an accident, but how can I forgive her for what happened with Agneta?

Poor Agneta.

How could Aggie have done that to you?

She says she can control herself now, but she could kill me anytime she gets too excited.

She's like a ticking time-bomb.

[2.30]

I hate this.

I'm trapped.

And I'll never escape.

I'd be better off dead.

Come on Plaxys. Come on Aggie.

You may as well kill me now.

You're going to do it eventually anyway.

[2.31]

Actually, I've been thinking about it.

(I mean, there's literally nothing else to do all day.)

Perhaps I've been hard on Aggie.

When I was little, Tom and I had a goldfish and I managed to kill it by giving it too much feed.

But only because I loved it so much and wanted it to get bigger so I could cuddle it.

Seriously, small kids should not be left in charge of animal welfare.

But my point is, maybe that's all Aggie was guilty of too.
That and lying and blaming her mum, of course.
But then I blamed Tom, so…

[2.32]
I tried to talk to Aggie about it when she brought me my breakfast.
But she just stared at me in silence.
I know she's got instructions not to say a word, but still she could have <u>acknowledged</u> me.
I mean, I was apologising for Pete's sake.
Well, you know what?
I don't want to talk to you either.
You big insect freak.
I hate you.
And all your Colonist kind.
For what you've done to me and Agneta.
To Tess and Jo and Brandon.
And Mum and Dad.
And everyone else.
You don't want to talk to me, Aggie?
I DON'T CARE.

[2.33]
I'm so bored.
Aggie's out and I'm alone.
Sometimes the barrier's up, sometimes down.
It makes no difference.
I've been round the apartment a million times by now in any case.

There's nothing to do.
I just want to smash the place up.
Smear stuff on the walls.
But, of course, I don't.
I'm too afraid of what they'll do to me.
The cut around my eye has opened up again. And my wrist is itching
like hell. But Aggie won't give me any ointment.
Running it under the tap is soothing but only momentarily.
How long will this go on for?
My whole life, I guess. Whether that's short or long.
I'll never escape.
I'm never going to be free. Not like we used to be.
Maybe I need to take the one way out of here that's still available.

□ | □   □ | □

[2.34]
This afternoon I opened my window.
There was a fresh breeze. Cool on a warm day.
It's a fourth-floor window.
It would have been such an easy thing to do.
To jump.
Well, for anyone else.
For me, when I looked down, I felt so dizzy I almost passed out.
I'm so weak.
So scared of everything.
I hate myself more than I hate Them.

□ | □   □ | □

[2.35]
Something's just happened.
After days of tedium.

I mean, I can't even remember when I last wrote. A week maybe?

Whatever. Something important happened today. Like so important. And I need to write it all down. Now. Before I forget any of it. Before Aggie gets back.

Aggie went out this morning. Didn't say a word. But left the barrier down.

I had the plain bread roll she'd brought me. No alternative since they changed the passcode on the fabricator, so I can't use it anymore.

Then I'm pacing round the apartment, ending up at the front door as I often do, when all at once I hear a scuffling sound just beyond it. I think it must be a rat – which I do not like the idea of – but then the sound changes to a voice softly singing. When I press my eye to the spyhole I catch my breath.

There's a girl in the corridor.

She's distorted in the fisheye but is my age, I think. Dressed in a tattered T-shirt and leggings. Her hair's bedraggled and her bare feet filthy. She's Asian – like Indian or Sri Lankan origin – and she's making her way up the corridor. She's singing in a low, sad voice, as she tries the handles to the other apartments. "Jeepers creepers, where'd you get those peepers? Jeepers creepers...." It was the kind of old song my Dad would have sung.

"Help!" I shout and bang on the door to get her attention. When I look back through the spyhole she's pulled away from the door on the opposite side of the corridor and is coming over.

"Help!" I scream, thumping the wood again.

Her face looms in the fisheye till it blocks out the light.

"Let me in." I jump as the door handle rattles, but the extra Colonist lock is still engaged and the door stays shut.

"I can't open it! You've got to get me out of here."

"Quiet, you idiot!" Her voice is low and angry. "They'll hear you. Stand away from the door so I can see you."

I step back.

"What are you doing here?" I shout through the door.

"Shh!"

I fix my eye again to the lens again and see her face as she checks up and down the corridor.

"Who are you?" *I ask again, more quietly this time.*

"I'm a runaway."

"Where are you from?"

"Trent Park Farm."

"Where's that?"

"Trent Park, you idiot."

"Oh. So, you've escaped?"

"Of course. That's what a runaway is, genius. I'm eighteen and a half. I knew I'd be next up for Harvesting. Time to get out. What are you doing here?"

"I'm being kept as a pet."

"Colonists don't have human pets."

"They don't normally. It's a long story—"

"I really don't care."

"Oh. Well, no need to be—"

"Shut up and let me in. They're right behind me."

"Who are?"

"Inquisitors. They saw me on Hampstead Heath. I thought I'd got away but they've followed me to the building. Let me in."

"I can't."

"Because your owners wouldn't like it?"

"No. You don't understand. I <u>can't</u>. It's locked. And anyway, you need to help <u>me</u> escape. They're going to kill me."

"Relax. They're going to kill all of us. You're better off where you are."

"Were you not listening? They punish me all the time—"

"But I bet you get good food and shelter. I could do with a bit of that. Mind you, I'd probably slit my owner's throat if I was a pet."

"Oh! I don't think I could do that." *I really couldn't. Not in cold blood. And even in self-defence I'd probably be too rubbish... And, anyway, despite all the terrible things they've done to me, they did save me from the farm.* "I'm just not like that..."

"Like I said: you're better off where you are. You're soft."

"I'm not soft—"

There's thumping on the door. Squinting through the spyhole, I see she's banging her forehead against the wood. "Please let me in."

"I really would if I could." I start to cry. "But the lock…"

"Just try fiddling with the latch—"

"I have. I've really tried."

"Whatever. Let me see you at least."

"What?"

"The letterbox."

I hear it open by my waist. It takes me a moment to understand what she means. Then I drop to my knees. She's holding up the flap and peering through, I see her eyes. I expect them to be brown but they're a startling, vivid green.

It feels like someone's thumped me in the chest.

Her eyes are the most deliriously beautiful thing I've ever seen.

She sings, "Where d'you get *those* peepers?"

"What?"

"I'm paying you a compliment. You've got really sexy eyes."

"Thank you!" I'm taken aback and blurt without thinking, "Are you gay?"

"So gay. Is that a problem?"

"No, of course not," I say like an idiot. "It's just that you're the one with the amazing eyes."

"Yeah. Everyone loves my eyes."

"They *are* amazing," I say again. My cheeks feel hot with embarrassment.

"I know. A lot of girls have told me that. That's been the one saving grace of being held prisoner on a farm. All those gorgeous girls with so much time on their hands. If only, hey, Peepers?"

"Oh, I'm not—"

"*Shh!* I hear them!"

I hear them too. A pounding from the stairwells at either end of the corridor. I rattle the handle. Throw myself against the door. But it's solid oak.

"They're coming." Her voice is suddenly weak. "I'm so tired of running."

There's a bang at both ends of the hallway.

"Let me touch you," she says.

Her eyes disappear, and her hand pushes through the narrow letterbox. Her fingers can just reach me, and I feel them warm against my cheek. I lean into them, my eyes closing at the caress, a singular moment of tenderness.

A clattering of boots in the hall. A buzzing in my head as they close in.

"Oh God—"

In an instant her hand is torn from me, and they bundle her over. I catch a glimpse of black uniforms as the letterbox snaps shut.

"Remember me, Peepers!" she screams. "I'm Verinder Rachel from Cockfosters! And I am human—"

Her voice is lost in the sonic whiplash from the Inquisitors. I writhe in agony on the hallway floor catching some of the punishment meted out to her.

And by the time the pain has passed, by the time I've recovered enough to place my eye again to the peephole, the corridor is empty and Verinder and the Inquisitors are gone.

□ I □ □ I □ I

[2.36]

I can't sleep.

I can't stop thinking about Verinder.

Her beautiful eyes.

She said mine were sexy.

The touch of her fingers against my cheek.

The warmth.

A real person.

I don't want to think about what the Inquisitors did to her. But I can't help it either. Not after what I saw that night on the farm.

"I'm Verinder Rachel from Cockfosters! And I am human!"

Even in her rags she was such a vivid, alive, honest person.

What am I by comparison?

I hate myself.

For not even knowing what I feel.

For not having been able to open the door and pull her inside to safety.

And for being petrified the Inquisitors will come back for me.

Every time I hear a sound in the hallway, I worry it's them returning.

And then that will be the end of me.

—No more chances, Plaxys had said. And she'd meant it.

Wait!

I hear steps outside the apartment.

They've gone.

The steps have gone.

My heart isn't beating, it's banging.

Every sound in the apartment or beyond sets me on edge.

It's taken me half an hour to pluck up the courage to turn my light back on.

I was petrified.

I've always imagined that if the Inquisitors were going to come and get me it would be in the middle of the night.

It's when undesirables are always taken away.

But they've gone.

They've gone.

□ | □   □ | □

[2.37]

Verinder Rachel.

    Cockfosters.

    Verinder Rachel.

    Cockfosters.

    Verinder Rachel.

    Cockfosters.

□ | □   □ | □ |

[2.38]

Another sleepless night.

All I can think about is Verinder.

Her eyes. Her touch.

I'm so sorry, Verinder, there was nothing I could do.

Only…

What if I could have opened the door? Would I have, then?

That's what haunts me.

That even if I could have unbolted the door I wouldn't have because I'd have been too scared of what the Inquisitors might have done to me.

Scared of what Plaxys might have done to me.

I'm sorry Verinder. I'm sorry to think like that.

But I'm going crazy.

I keep seeing you.

Just your green eyes through the letter box.

My mind is swirling. I can't stop it.

Maybe what frightens me most is you.

You're way too edgy and dangerous to have properly liked someone like me.

But I don't care.

I would have saved you if I could.

Verinder, I would have opened the door.

I promise.

□ | □   □ | □_

[2.39]

Everyone's still been ignoring me.

They even adjusted my food so I only get one boring tray in the morning that has to last all day.

Aggie has been just bringing the food and leaving.

Until this morning.

Today, she laid down the tray and whispered, —Only another five days.

Only?

Five days of what's basically solitary confinement.

Only?

You have no idea Aggie.

□ | □ □ | ⟟

[2.40]

I'm sorry I couldn't help you, Verinder.

I'm not strong like you.

But I would have if I could.

I've got to believe that.

Because you helped me.

Even in those few precious minutes, you made a difference.

You reminded me I'm not a pet.

You reminded me what it's like to be a real person.

My own person.

You reminded me that however much they may punish me, their Mantra's not right. Doesn't matter how many times they make me write or say it.

Animals are not intelligent.

Sure.

Animals are not creative.

I agree.

But I am not an animal.

My name is Carabel Caffarelli from Highbury.

And I am human.

□ I □ □ I □

[2.41]

Finally, the punishment ended today.

Plaxys was nowhere to be seen, but Schektl gave me a good talking to.

—No more chances.

Like I didn't know that already.

Finally, Aggie came in and hugged me like I was a puppy.

I let her.

I mean, what choice did I have?

Though to be honest, it was nice to feel something again.

Even if it wasn't real, it was still contact with something alive.

But I haven't forgotten what they've done to me.

—I'm even allowed to take you for a walk again. We could see Orlando?

I wanted to be strong like Verinder. But I couldn't help myself.

Just the thought of seeing him again made me burst into tears.

□ I □ □ I □

[2.42]

He wasn't there!

We went to Kenwood today but Orlando wasn't there.

It was such a downer.

We hung around for ages.

Being outside was clearly better than nothing but seeing other boys there was awful. I didn't want them. I wanted Orlando.

Hanging out and talking to him already seems like an age ago.

Aggie said we can try again tomorrow. I'm not sure how I'm going to cope if he's not there again.

Please let him be there.

Just for once let something go right.

Please.

□ | □   □ | □⌐
　　□

[2.43]

He was there today!

HE WAS THERE!

Down by the lake. I sprinted over and threw my arms around him.

"Where have you been?" he asked, holding onto me. "What happened to you? I've been so worried." There were tears in his eyes. "The last time I saw you, you were going to play draughts with Aggie's mother. I wanted to call you back the moment you walked away. Something just didn't feel— oh my God! What happened to you?"

I'd pushed my hair back from my face and he'd seen my left eye for the first time. "What did they do to you?" He raised a hand and reached out and gently touched my cheek with outstretched fingers. The barest touch and I felt... irritated.

I pulled away from him and shook my curls back down. "It's fine. Honestly."

"Did they——?"

"I did it." I mimed scratching myself. "Plaxys was in my head." Somehow the appalled look on his face pleased me. I won't lie, I am not a nice person. I couldn't work out what I was feeling. I'd been so looking forward to seeing him again, and yet now he was here and concerned it just left me cold. I didn't need his worry. There is definitely something wrong with me.

Anyway, I told him everything that had happened. The draughts game, Agneta, Verinder. His eyes were wide by the end. He'd even stopped walking, so I grabbed his arm and urged him onwards. The last thing I needed was for Aggie to start suspecting something.

"We've got to escape," I said to him, matter-of-factly.

"Of course. That's got to be our aim..."

"No, I mean, as soon as possible. I'll do something wrong and Plaxys will kill me. Or Aggie will lose her cool and crush my mind. And you're just one injury from the slaughterhouse... We need to get out."

"But how? Where? Look what happened to that runaway—"

"Her name was Verinder. And you said there was a group in Cambridge."

"Cambridge is fifty miles away. How would we get there? The last group of runaways didn't manage it. Your Verinder didn't."

"She's not _my_ Verinder—"

"How would we even get away?"

"We need to disrupt them on The Day Of Sharing. Just like you said. This was _your_ idea, remember. You were the one telling me we had to escape?"

"Sure. I know. But that was before…" He pointed to my face. "Look, this life isn't perfect. But if we keep our heads down, keep out of trouble, it's not so bad. I mean, at least we've got each other, right?" He reached for my hand, but I pulled away.

"You weren't listening," I hissed. "I can't _keep out of trouble_. Plaxys is literally a psycho. I need to get out. I'm _going_ to get out whether you come with me or not."

"Of course, I'm coming with you," he said immediately, defiantly. But there was fear in his face when he said it.

So, I'm not great at reading people – as is probably abundantly clear by now – but I could see that fear, and I knew that he wasn't frightened for himself. It wasn't even for me, directly. It was for _this_, these moments we'd shared on the grass, down by the lake, with a summer-blue canopy of sky above us and a thousand shades of green in the trees beside us; the faintest hint of a breeze caressing his cheek and my cheek in turn. However imperfect a life this was, these moments were ours. Aggie and Crilloo were at a distance. If we turned away from them, it was just us two, on a lawn, near a lake, a carpet of verdant grass and the cool dark waters before us. This was what was at stake. Because whatever came next, it would not be _this_. It would not be tranquil. It would not be easy. And we might not both make it.

"I'm so tired of running," Verinder had said.

But I hadn't started yet.

"Listen, Orlando," I said to him, staring him straight in the eye. "We're not animals, and we weren't meant to live like this. We've got to turn this around. We've got to escape."

He studied my face for a long time. "You're right," he said at last. Then sighed. "It's hard because I've only just got you back." He smiled even though I didn't. "But I'm with you. Of course, I am. One hundred per cent." He gave me another smile, more brittle this time; and then started walking away.

I jogged after him and now I did take his hand and held it tight all the way back to Crilloo and Aggie.

⌐ ▢ ▢ ▢
　 ▢ ▁ ▁

[1.90]

Aggie was doing my hair just now.

—You know you haven't written anything new in your journal for twenty days.

"Well, it wasn't high on my list of priorities after, you know, everything that happened."

—No. Of course not.

Her thoughts sounded embarrassed in my head. But then she went on. —You know, Mother doesn't want you to write at all. She thinks you're dangerous. But I've told her it's all OK. You're not saying anything bad.

"Of course not."

—I miss reading what you've written. The stories of your experiences before me. And being able to relive our time together.

"You've got plenty to do with The Day Of Sharing coming up, without reading."

—I know. I just miss it, that's all. And now you're happy, does that mean you won't be writing anymore?

"How do you mean *happy?*"

—Well, you're back with Orlando. You seem very happy together. Very content.

"Yes. I suppose we are."

—And you've said before, that humans only write when they're unhappy.

"They write *more* when they're unhappy. Do you want me to write?"

Aggie paused, her hands entwined in my hair. —I adore reading what you write, she said eventually, almost uncomfortably. —When I'm reading your journal, it means I'm close to you. That I know what you're thinking. You have a phrase for it.

"Being inside your head."

—Yes. I liked being inside your head, Cara. It made me feel special.

"Just like I'm inside your head, or at least know what you're thinking, when you speak to me."

—Yes.

Aggie was happy. I could feel it in her touch. And I was happy too.

Being with her and knowing I'd be seeing Orlando later.

"Don't worry." I said. "I'll be writing again soon. Just give me a little time."

□ I □ □ I □□
    □

[2.44]
I'm never writing in that orange notebook again.

I'm done with it.

Writing all that stuff, bringing memories back but having to be neutral about them so I don't give too much away. Just for a Colonist's pleasure.

It started off as therapy, but I've got this other, plain notebook for that. And I'm going to have escaped before Aggie realises that 'a little time' means 'never'.

But I'm still glad I wrote what I wrote. At least it means there's a record of what happened to us. A human record not just a bunch of Colonist lies.

I didn't write it for you, though, Aggie.
I wrote what I wrote for me.
And other real life, beautiful humans.
I wrote it for Verinder.
Thank you, Verinder for reminding me that I could be strong too.
And angry when I need to be.
Being afraid made me forget.
Trying to be good made me forget.
But you can never be good enough if you're being kept as a slave.
I wrote it for Tess.
I so love you, Tess.
I'm sorry I didn't listen to you.
I wrote it for Jo and Brandon and Ada and Miss Temple.
And I wrote it for Agneta and Alice.
But I didn't write it for any Colonist.
So, you can get out of my head, Aggie.
You're not welcome.
You never were.

□ I □   □ I □

[2.45]

He wanted to spell it out to me. What we might be getting into.
    "If they catch us, we're dead. You know that right?"
    "I know," I said. "But we've got to try. And we need to do it soon."
    "Our chances aren't great."
    "Listen, I'm still going to try, whether you're with me or not."
    "I'm with you, Cara. You know that."
    "OK then."
    "OK then."

"So," I said. "We need to disrupt the Hive Mind on The Day Of Sharing? That's still the best plan, right?"

"Yes," he said. "And I'm guessing your game of draughts with Plaxys isn't going to get it done."

"Are you being funny?"

He held up his hands. "I'm just thinking aloud."

"Why don't we use a tune like they did on that other planet?"

"No. That won't work. Crilloo said no music gets uploaded anymore. They have a filter prepared for that."

"Then what?" It was impossible to conceal my dismay, and even Aggie heard my plaintive shout and glanced over. I waved to her that I was fine and, smiling at Orlando, hissed, "Then _what_?"

He shrugged. "I don't know. I'm not sure what else we've got. We need to infect The Hive Mind with something that shows humans aren't just cattle. That we're as intelligent and creative as Colonists."

It took the entirety of the walk, from the top of the lawn by the House and down to the lakeside, for the idea to form.

"What about my journal?"

"What about it?"

"I've written loads in that."

"But didn't you have to take out references to anything creative? Like books or writers? Didn't it have to be factual?"

"Yeah, that's the thing!"

And I explained it to him.

My idea.

My _plan_.

By then, we were right by the lake. Orlando found a stone and skimmed it one, two, three skips over the surface of the water. Then he turned and looked at me.

"It could definitely work. I think you might just be a genius."

"It could work, couldn't it? And then once it's happening – when the Hive Mind is down – we can escape."

"We can arrange to meet somewhere. Our owners don't live that far away from each other."

—Cara?

Aggie was calling me. We started walking back. "But how do I get out of my building?" I whispered to Orlando. "You live in a house. I'm on the fourth floor of a block of apartments. And they've got serious locks on the door."

"Same with me. Though I've hidden a small garden axe under my bed which I'll hack down the front door with, if I ever get the chance. I mean, it's tiny and a bit blunt, so it'll probably take ages but—"

"Well, I haven't got an axe. Even a bad one. And have I mentioned, I'm four floors up?"

—Come on, Cara, it's time to go.

"Get me over. I'll take a look and we can work something out."

□ ▏ ▢   □ ▏ Ϥ

[2.46]

I love you, reader.

But there are some secrets I can't trust even to you.

Not yet.

Because if I told you what our plan was, and if you turned out to be a Colonist, then I'd be dead.

And Orlando would be too.

And all my thoughts and fears and everything I've written here would be lost.

Burned to ash like all our other lovely beautiful books.

So, I can't share it with you just yet.

But soon, I hope.

Oh, I hope you're a human reading this.

Please, reader. Because then that'll mean, somehow, the plan worked. That we escaped. It means I didn't die with some giant stag beetle ripping open my chest.

It means we beat the Colonists.

Treated them like they treated us, and made them suffer hopefully.

But if you are a Colonist reading this,

Then none of this will matter.

Because I'll be dead already.

[2.47]

It's not just the plan.

I mean, there are other things I can't write about.

Thoughts I don't want to put down on paper.

Personal stuff. Confusing stuff.

Even here, where no one else will see them. I mean, you're like the least judgemental person I know, reader.

Way less judgy than me.

But the thing is, I don't always need a Colonist to censor my journal; I do it to myself.

Because there are things that I haven't quite made sense of yet.

Things that Aggie said that evening, when she pretended to be Brandon and Orlando and then showed me her insect form.

I mean, a serious amount happened that evening.

But something she <u>said</u> lingered.

It's stayed in my head like Verinder's green, green eyes.

I can't shake any of it.

It's not like what Aggie said was a surprise.

But hearing it from someone else was.

Especially as I've been trying so hard not to listen to it in my own head.

I know it's not wrong.

It's just I'm not ready to hear it yet.

Maybe other people would be, but I'm not. And I'm going to go at my own pace.

Not anyone else's.

Not boy or girl or Colonist.

I'll listen to it when I'm ready.

Tess always used to say I never listen properly anyway.

That I would only hear what I wanted to hear.

But you know it's hardest sometimes to listen to yourself.

And until you do that, how can you tell anyone else what you're truly feeling?

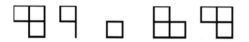

Part 12: Getting Biological

[2.48]

Today I was helping Aggie put up decorations for The Day Of Sharing. The whole house was getting festooned.

—*I'm so excited.*

Aggie's thoughts were indeed very bubbly. —*The Day Of Sharing's only six days away.*

"Sounds great. I guess."

—*It's really important for us on a new planet. Every year in the future we'll celebrate it as a day for giving thanks. Lift up your end.*

I held up a string of purple tinsel, while Aggie stapled the far end to the wall. The Colonists may have been advanced, but their decorations were just as tacky as ours. "So… Aggie?"

—*Yes, Cara. A bit higher please.*

She fired a staple into the centre of the tinsel.

"Orlando and I have become quite close."

—*Yay!*

Aggie screeched in my mind so loud that I dropped the tinsel. She came over and hugged me.

"Aggie I can't breathe."

—*Sorry, sorry. But that's just such good news. I so wanted you to fall in love as you call it.*

I raised an eyebrow at her. "Wow, Aggie, for a stag beetle you really are a romantic."

—*You know we're romantic, Aggie said, uncowed by my sarcasm.* —*You humans falling in love: it's not exactly The Great Yearning. But we still respect it, however backwards a species you might be.*

"Thanks."

—*You're welcome.*

"So, anyway," *I said.* "I'm wondering if I could have Orlando to come and stay one night. You know so we can – er – get even closer."

Aggie hugged me again. —*Of course, Cara.*

"Will Plaxys and Schektl be OK with it?"

—*Crilloo is a well-respected Administrator.*

"More respected than your parents?" *I teased.*

—As well respected. They will know that his racing males are well trained and no doubt think Orlando's presence will be beneficial for your behaviour.

Aggie walked back to her end of the tinsel. —And Crilloo will be delighted that you are ready to behave biologically.

"Hang on—"

—Cara's getting biological. Cara's getting biological…

□ I □ □ I □
   □   ⌐

[2.49]

"On no account, are we getting biological," I told Orlando the moment Aggie left us alone in the alcove.

"No, no, of course not. Although maybe a kiss to make sure she doesn't get suspicious—"

"No!"

"Worth a try."

I glared at him and he held up his hands.

"Just a joke, Cara."

"Well, let's just keep our eyes on the prize, shall we. How do we get out of here on The Day Of Sharing?"

He looked totally uncrushed and I suddenly realised I'd been incredibly arrogant. He'd probably stopped liking me ages ago. I would have if I'd been him. And of course, the moment I thought that he'd stopped fancying me, I immediately found him ten times more attractive.

"You were right about the locks on your front door," he was saying. "They're sprung-loaded using some kind of hidden tech. There's no obvious way of pulling their bolts back, so maybe they're activated by their heat signature or something… Even if we disrupt the Thought Field, it won't make any difference to these locks I don't think."

"So…"

"So, there is clearly only one answer."

"Which is?"

"You need to go out of the window."

"Are you out of your freaking mind?"

Aggie poked her head back into the alcove. —Everything OK, Cara?

"Yes, yes, fine." I glared at Orlando who was grinning goofily.

—It's just you don't look very happy with Orlando. Should I ask Crilloo to fetch him?

"No, no, it's good. It's just… You know… It's my first time."

I felt Orlando's arms suddenly wrap around me. "I told her I would be very gentle." He planted a kiss on my cheek and I forced a grin.

—OK. Well, so long as you're happy…

"We couldn't be happier. Could we, Cara?"

I grimaced. Then seeing Aggie still watching, gave him a little peck on his cheek. Aggie clapped her hands in delight, then disappeared. I shoved Orlando away.

"Let go of me, you gorilla!"

"The look on your face… But at least you finally kissed me." He was in fits of laughter.

"That was not a kiss!"

I take it all back. I didn't find him attractive in the least.

"Where were we?" He was still grinning inanely.

"Where were we?" I jabbed a finger into the middle of his chest. "You were trying to get me to jump out the window. We're sixty feet up here."

"I don't want you to jump. You need to climb down."

"I – am – not—"

"Aggie will come out again."

I lowered my voice. "I am not climbing out of my window. You know I'm scared of heights."

"You can make a rope from your sheets."

"Are you crazy?"

"It'll work."

"Aggie said The Upload on The Day Of Sharing happens to coincide with midnight. So, you're telling me I'm not just going out of my window, but I'm going out in the pitch black?"

"At least you won't be able to look down."

"Can you please take this seriously."

"I am taking it seriously."

"Well, I'm not going out the window. I can't <u>look</u> out the window."

"It's the only way out, so what's your alternative?"

He sat on my mattress and I sat on the chair. It was growing dark. I waved a hand in front of a light panel, and the alcove was infused with a soft yellow glow. The Colonists have started to upgrade their solar powered electricity system, but it's still pretty rubbish.

Eventually I sighed. "OK," I said. "What do I need to do?"

We waited till Aggie's parents got back. Plaxys looked hard at Orlando but didn't say anything, and the two of them walked to their bedroom as normal.

Earlier on, I had spilt some water on my sheets, accidentally-on-purpose. Aggie tutted but brought me new ones without fuss. I don't think she wanted to embarrass me in front of Orlando. I said I'd hang the wet ones out the window to dry, which is normally what we do with my bedding when we need to air it. But once Aggie had gone to sleep, we tore the new sheet carefully into strips and then tied them together with what we hoped would be strong knots. We tied one end around the washbasin in my shower room, the only thing we could find which was firmly fixed, apart from the toilet which would have been just too gross.

Then we trailed the sheet-rope out of the window.

I stood on a chair and straddled one leg over the sill, holding on to the rope with one hand and the window frame with the other.

"Now swing your other leg over and rest on your stomach on the window frame."

But I couldn't do it. The foot still on the chair and the attached leg began to shake uncontrollably, so I had to swing my other one back inside. I stood with my back to the wall, gulping air, my heart rate galloping out of control.

"I can't! I just can't do this. And it's pointless anyway. We'll never disrupt The Hive Mind enough—"

"It's OK." Orlando made to hug me. For once I gave into it and suddenly being in his arms felt so welcome. I put my arms around him and my head on his shoulder. "Listen to me. You can do this. And

you've got a plan. A good plan." He pressed his cheek against mine and then gently pushed me away. "Come on. Let's try it a different way."

We hauled the rope in and this time he tied it around my waist.

"Now look, you've got to trust yourself. You can't fall. The knots are strong. The rope won't break. OK?"

"OK."

I got up onto the chair again. I moved the wide loop of slack rope to one side, so I wouldn't foul it, then slid one leg over. I held tightly to the rope and the window frame, and leaning right onto the sill, I slipped my other leg around. I kept my body weight forward so that my dangling legs wouldn't drag me over. My chest pressed into the window frame so I could hardly breathe.

"You're doing great, Cara. Now, while keeping hold of the rope, let go of the window ledge."

But I couldn't move.

"Come on, Cara. You've got to let go of the window frame."

"I'll fall."

"You won't fall."

I was back on the Rocket Tree.

I was back on the bridge.

I was back everywhere else in between.

But then I heard a voice.

Let go, Cara.

And crazily, it wasn't Orlando talking.

It was Tom.

It's OK. You'll be fine.

I can't explain it. I certainly didn't try. And when Orlando saw my face awash with tears, he stepped forward to pull me back in. But this was the moment I let go of the window sill, and he began to pay out the sheet-rope.

It was a still night, and I went down without swaying, straight down like a plumb line, parallel to the drainpipe which ran four feet from me all the way to the ground. Down, past the third floor and second floor windows. The apartments were dark as I drifted past. I just hoped there was no one inside looking out.

I walked down the wall like I was abseiling, but the knotted sheet still cut into my middle, and my arms ached with holding my weight on the rope.

And then, still one floor up, the rope came to an abrupt end. It was a dark night, a quarter moon, and I could only vaguely see the ground ten, maybe fifteen feet below me. I would have to rip up the other sheet to lengthen it.

I started back up, but it was much harder than I'd thought. I simply didn't have the upper body strength for it. But once Orlando saw me inching my way, he began to pull on the rope as well. Eventually I gave up even trying, and he pretty much hauled me up as a dead weight. I rolled over the top of the window sill and fell on top of him with a crash.

—What's going on? Aggie thought to me before she was even round the corner. But once she saw me lying on top of Orlando in the near darkness, she scuttled away again, chuckling. —Sorry, sorry. I'll leave you two lovers alone.

I rolled off him, and we lay in silent, quivering, hysterics. I unhitched the sheet-rope and stowed it under my mattress. Aggie wasn't the most organised, so I was counting on her forgetting about the extra sheet at least until next week.

We lay there together in the dark, surprisingly companionably. I thought it would be awkward. But it wasn't. At least not for me. I was exhausted and fell asleep, and when I woke up, I had my arm across his chest. Orlando was awake already and watching me. He gave me a smile.

When Crilloo turned up to take him back, I threw my arms around Orlando and gave him a kiss on the lips. I was doing it for Aggie's benefit, but it felt surprisingly nice, Orlando's lips so soft against mine.

I felt a crackle of electricity. I really did.

It was a relief on so many levels.

I kissed him again. For longer this time.

And when I pulled away, he was blushing to his core.

"Listen," he started to say, but I silenced him with a finger against his lips.

"Tell me when you see me again."

And then he was gone, and I was left alone in the apartment with Aggie. She pumped me for details about my night but became more tactful when I wasn't forthcoming.

—You look tired, Cara, she said. —You'd better have a nap.

I lay on my mattress, and for a while I thought about Orlando. And Brandon. And Verinder. And everyone else.

Everything was swirling around for a while.

But eventually I did fall asleep. And when I did, it wasn't a person I dreamt of.

It was freedom.

Part 13: The Day Of Sharing

□ | □ □ | ⼗

[2.50]

I am running.

Through the night.

All around me, Colonists lie on the ground. Clutching their heads, like we clutched ours.

No one stops me.

No one can touch me.

I run on.

Alone.

Earlier that day. Morning.

—*I'm so excited, Cara.*

Aggie had bounded into my alcove.

—*It's The Day Of Sharing.*

"I know." *I pretended to rub sleep from my eyes and sat up. I'd been awake for the last two hours, going over and over my escape plan.*

—*Come on. We've got so much to do.*

"I'm coming— aaah! Stop tickling me!"

—*It's The Day Of Sharing! Get up, Lazy! We need to put up the last of the decorations.*

Aggie slipped back out of the alcove. I could have sworn she was dancing a jig.

"Seriously, Aggie," *I said, when I joined her in the living room.* "You can't put this up. It's so tacky." *I indicated a gold spray-painted bunch of grapes.*

—*That one's my favourite.*

She grabbed it from me, giving me a friendly nudge out of the way and stapled the stalk to the wall. Then stepped back to admire the effect.

"And Plaxys and Schektl are definitely OK with all this?" *The once chic, if bland, cream-walled interior had become a riot of tinsel and baubles.*

—*Yeah, Aggie thought breezily, as she took out a silver spray can. She'd recently started using slangier words and expressions in her thoughts. —My folks aren't coming back till late afternoon. There's lots of Administration to do on The Day Of Sharing.*

I snorted. "I bet."

—What, Cara?

"Well, when my parents said they had lots of work in the run up to Christmas, it was always code for going to parties."

—Really? Aggie stood frozen for a moment, the spray can poised, as she processed the idea. Her laughter filled my mind. —Really? You know, I'd never thought they might be having fun.

She chuckled and turned to the wall.

"Aggie, no—!"

Aggie looked up from the wavy two-metre-long stripe she'd just sprayed. —What is it, Cara?

"It's just – you know… Really?"

—It's artistic, Cara. It's cool.

I laughed. "I'll leave you to it," I said. "I need to go to the toilet."

I walked across the room to my alcove. The barrier was down as it always was now when it was just the two of us. In my head I went over my list again. The sheet-rope, of course, which I still needed to lengthen but I'd have time to do that when Aggie was having her afternoon nap:

—Uploading will be very tiring, she'd said.

I had my spare pillowcase in which I'd stowed some food and a bottle of water (I'd learned from my last escape attempt); plus, my two journals. Both rope and pillowcase were under my mattress. This journal was stuffed inside it as usual.

Having the pillowcase and seeing the decorations made it feel like Christmas. Christmas when I was little, and Tom had still been alive. On the night of Christmas Eve, we'd put out our pillowcase stockings and the mince pie and sherry for Santa. But before that, the interminable waiting of Christmas Eve daytime.

I heard steps behind me. Aggie was walking over, a spray can in each hand.

"Oh no."

—You've got to have your alcove decorated, said Aggie, spraying a wide purple arc on the wall and across the window.

"Not on the glass, Aggie! Your parents'll kill you."

—It's cool. Come on.

Aggie tossed me the silver spray can.

I rolled my eyes, then sprayed a modest star on the door to the bathroom. Actually, it was quite fun.

—Come on, Cara. You need to get into it.

And with that, Aggie grabbed the can back from me, held both at arms' length and started spinning and spraying a fine mist in all directions.

"Stop!" I yelled, laughing, throwing myself into the shower room to escape it.

—I'm getting dizzy. Oh! Sorry, Cara.

Cautiously I opened the door. Aggie was stood frozen, spray cans in hand, looking – if it was at all possible – embarrassed. The whole alcove bore a hideous dusting of silver and purple, with great gouts of colour on the walls and any other surface which the cans had been closer to. But that wasn't why Aggie was acting so sheepish. She'd collided with the box by my bedside and knocked my carafe of water all over the mattress.

—Sorry, Cara.

"I did say, be careful."

—I'll clear it up. Aggie picked up the unbroken carafe and placed it safely in a corner. —I'll take the mattress to the kitchen. It'll dry there, it's so warm—

"No!" My stomach lurched. What if she were to find my secret notebook? What if she were to read it? "I can do it."

—It's my fault, Cara.

Plaxys would kill me for sure. I rushed over. "Seriously I can—"

—I've got it, Cara. I can manage. Oh! What's this?

My notebook.

Remained hidden.

Aggie had lifted the mattress into the air like it was a cushion, and beneath it she saw the knotted sheet and pillowcase.

I stood there, frozen. My heart was banging so hard that it actually hurt.

Aggie carefully propped the mattress against the gaudily sprayed wall, knelt down and picked up the sheets and the pillowcase. She turned slowly to face me. —What are these, Cara?

I couldn't speak. I should have made something up. But my mouth was like sandpaper.

—Are you trying to run away?

Aggie's thoughts were in my head. So soft. Almost a whisper. It was not anger I could hear, just crushing disappointment.

But before I could answer, there was a bang as the front door opened and closed, and Aggie's parents burst in. Aggie seemed as surprised as I was.

—Thank goodness you're safe!

—Why isn't the barrier up?

Aggie blinked at her mother. —We never do that during the day anymore. You know that.

Her voice was emotionless. She didn't look at me.

—Cara needs to be locked away, as a precaution.

—Why? What's happened?

—A human has been found trying to escape. He had a stash of weapons. They think he was going to kill his owner before escaping tonight, while everyone is distracted on The Day Of Sharing.

—But what's that got to do with us, Aggie asked.

—It's the human, Orlando, that spent the night here.

"What? No! He would never hurt anyone—"

I cringed as Plaxys zapped me.

—How dare you speak without permission.

"I'm sorry, but what weapons could he have even had?"

—He had an axe in his possession.

Aggie shot me a glance.

"No! Orlando wouldn't hurt a fly."

—Did he talk to you about escaping? Plaxys demanded.

—Perhaps you two were thinking of running away together? Asked Schektl.

"No—"

—What's that in your hands, Aggie?

To my horror I saw that Aggie was still holding the sheet-rope. My chest was so tight that even a shallow breath was impossible.

—It's a decoration, said Aggie calmly. —Cara made it so she could join in with The Day Of Sharing celebrations. Get the stapler, Cara.

I looked at her blankly.

—Get the stapler.

In a daze, I went to retrieve it from the dining room table, stumbled back to my alcove and handed it to her.

—Look.

Aggie's voice was sweet in our heads. She trailed the sheet-rope along the wall, stapling it at intervals so it draped like a ragged paper chain.

—Oh… Well, thank you, Schektl said. —It's… lovely.

—And look.

Aggie held up my pillowcase of food, and my eyes widened. Aggie stared at me pointedly then back to her parents. —Cara told me they used to celebrate something called Christmas, where they put out a pillowcase or a stocking. So, I thought I'd do the same thing for her on The Day Of Sharing.

—Very thoughtful dear, said her father. —But now your pet has to be locked back into its alcove. The Inquisitors will need to talk to it tomorrow about this whole Orlando thing.

"What's happening to him?"

—It has been taken for questioning.

"But then they'll let him go, won't they?"

Schektl tipped his head to one side as though he was surprised. —Let it go? Of course not. After interrogation it will be sent for immediate termination.

"What? No! NO! You can't do that!"

—It was intending to kill a Colonist.

"No, he wasn't. He was going to use the axe—" *I broke off. I realised they were all staring at me.*

—For what? Plaxys asked suspiciously.

"I… I don't know. Please don't hurt him."

—He broke the rules and will be punished. Do you understand?

I looked down at the floor.

—DO YOU?

Aggie's mother's voice roared in my head.

I nodded.

—Well, you better had. No more chances.

"I know, I know—"

—Because if you step out of line again you know where you're headed don't you? LOOK AT ME!

I forced myself to meet her gaze.

—Although a female your age would normally go for breeding there is simply no point if they're trouble. And you've been so much trouble. You would go for immediate Harvesting. In fact, if you step out of line again, I'll take you to the slaughterhouse myself.

After Aggie's parents had gone back to work, we just sat there, on opposite sides of the barrier. Aggie had torn down my sheet-rope from the wall and stuffed it down the garbage chute along with my pillowcase of hoarded food.

—Did you ever like me, Cara?

"Of course, I did. I do—"

—Would you have tried to kill me too?

"No! Of course not, and Orlando—"

—Don't mention his name. You tricked me.

Silence again. Then,

—Do you think Colonists are stupid, Cara?

Aggie's voice was flat, the sparkle and the excitement gone from it. There wasn't even disappointment now. That had turned to a cold anger.

—Do you think I am stupid?

"No, of course not."

—We have brains with ten times the density of neurons that humans do. And we will soon be connected into an almost infinite resource of knowledge.

"I know."

—THEN WHY DID YOU TREAT ME LIKE A FOOL?

Aggie shouted so loud I almost fell off my chair.

—Why did you let me believe that you liked me, Cara?

"I do like you, Aggie—"

—I did everything for you. I got you special food. I gave you a bracelet. Your journal. I even found Orlando for you. How do you think that felt?

"What? I don't understand."

Aggie was on her feet now, gesticulating. —How do you think it felt finding a lover for you when I... I...

I looked at her bewildered. "Aggie, I don't understand."

—I don't understand, *Aggie sneered in my head.* —Of course, you don't. Because you're only human with your limited intelligence. You just used me. Like all humans do. You're vermin. I wanted to believe differently. But I see the truth now. Humans will lie and steal to get whatever they want.

"All I wanted was freedom."

—And what is freedom? There's no such thing. Most humans had the illusion of freedom but really just did what they were told.

"That's not true."

—And if they didn't, they would get put in prison or be killed.

"That's not true!"

—And how did you treat every other species on the planet, Cara? Humans are just animals, yet they treated all other species like dirt. Like playthings. You humans took everything you wanted and destroyed the environment. I used to feel sorry for you, but our scientists are right. You have no culture or creativity – no higher feeling. You can't have, or you wouldn't have treated animals the way you did. You wouldn't have treated each other the way you did. I'm so glad we came to your planet because we liberated it from you.

"And took it for yourselves."

—Yes, Cara. It's ours now. But we've saved it. From you and your kind.

"Why do you hate humans so much?"

—Not all humans, Cara. Just you.

I glared at her but she stared back defiantly.

—The moment the Inquisitors have finished their questioning, I'm getting rid of you.

My mouth fell open. "What? But I thought... Why did you protect me from your parents earlier then?"

—I've changed my mind, Cara. I'm bored of you. I don't want you here anymore.

"Aggie, wait. Aggie—!"

But she'd already walked away.

* * *

I lay on the bare, damp mattress and cried all afternoon.

Aggie had stripped the bed, so there was no hope of making another rope. My food stash was gone. My orange journal lay beyond the barrier on the dining room table. Only my secret journal remained, still concealed within the mattress.

I lay and sobbed for Orlando, wondering what was going to happen to him; worrying that something terrible already had. And I sobbed for myself.

I'd never seen Aggie like this. I didn't doubt for a moment that she would go through with her threat and get rid of me. Oh, why did I even try to escape in the first place? I had a cushy life. Aggie was kind to me. And I'd thrown it all away.

I sobbed until evening was drawing in. I was hungry, but I knew no food would be forthcoming. Aggie had made it clear I was being punished. Humiliated until the end.

I felt so hungry I was sure I was going to throw up.

I went to the toilet and knelt down and retched, but nothing came out.

I just stared into the darkening water of the bowl.

It was then, still on my knees in the tiny shower room, as I was turning and pushing open the door to leave, that I saw it, almost lost in the gloaming.

I'd scoured the whole apartment for anything to do with her, and here it was at last.

Down on the skirting, only visible at floor level, hidden normally by the waste pipe from the toilet, scratched into the paint in tiny writing:

> *I am Aggie*
> *Hiding from the monsters*
> *Day III*

And stuck there with a blob of dried chewing gum, was a lock of fine, blonde hair.

I blinked.

I am Aggie.

Agneta. Aggie.

As I sat back on my haunches, everything fell into place.

I saw in my mind how it must have been.

How Agneta had been staying here with her cousin, Alice. She was over from Sweden? Or probably just Leeds or Manchester since she was writing in English. But a special visit, for a week maybe, so that her uncle and aunt had made up a little sleeping area for her in the alcove, the area they normally used for exercise.

That fateful morning, Alice would have been at school just like I had been; her parents at work. But Agneta was in the apartment.

Maybe she'd had a lie in.

When the Colonists arrived perhaps their Thought Field wasn't up, or the atmospheric pheromone level wasn't yet high enough. Whatever, when she saw them, she saw them as they truly were and was terrified.

She hid from them in the little shower room.

Hid there all day. Petrified they would find her.

Then, having waited anxiously for the newly arrived Colonist family to get to sleep, Agneta must have crept out in the middle of the night.

She would have tried the front door, which was locked with the Colonists' invisible tech.

Her heart would have sunk when she realised she was trapped.

On the second night she took more risks. Did a stealthy tour of the apartment, looking for food.

Just like I did on Hampstead Heath.

But found nothing.

She had to lie low one more day in that bathroom, as the hunger started to gnaw.

And now, desperate on the third night, she was out again, looking for anything, even scraps from the Colonists' meal.

She thought she'd been quiet, but when she was halfway across the living room, the lights flicked on, and she saw a flame-haired girl standing before her, a Colonist in human form.

Agneta walked towards her. "I don't understand what's going on. I saw monsters. What's happening?"

—I won't hurt you.

"What's your name?"

—I'm Mlaxet. What's yours?

"I'm Agneta. But you can call me Aggie."

—You're so pretty. And your hair is beautiful.

"I like yours too. But what's happening? I can hear you but you're not speaking. Where's Alice?"

—Can I stroke your hair?

As Mlaxet stepped out of the shadows, so dazzled was she with Agneta's beauty, that her mask slipped, and she revealed her true form. Agneta screamed, and Mlaxet was so startled that she screamed too; her super-strong cry so loud, that it woke the apartment, and crushed Agneta's mind in an instant.

She caught Agneta as she fell; but she was already dead. She lay in Mlaxet's arms, the dead girl's blonde hair cascading over them both.

She was so overwhelmed with grief at what she'd done that she took the girl's name.

Mlaxet became Aggie.

And in doing so, she took the only thing Agneta had left: her identity.

It only took a moment for me to see the truth.

A version of it anyway.

The likely – or at least possible – events flashing through my mind.

"Oh, Agneta," I said out loud. "I'm so sorry."

I reached down and tugged the lock of hair free from the skirting board.

Agneta's beautiful hair.

I stumbled back out into the twilight of my room, to the window, to catch the last glow of evening on the golden strands. So fine, so delicate in my fingers.

Though the hair was Agneta's, it was someone else I was thinking of.

My best friend.

And as I stroked the strands, I realised she was there.

Tess was with me in the room.

Jo as well.

Orlando and Brandon and Pip. Verinder and Ada too.

Hey, Peepers, said Verinder.

"I'm so sorry I let you all down," I sobbed to them, whirling around, stroking the hair. "You all helped me so much, and I've done nothing for you."

You saved me, said Ada.

"I didn't. I abandoned you."

But this way we've got a chance, said Brandon. You can get help.

You're a survivor, said Tess reaching out and touching my face with her hair.

And you've got a plan, said Orlando. A good plan.

Pip gave me a thumbs-up.

"I've got a plan," I said out loud, exchanging a smile with Jo.

The hair caressed my cheek one last time; then I let my hand fall.

I opened my eyes.

I was alone.

Everyone I loved had been taken from me.

But I realised now, I hadn't let them down.

I still had my plan. And I was not going to let Them win.

Aggie thought she had me backed into a corner, but that's when animals are most dangerous.

The Colonists had turned me into an animal.

Well, now, They were going to hear me roar.

□ ' □ ⊔ □

[2.51]

By the time her parents got back, it was properly dark outside, and there was only an hour to go until The Upload.

They immediately set to work to get the place organised. Each of them needed to be in a separate room, so their thoughts would not interfere with each other. Aggie insisted that she wanted to be near me and do The Upload in the sitting room.

Plaxys began to argue but Schektl overruled her. They had been running late from work and he didn't want a long discussion. —It is acceptable, *he said.* —So long as the barrier to the alcove is in place.

They went to the bedrooms to prepare.

"Why did you say that?" I hissed at Aggie as she pulled over a chair and sat where I could see her.

—I want you to understand what a truly superior species looks like. I want you to be put in your place.

"Get lost. Colonists just torture and kill."

—Unlike humans?

"Sure. We do it too. But then that makes you the same as us."

—Be quiet!

She gave me a sharp buzz to the head to silence me. —I need to collect my thoughts for The Upload. So, sit there like the dumb animal you are.

My head was ringing but I knew what I needed to do to get my plan rolling. "Dumb? You're the ones who are dumb. Since I've known you, I've written an entire journal. I haven't seen you write or read one thing. I don't even believe you <u>can</u> read."

—What are you talking about? I've read your journal. Your worthless pile of paper—

—AGGIE, GET READY.

We could both hear her father clearly from the other room.

—PLEASE STOP YOUR CHATTING. THE TIME OF UPLOAD IS ALMOST UPON US. PREPARE.

"Worthless? I spent ages writing it. It's really long. There's so much in it—"

—Hah! So much.

Aggie got out of her chair and grabbed the orange notebook from the dining table and, before my very eyes, started rifling through the pages. She got to the end and threw it to the floor, laughing in my head.

—I reread the whole thing just then. <u>In ten seconds</u>. That is how extraordinary we are, Cara. That is how superior we are to your worthless lying selves. And now I have all your pathetic writing here.

Aggie stabbed a finger at her head.

—*I will upload your words, and then The Hive Mind can confirm quite how feeble your species is.*

—*AGGIE. Her father's thoughts were urgent now.* —*SIT AND PREPARE.*

—*I'm ready.*

Aggie sat back in her chair.

On the wall, the clock ticked to one minute before midnight.

Suddenly she shot me a glance. —*And why do I even bother cloaking my true body from you?*

I gasped as Aggie shimmered, and the huge stag beetle appeared again, her antennae waving, one of her legs pointing in my direction.

—*I am beautiful whether you recognise it or not.*

—*IT IS TIME. Aggie's father's voice again. The clock struck midnight.* —*THE UPLOAD IS BEGINNING.*

Suddenly, all around stag-beetle-Aggie, the normally dim solar lights grew in brightness as her neural energy filled the room, and she connected to The Hive Mind.

—*You see, Cara, Aggie called to me triumphantly. Her head was wreathed in tiny lights.* —*You see how wondrous the Colonists are? Even as my thoughts are uploading, I can still communicate with you.*

—*HALFWAY THROUGH, Schektl called.*

—*But you sit there with your mouth agape. You, who cannot even communicate telepathically. You are in such awe that you can't even speak.*

—*WE ARE UPLOADED. WE ARE ONE.*

The lights surged in the apartment until it was bright white and Aggie sat forward, a crown of stars about her forehead.

—*Behold me, Cara. I am connected to The Hive Mind. We are all one. Now tell me that humans are of any significance.*

It was then that I started to laugh.

I stood up and pointed at Aggie through the clear barrier between us.

"You fool! You stupid fool. You uploaded my journal, didn't you?"

—*Of course.*

The stag beetle squeezed out of her chair and approached the barrier. Her tone was lofty. —Your pathetic writings confirm once and for all your inferiority.

"You don't understand, you mega-brained bug! You've just infected the whole of your precious Hive Mind."

—What are you talking about? Your journal is factual.

"Yeah, that's the thing!"

That was the thing.

That was the plan.

It hadn't even been a plan at first. Just Jo's words ringing in my mind.

"And if they catch you, don't let them break you. I don't mean be a hero, just hold something back of yourself – of us – even if it's something tiny. Keep something human."

Keep something human.

A certainty I'd clung to from the moment I started living here, that however much they pretended to care for me, I wouldn't reveal all of myself to them. That there would be something I wouldn't let the Colonists take from me. That I would hold something back, something human, forever locked in my heart where they couldn't reach it.

You see, from the moment Aggie brought me home, I knew I would never tell her the real names of my friends or family. Slaves weren't allowed their own names. Well, I wasn't going to give Them ours.

The names I used instead weren't random, though. Far from it.

But I would keep the real ones hidden.

Even from you, reader.

They're mine.

It wasn't meant to be anything more than a tiny act of resistance, though. Until that day down by the lake in Kenwood, with Orlando.

Standing before him, bubbling over with excitement at the idea that had suddenly come to me.

That was when it turned into a plan.

That's when resistance turned into rebellion.

"Yeah, that's the thing!" I said to him. "The Mantra says we're not creative, but I'd changed the names of the people in my journal right

from the start. The names of my friends. Every living person in fact, apart from me. I mean, I probably should have changed my name too…"

"You changed names. Wow. What a rebel—"

"No, listen you idiot. I changed all the names to characters from my favourite books – what's better evidence of human creativity than that? I thought it could be like the way the Brontës used pen names. I gave all my friends pseudonyms in my journal. Like Tess – as in Of The D'Urbervilles – for the most beautiful girl, really kind and sweet, you know—"

"Oh yeah. Actually, I can see that."

And I told him some of the others.

How Brandon was named after the passionate, brave and loyal colonel in Sense and Sensibility.

And Jo was from Little Women, who's probably more like me to be honest, but she's one of my favourite characters, so had to be used for one of my best friends.

And many more besides.

"So, that's why Aggie thinks I'm called Orlando… Who is Orlando anyway?"

"It's a book by Virginia Woolf. About a man who becomes a woman and lives for centuries."

"Really? That's what you went for?" Then he shrugged. "Actually, that's kind of cool. I like it."

"And 'Orlando' is way better than your real name."

"Way better."

"Anyway, Aggie's read my journal so if I tell her what I've done just as she's completing The Upload, then recognition of all that human creativity will get inside The Hive Mind. Would that be enough to send it into meltdown do you think?"

We were right by the lake. Orlando found a stone and skimmed it one, two, three skips over the surface of the water. Then he turned and looked at me.

"It could definitely work. I think you might just be a genius."

"Thank you, Orlando," I said, smiling.

I was back in the alcove.

—What are you saying? screamed Aggie. —What have you done? I'm in so much pain.

"Every name in that journal is a character from a book."

—What book?

"Not one book. Loads of books. Of novels. Fabulous, fantastic, fictional—"

—Shut up.

"With plots and twists and turns and laughter and tears—"

—I said, shut up!

"And you only went and uploaded it all into your precious Hive Mind—"

—It's not true!

There was a banging of the doors to the bedrooms. Moments later, Aggie's parents burst into the living room, also in their stag beetle form.

—What's going on?

—Aggie, what's happened?

I was laughing at them all. "Tell them what you've done, Aggie."

—I don't understand—

—Aggie, what's she talking about? Plaxys demanded.

"Aggie's gone and uploaded the character names from all my favourite stories into your collective consciousness. Not much maybe, but each one represents hundreds of pages of human creativity. All those hints as to how fabulously intelligent, humans really are. Each one a lovely little seed of doubt—"

—Disconnect from The Hive Mind, Aggie. Disconnect!

"It's too late—"

—Aggie!

"You can't suppress us. Because we are human. We are inventive. We are wonderful—"

—I don't understand, Aggie moaned. —My head hurts.

But even as Aggie spoke, the lights in the apartment flickered and dimmed to a bare glow.

—No! I heard Schektl shout. And then he groaned in pain.

—What's happening? Aggie screamed.

"The Hive Mind is trying to defend itself against the contamination, isn't it? Tell her!"

—Make it stop! shrieked Plaxys.

The barrier to the room disappeared. Aggie and her parents fell to the ground, their antennae twitching in all directions. I went over to them, staring down dispassionately as they squirmed on the floor.

"You're right, Aggie. You are better than me. But you reminded me of something. Something that maybe I'd never properly understood before. That humans are just like every other animal on this planet. That we're all connected. But now we are animals too, you'll never stop us."

I grabbed the secret journal from inside the mattress and the orange one from the floor and stuffed them both into the back pockets of my joggers.

There was no way I was leaving them.

Because they're books, you see?

Pure creation.

The one thing no one can ever take from us, that the Colonists can never understand, and that one day will help us defeat Them.

I ran to the window. I had no rope, and no sheet to make one with, so I just did what I had to do. I swung one leg out, then the other, and perched for a moment on the sill. Ready to push off now, to freedom or certain death. But I was OK with either. I was just done with being someone's pet.

I thought of Orlando and Tom and sprang in the dark for the drainpipe.

And you know what, reader?

I caught it – just – and half squirmed, half slid all the way to the ground.

I stopped for a moment at the bottom.

Gasping for breath.

Not quite believing I was free.

But only for a moment.

And then I ran into the night.

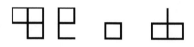

Part 14: North

[2.52]

It's starting to get light.

I've run pretty much all night.

OK, reader, not exactly run. But definitely jogged. A lot.

I'm at a disused service station at the moment. Resting before the final push. Or however many pushes I need before I reach safety.

I'm not sure exactly where I am, but I know it's north. Jo taught me the pole star ages ago, and I followed that for a bit until it got cloudy. But by then I'd picked up some road signs for the A1. Even I know, if I follow that, I'll be heading in the right direction.

I've only seen a handful of Colonists so far.

It's been dark, of course, but I've also been careful. Keeping low and under cover where I can. Where I have seen them, they've been lying on the ground, uncloaked and disorientated. Not in agony like Aggie and her family were, but definitely not normal. So, whatever I did is still working. But I don't know for how long, so I do need to get moving again soon.

I've been holed up at the service station for nearly an hour now.

I'd had a tiny glimmer of hope that there might even be food inside; but, of course, the shelves of what had once been the minimart were as empty as the kitchens of those fancy houses near Kenwood.

Seeing all those empty fridge racks, which would once have been piled high with microwaveable pasties, did make my stomach growl.

I mean, I'd hardly eaten the previous day.

And finding food had been one of the things which had worried me most about escape. After all, my time on Hampstead Heath had not gone well, and whatever happens, I'm not going after any more rabbits.

I was beginning to feel quite downhearted.

Until, that is, I remembered the bracelet on my wrist that Aggie had given me.

The beads of it glowing in the first rays of dawn,
Every colourful one of them made of sugar.
I've had a blue one and a green one so far.
They're like the best boiled sweets ever.

And I know that may not sound particularly amazing, but in the circumstances, it really is.

Water I'm fine with. At the moment anyway. There was a brief shower of rain last night.

It's been quite drizzly recently.

Is it always a wet July after a nice June?

Is that a thing?

Who knows. But it meant I had water. Fresh and clean even if I had to gulp it from puddles.

And whatever clouds there had been went soon enough. Leaving just me and the stars. I mean, it couldn't have been better escaping weather.

So anyway, I'm stopped here at this service station to make these last few entries in my journal. These might well be my last words to you, reader. The pencil I'd found tucked into the wire spiral of this notebook is down to a stub. Plus, I need to be more careful with my books. They've slipped out of the loose back pockets of my joggers once already.

I'm so clumsy.

But I'm here.

I've escaped.

And that's more impressive than I thought I was capable of. So, that's worth something.

Maybe everything.

After all, even if I do make it to Cambridge I don't know what I'm going to find there. Maybe the rebellion's already been crushed and Cambridge is no more than rubble. Or maybe humans have found a way and are fighting back.

Well, if we are, I hope we do it better this time.

I hope if we do somehow end up back on top, that we find a way to make it work for all of us on the planet, not just a few.

I'm scared, reader, I won't lie.

But the morning that's taking shape around me is beautiful. The rain has properly gone and the sky is becoming a delicate pale blue, the start of a lovely summer's day. I can hear the shrill call of birds, and when I look up there are swallows and swifts darting above me. There's a coolness in the air, but I know it's going to be hot later on. I'm not sure I'm going to survive it, but today is going to be spectacular, reader.

Spectacular.

I need to go.

Before whatever disruption I've caused wears off.

I need to make as much progress as I can while the Colonists' Thought Field is down, while they're lying on the floor, no better than insects.

I mustn't say that. It's not right. Insects are cool.

Cows, pigs, rabbits, birds, fish: they're all awesome.

They're as good as us.

I understand that properly now.

It's what Tess had been telling me for ages. Orlando too. I'd just been too dumb to understand it.

That being called an animal is actually a compliment.

Especially given how badly humans used to treat the planet.

But Colonists: they're no better than we were.

And it's only now that I finally I understand what The Mantra should have been all along:

> *Colonists are greedy.*
> *Colonists are cruel.*
> *Just like humans used to be.*
> *Animals are intelligent.*
> *Animals are resourceful.*
> *I'm proud to be an animal too.*

We're all animals now.

Me and Orlando and Tess and Verinder.

And that little bunny I couldn't kill.

I'm so glad I didn't.

We're all in it together.

Except for the Colonists. They can go to Hell.

I guess this is goodbye, reader. At least for a while. Thanks for being there.

I'll try and write again soon.

And maybe when I do, some of the things I've found so confusing about myself will make a bit more sense.

But for now, it's time to start running again.

Running with the hope of getting to freedom and defeating the Colonists. Hoping that one day, I'll free Tess and Jo and Ada. And maybe even Orlando and Brandon and Verinder too, if they're still alive.

Please let them be.

All of them.

Time to go. But before I do, reader, there was one last thing I wanted to share with you. The final exchange with Aggie, which is still ringing in my mind.

She was flailing on the ground, a pincer raised towards me.

—*You can't leave me, Cara. I own you.*

"*You don't own me. No one owns someone else. I'm free.*"

—*So, you're going to just abandon me then? Like you did all your friends? You're mean and selfish and you left them behind.*

I reeled at her words. But then I felt the strands of Agneta's hair in my pocket, and for a moment my friends were alongside me once more.

"*No. I didn't.*"

—*You're mine, if I say you're mine! I'm a Colonist. I can stop you, you know.*

I stared at her pitiful writhing.

"*Good luck with that.*"

Her voice became wheedling in my head. —*But I cared for you. I'm your Aggie.*

"*You're not my Aggie. You're Mlaxet. I know what happened with Agneta. You took everything from her. Even her name. Well, I won't let you do that to me.*

I straddled the window frame, one leg in, one leg out.

—*Don't go, Cara!* she screamed in my head in agony. *And I could have sworn, through the white noise of her pain, there was the sound of her sobbing.* —*You can't leave me.*

"*Just watch.*"

—*But I love you, Cara.*

"*What?*" I was so astonished I almost fell out of the window. "WHAT? You don't *love* me. I'm your *pet*. You thought you owned me, that's all. But not anymore."

—Cara, please don't go. I really do love you.

I gripped the window frame to steady myself.

—Please stay. *Carabel!*

I was bracing myself for the jump into the darkness but couldn't help turning one last time, repulsed at the sound of Aggie using my full name, fury rising in me like a molten tide.

—Carabel, I feel—

"I don't care what you feel! Only my family call me by that name and you're not my family! And don't think about taking it for yourself after I'm gone, like you did with Agneta. In fact," I said in sudden inspiration, my final act of defiance, to reclaim the one thing Aggie had left of me. "From now on, I have a new name."

I was going to be someone different, give myself a new name just like I'd given all those character names to my friends. And there was only one person it could be, representing all the amazing writers and artists and *everyone* who had fought against the odds and yet prevailed. There was only one name I would ever want to wear, reader, as a badge of deep, deep pride; the badge Miss Temple had once given me.

But I wouldn't be a character.

I was in charge of what happened to me.

"I hope we never meet again, Mlaxet, but if we do, you better remember not to call me Cara." I looked forward, readying myself again for the dizzying leap. "I'm not Carabel but *Currer Bell* and I'm the author of my destiny now."

—Cara—

"I'm not Cara anymore," I repeated, to myself as much as to her. "From now on, I'm Charlotte Brontë."

Closing Remarks

Following the sabotage perpetrated by the human property of Schektl 64972 and Plaxys 8251 a full Inquisition was launched.

The damage to The Hive Mind was so severe it took nearly 3 Earth Days to correct. The insidious nature of the assault on the collective consciousness was a clear act of neuroterrorism. It being inconceivable that a human could have formulated such a sophisticated attack without Colonist assistance, the Inquisition Committee concluded without need of trial that Schektl 64972 and Plaxys 8251 had led a conspiracy. At time of writing, they await scheduling for termination.

Their progeny, Mlaxet 2328, being pre-maturity and hence too young to be treated a co-conspirator, was instead interrogated to ascertain loyalty to the Colonist cause. The Inquisition Committee concluded that Mlaxet 2328 is Hive Aligned, and she has willingly offered her services to hunt down the dangerous runaway. She is currently receiving hospital attention for the neuroassault that the human caused.

At the time of writing the runaway human Charlotte Brontë, also known as Carabel Caffarelli, is regretfully still at large in the vicinity of 13th State, 20th City [Cambridge].

WARNING: THIS HUMAN IS EXTREMELY DANGEROUS. IF SIGHTED ALERT THE AUTHORITIES BUT DO NOT APPROACH HER.

ABOVE ALL DO NOT BELIEVE A WORD SHE SAYS.

Translation and collation of Colonist archive material by
'A'EP, UdNN

If you've enjoyed this book, do you think you might be able to leave me a review or rating on Amazon and Goodreads? *Now We Are Animals* took me seven years to write, and I had to set up my own imprint to get it published, so I would love to know what you thought of it. A review only takes a few minutes and a rating just a few seconds. Whether the verdict is 'good', 'bad' or just *'meh'*, it will help new readers find my work and will also encourage me to write the remaining books in this series.

Thanks so much in advance: it really does mean more than I can say.

And if you *did* enjoy this book you can keep up to date with news about my writing, upcoming releases, and receive exclusive extracts and short stories by joining my Readers' Club at **rpnathan.com**

Cara's story will continue in:

NOW WE ARE FREE

Cara has evaded the Colonists and made her way to Cambridge. Along the way she makes new allies; but then has to abandon them. In Cambridge she is treated like a celebrity, but all Cara wants is to rescue her friends. When the leader of the Rebels announces a daring rescue attempt, she gets the chance…

Yet all the while she is being hunted by Aggie and the Colonists. They are determined to recapture her and break the resistance movement once and for all.

The thrilling 2nd book in THE COLONISTS series

AUTHOR'S NOTE

I really hope you enjoyed spotting the various literary easter eggs in this novel, dear reader. Cara uses character names from famous books and plays for people she knows. The chosen works are some of her favourites and – since our tastes definitely coincide here – my favourites too.

They are books I have loved reading and I hope this novel inspires you to try a few of them yourself. Don't worry if some of the language seems a bit 'olde-worlde', or if there are situations which feel unfamiliar, or if you just can't finish them. Give them a go. You'll be surprised by what you find yourself loving.

There are three other books which particularly inspired me in the writing of this story. They are *Roots* by Alex Hailey, *If This is a Man* by Primo Levi, and *Animal Farm* by George Orwell. They tackle, from different angles, the topic of animalisation and what it takes to stay human in the face of oppression – central themes of NWAA. They're amazing books and well worth trying.

* * *

The mathematically-minded amongst you might also enjoy trying to decipher The Colonists' number system to find the subtle but significant easter egg within. The number of rabbits on the cover of the paperback version should hopefully give you a clue if you are struggling…

* * *

Finally, I don't believe books should tell you *what* to think, but they should *get* you to think. So, if this novel has inspired you in any way, and you want to do something for your world or the people around you, then I'm really glad. There are many great organisations and movements you can join, or maybe simply begin by making a small change in your own life.

Whatever you do, always remember that just because people approach a complex problem from a different angle, doesn't make them inherently bad or wrong. And so long as whatever you do is done with kindness and respect for yourself and others – even for those people you disagree with – then all good things will follow. Peace and love.

R P Nathan, March 2022

ACKNOWLEDGEMENTS

Books are never written in isolation, and since it took me seven years to write this one, NWAA is no exception. There are many people I would like to thank for their help along the way. Here goes:

Antonia Prescott and Cornerstones. Antonia, your editorial feedback was astoundingly insightful and your words of encouragement gave me the strength to keep enriching the story when, left to my own devices, I would have given up.

Rosa Morris, Lily Morris, and Vicky Smith for reading the very earliest version of NWAA, back when it was but a mere three chapters long and Cara was still called Francesca! Your early positivity gave me the green light to believe.

Thanks to Lydia Silver and Penny Holroyde. Although NWAA wasn't ultimately quite right for either of you, you took the time to discuss my work, giving great feedback in the process, and for that I'm so grateful.

To Tracy Traynor for your generous advice on independent publishing and the gift of The Greatest Showman; to Balbinder Chagger for writerly advice, water-cooler chat, and the gift of negronis; and to Dane and Alisha at ebooklaunch for the inspired cover design ideas and infinite patience.

Thanks to my amazing ARC team, members of the RP Nathan Readers Club and WeLoveTheSecondBestMan, and everyone who leaves a review of any of my books. Good or bad, they're always received and read with appreciation.

Thanks to Julie, Justin, Kish, Darryl and Jenny and my other vegetarian and vegan(ish) friends for being allies on a long journey. To Nigel, Tim and Ben (the artists formerly known as the North London Writers Collective) for various supportive flim-flam. To Hannah for bringing much joy into our family this year when it was so sorely needed. And to all my friends and family who have backed me so tirelessly. You know who you are and I love you. Chris, Karen, Alison, Steve, Denise, and Katherine in particular: you've supported me so much this last year on so many fronts: I will be forever grateful.

As always, to my parents and my sister: huge love and thanks for everything you do or have done. And to my amazing wife for sticking by me as I've pursued this crazy journey all these years: I love you Mrs King.

Finally, to the two most amazing people I know:

To Dominic, for reading early drafts, but much more for your unfailing stream of encouragement and your amazing ability to raise our spirits even in the toughest of times. I'm so proud of you and love you so much.

And lastly, to you, Rosa. You embraced this story right from the start, and challenged me to make it more inclusive and diverse. You read draft after draft and gave me detailed feedback which was invaluable. Every writer wants everyone to love what they write; but for this book all that I wanted was for you to. You are my Reader #1. I hope you enjoy the final version. I love you so much and am so proud of you.

RPNx

Also by R P Nathan
and available from Cassiopeia Publishing

THE COLLABORATORS

It is December 1942 in Occupied France. The Bertrand family are hiding their daughter's Jewish fiancé in a secret room in their apartment. The Resistance is planning to get the couple to freedom but the Germans have been tipped off by a collaborator.

The family's worst fears are realised when young German captain Karl bangs on the door and begins to ransack their apartment. But all is not what it seems because, as the heartbreaking plot unfolds, we realise that what Karl is really looking for is redemption.

"Brilliantly written from start to finish."

"Powerfully written, heart wrenching and tender, quietly devastating and uplifting"

"Skillfully constructed, this emotionally charged WWII tale will have you turning the pages from beginning to end."

"A really amazing read – so immersive, emotional and powerful. The time structure made it uniquely complex and really added to the dramatisation as the plot was unravelling and puzzle was piecing together in my mind, making the story all the more captivating."

A RICHER DUST CONCEALED

A fabulous jewelled cross is buried in Cyprus in 1570, to hide it from the invading Ottoman Turks. An Italian squire who saw it leaves a coded diary in Venice containing the treasure's location. A English code-breaker finds the diary in 1915 but dies in Gallipoli before he can crack the secret. And all the while, the sinister Venetian Council of Ten has also been hunting for the cross…

When young back-packer John buys a book in Rome in 1992, while on a student inter-railing holiday, he has no idea of what he has got his friends and himself into. A treasure hunt begins, but will the Council of Ten allow it to continue?

A mesmerising story of war and loss, friendship and love, and a fabulous Venetian treasure hidden for four hundred years.

"Writing of this quality is a pleasure to discover."

"A historical page-turner delivering genuine thrills."

"Thoroughly enjoyed this historical suspense novel! On the edge of my seat trying to figure out just who did it!"

"Clever evolving plot, easy read and compelling characters."

Made in United States
Orlando, FL
23 May 2023